I0589589

THE ASCENSION:
BIRTH OF A PHANTOM

THE ASCENSION:
BIRTH OF A PHANTOM

Joel J. Bledsoe

ISBN-13: 978-0-9968427-0-9
ISBN-10: 0-9968427-0-X

TABLE OF CONTENTS

PROLOGUE

"FOR THE RECORD, I didn't want this. Many will call me a traitor, but to be so, you must first betray. I followed orders, even sacrificed good men for the terrible ambitions of evil men. You cannot be a traitor if you are betrayed first. Anything after that is war. To my men, the fading faces of my memory, I will never stand against you. To my enemies, the faces that I never stop thinking about, I won't rest until I've slain you; only then do I give myself permission to die. This is Commander Jack Harrison, my enemies will know me by the name, Stormtrooper. A name I wore with shame, I will now wear to strike terror into those responsible for my dead men. Being a good man doesn't pay, being a bad man doesn't pay, the only thing that pays is doing what's right. But what is right or wrong, I now wonder. One man's right is another's wrong."

LOGGED, NOVEMBER 6th, 2025

The year was 2025. The world was on the brink of an unprecedented technological golden age not seen since the industrial era of the early 1800's. It became known as the Ascended Age. Mars, Mercury, and Venus were struggling to be terraformed to support human life, but progress had been made. Hundreds of thousands flocked amongst the stars, leaving the working class, poor, and uneducated to fend for themselves in an ever-crowded Earth. It was not strange to hear the loud *whooshing* amidst the sky, as space shuttles taking off were commonplace. The world population bloomed into the danger zone. Fourteen billion people existed on Earth at the time. Most lived on top of each other in urban cities. Open country was disappearing and living outside of a Skyliner city was rare. The world was in the gray area between the modern and the future. Artantium—a newfound mineral discovered in 2021 was the backbone of new inventions such as Nano technology, advanced robotics, and nuclear car engines. The first flying car was unveiled in 2024, diseases were decades away from not existing, and the future was no longer in the far distance, but on the horizon. It seemed that humanity was poised for a golden age of marvels and wonders. Chairman Gale, head of the international space committee, was famous for saying, "Mankind knows no bounds. What we can touch, we will grasp. What we cannot touch, we will reach for."

War and the weapons of war, however, advanced rapidly. Countries raced to find new and advanced weaponry with the idea of becoming the new superpower, as the United States was still on top. Planetary expansion was a hot spot for debates and feuds between countries over who had rights to what. War seemed inevitable. The American government had become obsessed with finding the next generation of soldiers, weapons, and weapons of mass destruction. An arms race not seen since the cold war had erupted. Under Article 331, the funding for advanced weapons research was tripled under one condition: human experiments were illegal. Facilities were erected in the dark corners of the country in secret and their orders were simple: make sure the United States stays superior to all foreign countries, no matter the cost. A facility lay in the deep snows of northern Alaska, Hope 7, the first of its kind.

The walls were as cold as ice. If someone listened hard enough, they would be able to hear faint screams under the chilled floors. No one tried to listen though. They went about their business as normal, completely ignoring their curiosity as to who or what was screaming. The view through the window revealed a forest of tall oak trees; their branches wet with dew, towering snowy mountains, and a valley covered in mist. The noise of gusty winds could be heard sweeping through the land. It was a dark Thursday night, November the 4th. The word "hope" was often thrown around, but on this night, there was no mention of the word. No one could have prepared themselves for the cry of the banshee, or the terror behind the red eyes. It was here where the ambitions of mankind would be its undoing. Inside, two janitors were doing their routine clean on Sub-Level One. The Holo-Screen gleaned in blue illumination on the wall. It was the final inning of the Rocket Ball game in the 2025 Rocket Cup. The announcer energetically described the game.

"Timmons passes the rocket to King... King, not letting the zero gravity slow him down, punches his rocket shoes, dodging the New York Shark defenders in a stunning spin!"

The Janitors stopped what they were doing and gave the screen their attention with wide eyes.

"There he goes... full speed... and uh, oh! Glass intercepts him with a full mid-air tackle, but what's this, folks!? King isn't stopping! He's holding onto the rocket!! There's ten seconds left on the clock, Sharks are up by one! This is it! Will the Los Angeles Titans win the game? And... Impact!!!"

"Yes!!!" One of the Janitors yelled out loud. He quickly covered his mouth.

"Titans win the game!! The 2025 Rocketship trophy goes to the LA Titans, what a game!! There ya have it, folks, we have one last treat for you; the closing performance by none other than Red Talbridge and the Fallen Stars!"

Loud rock music took over the hallway. Red Talbridge was an upcoming metal guitarist and singer. Everyone of the time knew his name and his music inspired individuality, rebellion, and freedom of expression. He was an icon of the Ascended Age; equivalent to John Lennon in the 1960's, or the NWA in the 1990's. He always wore light suits, had black skin, red hair, and his raspy voice couldn't be mistaken. He performed his most famous song, *Seven Shades of Personality*. When it released in 2021, it sold twenty-five million copies, worldwide, in the first week.

"Pay up!" Said the Janitor named 'Jackson.'

"Lucky win! But a deal's a deal!" Said 'Bill,' bitterly. He gave Jackson twenty dollars.

Talbridge's voice took over the hallway with slow rock music, "I'm just a, Metal man!! Metal man!! Metal man!!

They say, why are you so upset!?

Why can't you just be happy!?

And I say, listen to my metal boots as I'm walkin,'

I got no care for your talkin,'

They say sit,

I say stand,

My destiny is in my hands,

My metal heart must be tempting,

I just feel so empty!

'cause I'm a, Metal man!! Metal man!! Metal man!!"

"...I'm telling you, pal—they don't pay us enough to be all the way out here just to mop." Said Bill. He was a middle-aged white man who wore a gray janitor's uniform, had a hat over his bald head, and had a white goatee. He dipped his mop into the steamy water.

"Yeah, I'm twenty bucks richer so I can't complain." Said Jackson with a smile. He was a skinny black man who had short black hair and likewise wore a gray janitor's uniform.

"Hardy, har har," Bill said. "All I'm saying is that it's a strain coming all the way up here..." Bill was interrupted by a woman, dressed in white.

"Quiet!" The woman softly spoke as she walked by the janitors. "Turn that hologram off, now! If I see it on again, I'll have you both fired!"

The security mechs marched behind her like trained assault troops. Their metal feet clanged against the tiled floor. *Left, right, left, right.* She was wearing an all-white business suit; had short blonde hair and green eyes. The woman swiftly powerwalked past the janitors with two security guards in front of the mechs. They were armed with assault rifles and body armor. They punched in a password into the security console. *Click, click, click, click.* The elevator door opened, they all walked in, and the shiny steel door closed. Jackson could see his reflection from the door.

"Talk about a heavily armed detail! Man, she is one mean lady." Said Bill, licking his dry, crisp lips. He twisted the top of the small projector on the floor and the hologram shut off.

"No Kidding! It looks like someone dug her out of the grave!" Said Jackson, quietly.

Abrupt silence was followed by a long laugh. The sterile lights flickered.

"Whew! Ah, God—that's hilarious." Said Bill.

The flickering intensified.

"She needs to have somebody come out and fix this power surge! That's the third time this week." Said Jackson. Or I could just fix the damn thing myself. He thought. If the price was right. I'm not doing nothing for free! These over-budgeted money hounds barely pay me as it is.

"Seriously, man!" Said Bill. "This place gives me the creeps. A couple days ago when I was mopping the tile on the fourth level, I heard someone screaming—I mean a loud and terrible screaming. I peeked over the corner and I saw the security staff rush into a room. They were your regular macho men, tough guys. Broad shoulders, skillets for pecks, and bulging biceps. A few moments later a guy was thrown out with incredible force. I mean he shot outta that room faster than a Rocketship. He scared the daylight outta me. His face was bleeding badly. I watched him slowly turn his head towards me. I wouldn't have been surprised if he had a broken neck. I looked into his eyes and saw raw terror, man. You best believe that I jumped back in the elevator and high tailed it outta there."

"Really? Who do you think was screaming?" Asked Jackson.

"Hell, if I know!" answered Bill. "The boss lady raised hell when she found out that I'd abandoned my cleaning post. Screw her. I don't get paid enough to witness their top-secret mistakes."

"Too true! Hey, did you get any mail via the Mainframe? I'm a day overdue."

"Nah," said Bill. "From what I hear, they still haven't even sent my letter yet. It still needs to be 'processed,' they say—bullshit!"

"Well, this is a top-secret facility—they gotta keep it secret right?"

"Yeah, but all I need them to send is a letter to my wife. It shouldn't take them five days to process that." Bill complained. "I have a life outside of this hell hole ya know?"

"That's true," Jackson admitted. "A couple more days and we won't have to see this place until next month."

The conversation slowly died out like a flickering candle.

Jackson didn't say anything, but he had an unsettled look on his face. He didn't know what went on in the bowels of the facility, but he heard rumors. Talk of unsanctioned experiments, rumors of torture, even a rumor of a child experiment. Can't be, they're not allowed to do anything like that. Jackson thought, trying to convince himself that there was nothing out of the ordinary.

An hour passed.

Jackson stood back and smiled at the clean hallway. "Well, another hard day's work and another job well done!" He said, rubbing the sweat off his forehead.

"Sure," Bill replied. "Until we get called in next month to clean the same dirty floors... the same dirty walls... and the same dirty windows!"

"Yeah—It's time to find a new job, I think. They'll probably have us replaced with those damn mechs soon anyways. Us janitors are a dying breed, let me tell ya." Jackson said. He leaned against the wall and rubbed his arms. "Man, it's getting cold down here! Someone needs to turn on the heat. That draft has me feeling like I'm standing outside! Whoever the technician is, HE needs to be fired."

A cold air rushed into the hallway, the lights flickered more, then the lights burst in sync; creating a loud popping noise and leaving the janitors in the dark. The windows cracked and glass sprinkled onto the floor.

"Geez!" Jackson shrieked. "What the hell was that?" He said, pushing his shoulder off the wall.

The two men shuddered when they heard an automated voice. It sounded like the AI in a GPS system. "Emergency shutdown in effect! Please proceed to the control center!"

The voice kept repeating itself every ten seconds, emergency red lights came on, and the hallway was illuminated in red. The wind blew specs of snow in and the air was all too happy to get inside.

"What the hell's going on?" Asked Bill, wrapping his arms around his body.

A noise was heard and this time it was too loud to ignore.

"Wait—you hear that?" Cautioned Jackson.

The janitors brought their heads low and listened hard—they heard faint screams; like people were going down a rollercoaster a half mile away. The noise got louder and louder until the frightening barrage of screams became deafening. After about a minute, the noise eerily stopped. There was nothing but silence. The men could hear themselves exhale and inhale rapidly. The only way to the top of Level One was through the door where they heard the screams, but no man dare turn the handle. Another scream could be heard but it sounded different. It was very high-pitched. Jackson couldn't tell if it was screaming or the amplified noise of a whistling tea kettle. The doorknob began to rapidly jerk up and down. Jackson slowly reached for the handle. As soon as he touched it, he felt a painful shock zap his hand. He pulled himself away from the door. The knob stopped moving.

"Let's get out of here, man!" Bill said with wide eyes. He rushed back, knocking over his red mop bucket and spilling water all over the floor. He ran to the elevator door, but it was shut, and the security console needed to open it wouldn't turn on. Bill could see how terrified he looked in the door's reflection. He looked like he saw a ghost. The hologram suddenly turned on followed by loud rock music.

"I'm just a, Metal Man!! Metal Man!! Metal man!!"

A terrible static filled the hallway. The automated voice began to sound corrupted; randomly speeding up and slowing down.

"Emergency... in effect... control center." The automated voice sounded.

Then, a terrible, gut-wrenching, wail filled the hallway—unmistakably an expression of pain. It sent chills up their spines. Jackson swore this was all just a nightmare. A shadowy figure appeared at the far end of the hallway, opposite the elevator. It seemed to just warp through the wall. It was a small, shadowy, black outlining of a person that slowly grew in height. When it was done rising it had to be at least six feet tall. It let out a piercing shriek. The shriek broke the windows completely and the janitors covered their ears in agony. It was a high-pitched wail that would make even a corpse moan in agony.

"Make... it... stop..." The automated voice said with static.

Talbridge was having the concert of his life, "Red Man!! Red Man!! Red Man!!

Who are you to talk about me,
You've brought nothing but damnation,
You talk to me about salvation,
While only speakin' condemnation,
You're always cheatin,'
Now you've provoked my inner demon!
Red Man!! Red Man!! Red Man!!"

It looked like lightning struck the figure; a bright flash occurred, illuminating the dark hallway. Before Jackson knew, it had lifted Bill ten feet into the air and tore him in half in a quick and violent moment. So quick, Bill didn't even have time to scream. Just a sickening *slush* noise followed by the sound of blood being splattered on the no longer clean walls and floor. Jackson had felt the rush of air blow against him; his face physically shocked as it passed him. His friend's blood scattered along his left cheek like rain droplets. Horrified, Jackson ran past the figure, to the stairwell door. What the hell is that thing! He thought. Where do I go? What do I do? He could feel the bottom of his feet being shocked by the electricity as he stepped in the water. Jackson's mental shock began to wear off.

"Oh, God, oh God, oh God!" He blurted out.

Jackson reached the doorway, but the door was jammed shut. He frantically threw his body against the door, but it wouldn't budge. Something seemed to block it from the other side. He felt the cold air bite at his neck; his heart racing. Red Man!! Red Man!! Red Man!! Again, he threw his weight at the jammed door and it burst open. He started up the stairway, but quickly tripped on a step. He fell face first into a dead woman's breast. The skin was sagged and the force of Jackson's impacting head caused a little blood to spurt on his face. He quickly lifted his head and saw that the woman had been fried. She couldn't speak, but her waterless, dry eyes did. They spoke one word to Jackson's heart, *fear*. He didn't have time to mourn.

He kept running up the staircase that was littered with mutilated bodies scattered everywhere. They were either fried or torn apart; steam could be seen rising off the corpses. Most of the bodies had on white-lab coats with black burn marks on them. There was a ghastly smell of burnt human flesh that almost caused Jackson to vomit. He kept running, looking behind him, stumbling all the way; terrified that he was going to suffer the same fate as his friend. His ears were slightly ringing from the shriek. Before he reached the door, he slipped head-first into a puddle of blood. It shocked his face. He quickly got up, wiped the blood off with his sleeve, and shoulder bashed his way inside the control center. It was a mess—tables overturned and papers littering the floor. A bloodied security guard was leaning on the wall. His eyes turned wide when he saw Jackson. He was slightly shaking. Jackson shut the door behind him.

Barely able to speak, the security guard moaned, "You have to help me... fix this... please."

"Fix what? What do I do? What in the hell are you people doing here!?" Asked Jackson.

The security guard was panting in fear. "We screwed up... no time to explain... get this message to Baseline Security—Hellfire. Use the terminal over there... hold the red key to send up the distress beacon when you send the message... God help us all."

With those words, the security guard was dead. He let out a forceful exhale. His body slumped over to the side slowly like a dead cowboy slumping off his horse in a 60's western film. Jackson did as the man had asked. The keyboard was on the ground and the letters were bloodied. In a hurry, Jackson picked it up and prepared the audio message. From the elevated control center, he could see the lobby down below. It was filled with motionless bodies. The doors and windows were covered with steel barriers; a result of a shutdown. It was clear to Jackson that the shutdown had inadvertently prevented everyone in the lobby from escaping. He stopped taking in the sights and began speaking into the computer monitor.

"Please send help—something terrible has happened! Hellfire! Please help! God, I... I don't wanna die! I repeat Hellfire! Send help."

Jackson pressed the send button. He figured that he would have to lift the shutdown from his monitor if he wanted to have a chance at escaping. He prepared to do so. A noise from behind was most unwelcome. The shrieking wail pierced the air again and the console froze shortly after the message was sent. A cold rush blew past him; kicking up papers. It sent a terrifying shiver through his spine and heart. Jackson panted; feeling as if he was about to die from a heart attack. He wasn't that lucky. There was more screaming, wailing... then silence.

PART ONE

SOMETHING IN THE AIR

More than 300,00 children are diagnosed
with cancer each year.

CHAPTER 1: TASK FORCE X-RAY

One day before the distress message, November 3rd

THE SUN WAS high in the sky, the deserts of Nevada were baking in heat, and there was nothing but sand for miles. The wind carried the sand in the air; often creating small sandstorms against the unmercifully bright sun. *Whooshing* sounded as the space shuttles ascended into the atmosphere over the Nevada deserts. They were the lucky ones. The people on board were colonists entering the final frontier of space in search of new homes. It was old news; the earth was overpopulated. Resources were being depleted; plants and vegetation were on the decline, and there were theories that most vegetation in the northern hemisphere would be gone by 2040. In this era, people were seeking to fill holes and when they were filled, they just made new ones. It was a time of selfishness and self-image; higher thinking, freedom of expression, and body modifications. Everyone was reaching for something greater. Turmoil and civil unrest were on the rise. Some protested the creation of machines; others, the exploration of space. Constant meddling in the Middle East by multiple foreign powers led to quicker depletion of resources. It was a post-war on terror environment. To avoid any more quagmires in the Middle East, or anywhere for that matter, countries adopted the idea of using small, elite forces to deal with agents of chaos; opposing the large mobilization of conventional troops. These units were small, had minimal supervision, and were able to fight anywhere. In 2020, The US created a new military command called, GUARD. It consisted of a fighting force of its own, separate from the traditional military.

Gunfighter

Universal

Authority

Reconnaissance

Division

The division was still in its infancy and was made up of various special forces units, black-ops, counter-terrorism cells, spy rings, cyber, and space security. A small but deadly part of GUARD was Task Force X-Ray, a band of warriors that made a name in special forces for themselves by doing the impossible. In the year 2023, a Russian terrorist cell, the Artemis Hounds, overtook a nuclear reactor with the intent of detonating the facility—endangering tens of thousands of lives. An eight men team led by Commander Jack Harrison, were inserted by helicopter. They were shot down close to the perimeter. The helicopter blew into a ball of fire upon impact. The terrorists were so sure that the men were dead that they didn't bother searching the crash for survivors. It proved to be a fatal mistake. Officially, a team of army troops eliminated the terrorists and rescued the hostages. Unofficially, Task Force X-Ray, an eight men team, killed forty enemy insurgents. The truth never reached the public. Each man had been shot at least once, but it didn't stop them from getting the mission done. Of the few military units who knew of Task Force X-Ray, they nicknamed them, *The Undead Corpses* or *The*

Men of Metal. Deep in the Nevada desert, east of Las Vegas, their base, known by the name "Compound X-ray," was located.

A man stood on a sand mound overlooking the desert. He looked at his watch, it read, *2:58*. He prepared his blue eyedrops. The ground trembled. When the watch read *3:00,* he dripped a drop of Interstellar into both eyes and closed them. His knees lightly shook with pleasure and it felt as if his spine was the center of an orgasm. There was a loud eruption in the distance. He opened his eyes and beheld the spectacle of multiple space shuttles blasting into the atmosphere, seemingly in slow motion. The view was sparkling to his sights. He reached for one of the shuttles with his right hand.

"Taylor!" A voice sounded.

Shhh. I can almost feel it. He thought; his lower back tingling with ecstasy.

"Taylor, what in the hell are you doing!?" The voice sounded again.

Taylor broke from his serene trance, looked, and saw his friend, "Ramirez."

"Seriously, dude!?" Taylor said, flipping him off. "You ruined my moment!"

"Oh, I'm sorry princess! How about I take you to get ice cream and you can talk to me about your feelings!" Ramirez said, walking closer to Taylor. "What in the heck are you up to?"

"I was admiring the view."

Ramirez placed his hand over his eyes and looked at the launching space shuttles. He too stared for a moment before saying, "Well, the only thing stopping us from getting outta here is five-hundred-thousand dollars. You got that kind of money?"

Taylor didn't respond.

"Yeah, neither do I. Come on, let's have a go on the range, yeah?" Ramirez suggested. "Somebody has to kill the bad guys."

"Seeing how my peaceful meditation has been spoiled, sure, I'll kick your ass on the range."

Taylor hopped down the mound and the duo walked towards their destination. They stopped at the armory and equipped their M-4 rifles.

They loaded their magazines by hand with 5.56mm rounds. When they were done, they stepped back outside. A loud *Vroom!* sounded and Ramirez became starstruck. A matte black, Zeltsman 420 Raptor, speedily pulled into the compound and parked. It looked like a Ferrari mixed with an old school muscle car, maybe a 70's challenger. Ramirez stopped walking towards the range and moved towards the car like it magnetized him. A tall, black man exited the Raptor.

"Carter? You lucky bastard! How did you get your hands on one of these bad boys!?" Ramirez asked.

"I work for a living." He bluntly responded.

"Yeah? My step-sister's a prostitute, can grow a mustache, and juggles balls, but she can't afford a car like that."

Carter tried to refrain from laughing but his defenses gave way. His crisp lips lightly quivered before he let out a big laugh. "I tell ya," he started, "when you drive for thirty minutes behind someone going twenty-miles per hour on a one-way road, it tends to be vexing."

"Blah, blah, blah! Details, man!" Ramirez said, walking towards the front of the car, "You have a J-1 nuclear engine, giving off at least a thousand horses. All you're missing now are your flight thrusters."

"I said I worked for a living; I didn't say I was rich."

"Well, we're not due for briefing until 18:00, wanna take us for a spin?"

Carter looked at the ground a moment before saying, "Hop in!"

DANIEL RAMIREZ
(2018)

I looked out of the red Camaro, eyeing the quiet neighborhood. Carlos drove; Robert and Philip sat in the back. We saw the midnight Bentley that we'd been scoping out all week. I felt a tap on my shoulder. I looked behind and saw Robert handing me a black ski mask. I took it from him and donned it. Carlos and Robert were the oldest; both were twenty-one. I was seventeen and Philip was eighteen. Carlos parked the Camaro at the curb across the street from the Bentley. It was a Sunday night; garbage cans lined up along the curbs of the narrow, Los Angeles street.

Carlos turned off the engine, put on his mask, and said, "Listen up, fools! Robert and I are going to grab the tires. Philip, you pop the trunk. Daniel, you search through the car. Let's roll!"

We all exited the Camaro. Philip's fat ass took longer than the rest of us as usual. We rushed the driveway under the cover of night. Carlos and Robert, with socket wrenches in hand, quickly loosened the tire bolts. Philip rushed over with the jack and pumped up the car, so the tires were barely touching the ground. I used a thin piece of sheet metal, slid it through the window slit, and unlocked the driver's door. Like clockwork. I popped the trunk from inside and I looked for anything I could find. I opened the glove compartment; nothing but CDs. I took 'em anyway. There was a money clip in the cup holder. I put it in my pocket without counting. Carlos and Robert rolled the tires back to the Camaro. We only took two because we couldn't fit the rest. I exited the car, slowly shut the door, and went to the other side. Philip slashed the upper right tire and I slashed the lower tire. Our trademark, I guess.

As we did so, I heard a sickening 'chick-chick' sound. Out of raw instinct, I dashed for the Camaro without looking back; Philip followed. A gunshot went off. I heard Philip grunt in pain. I looked behind me and saw that he was still running; holding his back. The noise of skidding tires sounded as Carlos pulled the Camaro towards us. Robert opened the back door and we both crammed ourselves inside. Another gunshot sounded. I could hear the pellets scatter along the car. Carlos sped off. We all sat in silence even after clearing the street for fifteen minutes. We'd stolen a lot of things, but we'd never been shot at. Philip had three scattergun pellets in his back. He twisted and turned in his seat.

"We gotta get him to the hospital, Carlos!" said Robert.

"Nah," Carlos started, "I'll drop him off at the big homie's house. He'll patch him up."

We drove for about twenty minutes before getting to Ricardo's place. We all helped Philip to the front door. I could smell Ricardo's grandmother's tamales before we even rang the doorbell. The door opened and Ricardo didn't ask any questions. He was a chubby guy; had a thick black mustache, short black hair, and he wore glasses. We handed Philip to Ricardo and he closed the door. We all walked back to the car; Carlos lit up a cigarette.

"Good job, guys!" He said, blowing out smoke. "We'll get this merch sold and get paid later this week. What did you find in the car, Daniel?"

I pulled the money clip out of the bag and counted it.

"Two-hundred dollars in all twenties." I say. "I found some crappy CDs too."

"Better than nothin.'" Carlos said, examining the shotgun pellets in the car's side door. "That's sixty bucks each. You can keep the extra twenty, Daniel. Tell your mom I said hey."

"Thanks, Carlos."

"No problem, holmes. I got some weed I want you to push tomorrow, you down for that?"

"Yeah."

"Cool. I'll drop you off at your house. Me and Robert will store the goods at our usual spot. Let's get going."

We got in the Camaro and left.

Later that week.

"Daniel, look at me!" Yelled my mom.

I didn't want to face her gaze. I'd never been busted. In a way, I refused to accept that I was busted now. My backpack was emptied onto my bed; littered with bags of weed and money. I kept my eyes on the white, carpet floor.

"Look at me!"

I stood up and broke my silence, "Ay! Why don't you leave me alone! This ain't none of your-"

Her hand smacked me across my face. I shut up and sat back down. No words were said but the pain was there. My brother, Julio, was killed in East LA a few years ago, and my mom was doing her best to keep me out of trouble. I went after it though. Trouble was fun. With my gang, I was next to untouchable. Nobody messed with me. I had a group of loyal homies and we raised hell together. We were thieves for a living; full time. We were like kings. I turned to face my mom. Tears rolled down her face. That was the real painful part. She was my only real love in the world. I hated my deadbeat dad for leaving her to deal with me. More importantly, I hated hurting her.

"You're a grown man now, Daniel." She said, wiping her eyes. "I put a roof over your head, fed you, kept you clothed, and made sure you got through school. Why are you doing this, huh!? You want to be like your go-nowhere friends? Or is it Julio?"

"Ma-"

"It's Julio, isn't it!? Whichever it is, you're not going to be living under my roof and disrespecting me with this garbage! When you graduate in the next few months, you have two options: you can go to college, or you can go to the Army. I want you gone from this neighborhood. It's for your own good!"

She packed the bag with all my contraband and stormed out of my room with it. My life was forever changed and I knew it. Running away crossed my mind, but I knew that would only do more harm than good. I had nowhere to go; I was going to have to say adios to all my homies and eses. I didn't want to. They were my childhood friends and I was literally friendless without them. I paced back and forth in my room. I was a terrible student. I was going to graduate from high school by the skin of my teeth. Army it was. At least I'd get to fight and get paid doing it. Maybe come back and show Carlos my medals.

PRESENT DAY

Carter's car rushed down the lonely street. The speedometer was at 160mph. Everyone was amazed at the raw power of the car; amazed and slightly terrified. The engine was relatively quiet. 160mph turned into 200mph. The car was like a light train in its design; the feeling of actually moving was minimal. When they approached the Vegas strip, Carter slowed down. Talbridge's *Freeway Express* played in the car.

"California sunshine's got my visors gold,
I'm not shit so I'm told,
Who are they to judge me,
I gotta one-way ticket down the freeway express,
Where my metal head can't be compressed,
Where moving at your own pace is the law of the land,
Come on I'll give you my hand,
We'll roam free together,
Let the blind remain tethered,
We have dreams to follows, and ambitions to be treasured!"

Traffic began to pick up and the trio immediately regretted their decision to go to the bustling *Sky-Liner* city. Sky-Liners were cities with at least a population of ten million. They were distinguishable by their giant skyscraper buildings and housing. At night, the cities seemingly partied with no end in sight. The city lights could be seen for miles on end. Clean, nuclear energy made the atmosphere clear. After clearing the traffic, Carter pulled into an alleyway and parked his car. The trio exited and Taylor made sure to don his black sunglasses.

"Drinks before we get back?" Asked Carter.

Ramirez said, "Sure."

Taylor nodded his head in agreement. They walked through the wide alleyway, littered with beggars and drunks.

A middle-aged man who wore a ragged, duster coat asked, "Spare change? Spare change, boys? Spare change?"

Carter ignored him. The man stood up and walked backwards in front of Carter. "Spare change? Please, I need money?"

"Hell no! Get a job and get the fuck out of my face!"

The man dropped to his knees, "Please, if you'll just…" he started, while grabbing onto Carter's lower pants.

Carter snapped. He kneed the man in his chin and pushed him to the gravel. He got ready to deliver another blow when Ramirez stayed his hand. "Easy, you got him! Leave him be."

Carter calmed himself and he kept walking.

ROMAN CARTER
(2015)

I opened my busted locker to see cracked egg yolks over my hat and baseball glove. My former teammates laughed as they passed my aisle.

"Hey, Roman!" One of them said. "You got a chicken in there?"

The laughter made me feel small.

"Yeah," another started, "Didn't your dad teach you that the only good chicken is a fried chicken!"

I slammed my locker door and stormed towards him. The coach seemed to come out of nowhere. An older, white, fat bastard with a wrinkled face. He never took my side and I hated him as much as I hate getting dental work done.

"Hey, enough!" He said.

"Did you hear what they just said!?" I yell at him.

"Irrelevant, son. I-"

"I'm not your goddamn son!"

"Roman that is enough! You are off this baseball team! Clear your locker and get out of my sight!"

I walked back to my locker and began unpacking. Some of the

yolk had gotten on the picture of my dad. I rubbed it off and gently put it in my sports bag.

Later that day.

The waterfall next to the ravine sounded loudly. I dried my eyes and threw the next rock at the quicksand. It slowly smooched into the ground. With each throw, I felt a little better. It was a hot summer day in Atlanta, Georgia. I grabbed a tennis ball from my sack, threw it in the air, and hit it with my metal baseball bat. The tennis ball landed in the ravine; a little distance away from the quicksand. My baseball bat was all-black and had the word 'Ranger' on it in all-green lettering. It was a heavy, metal bat. I loved it. Despite all the crap I put up with on the team, I was the best hitter. That's what made the jerks jealous. The 'thumping' sound of a seventy mile per hour baseball was the best noise I'd ever heard; followed by cheering in the stands. I hit another ball towards the quicksand puddle. I heard cheering that wasn't really there. It went too far and flew into the wilderness beyond the puddle. I sorely missed it when my dad would take me to baseball games. I'd always laugh when he would enthusiastically sing 'take me out to the ball game.' I'd laugh, he'd laugh, and now no one's laughing. I got ready to hit another one when a voice startled me.

"What'cha up here doin,' boy!?" A man said.

I turned around and saw a short, old, white man approaching me. He had on a dirty white tank top and wore blue jeans. He looked like he spilt mustard on his white beard. He smoked a cigarette. I didn't say anything.

"I said, what'cha up here doin'?"

"Uh, nothing, sir!" I clumsily say.

"Well, you ought to know better than to be out here all by yourself! You didn't see the quicksand sign? Or did your daddy not teach you how to read?"

What did you just say to me? I thought to myself. The man

walked past me and looked at the ravine. I tightened my fingers around the bat.

"Ah—who am I kiddin,' daddy is a foreign word for you negro boys anyhow! Why don't you skidattle before you hurt yourself. Go on!"

Fuck you, old man! I think to myself, struggling to make a stand. He was of a dying breed; someone who probably donned a Ku Klux Klan hood back in his day. There was a lotta blacks in Atlanta, but you had the occasional few who were not only white but stuck in their prejudice ways. I gripped my baseball bat tightly. He turned his back on me. Big mistake. Anger was an understatement; I was livid. You picked the wrong day! My heart accelerates. With both hands, I lifted the baseball bat up high and instead of hitting a seventy mile per hour ball, I strike the man in the back of his head; right on his bald spot. The cracking noise was like none I'd ever heard. He dropped his cigarette, fell to the ground, and crawled towards the ravine. *What have I done?* Blood pooled from the back of his skull and leaked down the back of his neck. When he reached the water, he turned around and I saw fear in his blue eyes. I felt like I couldn't stop; like I'd gone too far. I swung the bat again. He tried to block it with his hand but was too slow. The bat struck him at his jaw and made another sickening cracking noise. He turned to face me again; his jaw hung low and was bloodied. His beard no longer had mustard on it, but ketchup instead. I could see exposed, broken, and bloodied teeth.

"Pease, on't kill me!" He mumbled out, spitting blood on my Chuck Taylor's.

I wanted to stop. Worse, I wanted him to stop. I brought the bat behind my head and swung with full force. His head slumped over into the ravine and I was certain I killed him. I could see the water carry away his blood. When the adrenaline passed and I finally realized what I did, I threw up. I murdered a man. I'm going to go to prison for life. The newspaper is going to read, 'teenager commits murder.' My grandparents will be heart broken and I'll never see them again. Not if no one finds out.

"Not if no one finds out!" I say out loud.

I decided to hide my crime. I wrapped my arms under his armpit, dragged his body through the shallow ravine, and towards the quicksand puddle with my bat around his body. I took a deep breath. *One... two... three!* I tossed him into the quicksand. He was slowly devoured by the sand; headfirst. I hoped that the quick-sand would end my problem and fast. I got ready to turn away when his hand suddenly grabbed my leg. I yelled in terror. He tried to mumble out words, but his head was already under the sand and I couldn't make out what he was saying. His legs kicked through the air like he was riding a bicycle. I grabbed my bat, knocked away his hand, and fell flat on my behind. His hands flung into the air wildly. Each second I witnessed his panicking felt like an hour. After about fifteen seconds, he stopped moving. Another fifteen seconds and his body had disappeared.

PRESENT DAY

The trio were in the heart of the city. Holograms played on city walls and buildings; showing various ads, or the replay of the 2025 Rocket Bowl. There were flying cars in the air; maybe about fifteen total. All throughout the street they walked on, there were vendors trying to sell their products. The air smelled of food and cigarettes. A couple of kids could be seen playing Rocketball in the alleyway; their rocket shoes activated.

To the trio's right, half-naked women taunted them from a building balcony, "Hey, boys! Where you off to so fast!? Lend me your hammer and I'll lend you a screw!"

Taylor thought about how much money he had. When it appeared that the trio were ignoring them, some of the women pulled down their pants and full mooned them. Some had various 'light tattoos' depicting various sexual acts on their bums. They whooped and hollered.

Taylor stopped when his mind was made up. He said to his comrades, "I'll catch up with you guys in a bit."

"I was waiting to see when you'd give in!" Carter joked with a smile. "Go on, catch up with us at the Diamond Bar, yeah?"

Taylor nodded his head and entered the building. The women on the balcony rushed down the stairs to greet their potential customer.

<hr />

RICK TAYLOR
(2022)

The room was dark and illuminated by blue lighting. I sat on a leather couch; my usual spot and examined the blue liquid. I was in need of something new... something that could better dampen the pain. Cocaine didn't seem to be enough anymore. Then again, nothing can quite reach emotional or even mental pain. Nothing can quite scratch that itch.

"Interstellar is the trip of the future, my friend." Raved Swordfish. "It's twice as powerful as cocaine, has no side-effects, and you'll experience no crash!"

Swordfish was a crappy name for him. His codename should've been gibbering hamster; more fitting for his rapid-fire speech. Sometimes he'd talk so quickly, I'd have to take ten seconds to process what he'd just said.

"Bullshit!" I said with a smirk. "Sounds too good to be true."

"That's just the thing, Rick, IT IS TRUE! Not only that, it's a hard drug to trace, which is good for you Army man! Just take one drop per eye; that's two in case you couldn't count, and feel the magic, baby!"

I sat back and thought hard for a moment. "I'll bite. Give me a sample."

"My man! Lie back and keep those eyes open for me!"

I did as he asked. Swordfish put one drop in both eyes. I couldn't believe the feeling I experienced. My neck was the epicenter of mad pleasure. The tingling, cool sensation trickled down my spine until my whole back joined the party, my ass followed. Everything I looked at was illuminated in blue, like a light blue tint on a car windshield.

"So… what do you… think?" Swordfish asked.

"Why in the hell are you talking so slow?" I responded.

He laughed like a retarded person and said, "I'm… not slow… Rick… you're just fast! Don't worry… though, that's… just the drug… speeding up your… senses."

Swordfish was a fast-talking person but, in this moment, I felt like I could've run a circle around him before he finished his sentence.

PRESENT DAY

Back at Compound X-Ray, Commander Jack Harrison sat at his desk; the leader of Task Force X-Ray. The shutters were closed and he sat in relative darkness. He was about 6'2," Caucasian; his face sunbeaten, and had short black hair with tapered graying temples. He had blue eyes and a long scar that stretched from his lower forehead, parting through his right eyebrow, and stretching down to his lower chin. His voice was deep and rugged. He was forty-six years old; a career Army soldier with a special forces background. He'd been an officer his entire life; entering the Army as a Second Lieutenant after graduating from West Point. Whenever he'd take off his shirt at a gym, people would question how old he was. He was in phenomenal shape; had a six pack and well-defined muscular physique in his arms and chest.

He had wrinkled patches on certain areas of his body from past gunshot wounds and shrapnel punctures. His hands were rugged and lined with callouses. He had an 82nd airborne tattoo on his right shoulder, with a green-beret, American flag bandanna wearing skull under the unit patch. On the right side of his back he had tattoos of his family member's birthdays, on the left, a list of names with a cross over them. Smoke seemed to line the room like fog. The cigar gave off a bitter, nicotine smell. His knees were aching. Medals and commendations made the left side of his desert-camouflaged uniform sag. In the dark room sat all his demons. He could hear the gunfire. The screams. The last words that were spoken. Worst of all, the dead faces that wanted to speak but couldn't. All of them were bloodied and no matter how hard he tried he couldn't turn away from their gazes. He gripped the cigar tightly with his teeth. A shattering noise startled him. He looked down and saw that he broke his drinking glass from squeezing it so tightly. The Whiskey quickly stung his fresh cut.

COMMANDER HARRISON
(2002)

I lifted his head out of the mud and saw that he was quite dead. Captain Sargento. A friend. A mentor. A dead man. The medics carried my best friend, Ron Turner, in a body bag. I looked around and took in the carnage. Thirteen men lay dead, exposed, or in body bags. Helicopters circled the area. A news reporter covered the event. I looked down at myself and saw that I had no bullet wounds or shrapnel; just minor cuts and bruises. I hated myself. I wish somebody shot me; killed me even. Because the guilt was more than I could take. I holstered my Desert Eagle.

"Hey, Stormtrooper!" Someone shouted from behind.

I turned around and saw a couple of Army privates walking my way and smiling.

"What did you call me?" I asked.

The private paused and made an explosion gesture as he yelled out, "STORMTROOPER! That's you!"

I blankly stared at the goofball kid.

"That's what they're calling you! Fitting ain't it? Seeing how you-"

"Don't call me that!" I shout.

"What? Come on! That's a cool name! I'd kill to get a nickname like that!"

I could feel my eyes widen. I walked up to his face and said, "You'd have to do more than kill, boy!"

Boy? The kid was probably my age, maybe a couple years younger. I felt like I said a Clint Eastwood line while in my underpants. Even so, after what I'd seen... after what I'd done, I had gained thirty years in a single day. I started to walk away.

"Stormtrooper's got a stick up his ass!" The private muttered to his friend.

Expecting a Whitty remark, I did a 360 turn and sucker punched him in his nose. Such force, I wouldn't have been surprised if someone told me I knocked him out. His friend threw a punch at me. I dodged it, gave him an upper cut, wrapped my arm around his throat, and brought him to his knees by kicking the back of his legs. It was systematic. I pulled out my knife without instinct or sense of my surroundings. When in training I was trained to kill, when in war I've killed, to survive I've killed. What's another casualty? Another kill?

"Don't do it!!" Yelled the Master Sergeant.

PRESENT DAY

A knock on the door broke Harrison's trance. He set his broken glass in the trash can and wrapped his hand with a white towel.

"Come in." Harrison calmly said.

The door opened and First Lieutenant Roger Jacobs entered. He was wearing a white buttoned-up shirt with blue jeans. He stood up straight and looked above Harrison's head. He gently closed the door behind him and informed the Commander of some news.

"I just got off the phone with Washington. The body arrived thirty minutes ago..."

Harrison stared down at his papers. Nothing but silence filled the room.

Jacobs said, "...Sir, it's not your fault. Diaz died a hero. You didn't kill him—the enemy did."

Looking up from his papers, Harrison said, "I didn't save him either. That's what matters, son. You can kill a thousand bastards and sleep it off, but the ones that you lose... you can never sleep those ones off."

After a long pause, Harrison asked, "Is that all, Jacobs?"

"Yes, Commander. I just want you to know, that me and the squad will always have your six, sir!"

"I would be disappointed if you didn't."

The lieutenant shut the door and left the room. Harrison stared blankly; reminiscing a battle. He faded out from reality and remembered his memory vividly. A single, long, tear trail ran down his scar and landed on the after-action report detailing the death of Diaz.

CHAPTER 2: CALCULATED VIOLENCE

Three days prior to the distress beacon, November 1ˢᵗ

WITH ALL THE talk of cures for diseases and cancers, humanity could not cure the terrible disease of war. Technology advanced many people to high positions of power and self-expression, but those people still needed bilingual men and women who spoke the language of violence to those who could only speak it. War was as ancient as humanity itself and Task Force X-Ray were warrior artists; masters of their craft. Each man was battle-proven; elite. They were quick to reload, accurate in their aim, covert when need be, and deadly when required. They were well-versed in firearms from assault rifles to light-machineguns, shotguns to pistols, and heavy weapons to explosives. Each man was a formidable hand-to-hand fighter. They were the shadow of the American military; able to operate behind enemy lines and execute swift violence of action at their government's orders. Gusty winds breezed over Compound X-Ray as two specially modified Blackhawk helicopters appeared in the night sky and landed on the base's helipads, kicking up dust.

Commander Harrison and the entirety of Task Force X-Ray were inside of a briefing room in full combat gear. Eight men in total. They held various assault weapons, wore all-black swimsuits, and each wore body armor. Night vision optics were latched to their helmets.

"Wheels up in fifteen minutes, gentlemen—be ready!" Harrison ordered. "Our mission is to hit the Italian cargo freighter named *Andolini*. As you guys know, the freighter was hijacked two days ago by terrorists."

"Artemis Hounds?" Asked Diaz.

"That's correct, Diaz. Same assholes that took the Birmingham reactor in '23. They are heavily armed and have already demonstrated their ability to kill hostages. Check your fire and take them down clean. Watch your corners and background."

The squad all shouted, "Yes, sir!"

Everyone checked their tactical vests and weapons; patting their fatigues, making sure they had all their gear. Each man checked each other as well.

Harrison said, "The LT will fill you guys in on the plan of action. I'm going to have a debrief with our pilots. Keep your edge, X-Ray!"

He gave Jacobs a pat on the shoulder as he walked outside the room. Jacobs stood in front of a briefing screen. He continued to fill in the squad, occasionally clicking the remote, changing the power point slides.

"OK. I will lead the main fire team. We will fast-rope from the helicopter down to the top deck and secure it. Our call sign is 'Shark-1.' Ramirez and Taylor will be with me; Carter will provide sniper support from the hovering Blackhawk. The rest of you will go with the Commander, secure the lower part of the ship, and search for the hostages. You guys are 'Shark-2.' When we're en route to the freighter, a Chinook will join us from Camp Solomon. The hostages are to be loaded onto the bird for extraction, while we exfil with the Blackhawks. It is believed that two hostages have already been executed. That leaves us with at least twenty-eight crewmen that need rescuing. Any questions?"

"Do we have any confirmation of explosives?" Asked Ramirez.

"Artemis Hounds always have explosives, Ramirez. Stealth is going to be our best ally. The moment they are alerted of our presence they will likely try and detonate the bombs. If you ask me, they're probably just luring in a military unit to inflict greater casualties. We've seen this before. Anything else?"

A confident silence filled the room.

"Good! Let's do this!"

The soldiers walked out of the briefing room and loaded into the helicopters. The Blackhawks were modified to reduce sound. The rotors smoothly whipped through the air, but it wasn't as loud as a traditional helicopter; courtesy of Artantium lacing. They lowered their heads and covered their faces as they entered. They closed the side doors and the helicopters lifted into the air. They flew over the compound and towards the cargo freighter in the Gulf of Mexico.

Shark-1 readied their night vision goggles. The Andolini was in sight; a large cargo freighter stacked with multi-colored, steel cargo crates. The ship slowly moved as huge waves pounded against its hull. The Shark-1 helicopter hovered over the back of the ship with its side door open. Some poor guy was puking his guts up over the side of the ship. Carter inhaled. When the man was done vomiting, Carter exhaled. The terrorist turned around but was met by a bullet from Carter's sniper rifle. He was tossed over the railing from the round's impact.

"Tango down!" Carter reported. "LZ is clear for the moment."

The Shark-1 squad, led by Jacobs, fast-roped down to the back of the ship. They all wore gloves to protect their hands from the leather rope as they descended. The storm angrily shot lightning down from the sky, rough seas pounded against the ship's hull, and rain filled the air. Through their eyes, everything was illuminated in green; adrenaline pumping through their hearts. Jacobs led his men to cover, next to a stack of red cargo boxes. He peaked over and saw two terrorists in the distance patrolling the top deck and smoking cigarettes. One carried an AK-47 assault rifle, the other appeared to be unarmed. They could be heard laughing. Jacobs and Taylor took aim with their suppressed M-4 rifles and they synced their shots.

Jacobs quietly counted, "Three... two... one... *fire!*"

Both hostiles fell with single shots to their heads. The suppressors, mixed with the loud sounds of thunder and water, made the gun shots almost completely silent. Shark-1 continued to move up the ship. It was cold. There were dozens of steel cargo boxes that they had to maneuver through before reaching a steel stairway that they took up to the control room. While crouched, Jacobs peeked through the water-speckled window and saw that there were seven hostiles in the room, one at the helm. Most of them were manning the machinery. One looked out at the sea with a pair of binoculars. The storm ramped up. Between the huge ocean waves and the rain, visibility significantly decreased, and the ship tilted left and right. The ship would rise and sink as it treaded on the ocean's mighty waves. Using hand gestures, Jacobs ordered his men to stack up on the door.

He commanded, "Quick and clean!" Then, over his radio, he said, "Carter—get ready to take your shot. We're moving in thirty seconds."

Jacobs turned the valve and slowly opened the door to a crack. As he did, one of the hovering Blackhawks slowly declined its altitude and Carter lined up his shot. Jacobs threw a flashbang into the room. It exploded; causing a bright flash that blinded the hostiles and burst the room's inner lights. Carter took his shot and the terrorist at the helm was blown back by a bullet to the head. Didn't feel a thing. Jacobs and his men entered the room while all the hostiles were dazed by the flashbang. He and his men killed them with quick, controlled, burst of gunfire, and seized the control room. Diaz made sure each enemy was dead.

Over the radio, Jacobs said, "Shark-2—you are clear to descend!"

The second Blackhawk broke through the darkness as if part of the sky itself was descending onto the ship. Shark-2 lowered themselves onto the deck and quickly made their way up to the control center, while Shark-1 kept the top deck secure. Shark-2, led by Commander Harrison, made their way down to the lower decks like lions stalking their prey from the shadows. The flooring was metal and had little holes that a finger couldn't go through. They kept close to the walls and stayed out of the light whenever possible. It smelt of cigarettes. A terrorist stepped into the hallway from a room, but before he could turn around, he was shot three times through the back. He rolled over the floor in pain.

As they stepped over his body, they shot him again in the head. Shark-2 methodically searched all the rooms and eliminated any terrorists found inside. Most were sleeping or puking their guts up from the sea storm. They made their way down to the second lowest deck; right above the engine room. Commander Harrison saw a double door with two holed windows in them. He crouched and peaked through the window. He scanned the room and saw the hostages. They were sitting side by side; hands were bonded together, and they had brown bags over their heads. The team confirmed that the hostages were being kept in the ship's mess hall, where the sailors would eat. There were four armed guards in the room and one had an explosive vest on his body. The room was well-lit; an advantage to a defending enemy. Harrison reasoned that killing the lights would take out their eyes, while the squad's night-vision would allow them to make short work of the blind hostiles.

Harrison whispered, "Head to the power room we passed by and hit the lights when I give you the go-ahead, Diaz."

The soldier responded, "You got it!"

Diaz was about 5'8." He had black, wavy hair, and light-brown skin. He held a Scar-H assault rifle with a laser sight only visible with the night vision goggles. He powerwalked through the hallway and went up the stairs. As he was rushing past a room, a terrorist tackled him to the wall. Diaz's weapon was knocked out of his hands. He tried to stab Diaz with a knife, but he blocked the attempt with his forearm. They tumbled back and forth, slamming each other to the wall, and punching each other.

The terrorist was a bearded, mountain of a man, and used his superior body size and strength to pin Diaz down to the floor. Diaz stubbornly punched him in the ribs multiple times, knocked the knife out of his hand, and flipped him to the ground. Diaz delivered blows to the man's face. The hostile reached for the knife, grabbed it, and managed to stab Diaz, but the knife hit the armor plating of his tactical vest. Diaz prepared his fingers and grimaced as he gouged into the eyes of the terrorist. He screamed and his once-tough punches turned into pathetic slaps against Diaz's armor and arms. As the man withered, Diaz pulled the knife from his vest, and stabbed him in the throat, killing him.

The noise of the screaming could be heard throughout the hallway. After Diaz stabbed him, he could only hear a gurgling noise as the man drowned in his own blood. He pulled his hands away, looked at his black gloves, and saw that they were covered in blood. He looked at the man's face and examined the black, gaping holes that used to be where his eyeballs were.

Harrison asked over the radio, "What the hell is going on over there, Diaz?"

Diaz stood up and struggled to catch his breath, "Sorry, sir—ran into an inconvenience."

There was an eerie silence at the door where the rest of Shark-2 was waiting. Harrison knew that the jig was up. He signaled to Bradley, *prepare to breach.* Suddenly, an explosion blew the steel door from the mess hall into the hallway. The entire team was knocked down, as a ghastly inferno of fire and shrapnel briefly engulfed them. Loud automatic weapons fire sounded shortly after. A good sign; as this meant the terrorist had not yet detonated his bomb vest. The hostages screamed. Jacobs and the Shark-1 team heard the explosion. They felt a harsh rumble and some piping vibrated.

Jacobs asked over his radio, "Shark-2—what's your status?"

Nothing but static filled the radio.

He repeated, "Shark-2—do you read me? Over."

Nothing but static.

Jacobs shook his head. "There's trouble! Taylor with me. Ramirez, you stay up here and keep the ship steady."

Ramirez returned with, "You got it, boss!"

Jacobs and Taylor proceeded down to the lower decks.

Meanwhile, Diaz made his way back down the now smoke-filled hallway to his squad. Bradley, the man closest to the door, was laid out on top of Harrison. Garnome, the third teammate on Shark-2, had shrapnel punctures through his vest and reached for his MP-5 sub-machine gun that had been blown out of his hands. Three terrorists emerged from the smoke; a clear sign that the vest had not been detonated. In what seemed like a slow-motion moment, Harrison grabbed Bradley's M1911 pistol from his holster and fired three rounds through the lead terrorist's chest. As the second hostile aimed his weapon, Bradley quickly flipped over and hurled a knife; hitting him in the stomach. The third terrorist, still in shock from the sight of the first man dying, drew his weapon to his shoulder. But before he was able to fire, a hailstorm of machine-gun bullets tore him apart as Diaz jumped over his wounded comrades, guns blazing. Behind them, two more terrorists entered the hallway. Garnome grabbed his MP-5 and rolled over on his belly and killed both with messy shots to their chests.

As soon as Diaz turned to face the mess hall, the fourth hostile, with the bomb vest, was just walking out; a radio in his right hand and a high-powered pistol in his left hand. He had the look of someone who wanted to die and had a black tattoo around his eye. Diaz didn't have time to reload, so he pulled out his combat knife and rushed the terrorist before he could detonate his bomb vest. The terrorist fired one round that ripped through Diaz's shoulder and splattered blood on the hallway. Diaz, undeterred by the wound, pushed the hostile deep into the mess hall; repeatedly stabbing him in his stomach right below the bomb vest—but the combatant was able to shoot Diaz multiple times in the process. The high-powered pistol rounds burst through Diaz's body armor and with each shot, he felt his life draining out of him. With one last heroic effort, Diaz choke slammed the terrorist to the ground, finishing him. He looked at the blood oozing out of his vest, stumbled back, and collapsed onto the floor.

As Taylor and Jacobs helped the squad to their feet, Harrison, with one thing on his mind, rushed into the mess hall, threw Diaz over his shoulders, and carried him out.

Harrison ordered, "Taylor, take the squad and get those hostages out of there! On the double, soldier!!"

The men cut the binding on the hostages' hands and feet; their blindfolds next. They never stopped screaming. A total of twenty-five hostages were led out of the mess hall by Taylor, followed by the squad, into the hallway. The terrorist with the bomb vest whispered—in Russian—into the radio attached to his vest, "Until Valhalla, my brothers!"

The "radio" in his right hand turned out to be a detonator for more than 3,000 pounds of explosives located in engineering. With his last gasp, he clicked the detonator.

The ship violently shook; sending shockwaves through the entire vessel. The man's bomb vest likewise detonated.

The squad had made it to the third level, but were knocked off their feet by the sheer force of the explosion. Chaos ensued—railing and pipes collapsed; the once-mighty ship quickly turned into a wreck of twisted metal. The vessel was filled with a ringing noise. The team continued to make their way to the deck, fumbling and slipping every step of the way, while trying to keep the civilians together. They ran into walls and lost their footing often; a clear sign that the ship was capsizing. The men started to pick up a faint background noise as they continued moving through the dying ship. They made their way onto the second deck and an entire hallway collapsed; forcing them to find an alternative route around it. Bradley felt a pipe smack him against the back of his head. Oh! The pain! He thought to himself as he kept moving. The background noise grew louder, edging out the ringing sound. It sounded like an overloaded pipe was about to give way.

It was the noise of rushing water.

The water swooshed past the squad, who were still trying to get themselves, the civilians, and their wounded men to the top deck. They rushed towards the door that led to the staircase up to the helm, but the door was sealed shut. It was horizontal, not vertical. The ship was capsizing quickly and the squad was running out of time.

Taylor shouted, "We've got to get this door open! Give me a hand, Bradley!"

They both pulled on the valve handle, trying to turn it, but the door defiantly remained shut. Crates were flying around the room, smashing against the walls, and hitting the men. Cold water rushed up the stairwell and into the room, like the devil was rising to collect his due. The room quickly filled with freezing-cold water.

Jacobs yelled, "Get it open!"

Bradley shouted back, "We're trying—it won't budge!"

The water forcefully slammed against the wall and doorway; pinning everyone up against the wall. The room was now fully submerged.

An unspoken feeling of despair engulfed them.

The lights in the room clicked off. Seconds passed, but it felt more like hours. Underwater, Taylor and Bradley courageously continued to try to get the door open, but to no avail. Some of the civilians already began to drown. Garnome tried to calm them while underwater. The door showed no signs of opening and hope was fading quickly as they faced their cold doom.

Suddenly, a brief, bright flash shone through the water.

It was Ramirez, who had detonated shape charges on the door, blowing off the hinges.

He lifted the door open, water poured out, and the soldiers all climbed out with the hostages and made their way to the side of the ship. The Blackhawks were hovering, along with a huge Chinook helicopter. Bradley and Garnome carried the hostages who were unable to move on their own. With the ship sinking rapidly, the hostages were led onto the Chinook, which then immediately lifted off. Task Force X-Ray loaded onto the Blackhawk helicopters and they took flight. Harrison and Jacobs sat in the Blackhawk with Diaz, while Garnome, the medic, frantically worked to stop his bleeding. Diaz was laid out on the floor. Garnome kneeled over him, his upper body rested in Jacobs's arms, and Commander Harrison held Diaz's shaking hand.

Diaz choked out, "How did I do, sir?"

Harrison looked at him and smirked. "Quiet now, Diaz. You're going to be just fine, son."

Although the Commander knew it didn't look good. Diaz was pooling blood over the floor of the Blackhawk. His black, scuba outfit was bloodied. The left side of his face had blood that stretched down his neck. Diaz seemed congested. Each breath was a struggle and he sounded like someone who was having a bad asthma attack. Oh! Diaz, Commander Harrison thought. You weren't supposed to die, not now. You were on your way. You were going to finish college, what was it? USC? You and your family were going to buy that house in Los Angeles; the house I advised you not to buy, but your stubborn ass wouldn't listen. You have kids. Don't die now, son.

Diaz in a voice that was little more than a whisper, said, "Never... never lost this much blood."

Jacobs wiped the blood off his neck. "Just hang in there—all you have to do..."

Diaz coughed up more blood, the shaking in his hand turned to a tremble, and he gasped for air. He put his hand on Jacobs's chest and moaned, "Oh God! I don't think I'm going to make it!"

Harrison whispered to Garnome, "Talk to me. How does it look?"

Garnome kept his hands still on Diaz's chest and shook his head. "Two rounds punctured his chest cavity. I think one might have hit a lung..."

There was a long pause.

Garnome admitted, dejectedly, "...I don't think he's going to make it, sir." Garnome glanced up at Diaz's face. He was fading. Garnome felt a sense of self-hate come over himself. My friend is dying and I can't save him. I'm the medic. It's my job to save my guys.

Diaz weakly looked up and faintly called out "Jacobs..."

Jacobs acknowledged him. "Yeah, Diaz?"

"Would you... say a... prayer for me?"

Jacobs sucked in his lips and felt his eyes water. He softly replied, "Okay, buddy." He gripped Diaz's left hand. Sure, I've seen people die but never like this. Never has anyone died in my arms... never have I been so close to someone who was fading from life... never has it been such a friend. I've lost count of how many bad guys we've put in the ground. So many missions. For a while I believed that we were indestructible... you especially. What a fool I was.

"Dear father, I ask that you watch over Steven Diaz. Embrace him as we embrace you. Love him as we love you. Take him into your arms and watch over his family..."

Diaz interrupted Jacobs, "Oh, Roger... you sound like an angel. Take care of Sophia for me. Take... take... care..."

Tears leaked down Jacobs's face. He continued to pray.

Diaz's eyes went blank. He stopped shaking and quietly died in Jacobs's arms. No words were spoken. Garnome held his face in his blood-soaked hands, Jacobs closed his eyes, and Harrison, the only one left with any resolve, gently closed Diaz's eyelids and looked out at the storm. The cargo freighter was angrily sinking to the bottom of the ocean. What a life we live. Harrison thought. Kill and die... kill and die... kill and die. When does it end? This life is a curse... a burden. It ages you twice as fast; turns your hair white. I'm too old for this. I've seen this too many times. Young guys who give up everything for the adrenaline of combat. The promise of patriotic duty.

Think Diaz cared about patriotism a couple seconds ago? No. He cared to live. I can't do this anymore. I'm forty-six years old but it feels like I'm ninety.

The helicopter continued its route back to Compound X-Ray. Jacobs finished his prayer.

Drying his eyes, he quietly said, "In Jesus name I pray, Amen."

Only the windy Seabreeze through the sky could be heard against the sound of the unforgiving ocean water below them. As elite as Task Force X-Ray was, they were only human. No amount of training could prepare a person for the harsh realities of war.

CHAPTER 3: SUNSET

14 hours before the distress beacon, November 3rd

Burton? Youngest face I'd ever seen. I ordered him to pursue the enemy through the parking structure... by himself. I caught up to him just in time to see the light from his eyes dissipate. I can still feel his mother's slap across my face when I informed her about his death. Yates? Jumped on a grenade to save me. He was barely old enough to drink. Thompson? Burned alive when the bomb detonated in the reactor. I can still smell the sweet, sickly smell of his burnt flesh and hair. I'll probably never eat barbecue again. Harrison looked out at the barren desert from his office and shined his pistol. Diaz? Died a hero but wouldn't live to see his medals. How will I tell them? How will I tell them that I'm leaving? How do I tell myself? Harrison downed a shot of Whiskey.

As the sun began to set over the now-quite Compound X-Ray, the team of Task Force X-Ray, excluding Diaz and Harrison, conversed over a fire in the middle of the compound, outside. Ramirez, Carter, and Taylor had just gotten back from Vegas. Their spirits were low and calm. They often tried to make jokes or rib each other to get the death of Diaz off their minds, but it didn't really work. Behind every laugh, there was an ache of sadness that Diaz's voice couldn't be heard laughing with them. Bradley sat next to Jacobs. He massaged his aching knees.

He asked, "You talk to her?"

Jacobs murmured, "Yeah."

"How's she holding up?"

"Like a trembling skyscraper on its last legs. She and the kids are moving to Nebraska to stay at her parents' place. She wants us to come visit when we're on leave."

"Wouldn't miss it for the world."

Bradley looked up at the moon. *That's where you're going. A few more years of this hell and you'll be there. Believe it. You're going to give your family a new beginning. Give them the life that you could never have.* Abraham Bradley laid back into his chair and began to sharpen his throwing knives. He was light-skinned, had a neatly trimmed black beard, a bald head, and brown eyes. He was about 5'8" and had a muscular physique. Bradley was a decorated Army soldier and held the rank of Master Sergeant. He was the close-quarters combat specialist of the squad; a master at hand-to-hand combat. He was thirty-five. His squad mates often made fun of his baldness and claimed that he could no longer grow head hair. He argued that he could if he wanted to. He was African American, born and raised in Chicago. Fierce and loyal, his ferocity on the battlefield was only matched by his fierce passion for his comrades. He was a 'steaks and weights' type of guy. Friends wanted to go out, Bradley wanted to lift weights. His favorite hobby outside of lifting weights was reading. Like his favorite movie, his favorite book was Tolkien's Lord of the Rings.

He had family in Chicago; A wife and three daughters. Bradley used to say, *I can beat just about any man in the world, but I don't stand a chance against my girls at home.* His dad was encouraging of him joining the Army, being a former Army man himself. He was recruited out of Franklin high school. He originally planned on being a technician but became attracted to the explosive career of a special forces soldier.

ABRAHAM BRADLEY
(2020)

The lights in the gym were dim. I struck the punching bag repeatedly; my face drenched in sweat. A couple times I threw my right arm a little too far and the wound under my right arm pit began to bleed. I could see it reddening the white gauze, but I didn't care. The TV played in the center of the room. CBS covered the new military mechs coming into service. What a waste of money. You can't send a glorified tinman into a Vietnam or an Afghanistan. They lack judgement. Sure, they might save lives in some cases, but would be too heavy handed in other situations. Could they make the distinction between a combatant with a machete and a child with a butter knife? I watched the sleek Model-2's march down Washington square for a moment before returning to my punching bag. My hand wraps were torn up pretty good, so I decided to unravel them and replace them with a fresh wrapping. I looked up from my bench and saw a figure standing in the dark area of the room, next to the vending machines. He blew smoke from his cigarette. At first, I didn't pay him any mind. I got up and resumed my attack on the heavy bag. *Right, left, right, left, right, right, uppercut, left hook.* I noticed the figure began walking my way. He stood into the light and I quickly made him out to be a General. The three stars on the shoulders of his army-green dress uniform gave it away.

I stopped what I was doing and gave him a sharp salute. He didn't salute back. He sucked on his cigarette and puffed out smoke. "Bradley, Abraham?" He asked.

"Yes, sir!"

"At ease, Sergeant."

I dropped my salute and resumed hitting the bag. *Left, left, right, left, left, right, uppercut, right hook.*

"I heard what you did, Sergeant."

It seemed that once he said that, the meds wore off, and I could feel the pain under the gauze.

He continued, "Major Dicks put in a recommendation for the Medal of Honor for your actions."

I sighed before responding. "I don't want it, sir. I didn't do anything that really mattered."

The General was visibly surprised. He made a half smile. "That's not what I heard. Word is, after Sergeant Lively was hit, you killed seven insurgents with your bare hands, carried the downed Sergeant to the extract, and was shot three times in the process."

"My plates absorbed two of those shots, so I only got hit once. I didn't kill seven with my bare hands, I had a combat knife in one. And..."

I paused as I reminisced those green eyes go blank; watching a soul pass right in front of me. That's one hell of a thing to see.

"And?" The General asked.

"Lively... he died, sir. I knew him well and I was close with his family. I killed insurgents and took fire, but none of that meant a damn thing at the end of the day because my pal lost his life. Like I said, I didn't do anything that mattered."

The General blew out more smoke, put his rugged, carpenter-like, hand on my shoulder, and said, "I understand, son. That's exactly why I'm talking to you and not Lieutenant Mike, or Sergeant Thompson. I'm putting together a special team to combat the threats of the future. There's no room for glory hounds or medal seekers. I need men who are experienced, and I need men who can work as a team."

"Special team? I don't know if you realized, sir, but I'm already in a special team."

"That you are. A damn good one too. This team is different though. Ever hear of GUARD, son?"

"No, sir."

"GUARD is a new division in our military. A rather radical step. It will be a division of our toughest and best warfighters and cyber security staff. The world is not what it used to be. Technology is exploding at a never-before seen rate. The gap between our superiority and our adversaries has shortened. Our enemies are evolving and thus, so must we. Unlike the rest of our armed forces, this division will not fight with one hand behind its back. It will fight anywhere, everywhere, anytime. The rules of engagement are practically going to be unshackled for this division; allowing it to unleash violence at its own discretion during missions."

I pondered for a moment. I thought about all my friends in special forces. I'd have to leave all of them behind and go through the pain of being a FNG all over again. To hell with that! I already fight with the toughest and best.

"I don't know, sir. I think I'm good with where I'm at." I say.

"I have one last card to use. If it doesn't sway you, then you'll probably never see me again. I'm sure you've noticed all those space shuttles launching into our atmosphere."

I nodded my head with intrigue.

The three-star continued, "What if I offered to put you on one of those shuttles?"

Never in my wildest dreams did I expect to hear that. Only people with large bank accounts could settle on the space colonies. That or necessary terraforming staff. I was neither. It dawned on me that I could give my family a new start. Life on the colonies were flourishing. Earth was an overpopulated mudhole; people living on top of each other like rats, criminals running amuck, and a war that was sure to come. Going to a colony was like buying a new life.

"What's the catch, sir?"

"No catch, son, only conditions. You serve honorably for at least seven years in this unit I'm putting together and upon retiring I'll book you on the next shuttle to the destination of your choosing. Mars? Luna? Venus? You name it. Your pay will likewise be doubled."

The General arched back and smoked his cigarette like the deal was already sealed. It was.

"I'm in!"

PRESENT DAY

Garnome limped his way to the squad and took a seat in a chair next to Jacobs. He had white bandaging on his right leg and left forearm.

Jacobs asked, "Hey, Jerry. What did the docs say?"

He made a small grimace as he sat down. "Everything checks out. Just a little sore—you know, shrapnel will do that to you, and last I checked, I'm the only doc around these parts!"

"Oh, I'm sorry. I was talking about the *real* doctors. You know—the ones who save lives and don't take them."

Garnome laughed but quickly snapped back at Jacobs, "Not funny. I'll remember that when you're bleeding out. Someone will yell "Help Jacobs," and I'll respond, "I only help 'essential personnel.'"

Jacobs smirked. "Ouch!"

Jerry Garnome was a career medical officer, in the military for twelve years, and had a master's degree in the medical field. His military record was outstanding, and he held the rank of Captain in the Army. Although he was a Captain, the way Task force X-Ray was structured didn't mean he was the second-in-command—just the second highest rank officially or, on paper. He was a white man from Miami, Florida, married, with two daughters, one four years old and the other, seven. His hair was brown with a bald spot in the back, blue eyes. His face was clean shaven. His skinny body always made his body armor look awkward, but he was nevertheless in fine physical condition. Garnome cared deeply for his men. He would put himself in harm's way and do everything in his power to save anyone who needed it; soldiers and civilians alike. He was a 'by the books' type of man. He brushed and flossed his teeth twice a day and went to the dentist once a month when not deployed.

He was preparing to leave the military when he was brought up to his superior's office. Garnome thought that he was in trouble at first. *Come on in, Captain and have a seat.* The Colonel casually said. Garnome asked what he was in for and the Colonel told him about a new high-speed unit being created to better combat terrorism and that they wanted him. *What did I do to earn such an honor?* Garnome asked. *You have an outstanding record. For all the years you've been with us, you've never been a troublemaker and your medical procedures are at a 93% success rate. You're a damn good doc. You've saved a lot of lives and well… you're up for promotion. Do you accept?*

There Garnome was, readying to fill out his DD-214 form and dreading the idea of entering the civilian lifestyle, when he was offered this new position that payed twice as good as what he was already getting. When he discussed everything that was expected of him, he signed the contract and joined Task Force X-Ray.

JERRY GARNOME
(2020)

I heard the crying of a young boy, maybe six years old. Minutes felt like hours in the crowded waiting room. My wife, Rachael, put her hand on my right knee. I looked down and realized that my leg was shaking. I stopped.

"Mr. and Mrs. Garnome?" A nurse called out.

We stood up and walked into the doctor's room.

"The doctor will be with you shortly." She said, closing the door.

We waited a while longer. I thought about my last patient, a young Kenyan girl who'd been shot during a Boko Haram assault on her village. It was a gut shot; blood profusely leaked out of her back and onto my hands as I dragged her to safety. Her mother begged me to save her life. I was at the top of my game. The last ten patients I'd helped all lived but this time was different. Her eyes were fading and she'd lost so much blood, I worried she might've needed a blood transfusion, which would've been impossible given the circumstances. Bullets landed near my position; hitting the dirt and nearby wooden huts. I took deep breaths and focused. The sounds of screaming and gunfire became a distant sound. The bullet went through her stomach and out of her lower back; good news, as I didn't have to remove the bullet. I pulled out my suture kit and sewed the wound shut. I used alcohol to clean the wound and I tightly wrapped white gauze around her abdomen.

She stopped moving and her beautiful, wide eyes went blank. Not on my watch! I quickly pulled out my defib kit. I rubbed them together. *3... 2... 1... Clear!!* Nothing. The mother began to weep, Ramirez had to hold her back while I continued. I rubbed it together again. *3... 2... 1... Clear!!* Her body jumped forward and she gasped for air. She hugged me. I don't know if it was instinctively or out of gratitude. Either way, I saved her life. The thought gave me comfort as I waited. The doorknob shook and I braced myself for what was to come. The door opened and the doctor entered the room. He was a tall, Asian man, with graying hair, and glasses.

"Good afternoon, Mr. and Mrs. Garnome." He said with a smile; shaking our hands.

"Doctor," My wife anxiously started, "How's our child? Is he going to be OK?"

His smile slowly faded. He sat down on his adjustable chair and held his clipboard tightly.

"I'm afraid I have some bad news. Your son, Michael, has Leukemia... I'm so sorry."

Rachael put her hand around her mouth and a river of sorrow poured down her face.

"However, we've had recent breakthroughs in treating various cancers including Leukemia. Michael has an aggressive diagnosis, but if we can keep him in chemotherapy and fight this thing, maybe we can keep him around long enough to cure him."

"Where is he?" I ask.

"Michael is currently in lab five, just down the hallway. We need to schedule a date for him to begin chemotherapy immediately. I know this is tough news, but we can do this! I'll make sure that the procedures are done as safely as possible."

"Thank you, doctor." Rachael said.

I strangely didn't feel too worried. I saved hundreds of lives and put my life on the line for total strangers. I rubbed the sterling-silver cross under my shirt with my thumbs. Surely God will see us through this difficult time and save my boy.

PRESENT DAY

The Interstellar had worn off. Taylor's body slightly ached and he felt tired. The blue tint went away and everyone moved at their normal speed. He got up and walked into the porta-potty and threw up in the toilet.

Rick Taylor was currently the youngest man on the squad at age twenty-six. He joined the Navy at age seventeen with his parents' consent and enlisted with the elite Navy SEALs for six years. He lived for the thrill. His expert marksmanship gained the attention of his commanders and they offered him a transfer to be a part of

Task Force X-Ray. Although reluctant at first, he eventually joined. He and his SEAL buddies got into a bar fight in San Diego. A man accused him of sleeping with his wife and Taylor responded by saying, *what can I say? I rise with the tide and plunge with the force of a riptide. Chicks dig me, bro.*

The man punched Taylor in the face and a chaotic bar fight ensued. The police showed up, but the SEALs slid out the back and escaped the scene. A couple days later he was called into his superior's office. Taylor was certain he was going to get chewed out for that bar fight. *Have a seat, Taylor.* The master chief said. Taylor sat down and thought to himself, and here we go. The officer looked up from his papers and said, *do you know how the world works, son?* Taylor felt like laughing but restrained himself. *I, uh, don't concern myself with questions like that, sir. I just go with the flow.*

The chief had a serious, unflinching face. *You just go with the flow, huh? Well that's poetic but that's a good way to get fucked over, son. The world works like this. You train a young man to be one of the best soldiers around. The soldier goes through the hardest training in the world and his superiors are certain he's there to stay. Then BOOM! The big bad Army comes in and steals away one of the Navy's top sailors.* Taylor didn't understand. When the chief explained everything, Taylor realized he was being offered a position in Task Force X-Ray, an official subdivision of the US Army. He accepted.

A California native, Taylor loved to surf. Everyone was a *bro* or *dude* to him, even the Commander, although he'd never say it to his face. Taylor was a 'too cool for school' kind of guy. He was the type of person who was the star football player in high school, the guy that got the girls, and the one who was always late with his homework. He served as the squad's weapon expert—there was no weapon he couldn't fire, clean, take apart, and modify. He was single, with no offspring, Caucasian, tall, blond curly hair, physically cut, and on his body and arms he had multiple colored tattoos. His left arm was a sleeve of various tatts. He convinced himself that he had no family. Only the members of Task Force X-Ray could resemble anything close.

Ramirez watched his clock, *17:05*. Forty-five more minutes and he'd be receiving his final briefing before heading home. He was excited. He was going to spend the holidays at his mom's place. He could smell the turkey, ham, tamales, and Corona.

Daniel Ramirez was a dedicated soldier and loyal friend. His men could always rely on him to cheer them up with jokes or just pure comedy. He served four years as a combat engineer in an Army tank company after he had served four years as a cyber warfare operator. He had strong tech expertise—he could send communications, hack computers, and anything in between. He was also unofficially considered the best driver in the squad, although Carter would always dispute it. Daniel grew up in East Los Angeles, California. He was of Mexican descent and stood at just 5'5". He was a troubled kid and young adult. Fortunately, he'd never been caught during his criminal deeds, thus he had no official record. The military shaped him to be a team player and better developed his social skills. He had short, wavy, black hair, tan skin, brown eyes, and, like Taylor, multiple tattoos. Although highly competitive, Daniel liked to see his friends do well, and would often take on extra slack to ease his teammate's burdens.

One day, Ramirez was changing out a machine-gun on an Abrams main battle tank. He took out the heavy M2 50. Caliber machine-gun and replaced it with the lighter M-240B machine-gun. He grabbed a belt of 7.62 caliber machine-gun rounds from an ammo crate and loaded the gun. He lightly sung to himself as he switched out the weapons.

"Only God can judge me! Will I succeed? Paranoid from the weed!"

When he turned to the side to grab a repair tool, he saw a General standing next to the tank. He wore an army-green dress uniform, had a black beret, and shades. Ramirez clumsily dropped the repair tool and stood to attention.

Sergeant 1st class Ramirez reporting for duty, sir! Ramirez shouted. The General removed his shades and said, *At ease, son. Come on down, I wanted to talk to you.* Ramirez never heard those words come from a General in his life. He stepped down the tank and the officer shook his hand. Ramirez remembered him having a rugged hand with a tight grip. *I'm putting together a special unit of high-speed operators. I've read your file and I want you to be a part of the unit.* Ramirez reminded the General, *Uh, I'm no special operator, sir. I'm just a regular technician, how am I even qualified?* He put his arm on Ramirez's shoulder and said, *Like I said, I've read your file. Before the Army transferred you to this tank company, you were a cyber warfare elite. You aced your tests and proved to be an effective counter-hacker. You're just the man for the job. You scored very high on your communications and repair tests and the unit I'm putting together needs a man with your expertise. You don't have to accept, but I need an answer, yes or no?* Ramirez said, *Yes.*

The sun was now completely set. Jacobs had been talking to his wife via laptop for the past twenty minutes. The laptop sat comfortably in his lap and the couple could see each other's faces through the screen.

Jacobs could be heard to say, "...Oh yeah, we definitely have to try that food spot!"

His wife, Alison, replied, "Yeah, it's really good. Best pizza I've ever had! You know it's good if a New Yorker says it is. So, when do you think you'll be coming home to me?"

"We're waiting for our final briefing and then I'm going to board the light train. I should be home around one in the morning. Which brings me to what I wanted to tell you... Diaz was killed a couple of days ago... it hurts. The men and I haven't completely recovered... I know I haven't"

There was a pause and Jacobs cleared his throat for the third time.

Alison said, "Oh, my god. I'm so sorry, Roger. He was a good man... I was just talking to Sophia a week ago..."

"Yeah... yeah it's a real bummer, but thinking of coming home and falling into your arms is what keeps me going, babe. We'll talk more when I get home. I guess I'll be going now. We'll see each other soon."

Alison pleaded, "Wait, Roger. There was something else I wanted to tell you..."

"Yeah?"

"I was going to wait but after hearing about Diaz..." she sighed before continuing, "Well, I thought I should lighten your night with some good news."

A suspenseful pause followed.

Alison said, tearfully, "... I'm pregnant!"

Jacobs almost jumped out of his chair. "What? Are you sure?"

Alison chuckled, "Yes, Roger—I'm sure."

Jacobs shouted, "Oh wow! That's *great* news! Oh, man—I've gotta tell the boys. I'll be seeing you very, very soon, darling."

"Alright and Roger—you be careful out there, OK?"

"Yes, ma'am. Bye now."

"Goodbye, hun."

Jacobs logged off the computer and jumped out of his chair. "Guys—you won't believe it! Alison's pregnant!"

Bradley seemed just as excited as Jacobs; a big smile emerged from under his beard. He was the first to speak up. "Oh, that's great news, man! I'm happy for you."

Taylor, still a little stoned, was next. He teased a bit. "Aww—Jacobs is going to be a daddy. Congratulations, bro."

Ramirez needled him, "What? I didn't think you had it in you!"

Jacobs retorted, laughing, "Screw you, Daniel!"

Ramirez said, in a more sincere tone, "Nah man. All jokes aside—that's terrific news. Congratulations, man."

Carter added, "Nice! You'll make a great father!"

Garnome chimed in, "Congratulations, LT! You have it set."

The squad all gave him handshakes and hugs.

Roger Jacobs was a dedicated leader and demolitions expert. He was one of a rare few to hold an officer's position in the military and still be tightly knit with his squad. The men looked to him for not only leadership but also for advice and counseling. Jacobs had short, wavy blonde hair, blue eyes, no tattoos, and he stood at 6'2" tall. After graduating from college with a bachelor's degree, Roger entered the military as a Second Lieutenant, and spent four years in the Marine Corps as an infantryman and platoon leader. He spent another four years in Marine Force Recon. He was 34 years old, married for three years and now he was expecting his first child. Jacobs, now a First Lieutenant, was second-in-command of Task Force X-Ray.

Right before he joined Task Force X-Ray, he had gotten into a fight with Walter, Alison's ex-boyfriend, a couple days prior and had recently lost a friend in a combat mission when he was with the Marines. He was depressed and at a low point when his friend, Tanner, told him that an Army General was looking for him. Here in Camp Pendleton? He thought to himself. I thought the Army wasn't allowed here, who let him in? Jacobs left the barracks and walked into his CO's office and sat down. The General leaned against his commander's desk before speaking. *I'm General Sampson and I presume you're Lieutenant Jacobs?* Jacobs wasn't in the mood. He had just lost a friend and gotten into a nasty fight with Alison's ex.

He thought Sampson was there to give him a medal for his actions in combat. *I am, sir. May I ask what this is about?* Jacobs asked in a low voice. General Sampson explained why he was there. When Jacobs found out about Task Force X-Ray, he was very reluctant to join. I'm already a part of the world's finest fighting unit. I can't leave these men I've served beside for so long. Jacobs was thinking to himself. *During your time in Helmand province, you destroyed an enemy weapons cache, repelled an ambush, and single-handedly carried two of your squad mates to safety.* The General raved. *You have proven that you are a good leader; someone who will always put his men first. That's the type of man I need for Task Force X-Ray.* He continued. Jacobs knew he was going to have a family with Alison and the corps' paychecks weren't cutting it. He eventually accepted Sampson's offer and did what he'd thought he'd never do: join the Army.

ROGER JACOBS
(2023)

Blood leaked in a long line down the right side of my face. I bashed my head against the glass again; leaving blood on the mirror. Alison banged on the door like a demanding police officer.

"Roger!! Roger, open the door!! It's not your fault!!"

"It's my fault alright!! I'm no damn good!" I respond.

"That's not true, honey! If it was, I would've never gone on that third date, let you meet my parents, or marry you!"

Damnit! Why can't you just let me be mad. That's why I loved Alison. No matter how angry or sad I could be, she always had armor-piercing words that could breakthrough into my heart. God, I love you. I opened the door and she damn-near tackled me to the ground. She wrapped her arms and legs around me and squeezed tightly.

"It's ok, it's ok, baby!" She started. "There's nothing wrong with you. We'll try again."

"How many times have we tried? I wanna have kids before becoming an old man."

"We will. There's a lot more life to us. Now we have an excuse to have more fun!"

We both chuckled. When she sensed my tenseness lower, she released her grip on me, and stood on her feet. Alison turned the water on and when it got hot, she wet a blue face towel, squeezed out excess water, and began wiping the blood off my face. We'd been married for about four years and we'd tried more times than I could count, but a child seemed beyond our reach. Sure, I enjoyed expressing love with my wife, but I'm getting older, and I want to be able to experience my time with my kids while being fairly young.

PRESENT DAY

Jacobs expressed his gratitude to his comrades. "Thanks, guys. It really does mean the world to me. I guess I'll go and let the Commander in on the great news."

He left the circle and walked inside the compound.

Carter said, "Yeah, you guys—I have some tinkering to do on my rifle. I'll catch you in the mess hall. Shots before we part ways."

Carter walked away from the fire and went to his quarters, where he adjusted the sights on his sniper rifle.

Roman Carter, at age twenty-eight, was as charismatic as he was deadly. After high school, he immediately joined the Army and attended sniper school. He aced his marksmanship training and was a renowned sniper. After spending eight years in the Army, he, too was offered a position on Task Force X-Ray, and unhesitatingly accepted the position. *You killed some thirty Iraqi insurgents during your time in Ramadi, and another forty-five in Afghanistan. I need a sniper like that.* General Sampson said. Carter was quick to remind him, *It's not about the bad guys, sir, it's about the good guys. I killed in order to save lives, no more, no less.* An African American, he'd been raised by his grandparents in Atlanta, Georgia, after his parents disappeared.

His aunt, who was looking after him before his grandparents, died from breast cancer when he was ten. When she died, Carter felt that he had no one left. He didn't have many friends and his family members seemed to leave him all the same. He spent much of his childhood feeling neglected. Feeling like no one cared about him. One day, in Arthur High School, a sharp-looking Army recruiter came to his school. At first Carter was too shy to talk to him, but he eventually made his way down to his booth. Carter, who was considering suicide, joined the Army, and the Army saved his life and strengthened his character. His granddad served in the Navy during the Korean war and was pleased to see Carter join. He was tall, skinny, physically sharp, with short, curly brown hair, and green eyes. Although sometimes distant from his squad mates, he had saved all their lives at least once.

This was Task Force X-Ray, an elite team of elite soldiers. They'd fought in many battles together, shared beers, battle wounds, good times, and bad times. Task Force X-Ray was a tier-one military team sent in to deal with their country's biggest problems. They were a dark, top-secret, special forces team, unknown. They were kept out of the news and there was no training to get in. You couldn't find Task Force X-Ray—they found you. Only the best of the best was selected to join this task force; typically those who had proven themselves in combat, and only the highest members of the US government and few GUARD units knew of their existence.

They were the tip of the spear for GUARD. All special forces units became enveloped into GUARD, but Task Force X-Ray was on another level. They were allowed to fight anywhere; even in other major countries during 'peacetime.' They gathered intelligence, captured or killed high valued targets, engaged in espionage, and on rare occasions, carried out assassinations. The rampant arms race invoked the government's needs of a black operative team that could operate with no limitations. A team that could fight just as dirty as the enemy. The answer was Task Force X-Ray, a group of individuals that could be sent behind enemy lines without any direct ties to the US. They were weary from battle and each man was anxious to go on leave. It was the night of November the 3rd and Thanksgiving was on everyone's minds. They didn't know it then, but, although they'd been through many hellish, tough situations, their toughest situation was right around the corner.

CHAPTER 4: "HELLFIRE"

The night of the distress signal, November 4th

IT WAS PAST midnight. Strong winds swept across the lonely Nevada desert and the moon was full as it casts its illumination onto the land. Blue lighting shone from Las Vegas. The bright trails of the space shuttles could be seen in the night sky. In Harrison's office, he and Jacobs were talking.

Harrison said, "If it's a boy, show strong leadership. Take him out hunting, fishing; teach him respect. Instill in him at an early age what it means to be a man, and in his teenage years, watch him closely. This is when they become more 'artistic.' They struggle to find themselves and they're looking for their purpose. It's up to you at this stage to help him find it, so that, by time he becomes an adult, he'll have an easier time knowing what he wants to do. If it's a girl—well, I'm afraid I can't help you, son. You're on your own!"

Jacobs laughed and answered, "Will do, sir. How are your sons doing?"

"They're all grown up now. The youngest one, Henry, plays for the Texas Wildcats in the Rocket League and I guess he got himself a girlfriend. The older one, George, is on his way to Ranger school. The oldest, Jack Jr, is a lawyer down in California. He's married, has two little girls, and has another kid on the way."

Jacobs loved serving under Harrison because he was never 'too good' to be right beside his men. He always charged into battle with his shoulder lined with the man next to him and never put himself first. It was easy to forget that Harrison was an officer and not just another grunt. Harrison held an 'open door' policy and all who served under him could talk with him whenever they were off duty. Harrison and Jacobs often held conversations like these whenever they had downtime. Jacobs's father passed away from cancer a few years back, but he saw a father in the Commander. He had missed the conversations he held with his dad. They would sit on the porch and talk about cars, women, food, and life. Jacobs remembered sipping his dad's iced, lemon tea. The sweet taste with the hint of lemon combined with talking about life was a much-needed meditation session. He never quite recovered from losing his dad, but the conversations he had with Commander Harrison reminded him of those talks he had with his old man. They conversed for thirty minutes and Harrison tried to keep each topic going.

Harrison paused for a moment. He decided to test the waters. "Well, as for me, Roger, I'm thinking of retiring." He spoke those words with an eager anticipation of a response.

Jacobs heard the words, but it took him a minute to process them. He paused before saying, "What? The great Commander Harrison retiring? I never thought I'd see the day."

"Yeah, son. Maria is tired of being alone and I can't blame her. Being gone all this time and constantly being deployed to battle zones takes its toll on you, and it has taken its toll on this old warrior. Besides, I've done my patriotic duty to my country. It's time I start living life for myself and my family." Harrison spoke those last words with a hint of bitterness. He downed a shot of Whiskey and grimaced as it went down his throat. "I'll let the young guys bust their knees and backs in my stead."

Jacobs took in the news.

He was happy for Harrison in the sense that he would be retreating from a life of violence and danger, but deep down he hated the idea of him leaving. He was so fond of taking orders from him, he couldn't bear the idea of having to take orders from someone else. He was the true source of Task Force X-Ray's mysticism. Without him, Jacobs worried that the unit would just be like any other special forces team.

Harrison said, "I guess that means I'll be leaving you in charge."

"Oh, I don't know about that, sir. I don't think I'm up for it."

"Wow—the great Lieutenant Jacobs shying away from an opportunity? Now THAT is something I thought I'd never see!"

Jacobs joked, "Ha, ha, ha, I just hope my face doesn't turn into yours!" Jacobs tweaked his voice to sound like Commander Harrison's and mockingly said, "You know, son.... When the day comes when you have to iron the wrinkles on your own face, you'll know what I had to go through!"

Harrison burst out laughing. "Ah, man. That really hurt my feelings, Roger. I have to ask, though: Why not?"

Jacobs continued, "Who'd want those wrinkles... that thousand-yard stare... that terrible scar?"

"I'm not talking about my face, son. My face has seen more battles, medals, and bedroom action then your face will ever see! Why wouldn't you want to lead Task Force X-Ray?"

Jacobs shook his head.

"Come on! You're a terrific leader. I've seen you lead men into battle without hesitation, completely covering any fears or doubts you might've had. More importantly, though, you genuinely care about the men. You've already earned their respect, admiration, and loyalty. You're perfect for the job, Roger. Or have you secretly been a pussy my whole time knowing you?"

Jacobs was slow to smile. Harrison could tell something was

eating away at him. He replied, "Sir... I just can't deal with seeing my men die—the death of Diaz proved that to me. Before that, my time in the Helmand Province. Leading them into battle is one thing but giving orders that cost them their lives and then having to live with those decisions... would be more than I care to bear. Sure, I've led guys during my time in the corps, but Diaz dying in my arms... I don't know."

After a long pause, Harrison said, "I understand, If I'm honest with you, Roger... Diaz's death is part of the reason I plan on retiring."

Jacobs slowly nodded his head.

Harrison downed another shot. "War is poison, son... it taints your soul... lives with you. I've commanded many men into battle and I've got a lot of 'em killed, too. I never stop seeing their faces. I remember the orders I gave that cost them their lives. But such is war. We're warriors. We poisoned our souls the minute we entered combat and Roger, we've both seen a lot of it. You could get men killed, but you could save them; save a lot of other lives as well. That's what I tell myself: 'I've lost a lot of men, but I've saved at least twice as many, if not more.'"

The office phone rang, but Harrison continued.

"So, think about it, Roger. I respect your reasoning, but I couldn't imagine a better man to lead the squad. If you don't do it, Washington is just going to send some goofball down here to take command. How many men will he get killed? And will he care for the men the way you do? Food for thought..."

The phone continued to ring.

"I have to take this call, give me a minute."

Jacobs nodded his head

Harrison answered the phone, "Commander Harrison speaking."

"Commander, we have a situation. This is General Michaelson."

"I understand, sir. Proceed."

"Listen, Commander. A Red Tier-One situation has just been passed to command—do you acknowledge?"

Harrison cleared his throat. "Yes, sir!"

"Good. General Sampson is en route to Compound X-Ray with a small delegation to brief you on your assignment. Expect him in roughly 30 mikes."

"Will do, sir."

"Oh, and one more thing, Commander. I'm sorry to hear you lost a man in this week's earlier operation. My condolences. However, to ensure Task Force X-Ray is at full operational readiness, I'm sending you a new guy. He's riding alongside General Sampson. I'll send you his dossier via email."

"Sounds good to me, sir."

Both officers hang up the phone.

Harrison shook his head, looked at Jacobs, and said, "Well, well, looks like we have a big one coming our way."

Jacobs felt his heart rate speed up. "A 'big one,' sir?"

"Red Tier-One." Harrison answered, standing up and looking out of his window.

"Shit!"

"The feeling's mutual, but we have our orders. General Sampson and his staff are en route to brief us on the mission. Head to the barracks and tell the men. Looks like the holidays are going to have to wait a while."

"Yes, sir!"

My retirement too. Harrison thought, gulping another shot.

The wind was now blowing intensely. Roughly thirty minutes passed, and a single Blackhawk helicopter appeared in the sky, and landed on the compound's helipad. General Sampson stepped off the chopper accompanied by a young man, a CIA operative, and an unknown person. General Sampson was a tall, skinny man. He had had short black hair with gray sides. He wore a crisp, army-green uniform, and had an army hat with three stars perched in the middle. He was a close friend of Commander Harrison and handpicked each member of Task Force X-Ray. Sampson was their handler; the unit directly reported to him. He had a face that seemed to say, *I've been doing this for too long.* Commander Harrison met them at the helipad, gave the General a sharp salute, and they walked inside the base while covering their heads from the gusty winds. They proceeded to the briefing room, where all the members of Task Force X-Ray were assembled. They stood to attention until they were told to sit. The briefing room was a large atrium, adjacent to the mess hall. The members sat in gray-steel, fold-up chairs.

No one knew what was going on. They hadn't been presented with a Red Tier-One situation since the terrorist attack on the Birmingham nuclear reactor; an event that threatened the lives of over thirty-thousand people. They had all hoped that the entire thing was a joke. Some had already ordered tickets on the Vegas light-speed train for the next day. They were tired and each man was thinking about home, as Thanksgiving was just a few weeks away. They all sat in casual clothing and waited in silence for the senior officer to brief them.

General Sampson stepped onto the stage in the front of the room and got right to the point. "Gentlemen, there is a high-priority mission that demands your utmost attention, so I'll be as brief as possible. Here with me is CIA operative Sonya Chrystal and Val Bridgeway, part of the Volaire science team. The man to my left is Chris Marilyn. He is a temporary addition of Task Force X-Ray and all three of these people will be accompanying you to your destination. Val, if you could fill them in..."

Val Bridgeway was a short white woman, dark orange hair wrapped into a bun, brown eyes and glasses. She held her notepad tightly and often adjusted her glasses. She was wearing an all-white button up shirt, under a grey jacket with a furred hood, and blue jeans.

She spoke in a soft voice, "Roughly six hours ago, we lost contact with our R&D facility in a remote valley in the northern slope of Alaska, Hope 7. The facility has top-secret, classified documents that are critical to our military infrastructure. The American war machine relies on the advanced inventions coming out of Hope 7. It is critical that we secure the facility."

Ramirez asked, "I feel a catch coming on. What kind of enemy insurgents are we looking at ma'am?"

Bridgeway replied, "Not insurgents. There may be multiple combatants, but all that we're sure of is "It.'"

"It?"

"After the incident, command sent in a security team—codenamed, Baseline Security. They were the team ordered to respond to any possible crisis at the facility and served as a quick reaction force."

Bradley was writing notes in his notepad. "You said, *'were'*?"

"That's correct. Sonya tells me that they were completely wiped out—a thirty-two-man team."

"Who managed to do that?" Carter asked impatiently.

"Listen—instead of me doing a Q&A, I'll show you footage from a security cam. This footage is labeled, "First Contact.'"

Bridgeway's hand shook as she inserted the disc into a projector. Carter thought that she would break the disc trying to insert it. The security-camera footage played onto the auditorium's screen. It showed two janitors talking in a hallway, a woman in all-white passing by with two-armed security guards and four mechs. The janitors appeared to be laughing, the lights flickered, the lights burst, the hallway was illuminated by red, and a strange looking figure appeared on the camera. Bridgeway paused the video and zoomed in on the figure.

There was a long silence in the atrium. Some leaned in close to get a better look at the screen.

Bridgeway continued the clip in slow motion.

The figure appeared to be a dark, shadowy outlining of a human; a moving piece of darkness. It was a black, static silhouette. A terrible wailing was heard. They could hear the words, *Make... It... Stop...* The static figure increased in height and zipped through the hallway. As it does, the security-camera footage becomes too distorted to see anything.

"This is all from the security camera, but shortly after this footage, one of the janitors managed to send a distress beacon," Bridgeway explained.

She started the distress video.

A man appeared on the screen. He was a black man, but even he seemed pale. He spoke like he'd just ran a marathon. "Please send help, something terrible has happened. *Hellfire!* Please help! God, I don't want to die. I repeat: *Hellfire!* Send help!"

The message froze up. The screaming and wailing continued until the footage shut off completely.

Ramirez murmured under his breath, "*What the fuck?*"

Sonya Chrystal was average height, Caucasian, red hair wrapped into a ponytail, and had green eyes. She was wearing all-black combat pants tucked into all-black combat boots, in addition to an all-black, long-sleeved buttoned-up shirt under a tactical vest. She had a combative look about her.

Chrystal said, "'*Hellfire'* was the code for 'Red Alert'. Once he sent this message, we dispatched Baseline Security to deal with the threat. We haven't heard anything from the teams and we suspect that they've all been killed. Hope 7 has officially gone dark."

Jacobs asked, "Just what kind of research do you people do at Hope 7?"

"Classified research—the kind of research that is above your pay grade, Lieutenant. Let's just say this facility and its research is critical to national security. It must be recovered or destroyed. If possible, we need to recover as much classified data as possible, and if necessary, we need to destroy the facility entirely to ensure that the research doesn't fall into enemy hands. This thing has been given the codename 'Phantom.' It is to be destroyed. It's too dangerous to try any other strategy."

Commander Harrison asked, "Just how do we deal with this 'Phantom'? And what can you tell us about it?"

"We do not have much information on 'Phantom,' other than that it uses some sort of electric power to speed across areas. There have also been reports of its ability to teleport. Val can give you more information..."

Bridgeway spoke up, "We are arming your team with special bullets for your guns. They are called 'proton rounds'—basically standard bullets but with electric micro-chips inside the tip of the ammunition. The micro-chips are electrically charged; using electric pulses and negative charge to create disruptions in the Phantom's electric frame. If you fire these rounds at the Phantom, it should cause it to flee, and it may possibly lose its powers. Maybe if you hit it enough times, you will kill it."

"Maybe? We don't operate on maybes." Harrison stated.

"It's all that we have. We're confident that these bullets will better assist you in dealing with this threat. Standard bullets didn't work out well for the security staff." Sonya said.

"However, we must be very careful." Val continued. "It is believed that the Phantom can infect electronics and corrupt electronic systems. The mere presence of the Phantom alone will probably cause your electronics to malfunction. We are also arming your team with specially modified plates to go on your armor. They act as electric micro-shielding, which will stop the Phantom from running right through you and ripping you in half."

"Any more questions?"

Commander Harrison didn't say anything, but he knew that something was amiss. For something that is such an unknown, they sure do seem to know a lot about it. He thought.

Carter said, "I have one, who's the lady in the white business suit?"

"That's Samantha Volaire, lead scientist of the Volaire science team, and overseer of all projects at Hope 7. Are there any other questions?"

Silence filled the room. Not a confident silence, but an unnerved silence. No one knew what to make of the creature. How did it come to be? Who created it? How do we beat it? Were among the questions inside everyone's minds. Ten minutes ago, they were thinking about turkey and being smothered by their lover's lips, but now they were being ordered to fight a seemingly super-natural being.

General Sampson broke the silence. "Excellent. We need the task force wheels up in an hour. Val will help get you men situated with the new tech. Commander Harrison—may I have a word in private?"

"Yes, sir. Team—assemble in the armory, gear up, and walk the new guy through the basics. I'll see you in fifteen."

Everyone shuffled down to the armory. They moved sluggishly.

Meanwhile, Harrison and General Sampson talked in the Commander's office.

Harrison said to Sampson, "I don't like it. What in the hell did we just watch? It looked an awful lot like a human."

The General replied, "I'm with you, Jack. I don't like it either, but these are your orders."

He paused and peeked out the door.

He popped his head back in and spoke in a low voice. "Between you and me, this operation is high level. It comes from the very top of command. Off the record, you do what you have to do. Just get you and your men out of there in one piece. Task Force X-Ray is too valuable to be lost on this so-called 'shadow op.'"

"You didn't answer my question, sir."

"In all honesty, Commander, I have no clue what's going on down there. All I know is that the US government has poured huge amounts of funding into Hope 7—billions of dollars. It's a critical research facility; they advance our weaponry and technology… that's all I know. It is absolutely imperative that the research be saved or destroyed. It's classified and with cyber-terrorists like the Artemis Hounds on the loose, we have to put a premium on protecting our technological secrets. Not to mention, China and Russia would jump at the opportunity to recover even a fraction of our intelligence in Hope 7. Above that, we need to find out what happened and ensure that this monster doesn't escape into the world."

"Can we be sure that these proton rounds will do the job? Same for the micro-shielded plates?"

"Fresh outta R&D, but test-proven. They'll work and the bullets will clear your weapon's barrel without issue."

"What if we find evidence of a violation of Article 331?"

"Download it and bring it back to me personally. We'll review it and pass it to command. We're soldiers not criminals, Commander. A violation of Article 331 is a crime against humanity, I expect you to record all the evidence you can find."

"What of Hope 7 itself? What do you want us to do if it is compromised? Or if the Phantom is beyond our combat capabilities?"

"Do what you do best, Commander: blow shit up! Pass 'Inferno' to command and I'll send bombers to level that place in under an hour. Just make sure you and your men clear the blast zone."

"Can we expect any other units from GUARD to assist us?"

"I requested a team of Army Rangers to assist you in securing Hope 7, but I was denied. All other units are either engaged in other areas or their clearance is too low. I'm afraid you men will be on your own."

Harrison nodded his head. "Well, sir, like you said: I have my orders. You can count on Task Force X-Ray to get the job done."

"Outstanding, Commander. Just watch yourself, Jack."

"Will do, sir."

The men saluted each other; General Sampson walked to the helipad and left in the same Blackhawk he'd come in on.

In the armory, the squad talked about the situation. Sonya, Val, and Chris were not in the immediate vicinity.

As he loaded his .45, Bradley said, "I don't know about this one, guys. Something feels wrong about this mission. I got bad vibes all the way."

Ramirez was writing a letter to his mom the old-fashioned way: pen and paper. He wanted to tell her so badly about what he had just saw, but he knew it was top-secret, and the letter would never make it to her. He made up an excuse on why he probably wouldn't be home for Thanksgiving without spilling any real details.

He replied to Bradley's comment, "You're preaching to the choir, brother. The whole mission feels sketchy—and what about that thing we saw, that 'Phantom'? Did you see how fast it shot through that hallway? How in the hell do you even fight something like that? It's like nothing we've ever fought—super-natural even. And don't even get me started on that scream: like nails on a chalkboard... and we weren't even in the hallway that was just through the audio track."

Ramirez didn't have a special forces background like his fellow comrades. He was an Army cyber-warfare operator before being an Army technician. Prior to the training he got in the task force, he didn't have any advanced shooting skills. He didn't even have much combat experience outside of his time in the new unit. Ramirez was often nervous between operations, but this time was different. The butterflies in his stomach seemed to be made of metal. He felt the urge to take a crap multiple times before even putting on his boots.

Taylor joined in on the conversation. "Yeah... it's no doubt that we're in the fight for our lives on this one, boys. I don't even think the legendary "Stormtrooper" Harrison will be able to save us on this one."

That was a statement. Commander Harrison saved Taylor's life more times than he could count. Taylor viewed Commander Harrison as an icon; a true, rough-faced, American war hero. Whenever he fought with him, he always felt assured. Even when the odds were stacked against the team, he knew that the Commander would always find a way to win. This time, however, Taylor didn't feel so assured. He slotted his Interstellar into his left magazine pouch.

Jacobs, fitting on his combat boots, added, "Come on, guys—we've got this! We've fought in countless battles, had many close calls—but we're still standing, aren't we? If anybody can stop this ghost, we can!"

Those words echoed back to the speech he gave his Marines before assaulting that weapons cache in Helmand province. It was a rally. Words of confidence bred from a mind of uncertainty. This time was no different. Jacobs played the clip of the Phantom over and over in his head. He would never say it out loud, but deep down he worried greatly that there would be heavy casualties amongst the task force. *What? We never suffered more than a single death on a mission. Surely, I worry too much. Maybe I should remind them of... no. That's not the same. Or what about... no that's not the same either.* Truth was, this mission was going to be like nothing they'd ever experienced. Nothing even came close.

Carter was loading the special bullets into his magazine. The 7.62mm rifle rounds had see-through blue tips instead of the bronze tips on standard bullets. Inside the blue tip, there was a thin, electric line in the center. The line reminded Carter of that Tesla coil lighter his brother sent him a couple years back. *These Toys R' Us bullets better work.* He thought to himself before saying aloud, "Damn straight. I'm more curious about that spook from the CIA. I never liked working with the damn CIA! They're always sketchy, with their 'shadow ops,' and political agendas. No, thanks! Gotta keep our eyes on her, that's for sure."

Garnome looked at Diaz's old locker. It had been cleaned out. He felt tremendous sadness come over him. He remembered how Diaz was always excited to go on a mission. He would energetically strap on his boots, slap his helmet a few times, lightly jump up and down a couple of times before saying aloud, *Let's kill 'em all!* Garnome always used to feel that Diaz enjoyed his job too much. Like he was a heroine fiend who was about to get his next fix; only instead of heroine, his drug was war. Garnome loved his tenacity though and he was going to miss that tenacity on this mission. He blamed himself for not being able to save him. He tucked away his picture of his son, Michael.

"Man, it just isn't the same without Diaz." Garnome said with emptiness in his tone.

A brief, sorrowful silence came over the room as the doc continued to load up his medical kits and equipment.

He continued, "Now we're stuck with some new guy that couldn't grow a beard to save his life. Probably can't fight either."

Carter nodded his head. "Seriously, that kid is too young to be on this op. I could see if we were fighting terrorists—but this crap? It's out of his league! What did this rookie do to get access to the most elite fighting force in the world? Is he even old enough to drink!?"

Jacobs broke in, "Yeah I don't like it either, but if we hold strong, we'll pull through, just like in every other mission. Now, walk me through your loadouts."

Bradley responded, "I'm taking the M-60 light machine-gun on this one. I'll have my sawed off, pump-action shotgun with me too. I'll keep my trusty throwing blades close. My .45 will be a last resort"

Ramirez chided Bradley, "You think those throwing blades are going to even faze that thing?"

Carter jumped in. "Forget that! Same goes for that dinosaur of a gun—the M-60? Come on, I'm surprised they still make those guns. The '60 belongs in a museum, bro. Vietnam ended in '75, time to let go of the past!"

Bradley had his mind made up. "Hey! Leave the '60 alone! That gun is battle tested—tried and true! What about you? Didn't you get the memo? We're fighting in close quarters. How well is your sniper rifle going to hold up in there?"

Carter sneered, "Very funny, close-quarters man. I'm taking my Scar-H assault rifle and I'll have my semi-automatic marksman rifle at my side, just in case we run into some long-range action."

Taylor held his weapon in the air. "Me? I'm taking the S-7 flame-thrower, bro. I'll fry that thing at close range. It feeds on napalm cartridges. This way, I don't have to carry that heavy tank on my back. When the napalm runs low, I can just switch cartridges, and it'll be as good as new. I'll be taking my MP-7 sub-machine gun as well."

Ramirez reminded the group, "Diaz always liked using flame-throwers. Rest in peace, brother. As for me, I'll be taking my M-27 assault rifle with grenade launcher. My G-18 will rest in my holster."

Taylor asked, "Long barrel or short?"

"Long."

Garnome inserted his shotgun shells by hand. "Unlike you guys, I don't want to be too badly weighed down, so I'm taking the tac shotgun with my M-9 Beretta."

Jacobs asked, "Going Italian, are we? I'm keeping my loadout American. I'll be taking my M-4 with my 1911. Make sure you guys bring your night-vision goggles, extra rounds, flashlights, etc."

Carter spoke for the group, "Don't worry, Jacobs. We got it."

Chris Marilyn, the new guy, entered the armory.

"Hey." He softly said.

The squad stared at him. The room went from loud with conversation to near silence. Bradley tapped his blades together. *Ting, ting, ting, ting.* Chris was just 19 years old and was expected to fill Diaz's role of heavy assault. The boots he had to fill were big. Diaz was a tenacious fighter; tough and loyal. Chris was obviously new and the squad was going to have to warm up to the unproven, young man. He was a skinny, white man; arms thin but cut, his blonde hair was defiantly longer than the rest of the men's hair. He had a thin, pale face.

Carter said to the new guy, "What makes you so special, kid?"

"Well, I . . . ."

"Forget I even asked you."

He went back to quietly prepping his weapons.

Jacobs asked, "You said your name was 'Chris'? Get loaded up! Wear both armor plates, front and back, and choose your weapons. You might wanna pack heavy, we're in for a hell of a fight. Fighting will likely be close-quartered, so load accordingly. You're new here, but we're Task Force X-Ray and we move quickly. I'm expecting you to match our performance and carry your weight, soldier. Is this your first op?"

"No, sir. I worked for a classified government organization..."

Ramirez budded in, "Yeah, and I worked for the president of the United States. I would stand behind him, catch his farts in a jar, and throw them at his enemy's faces!"

Everyone but Chris laughed. He had a serious face. If he walked onto a school campus, people would think in their minds, *School shooter!* There was an ominous glow about him. He didn't look intimidating, instead, he had a 'dangerous if provoked' vibe.

Ramirez continued, "Cut the act kid, what did you do?"

Chris didn't say anything.

Ramirez slowly walked over and got in his face.

"Can't hear you!"

The squad cheered, whooped, and hollered; tuning into the escalating confrontation. The duo stared each other down. Sonya stepped into the armory.

She said, "Hey!! That's enough! Chris—grab your gear!"

Chris broke the stare and went inside the open weapons vault. He walked out with an M-249 squad automatic machine gun and slung around his hips a single-barreled grenade launcher. He bumped Ramirez's shoulder as he walked by.

Bradley whispered to Jacobs, "Shit—the kids' stronger than he looks."

Harrison stepped into the armory and everyone went back to prepping for the mission. He walked to his personal weapons locker, where he equipped an M16-A3 assault rifle and a Desert Eagle .50AE pistol. The pistol was clean and silver looking; had a custom leather grip with the image of a jagged lightning bolt inside an eyeball. In his locker, he had a picture of his wife, Maria. It was a professional photo of her sitting on sand and holding her wooden guitar. The coloring was black and white. Harrison hadn't seen Maria in over two months and yet whenever he stared into that picture, he felt that he could smell her hair. A warm Jasmine scent came to Harrison's mind with a hint of cinnamon. She sat on the beach; the waves as a background, with her legs crisscrossed, and her black hair wildly covering the left side of her tan face.

He removed the photo from his locker and placed it inside his internal chest pocket, covering his heart. Harrison always carried the photo with him during combat missions. He imagined someday that he would be too slow and a shooter would get a couple lucky shots on him. He would slump onto a boulder or next to a building, and covered in blood, he would remove the picture and die with the image of his wife in his mind. The smell of Jasmine and cinnamon would give him peace before dying. Fortunately, no one has ever been quite lucky enough to kill Harrison. In fact, he had made a name for himself by being very hard to kill. He'd been shot multiple times, stabbed, pierced by shrapnel, and has had broken bones. In a strange way, he was known for not dying.

Sonya walked into the vault and equipped an MP-5 sub-machine gun. She held the weapon firmly, hinting to the others that she knew how to use it. Taylor caught a glimpse of a 'light tattoo' on her neck. It was two boxers throwing punches at each other and shuffling their feet. The motion would play out in real time and keep repeating itself. Light tattoos were a new invention and Taylor was always nervous about getting one. She took off her tactical vest and replaced the standard bullet-proof plates with the specially modified armor plates. They looked like the normal plates, but they had light green coloring on them, and there were four, thick, black wires that connected from the four corners of the plate to a small, bulky, dome in the middle. Everyone knew that the plates were prototypes, as they likewise knew that they were the only protection they had against the Phantom.

Val came in with an M1911 sidearm holstered at her side; the weight feeling strange to her. It was clear to the others that she didn't want to go. I'm a scientist, not a soldier. She thought to herself. Val had been chosen for this mission for a simple reason— she knew how to maneuver through Hope 7 and her knowledge of the facility's layout was going to be crucial to mission success. She looked around the room and saw tough men. They carried many weapons; had rough, unemotional faces, and were weighed down with equipment meant for death and destruction.

Sonya said to Val, "That's all you're taking?" Referring to her pistol.

"It's all I need." Val said, knowing that she had never fired a weapon in her life. She was afraid of them. The loud banging noise that they made and the aftermath. She was afraid that if she did take one of those big machine-guns or assault rifles, she would only be a greater danger to those around her. Not to mention, Val was a small framed woman, and the weight of those firearms would have probably been too much for her to carry.

Harrison walked over to Jacobs and said, "Jacobs, I want you to bring extra C-4 in case we have to level the place ourselves."

"Will do, sir."

The Lieutenant packed extra C-4 charges into his rucksack and slung it over his back. The squad had already loaded the special ammunition into their guns and spare clips.

Harrison said, "Bradley, I need you to pack extra ammunition into your rucksack."

"You got it, sir!"

Harrison spoke to the group as a whole, "Ok, guys. Do me a favor and take your American flags off your uniforms. This is a black op, which means the US government cannot be seen as being involved in any way."

The squad unenthusiastically took off their American-flag patches. Jacobs walked around with an empty helmet, collected all the patches, and left them in the armory. The originals still had their unit patches; a gray patch with a knife through a skull and the lettering, X-Ray below the emblem. The team was wearing woodland camo uniforms, knee pads, and they all had body armor with the specially modified plates. They had helmets with night vision lenses attached. The soldiers were loaded down with grenades, explosives, ropes, knives, flares, MREs, and water. Each rifleman had about eight, thirty round magazines. Machine gunners carried four, one-hundred round, magazine belts. Bradley carried about six hundred rounds of ammunition in his rucksack in the form of magazine clips and belts.

Harrison walked to the front of the armory and spoke again, "OK, people. We're taking two Blackhawks up to Washington state. After refueling there, we'll be taking the long ride to Alaska, Hope 7. Catch as much sleep as you can on the choppers, because once we set boots on the ground at Hope 7, it's game time. If we fail in our mission, we are to pass 'Inferno' to command, and they'll handle it from there."

"Do you think it'll be cold up there?" Asked Ramirez.

Commander Harrison looked at him and said, "You know how I said that there is no such a thing as a dumb question, Ramirez?"

"Yeah."

"Well there's an exception for you! Now let's get out there so we can be back in time for Thanksgiving. My Cowboys are playing."

"Yeah. Against my Rams! Sorry, Commander, but it might be a gloomy Thanksgiving for you!" Said Taylor.

Commander Harrison turned to Taylor. "It would only be fair, considering how the LA titans whooped those New York Kings in the 2025 Rocket Bowl! What was your team again!?"

"Whatever!" Taylor said, waving his arm to the side.

Jokes and laughter were used extensively in Task Force X-Ray. It was a coping mechanism and kept the thoughts of danger and fear at bay. The squad walked out of the armory and toward the helipads, where they loaded onto the Blackhawks. Ramirez, Chris, Carter, Garnome, and Jacobs entered one helicopter, labeled 'Blue-1'. Harrison, Sonya, Val, Bradley, and Taylor stepped onto the second helicopter, labeled 'Blue-2,' and both birds took off.

The mission was officially 'greenlit.' There was no turning back now.

CHAPTER 5: BAD OMEN

FROST STUCK TO the windows of the Blackhawk helicopters like a shroud. The noise of the rotor blades and the engines seemed strained, like tired horses. The choppers entered the valley where Hope 7 was located. From the windows, the squad could see tall oak trees that seemed to blanket much of the valley. Mountains stood guard over the valley to the far right and the not so distant left. Although it was mid-day, 5:03 PM to be exact, there was no sun—nothing but clouds and gloom. Inside the Blue-1 helicopter, the men took in the sights.

Through a yawn, Ramirez said, "Man, check out that view. Maybe I'll take a vacation up here."

Garnome commented, "It's beautiful, but I don't know about taking a vacation though. Too isolated. There could be a thousand murders up here and no one would even know."

Jacobs added, "Forget about the isolation. I'm more worried about the ghosts and ghouls that are on the prowl. I don't know about you guys, but I don't plan on getting possessed."

Garnome could feel his anxiety spiking. "Man, this is a trip!

Here I thought ghosts didn't exist, and now we're about to fight one." He let out a sigh, before saying, "I don't know..."

Jacobs put his hand on the medic's shoulder and assured him, "You'll do fine, Jerry. Your squad is going to have your back the whole time and remember—we're Task Force X-Ray!"

Garnome remembered that he was part of the most elite military unit in the world at the time. More importantly, he knew the legendary Commander Harrison was going to be leading the way. "You're right!" He said. "Let's kill this thing and get back home!"

"That's the spirit! My favorite killer doc is ready for action!"

Carter was sleeping.

The voice of the Blue-1 helicopter pilot crackled over the radio. "We're about fifteen minutes from the LZ. Descending now!"

Jacobs said, "Roger that."

The helicopter made a tight turn and slowly began to descend its altitude. Chris was playing a video game on his Nintendo mobile play device. His eyes were glued to the screen and his earphones were so noisy that Garnome could hear some of it.

Garnome told the newbie, "Oh, you're such a child!"

Chris shot back, "Just because you can no longer enjoy your youth and I can does not make me a child!"

Garnome was surprised that Chris could even hear him.

Jacobs muffled his chuckling. "Ouch! That was a burn! Clearly he's not worried."

Meanwhile, in the Blue-2 helicopter, Harrison's squad held a more tactical conversation.

Commander Harrison said, "As soon as we touch down, our first objective will be to secure the lobby, and regroup with Blue-1. Based on the schematics provided by Val, the facility descends six levels. Level One is where the lobby and control center are located. Level Two is where the medical and tech labs are located. Level Three is where they test their weapons and research. Level Four serves as some sort of security or surveillance area. We don't have any information on levels five and six—we'll just have to sort it out when we get there. If we deal with the Phantom, the rest of the mission should be a cake walk. Rescue and recovery."

Sonya added, "We can explore more options on how to deal with the Phantom when we get inside. I wouldn't count on your bullets being the sole savior on this operation."

"So, why did the CIA deem it necessary to send you on this mission, Sonya?" Asked Harrison.

"You know, to recover intel and send it back to Langley HQ." She replied. "Why? Do I make you uncomfortable, Commander?"

"Hardly. If you'd seen half the things I've seen, you'd realize that there isn't much to be uncomfortable about. Suspenseful, on the other hand, would be more accurate."

"We're on the same team. We both want to secure Hope 7 and deal with the Phantom."

"Yeah. How we do so, however, we may disagree on."

Sonya made a cryptic smile. "Some things are best buried, Commander. Dig deep enough and you're bound to fall into hell."

Harrison looked out the window and took in the sights; wild horses could be seen roaming the land. Deer and other animal life could also be seen in the forest. Smoke rose in the distance, past a small river. The scenery reminded Harrison of his time as a child in Texas. His dad was the ultimate outdoorsmen. He would never stand to let Harrison sit in the house for real long periods. Rather it was in the morning, after school, or at night, his dad always dragged him outside. He taught him horse taming, took him on mountain climbs and hikes, took him hunting, and taught him how to fish. He remembered the first time he killed an animal. It was an innocent, snow-white, rabbit. He held his dad's .22 rifle with shaken hands.

It was chewing on grass when his dad whistled. The rabbit quickly looked up. Harrison had his crosshairs on its head but due to the shaking of his hand, when he fired, he shot it in its lower stomach. The rabbit rolled frantically on the dirt. It stood up on two legs, coughed up blood, dirtying its white coat. It didn't know what hit it, or why it had to die. The innocent creature rolled in the mud and died. He remembered feeling tremendous sadness for killing the rabbit.

Bradley pointed at a string of huts overlooking the frozen riverbed and said to Val, "Are there civilians in this area? I thought this whole valley was top-secret."

Val explained, "The facility may be top-secret, but the valley is open to civilians, although we do not encourage it. We try to scare them away by telling them nuclear material is used in the facility and that it is highly unsafe to be exposed to the forest for large periods of time."

"Does that work?"

"For the most part. Some hikers come up here. Sometimes hunters looking for a good hunting ground. Alaska might be the wild west of the Ascended Age, but few have settled in this harsh region of the Alaskan Northern Slope. The weather can get as low as ten degrees Fahrenheit up here."

Bradley said, "Well hopefully we won't be staying long. I didn't bring a jacket."

Hope 7 was now in sight—a tall, wide, square-shaped complex with windows around the structure. There were two helipads at the top of the facility next to two large antenna arrays. The windows had been reinforced with steel barriers due to the shutdown. There was a road that led to a security gate and various concrete barriers. Beyond the checkpoint appeared to be a parking lot in front of the main entrance.

The Blue-2 helicopter pilot announced, "Seven minutes out!"

Harrison said, "This is it! Taylor, when we land, I'll need you-"

He was interrupted by a bright flash in the sky. The men had to cover their eyes with their hands. There was a loud beeping in the choppers. The helicopters began to violently spiral out of control; rotating to the right and left. The helicopters were dangerously close to each other and for a moment, Commander Harrison worried that there was going to be a mid-air collision. The rotor blades lightly grazed the side of the choppers. They'd gotten so close,

Harrison could see some of the men's faces from the Blue-1 squad. Thankfully for them, the helicopters parted and drifted away from each other. Out of the frying pan and into the fire.

The Blue-2 helicopter pilot said, with a shaken voice, "Critical systems failure... we've lost power... we're going down hard... brace for impact!"

The Blue-2 helicopter hit a thick oak tree. The back rotor was completely blown off and the helicopter was sent crashing into a blanket of oak trees. The bird's top rotors were also torn off, with the rotor blades flying and chopping through the air. The aircraft flipped over multiple times and they were thrown unconscious. The Blue-1 helicopter likewise spun out of control and drifted further away from Hope 7. They had their door open and the squad had to hold on extra tight, so they wouldn't fly out. Ramirez lost his grip and Chris reached after him. The helicopter landed at the base of a mountain, with the top rotors violently broken up; sending flying debris and pieces of metal shooting in every direction. Most of the crew were likewise knocked unconscious.

HOURS PASSED.

At the Blue-2 crash site, Harrison began to wake to the feeling of cold water dripping on his face. He was lying outside of the crashed helicopter, the ice at his back, and his fingers numb. He struggled to sit up—it felt like he was doing a sit-up with a 100-pound weight vest on his chest. Gloom turned to darkness and the dripping rain turned into a mad flurry. The wind picked up and a terrible cold descended over the valley. He managed to sit up; his neck and right shoulder in blistering pain. He looked to his right and saw Bradley tending to a wound on his leg. Taylor was lying unconscious inside the overturned, wrecked helicopter. Sonya was checking the pulse of the pilots, and Val was trying to get in contact with Blue-1.

He crawled over to the wreckage, and while still prone, he pulled Taylor out of the helicopter by his vest. Taylor fell out on top of Harrison. The Commander turned him over and checked his pulse; it was low, but Taylor was alive. Harrison began performing CPR— with no results. He tried again. Still no response. He kept trying. Suddenly, Taylor gasped for air; his eyes shooting wide open. He scanned his surroundings and trembled like a jackhammer.

Taylor, rapidly panting, said, "Oh, God... Abe... Ramirez... where are you guys?"

Harrison told him, "Calm down, son. Everything's going to be OK."

Taylor looked up at him and was relieved to see a familiar face. "Oh, Commander Harrison... I had this terrible dream. We were flying in the air and then something crazy happened. There was a bright light and we crashed."

"Hate to tell you, Taylor, but that really happened."

"What!?"

"Rest now, Taylor. Deep breaths."

Harrison stood up and grabbed a bottle of water from his torn backpack and gave it to Taylor. His hands trembled as he grabbed the bottle from the Commander's hand. Harrison propped Taylor up against the end of the helicopter, far enough so he wouldn't get burned, but close enough to keep warm. He had cuts on his face and a piece of metal sticking out of his arm. Harrison stood up and walked over to Bradley.

Harrison said, "How's that wound looking, Bradley?"

Bradley quickly glanced at him and went back to focusing on his leg. "It's nothing, sir!"

Harrison lifted Bradley's hands off his wound and saw a deep cut in his right leg with blood gushing out; turning the nearby snow into a ghastly red color.

Harrison shook his head. "Sure as hell doesn't look like 'nothing.' You always were stubborn."

Bradley managed a faint laugh. Harrison pulled his bandaging and alcohol from his backpack. The alcohol bottle had a hole in it, and most of it had leaked out, but enough remained for Harrison to bandage Bradley's wound with gauze coated in alcohol. He wrapped the bandaging tightly around his leg. Bradley had the face of someone who was getting his teeth pulled, but he didn't grunt once. Although the squad had an official medic in Garnome, they were all trained in basic medical attention.

"Sit tight, Bradley." Ordered Harrison, standing to his feet and walking over to Val.

Val said over her radio, "Blue-1—do you copy?"

She heard nothing but static on the com.

Harrison asked, "Any luck with the radio, Val?"

"Unfortunately, no, Commander. I've been at it for the past ten minutes—nothing but static."

"The EMP probably fried the electronics and that's just assuming that's what it was. So, go on, and give it a rest, Val. We're going to need to head inside the facility for shelter soon, anyway. How are your wounds?"

"A couple cuts and lacerations—nothing serious I can assure you."

"Good! Catch your breath a moment."

Sonya powerwalked to the Commander and reported, "Both pilots are dead, Commander!"

Harrison looked at the wrecked helicopter cockpit and saw the dead pilots. What a shit-show. He thought before saying aloud, "That's bad news! We're going to have a heck of a time getting outta here." He pondered for a moment before saying, "For now, I need you to assist the squad and help them get back on their feet. Taylor seems to be suffering from shock or hypothermia. Val seems to be fine. Don't let Bradley send you away. I'm going to check for our weapons."

Sonya nodded her head and immediately walked over to Val and offered any medical assistance she could. Harrison began his search by checking inside the helicopter. He saw Taylor's flamethrower sitting, ironically, inside the flames enveloping the helicopter's interior. He reached in, pulled it out, and threw it in the wet ice, cooling it. When he picked it up, he noticed that the handle and barrel were charred, but, surprisingly, the weapon still seemed functional, although damaged. He looked around the wreckage and found his M-16A3 lying in the snow. He picked it up and slung it over his shoulder. Bradley, Sonya, and Val already had their weapons.

Harrison walked back to the cockpit and removed the pilot's dog tags. He had to squeeze his hands through the metal debris. One read, *Keaton, Robert,* the other read, *Samuel, Josh.* He wanted to pull the men out, but the cockpit was partially buried into the ground, and protected by twisted steel. He had no choice but to leave them. He turned to Sonya and asked, "What's the squad looking like?"

Sonya said, "They'll be fine. I applied a tourniquet to Bradley's leg to help manage the bleeding, he's had the worst of it. The rest of them have only minor cuts and burns but nothing serious. Let's do what we came here to do."

"Good!" Said Harrison, relieved. He was no stranger to seeing men die under his command. He led soldiers on many missions before his time in the X. But losing Diaz changed something in him. It reminded him how much the men of Task Force X-Ray meant to him. They weren't just some paper men he led, they were family, even like sons.

Harrison handed Taylor his flamethrower and helped him to his feet. He could tell Taylor wasn't all there. His right cheek was bruised and colored dark purple. He had dark blots underneath his eyes and he slightly rocked his head back and forth like a Parkinson's disease patient.

Harrison asked, "You good, Taylor?"

"Yes, sir! Just a little cold, sir."

"We're going to make our way inside—hang tight. What about you, Bradley? You ready to move out?"

Bradley stood up with a slight limp and said, "I'm ready, Commander—let's do this!"

Commander Harrison loved working with Bradley. He was a tough soldier; always ready to fight, and always ready to get the job done no matter what. That cut on his leg wasn't minor, yet he shrugged it off, and was ready to continue the mission; no complaints. Any tougher, Harrison would've been convinced that he was a machine.

Harrison said, "Excellent! OK, everybody. Let's start making our way inside the facility. When we get inside, we can take a short rest and wait for Jacobs and the rest of Blue-1."

Bradley was quick to ask, "Shouldn't we head to the Blue-1 crash site?"

"Normally I would say 'yes,' Bradley, but we won't last thirty minutes in this storm, and Taylor already has early signs of hypothermia. We have to find shelter and quickly. If we don't hear from the Blue-1 squad after we get inside, and if the storm calms, we'll head out and search for them. We're not leaving them, but you men come first."

"Roger that!" Bradley responded. He didn't like the idea of leaving the rest of the team in the storm, but he understood the Commander's reasoning. The men directly under his command had to come first.

The Blue-2 squad made their way through the forest and headed towards Hope 7. They followed the muddy trail, marred by tire tracks. The storm only worsened. Rain poured unmercifully down from the clouds, high winds swept through the valley; turning the dirt and ground snow into a river of icy mud. Lightning began to angrily strike out amongst the darkened sky. The Blue-2 squad kept walking. Only the sound of the storm could be heard—everything else was quiet. The towering oak trees seemed endless. The smell of pine was fresh in the air. Bradley was thankful that the terrain itself was pretty easy going. There were few large boulders and rocks, and the ground was smooth; giving his wounded leg an easier time.

Taylor exclaimed, "Hell of a storm! Was it lightning that brought us down?"

Harrison answered, "Unlikely! No way lightning hit both choppers."

Bradley asked, "So it was an EMP?"

Harrison said, "Possibly—the real question is: What triggered it? Does Hope 7 have EMP defenses, Val?"

"None that I know of. The facility relies on secrecy and a heavily armed detail of guards for security."

Taylor pressed her, "So you don't know?"

"No, I don't."

"Bullshit!" Taylor murmured to himself. He signaled to Harrison and lightly spoke, "Sir, no way they're telling the truth!"

"We'll sort everything out when we get inside. Just focus on the ground in front of you." Harrison whispered.

Bradley asked, "Do you think it was the Phantom?"

Harrison answered, "I'm not sure. It would take an incredible amount of power to create an electromagnetic pulse and even more power to cause it to reach us, but I wouldn't put it past the creature. We'll find out soon enough—the facility is just ahead."

As the squad approached the parking lot, a snapping noise was heard—as if someone had stepped on a branch. The squad all halted and aimed their weapons to their right side, where the noise was heard.

Val asked, "You hear that?"

Harrison warned, "Shhh!"

Immense tension built as the team scanned the area looking for targets. They aimed towards a cluster of small trees. The noise of thunder and rain made it difficult to hear. They waited... and waited... Finally, they lowered their weapons and kept moving.

Harrison ordered in a low voice, "Keep your eyes open and keep moving forward-"

A man suddenly jumped out of the tree line. The squad aimed their weapons again. Harrison shouted, "Stop right there!! Identify yourself!"

The man was wearing gray pants and a torn, baby-blue, dress shirt. Half of his face was covered in blood. It dripped onto his black tie; giving the tie red stripes. He was a fat, white man; clean shaven, and had brown hair. His eyes were wide and filled with panic.

"Please! You gotta help! Everyone's dead... they... they..." The man started a terrible dry cough before continuing, "They killed them all... it was... it..."

Harrison said, "Slow down! It's OK. Just tell us what happened. Breath..."

"They... they..."

"Who's they?"

The man dropped to his knees. He stared at Commander Harrison in utter confusion before muttering out, "The eyes... they were... red..."

The man fell face forward into the mud, making a splatter noise. Harrison slowly approached the man. He was followed by Bradley. Harrison lifted the man's head out of the mud. His eyes were wide open and caked in mud. It quickly reminded him of Captain Sargento. He flipped the stranger over on his back and checked for a pulse. The man was dead. Bradley examined the body and saw that he had four gunshot wounds. Two in his chest, one in his right shoulder, and one in his lower stomach.

"Gunshot wounds!?" Bradley asked, surprised. "The Phantom doesn't seem like the type to use guns. Who do you think shot him?"

"Hell, if I know, son. Whoever did it was intent on making sure he was dead. Four gunshot wounds, center massed... too many to be an accident." Said Harrison. He wiped the mud off the man's ID badge and read it aloud, "Albert Ronson—security. Well, unfortunately there's nothing we can do for him, he's dead. Tread carefully. This wasn't the Phantom's doing."

The squad cautiously continued up the dirt road and approached the outskirts of the facility.

Harrison announced, "Almost there!"

The checkpoints around the facility were eerily empty. Dozens of cars littered the parking lot, but there were no signs of life. Harrison signaled to his men to keep low. They walked in a crouch as they scoped out the parking lot. Bradley and Taylor scanned the cars and nearby security checkpoints. Nothing. Harrison kept his eyes trained on the roof of the facility, keeping watch for snipers. When it seemed clear that there were no imminent threats, everyone rose to their feet and walked towards the entrance.

Bradley said, "I guess the security evacuated, huh?"

Val said, "The lucky ones I'd imagine, although they didn't have orders to. Their orders were to guard the outside of the facility until we arrived. Something is awry."

"That man we saw had gunshot wounds. Did someone assault the facility? Do you think that when the shooting started, they tucked tail and ran?"

"Maybe..."

"I wonder where all that wildlife went. We didn't see any on our way to the facility from the wreckage. I got a bad feeling..."

Bradley was interrupted by lightning as it violently struck the ground near the squad.

Harrison shouted, "Run!!"

The squad made a mad dash for the facility. Lightning zipped and zapped around the party. Oak trees were violently shattered; causing terrible debris of wooden shards and splinters to shoot through the air. Some men could feel painful pricks on their faces from the sharp splinters. Trees fell over, one on top of the security checkpoint, smashing the barricade. Car alarms went off. As the lightning continued to strike with abnormal intensity, there was a horrific, faint-but-definite, wailing scream. Its sound almost equally matched that of the thunder and lightning. The squad ran past a few cars in the parking lot before making it right in front of the facility and used the building as shelter from the lightning. There was a statue in the front of Hope 7. It was a white sculpture of a man holding a book in the air. A lightning bolt shattered the statue and only half the body remained. A minute passed and the lightning ceased. The few cars that were in the parking lot sounded off their alarms. The squad couldn't enter the facility. Due to the lockdown, the windows and doors had been reinforced with steel barriers.

Harrison said, "Taylor, pass me your thermite torch!"

Taylor reached inside his rucksack, and with a trembling hand, he pulled out a thermite torch and passed it to Harrison. He tried to cut through the steel barrier, but the steel was too thick.

"It's not working—let's go to Plan B!"

The Commander used the torch to cut deep fissures into the steel in the four corners and the middle of the steel door. While he made the cuts, Taylor planted thermite shape charges into the four corners of the door, connected to a high-explosive shape charge to the middle of the steel.

Taylor warned, "Stand back everybody!!"

Everyone moved back from the steel door, while staying close to the facility's walls.

Taylor yelled, "Fire in the hole!"

He detonated the explosives; the steel door was lit up by the thermite and blown away. Only a huge gaping hole remained where the proud steel door once stood. The squad hastily rushed inside with their weapons up.

The smell caused Taylor to almost instantly vomit. They looked around in shocked disbelief.

Harrison covered his mouth and nose. "Oh, my god... this is bad... this is very bad..."

PART TWO:
THE DESCENT

**Close to 610,000 people die of heart disease in
the United States every year**

CHAPTER 6: AFTER DARK

THE LIGHT OF day was gone and the storm continued to wreak havoc in the valley; the rain relentless. Thunder drum rolled amongst the stars. At the Blue-1 crash site, lieutenant Jacobs regained consciousness and began to crawl out of the crashed helicopter. The wreckage, like at the Blue-2 crash site, was on fire. Jacobs slowly crawled out; his head aching. There was ringing in his ears, and he felt a burning sensation on his face from lacerations. He managed to fall out; about a ten-foot drop. His legs were numb and he struggled making his way to his feet. He saw Carter about twenty feet from the wreckage, laid out on his stomach; his hand still tightly gripping his rifle. Jacobs turned to face the helicopter to see if he could find any of his other squad mates. He saw one of the pilots inside the cockpit beginning to wake, but he started to panic due to the fire. Smoke billowed and the pilot was fading into the smoke cloud; his hands loudly banging on the window. Jacobs struggled to climb up the small, muddied slope. When he did so, he tried to open the helicopter door, but it was sealed shut. Protruding pieces of steel guarded much of the door like a rose bush. So, Jacobs quickly pulled out his sidearm and aimed it at the window.

"Watch your head!" Jacobs shouted.

He shot out the window; shattering the glass. The pilot unfastened his seatbelt and Jacobs helped pull the pilot out through the window. The fire was hot on his heels. Jacobs and the pilot rolled down the muddied slope. Both the pilot's legs had caught fire and Jacobs frantically searched for a way to put it out.

"Quick! Roll around in the snow!" He instructed the pilot.

The pilot grunted in pain as he rolled over the wet snow and rain. The fire was put out and his legs smoked. Jacobs turned and tried to reach for the other pilot, but the fire had already taken hold of the cockpit. If the co-pilot survived the impact, he would never have the chance to wake up. Jacobs could do nothing but shake his head in anguish. His eyes were tearing from the smoke. The issue with many helicopter crashes is that the helicopter itself can turn into a wreck of twisted steel; making rescuing the pilots or retrieving their corpses that much more difficult.

"Are you OK?" Jacobs asked the surviving pilot.

The pilot answered, "I need medical attention. Where's Hawkins?"

Jacobs shook his head and pointed at the wreck.

"No!!" The pilot shouted. He crawled towards the wreckage while on all fours, but Jacobs held him back.

"He's dead! Crawling in there and burning with him won't bring him back!" Jacobs said.

When the pilot tired himself and came to the conclusion that his co-pilot was dead, he laid still on the cold snow; gasping for air. Jacobs hooked his arms under his armpits, dragged him down the slope, and set him against a rock formation.

"I'm sorry, pal, I really am. I tried to reach for him, but the fires had already beaten me. Just sit tight and rest easy, OK? I'll have a look for my men and we can see about what we can do about your injuries." Jacobs said.

He walked over to Carter, flipped him over on his back, and shook him. Carter didn't respond. Jacobs checked for a pulse—there was none. Jacobs's heart began to race as the cold water from the storm dripped down his face. He pulled his rucksack to his front and searched for medical equipment he knew he didn't have.

"Garnome!!" Jacobs yelled.

There was no response.

"Medic!! Man down!!"

Still nothing.

Jacobs shuffled around the wreckage; desperately looking for any kind of first aid. His legs gave out and he fell to his knees. He almost gave up when he noticed something in the corner of his eye. He was slow to stand up. He squinted and saw Garnome's medical bag hanging on a broken tree branch. It was a red bag with a large red cross—unmistakable to the naked eye.

Jacobs murmured, "Oh, thank God!"

He rushed over to the bag, pulled it down, opened it, pulled out the defibrillator unit, and rushed back to Carter. Jacobs unbuttoned his fatigues and vest until Carter's bare chest was exposed. He charged the defibrillator and pressed the pads against his chest. Nothing. He charged it and tried again—still nothing.

"Come on... come on!" Jacobs pled.

He tried for a third time. Carter sprang to life and took in a deep breath of air; gasping.

Jacobs exclaimed, "Yes!"

Carter looked around and asked, "What... happened? Where... where are we?"

"Settle down, brother, and breathe. I just took a defib to your heart three times. You really had me scared there. We were on our way to Hope 7, but we crashed in the wilderness. I estimate that we're at least five miles away from the facility. Here, drink."

Jacobs gave his canteen to Carter and he drunk the water like a man who'd been stranded in the desert for a couple of days.

"Easy, Carter." Jacobs warned. "We're going to need all the

water we got before this operation is over. Besides, I don't want you cramping up. We have a long walk ahead of us."

Carter, wide-eyed, scanned the devastation around him. "Where... where's everyone else?"

"I don't know. I'm about to look around for them. Can you stand?"

Carter gave the canteen back, gripped Jacobs's hand, and struggled to stand up. When he made it to his feet, he felt like his legs were made of jelly.

"I... I don't know."

"It's OK. Take it nice and slow."

Carter took a few steps forward... and a few more. The numbness slowly wore off and he felt comfortable enough to help Jacobs search for their comrades.

"OK. I think I'm good. Let's find our guys... thanks for saving my sorry ass by the way."

"Sure, buddy. This isn't the first time I saved your life, and, at this rate, it won't be the last."

Shivering, Carter said, "Man, its cold! You said we crashed, huh?"

"Nah! We just jumped out of a perfectly good helicopter and parachuted our way down!"

"Hey! We've done stupider things." Carter said while rubbing his forehead, nursing his headache. "So much for catching sleep on our way to the facility."

"Let's get a move on! The rest of X-Ray is out there somewhere, come on!"

"I'm right behind you!"

Jacobs picked up his M-4 from the cold ground, turned around, and gave a thumbs up to the pilot. The pilot responded likewise. They searched around the wreckage, looking for their comrades. There was nothing in the near vicinity, so they searched further away from the helicopter wreckage. As they walked, it got darker, and they could see oak trees cut in half and some completely snapped over from the crash. Some had deep gashes from the rotary blades. They walked down a slope for about five minutes, south of the wreckage.

Carter said, "Hell of a landing!"

"You said it." Jacobs replied. "Thank God we made it. It could've been a lot worse."

Suddenly, they heard a voice.

"Help! Help! Is anybody out there?"

Jacobs and Carter rushed toward the voice and found Garnome. He was pinned to the ground by a collapsed oak tree.

Garnome cried out to them, "Oh—thank goodness! I was starting to get scared."

Carter replied, "Don't worry, doc. We'll get you outta there in a heartbeat!"

Jacobs and Carter positioned themselves on both sides of the tree and tried to lift it. They grunted and gritted their teeth. The tree barely moved.

"Jesus, this thing is heavy!" Exclaimed Jacobs. "OK. Carter and I are going to lift. Garnome, help us by pushing the tree upward, and when you have enough room, wriggle your way out from under the tree."

They all lifted the oak tree with strain. Garnome crawled from under it. When he was free, the men let the tree down hard. The medic had mud on his face and uniform.

Jacobs asked, "Are you okay, Garnome?"

Catching his breath, he replied, "I could be better, but I'm squared away. No serious injuries."

"Good. Head back to the crash site and check on the pilot; he suffered some burns on his legs. Also, search for weapons and ammo while you're at it. We're going to need it." Jacobs said.

"You got it!"

Jacobs handed Garnome his medical bag and a flashlight, and he went to the wreckage while Carter and Jacobs continued their search.

Carter looked around and said, "What a mess!"

Jacobs agreed. "I know. I hope the Commander and the rest of the men fared better."

"Me, too. What do you think did this? Was it an EMP?"

"I *think* it was, but it's hard to say. There was a bright flash in the sky and next thing I knew, we were spiraling out of control."

"It must've come from the facility."

"No doubts there—it definitely came from Hope 7. Now we're faced with a dilemma, though. Getting out of here is going to be tough." Jacobs said as he assessed the situation.

Carter said, "Maybe we can raise communications inside the facility? Did you try contacting the Commander?"

"Yeah, but the radios are shot—the EMP must've fried them. Raising communications inside Hope 7 is going to be our only shot. Without comms, we can't call in a pickup, and, even if we could, we would have to make sure they don't suffer the same fate we did."

"True, that was some miracle—us surviving that helicopter crash."

Jacobs tried to lighten the mood a little. "I survived. Technically, you died. But, hey! You're alive now, so I guess that counts!"

Carter felt a shiver rush up his spine.

This wasn't the first time they had been in a helicopter crash, but it was the most surprising. Jacobs could recall three other times they had survived helicopter crashes. One time, during a mission in Nigeria, they extracted a Nigerian diplomat from a Boko Haram terrorist cell. They fought their way to the chopper and it took off, only for the bird to be downed by a concealed .50 caliber machine-gun nest. That was the 'softest' crash out of the three, as the helicopter didn't reach a high altitude. The other time, they had just extracted from the coast of Cuba when a heat-seeking missile locked onto the bird. The pilot dumped a set of flares, but the missile payed the flares no attention and rammed into the back rotor; completely destroying the tail of the helicopter. The blades stopped chopping and the bird went on a free-fall and plummeted into the warm ocean water. Lastly, the helicopter crash during the raid on the Birmingham reactor. That was the worst one.

Jacobs and Carter kept searching in the dark. It was quiet when suddenly, they stumbled upon Chris Marilyn, lying up against a tree with a pistol in his hand. He had a gash on the left side of his head, right above his temple. Multiple blood trails leaked down his face.

"Who's there?" He cried out. "Stay back! I have a gun—I'll shoot if I have to!"

Carter, without raising an eyebrow, said, "Easy, there, Junior. It's your team."

With a sigh of relief, Marilyn said, "Whew! What took you guys so long?"

Carter reprimanded him. "Excuse me? I see two legs in good condition. Why didn't you move your ass to the wreckage? Or search for the rest of us? Damn, kid, this is Task Force X-Ray not grade school! Do you want me to spoon feed your sorry ass some applesauce too?"

"Hey, no need to be a jerk, Carter! I don't have a flashlight and its dark as hell!"

Chris sighed. "To be honest, I'm a little scared. Main reason? I'm watching over *my* squad mate."

He pointed upwards and Jacobs shone his flashlight up. Ramirez was above them, tangled up in the branches of an oak tree. He was unconscious and clearly banged up.

Chris said, "When the helicopter spiraled out of control, Ramirez fell out of the chopper through the side door. I tried to reach for him, but I missed his arm by half a second and managed to fall out with him. We both got banged up by those trees pretty badly. I just fell through the branches, while he got stuck in them."

Carter was impressed by Chris's bravery. "...Whoa!"

Jacobs kneeled next to him and nodded his head. "What you did was brave, Chris. Now put away your gun and help us get Ramirez down."

Chris forgot he was still aiming his pistol. He holstered his sidearm. Carter helped Chris to his feet before giving Jacobs a boost onto the thick oak branches. Ramirez was knocked out cold. Jacobs could tell that he was alive; seeing his steamy breath exhale in the cold air. He put his hands on Ramirez's vest.

"Get ready to catch him!" Jacobs yelled.

He pulled on Ramirez's body and loosened him up from the branches. As Ramirez fell and landed in the arms of Carter and Chris, a branch that was being cocked back by Ramirez's body loosened and smacked Jacobs across his face. He lost his footing and fell down the tree. Each branch gave him a hi-five and he fell face first onto the cold ground.

Carter rushed over to him and helped him to his feet. "Yeah... so about those Christmas lights? You sure you're up for it this year?"

Jacobs spit out blood, wiped his face, and said, "Screw you, smart ass! Nice to know your sense of humor wasn't lost in the crash."

Carter looked him over more thoroughly and saw that he suffered no major injury or laceration. "You good, LT?"

"Yeah, yeah! Get your ass moving, soldier! Help me with Ramirez."

Jacobs and Carter picked up Ramirez and carried him back to the wreckage. On their way back, lightning struck next to them, and a creaking noise could be heard, as if a rickety door were being slowly opened.

Jacobs looked up and warned, "Look out!!"

Carter and Jacobs tossed Ramirez's body out of the way and dove to the side, as did Chris. A towering oak tree fell down and landed next to them.

"Whew! That was a close call!" Chris said.

Jacobs, trying to keep things moving, said, "Let's just get up to the wreckage before we get killed by trees."

The duo picked up their comrade's body and continued up the snowy slope; back to the wreckage. Garnome was bandaging up the pilot's legs and smiled when he saw the squad coming up the slope in their entirety. He was quickly alarmed by Ramirez's unconscious body.

Garnome exclaimed, "Oh, great! You found them! How's Ramirez doing?"

"He's breathing, doc. Time for you to work your magic and get him back on his feet." Jacobs responded.

They set Ramirez down next to the wreckage and Garnome examined him while checking for a pulse. Ramirez's face was bloodied and bruised. He had a cut that stretched down his lips and caused blood to leak down his chin. It was so cold, that the blood steamed amidst the cold air.

Chris asked, "How's he doing, doc? Will he pull through?"

Garnome nodded his head and said, "He's going to be just fine. I'll patch up his face the best I can. He may have a broken rib or two as well—nothing I can do about that. Hmmm. Seems like his left arm might be dislocated, but it's nothing I can't put back in place."

Jacobs said, "Good! What's the status on our weapons?"

"Well, I was able to find my shotgun. I found Chris's M-249 too. I set them next to the pilot. Sorry about your Scar, Carter. You'll have to make do without it."

The men picked up their weapons. A cracking noise sounded as Garnome set Ramirez's arm while he was unconscious. Any major lacerations on Ramirez's face he set band-aids on. Garnome dragged his body closer to the wreckage's fire; giving him some warmth.

Jacobs asked, "How's the pilot?"

Garnome answered, "As I started to work on him, he passed out. I think it's from shock. His legs are badly burned; we're going to have to carry him. The other pilot is dead, killed on impact."

Jacobs replied, "I know. The wreckage caught flame before I could do anything. Bad business. How much ammunition did you find?"

"I found one of our spare ammunition bags."

"Good. Everyone who's missing clips, check the ammo bag, and stack up!"

They all searched the bag and filled up on lost magazines before Jacobs handed the bag to Chris to carry. Garnome quickly checked on everyone. Those who tried to wave him off only succeeded in receiving extra attention. He deemed that everyone was ready for duty. Scrapes, minor burns, and bruises did little to slow the soldiers down. Jacobs's immediate concern was the weather. His temperature gauge was at 18 degrees Fahrenheit and declining. Not so immediate, was his worry for Commander Harrison and the Blue-2 squad. His time read, 20:33. The helicopters crashed around 17:08. That meant that he and his men were out for about three hours and Blue-2 never came for them. That's what made Jacobs worry even more.

Ramirez began to come to.

"Ah, man... my face... hurts."

The squad all surrounded Ramirez and helped him to his feet.

Garnome told Ramirez, "I applied some bandaging to your face, and I gave you an adrenaline shot to help you get conscious. Take a couple of these."

Garnome gave him two aspirins with a bottle of water. Ramirez threw the red pills into his mouth and chugged down some water.

"How do you feel?" Garnome asked.

"Like shit, but I can fight! Where the hell are we?"

"We're a distance from the facility so, we have a good walk ahead of us." Jacobs said. "It ought to be a stroll. We'll link up with Commander Harrison and continue with the mission. We need to get a move on. I think the Blue-1 crash site is north of our position. We overslept; its been about three hours since we crashed and they never came for us. Our priority is getting to that crash site. Anybody got their land navigation gear?"

Every soldier shook his head in the negative.

"Comms?"

The response was the same.

Chris said, "Nothing but static."

"Stay together, keep the chatter low, and your voices down. Somebody grab the pilot. He's had a hell of a night."

"Haven't we all?" Shrugged Ramirez, finishing the water.

Garnome turned around to grab the pilot, and, to his surprise, he was gone. His face was puzzled as he looked around the wreckage.

Garnome asked, "Where'd he go?"

Everyone looked around.

"He was just here!"

Ramirez asked, "Who's gone?"

"The pilot! He was just lying here!"

"Did he take a piss?"

"Doubtful. His legs were too screwed up for him just to stand up and walk away—and besides, he was unconscious."

Carter walked over to the rock formation and knelt over the snow, where the pilot was and noticed a trail followed by footprints.

He reported, "It looks like someone dragged him. We have to hurry—maybe we can still catch them. They couldn't have gotten far!"

Chris asked in confusion, "How did someone take him right under our noses!?"

Jacobs said, "We'll figure that out later. Let's just follow the trail before we lose them. Come on, double time!"

Carter led the way and the squad followed the trail in the snow with haste. The trail got fainter as they continued and then it ended in the forest. With a trickle of snow constantly blowing in, the footprints became harder to track as well.

Carter kneeled on the ground and said, "Either the trail was covered by more snow, or someone lifted him up and carried him the rest of the way."

Jacobs shook his head. "Shit! We can't leave him. Fan out and holler if you find him. We'll advance steadily forward towards the crash."

The men spread out about thirty feet from each other. They could see their breath in the biting cold. Lighting snapped like the snapping of a whip. 1…2…3…4…5…6… *Snap!* 7…8… *Thunder!* They scanned the ground and followed any leads. Evidence ranged from broken branches and twigs, when they picked up the trail, or when they saw splats of blood. After a few minutes, they picked the trail up again and converged into a single-file line as they followed it. Each man was left to his own endurance of the cold. They kept their weapons level and constantly scanned their surroundings. Chris felt himself begin to fall down a muddy slope. His arm was tightly grabbed by Ramirez.

"Gotcha!" Ramirez said in a whisper.

He pulled him up the slope. The men stopped and examined the layout. The slope was a good thirty-foot drop and the men found themselves on a ridgeline. Jacobs pulled out his binoculars and scoped out the area. Hope 7 had to be another four miles away, at least, he reckoned. The pilot was still nowhere to be found and the trail fell cold again. Jacobs was afraid that if they went down the slope, there was no guarantee that the pilot would be down there, and no guarantee back up. The men took a knee and drank water. Jacobs kept scanning with his binoculars. He saw a couple of snow-white wolves running towards something. Where are they off to so fast? He thought. They ran to the right; towards Hope 7. Jacobs lost visual. As the squad took a rest and he pondered, there was a loud snap behind the men. They turned around. Carter was the first to grab his rifle off the ground. Their night only seemed to get worse. A menacing, brown Grizzly bear had one paw on a broken log and one paw in the mud. Its brown coat was pelted with mud and snow. The bear stood up on two feet; it had to be at least eight feet tall on its legs. It let out a loud growl. The squad quickly rose to their feet and trained their weapons on it.

"What are we gonna do!?" Panicked Garnome.

"Easy, easy, easy!" Jacobs ordered. "Stay your ground!"

The bear put all four paws on the ground and started to walk towards the men. Each soldier slowly stepped back. Ramirez could feel his heels grinding against the edge of the slope. The bear rushed the men. They all opened fire on the 750-pound monster. The issue was that the bear was so close, that they had little time to effectively kill it before it reached them. When it was clear that the bear was not going to fall, Jacobs gave a daring order.

"JUMP!" He yelled.

The bear was less than five feet away. Each man jumped down the slope.

DANIEL RAMIREZ

"Ramirez! In my office, now!!" Yelled my CO.

I stood up and walked towards his office. The shitbag corporal had a smirk on his face. I almost punched him out again but decided that it could wait for another time. The door read, *Colonel Richardson*. I opened it, closed it, and stood to attention. The Colonel was a white man with a bristled brown mustache. This wasn't my first run in with him; he was a real Pendejo.

"Ramirez," he started, "you are a sorry excuse of a soldier if I've seen one! You've been in this cyber division for four years and you've been in eight fights. I've sat you down in this office for half of them but somehow the brass always seems to cut you slack! Well, not this time! I have to listen to how this altercation started but mark my words, you're not getting outta this one. Speak!"

"Sir!" I say, "Corporal Lars called me a beaner and I kicked his ass for it! That's all I have to say, sir!"

The Colonel already had his mind made up. "Not good enough, Soldier! That may be true, I will have Corporal Lars reprimanded for it, but you're just too much trouble! Too many fights and this division won't have it. I'm transferring you to the fifth tank company, third battalion as an engineer. If you don't clean up your act while you're down there, you'll be out of this man's army in a heartbeat. Dismissed!"

As soon as I cleared his office in soldier-like conduct, I stormed down the hallway like a raging bull. All my fights were genuinely not my fault. Sure, I might've been the first one to throw hands but always with reasonable cause. Like my brother Julio told me: never take shit from nobody! Don't care how big or little you are. I can take jokes and horseplay but outside of that I was all business. What can I say? I'm a child of the streets! I turned the corner and felt a tight grab on my arm. A sergeant pulled me aside into his office. I almost instinctively hit him but restrained myself until I figured out what was going on. His name badge read, *Sergeant Louis*.

"What's this about, Sarge?" I ask.

"You," He said with a mellow voice. "You, Ramirez. I want to know what your problem is. Care to discuss, Corporal?"

He offered me a seat and I sat down. He was around my height; had a light brown buzzcut and green eyes. He was probably in his late thirties. He strangely reminded me of Julio although they looked nothing alike. Maybe it was his voice or the way he talked.

"Why all these fights?" He asked.

I didn't say anything at first.

"OK. I understand, where are you from?"

"East Los Angeles." I tell him.

"Nice! I'm from East LA too!"

I felt a sense of camaraderie with him that I hadn't felt with hardly anyone in the Army. He was Hispanic like me, from the same side of town, and wore the same uniform. We talked for so long that I hadn't realize that almost an hour went by.

"So where is old Richardson sending you off to?" He asked.

"I'm being transferred to the fifth tank company, third battalion."

"No shit!? I'm being transferred to the same unit! I leave next week, you?"

"I can't say. It'll probably take a little while for them to process all the proper paperwork."

"Well, when you catch up, you know my name! Keep your cool, corporal! Don't fight over petty things. Believe me, I could've been spared a lot of trouble if I didn't let my fist speak for me."

I partially accepted the constructive criticism. "Definitely! I'll see you soon, Sergeant!"

I stood up and walked out the office door. I had briefly forgotten why I was mad in the first place.

PRESENT DAY

The Blue-2 squad dusted themselves off. They had sludges of mud on their uniforms and faces. Carter sat against the muddied slope.

"My arm... I think it's dislocated." Carter said, clenching his left hand into a fist.

Garnome kneeled over him and gently grabbed his right arm. He said, "You ready?"

"No funny games, Jerry, I swear to god!" Carter responded.

"I always get the job done. OK. Let's do this! On three. One..."

Garnome pulled his arm and placed it back in its socket.

"You son of a bitch!" Carter said with gritted teeth.

"There! Back in place! You're welcome, pal. Here, take a couple of these for the pain."

Garnome tossed him a pair of aspirins and helped him to his feet.

"Alright, saddle up, guys!" Jacobs ordered. "We have to keep moving. Hope 7 is going to be to our right. Keep your eyes peeled for the pilot but he can't be our priority anymore."

"We can't leave him!" Garnome lightly protested.

Jacobs sighed, saying, "I don't wanna leave him, but we have to get to the rest of our guys. They're going to need us. We'll keep searching, but it has to be in the direction of Hope 7. We gotta pick up the pace."

Garnome nodded his head. "Roger that, LT."

They kept moving. It was almost strange to the men to not hear any space shuttles take flight amidst the night sky. Alaska was one of the last bastions of the world to not convert to the Ascended Age. Millions of Americans fled to Alaska in hopes of fleeing the ambitions of technology. They were a people who valued the old ways of life; hunting for one's food and searching for one's water. It was equivalent to an old western town refusing to conform to a modern industrial city. Much of Alaska was untouched by the rest of the world. There were no Sky-liners, flying cars, or light trains. There were no lights; the moon cast its illumination onto the wooded forest. Most of the men wore their night vision goggles; none used flashlights. They stepped quietly and each man was mindful of nearby branches. The cold air made exposed cuts and wounds sting.

Carter stopped and said, "Hold up. What's that?"

He pointed to the ground. The snow was bloody and there was blood on the nearby oak trees. A ruckus was sounded in the distance; the sound of snapping branches. The men looked to Jacobs for orders. He used sign language to direct Carter to take position on the left flank, Ramirez and Chris further along the left flank, and Garnome would push up the middle. The formation was an 'L-shape' firing line. This would limit the chances of friendly fire. They got into position and followed the blood trail through the dense, vine-covered area of bushes, branches, and snow. As Jacobs moved forward, he noticed that some of the oak trees had been slashed or chipped; like something had been banged against them. When they pressed the position, guns at the ready, they saw a body being chewed on by wolves. Jacobs shot one of the wolves and the rest ran away. The team converged on the body. Carter kneeled in the snow and scanned the area with his rifle; protecting the perimeter. The body was a shirtless male with a hole through his chest; his face brutally smashed in. Garnome recognized the helmet that the man was wearing—it was the pilot from the helicopter.

Garnome tucked in his lips; clutching his fists. "Ah, no... no... it's the pilot. Jesus Christ!"

Ramirez shook his head. "Damn! Did the wolves do this?"

Jacobs knelt beside the body, examined it, and said, "His face has been badly smashed in—and that hole through his chest? No. Wolves didn't do this. Something else did."

Garnome examined the body further and said, "I agree. His jaw is broken, as well as his nose—the right cheekbone looks fractured or even broken. Ah—his eyes have been gouged out too!"

Chris said, "Geez! I could fit my fist through that hole! Maybe someone shot him?"

Jacobs explained, "No. We would have heard it, and, besides— that hole is too big to have been made by a gun. Whatever did this got up close and personal. Well... there's nothing we can do for him now; poor bastard's dead. Grab his tags and we'll make sure to send a BRS team to recover the bodies. Move out, X-Ray! Keep your guard up!"

Garnome grabbed the pilot's dog tags and snagged them off his corpse. The squad continued moving through the forest. Chills ran down the spines of the soldiers. The pilot had been horribly muti- lated, like he was a plastic toy at the mercy of a mindless child. What did that? Was it a bear mauling? No. If so, the wolves wouldn't have been present. What carried him off in the first place? Was it... no, couldn't be. The Phantom? Jacobs felt a shiver rush down his back as he tried to make sense of what happened. I thought it was contained to the facility. Another twenty minutes had passed and the storm temporarily calmed. The men of X-Ray constantly scanned the trees and their nearby surroundings. There was an eerie feeling that someone or something was watching them. They would walk for a bit, then they would hear something in the dis- tance. A cracking of a branch or light shaking of nearby bushes. Wolves could be heard howling and the temperature remained bit- terly cold. There didn't seem to be any end to the oak trees and a feeling came over the squad that they were officially lost.

Jacobs asked, "Does anyone know where we're going?"

Chris, in youthful ignorance, said, "To Hope 7, sir."

No way!? I thought we were going to the county fair. Jacobs sarcastically thought before answering aloud, with a slight hint of contempt in his voice, "I know that! But where are we? This forest is too tall and dense. I hate to admit it boys, but it appears that we're lost."

Ramirez said, "Great! How are we going to get to the facility if we have no clue where we're going?"

"We should keep moving and see if we can get clear of these oak trees. When we've done that, we should be able to spot the facility. I think we're on the right path, but I'm not sure and that pisses me off."

The men looked around for a high position, but the trees blocked their view. Jacobs led his team further through the forest; hoping that he could find an elevated position or a sign. Another ten minutes and there was a brief clearing where the trees weren't invading the men's space. A figure could be seen standing on the other side of the clearing. Jacobs kneeled to a crouch and aimed his rifle; his men followed. They slowly crept along the tree line. The figure stood in darkness and was looking in the opposite direction of the squad. Everyone hoped that it wasn't the Phantom. If so, men would die here. They had itchy trigger fingers. As they slowly advanced on it, they realized that the shadowy figure was a man standing against a tree. He was tall, his head was shaven, and, strangely, he didn't have a shirt on.

Ramirez whispered, "Doesn't something feel off? It's freezing and this guy is standing out here with no shirt."

Chris quietly said, "Remember that shanty town we passed by when we were airborne? Maybe he's a villager. Maybe he knows how we can get to the facility from here."

"Or maybe he's the same bastard that killed our pilot. We'll take him down and then we'll question him. Carter, on me!" Jacobs ordered.

Jacobs and Carter quietly moved up on the man. They stepped toe-first into the snow. He was breathing hard, as if he just got done running. Carter was instantly reminded of the time when he murdered the man in Georgia. He felt himself get hot; his palms sweaty.

When they were close enough, Jacobs and Carter tackled the man to the ground. They noticed almost immediately how strong he was. Carter was shoving his head into the snow and Jacobs struggled to zip tie his hands.

The man threw them off his back and Jacobs was shocked when he turned around to face him. His eyes were a ghastly bloodshot red. He was extremely masculine—and he had pieces of metal hanging out of his body. He spoke inaudibly; growled and angrily yelled at Jacobs. Before anyone could shoot, the man punched Jacobs in his vest. Jacobs felt as if he had been struck by a harpoon. The blow sent him flying; landing in the snow.

Carter shot the man three times in the chest, and the others fired and hit him simultaneously. The man shook violently as he was struck by the proton rounds but refused to fall. After another dozen rounds, he finally fell to the ground, kicked up snow, and stopped shaking after a few seconds.

Carter shouted, "Jacobs—are you okay?"

Jacobs coughed and moaned, "Ooh, my chest—that bastard can punch! We get him?"

"Yeah, he's toast!" Carter reported as he helped Jacobs to his feet.

To everyone's disbelief, the man slowly began to move again. It started with a trembling hand, his feet next, and then he stood up.

Ramirez was in utter disbelief. "No way!"

The man yelled and ran towards Carter. He was lightning fast. He ran side-to-side and moved with such speed that the soldiers struggled to lock onto their target. He threw a punch but missed Carter and hit an oak tree—leaving a gash in the thick tree. Ramirez got ready to fire but was tackled by another strange man from the side. Chris turned to fire at Ramirez's tango, but had his weapon knocked out of his hands, and too was punched to the ground. He turned back to Ramirez and got ready to strike but Chris jumped on his back and stabbed him repeatedly in his chest.

The combatant threw Chris over his back and clenched his hand tightly around his face.

He looked at the knife sticking out of his chest and angrily spoke, "You... know scalpel!?" He showed various cuts on his left arm. "I show... you scalpel! You die... inferior!!"

Chris was unnerved but didn't show it to his enemy. With a straight face, he pulled the knife out of the man's chest and ran his blade across his throat in quick fashion. The man panicked as the blood ran down his throat. Chris lifted his arm, stabbed him in the armpit, flipped him to the ground, and repeatedly stabbed him in his throat. Ramirez witnessed the whole thing. When Chris turned away, his face was peppered with dots of blood. You're not just some replacement. Ramirez thought to himself. The other combatant had his hands around Garnome's throat. Carter came from behind and bashed his head with the butt of his rifle. He did so continuously. When the cracking noise sounded and the head was no more than smashed cherry pie, he stopped. He gritted his teeth. There was wetness around his eyes. When he became conscious of it, he quickly wiped them.

Garnome said, "Good kill! You saved me!"

Carter didn't say anything.

"You alright!?"

"Yeah... yeah, tango down." Carter said, while walking to the side.

ROMAN CARTER

I ate my bowl of cereal tepidly as if I had a swollen throat. Gramps had the news on. I rarely looked up. I saved the lucky charm marshmallows for last. I got ready to take another bite when the news caught my attention.

"Welcome back, folks. This is Rosa Mendes and you're watching

CBS. Earlier this morning, approximately around 6:00 am, a group of construction workers noticed a white truck parked south of the Atlanta national park."

A picture of the man I killed took over the screen.

"The vehicle belonged to this man, John Tarbell. He was parked next to a forest with quicksand pockets inside. Some are already worrying that he may have stumbled into one of the pockets. There is a search party taking place."

The milk seemed to leak out of my mouth and back into the bowl.

"We're searching hour by hour looking for my dad." A lady spoke on the screen, teary eyed. "We refuse to believe that he's dead."

I stood up, rushed over to the bathroom, and puked up my guts. I could see my lucky charms fly outta my mouth. You stupid murderer! What were you thinking? Letting your anger make a killer outta you! When I was done, I could feel my granddad behind me.

"What's going on with ya, boy?" He said in his soft, raspy voice.

I hastily searched my mind for an answer. I told him a lie while also telling him the truth.

"It's just... it's my dad, gramps. I really miss him." I said, tears rolling down my face.

He stepped into the bathroom and gave me a hug. "Listen here, boy. Your father loved you! You were his greatest treasure."

"Then why did he leave me!? Huh!?"

"He didn't choose to die, Roman. Nobody chooses death. Truth is, he hated his life, but he would've done anything to spend another day with you."

I broke the hug and stormed out of the bathroom.

PRESENT DAY

Ramirez put a few more bullets in each hostile; two to the chest and one to the head. Chris dragged the man he killed and set his body atop the other man's corpse. Each person searched their minds for answers. How was it that two unarmed men almost bested a team of armed, elite soldiers?

Chris spoke aloud, "When the guy grabbed my face, he talked strange. He struggled to speak and he called me, 'inferior.'"

Ramirez said, "Forget that one second. Who the hell are you?"

"What?"

"You heard me. You took that guy down with a knife. Killed him like you'd been doing it your whole life."

The squad stood with their heads held high and waited for a response. Chris held his knife in the palm of his hand. It was an all-silver, skinny, fixed blade. The blade itself was about four inches long. The handle had a black imprint of a falcon at the bottom of it.

CHRIS MARILYN
(2016)

We all stood in the dark; maybe four hundred in total. Our heads were shaven. My bare feet were chilled on the cold, marble flooring. We faced the large, black falcon on the wall. The environment was concrete and cold. We could hear noise beyond the large door in front of us. Yells of anger and pain, and the thumping of the fallen bodies. The waiting was awful. I had butterflies in my stomach and my heart rapidly raced. The door opened and my friend, George, walked up the long hallway, escorted by an administrator. He walked with his head down; his face bloodied. The administrator congratulated him and escorted him to his holding room.

"Marilyn, front and center!" Yelled an administrator.

I felt like my heart did a backflip. I run around the group and stand to attention at the front.

"What is the purpose of this exercise!?" He asked.

"To kill my opponent!"

"How will you do this!?"

"By any means necessary!"

He removed the blade from the black box in his subordinate's hands and gave it to me; an all-silver, straight blade.

"I award you the falcon blade, student. If you survive, you may keep it!"

"Yes, administrator."

He pointed to the door. I walked down the long hallway. I was ten years old. This practice was known as, "The Trimming of the Tall Grass;" an exercise that would decide living from dead, boy from man, killer from assassin. When I reached the door, I used both hands to push it open. I was terribly scared but trained to hide it. I could hide it from everyone else but not myself. I entered the arena. It was underground, as was everything at the F-2 depot. The large room was illuminated in blue lighting. To my right, there were about twelve administrators sitting in the stands. Artificial waterfalls sounded on both sides. My opponent walked forward. He was tall, skinny, white face, and shaved head. We circled each other, slightly getting closer with each revolution. We readied our knives and charged each other. Each blade strike was fluidly dodged. He had a long reach, so I had to be mindful of keeping my distance. We tumbled and fought for about fifteen minutes; a record at the academy. We had cuts on our skinny bodies but no stab wounds. Until he landed a deep stab in my upper back, above my left shoulder. I punched him and pushed him away. The pain was excruciatingly sharp. My left arm limped and I could feel the warm blood running down my arm. We both thought that it was the beginning of the end for me. He started to smile until he realized a fatal mistake, as did I. He left his knife in my back. We were taught to never do that in training; always make sure to pull your blade out of each stab.

He was left defenseless. He rushed me, I lowered my head and blade and pierced his armpit with a deep stab. I flipped him over to the ground, stabbed him in the abdomen, and finished him with a blow to the back of the neck. I was a Falcon; a trained American assassin. It only cost me everything. Worse, it wasn't my choice.

PRESENT DAY

Chris tucked his blade into his knife holster around his hip and said, "I'm on your side, Ramirez, that's all you need to know."

Ramirez waved him off. He and Garnome examined the bodies of the strange men.

Ramirez shined his flashlight on the man's neck and said, "Wait—check this out! He has a barcode on his neck!"

Jacobs asked incredulously, "A barcode? Is it like a tattoo?"

"No—it's more like an engraving into his skin. It has blue illumination on it."

Garnome grimaced as he examined the body. "This is weird, man. The metal that's hanging out of his body seems to be attached to some sort of metal plating in his chest and abdomen!"

Ramirez said, "What? Is that even possible?"

"Possible—sure. I'm just as certain that it was beyond painful. These guy's have gone through extensive body modifications."

Carter examined the gunshot wounds and reported, "It looks like eighteen of our bullets hit him—but eight of them hit the metal plating. Doesn't explain how the other ten rounds didn't kill him. All I know is that he partly shattered that oak tree when he tried to punch me."

Chris said in disbelief, "Partly shattered an oak tree? This guy must've been incredibly strong!" He thought about the time he bet with his friends on who could hit an oak tree the most times before pulling out. Chris won, but after twenty-three punches, and bloodied hands, the oak tree didn't even have a dent in it. This man here literally took out a chunk of the tree with a single swipe.

Garnome said, "Looks like we know what got the pilot—this is what killed him."

Jacobs coughed and said, "His eyes were gnarly red. My guess? He came from Hope 7. He wasn't the only one either. There could be more out here. Keep your eyes open. Presume that all contacts are hostile until proven not. If there are more, I fear for Commander Harrison and the rest of our guys. We've gotta get there fast! Double time, X-Ray! Carter, take point!"

Carter acknowledged. "You got it!"

The squad advanced. Jacobs stayed in the back of the line. Suddenly, he was overcome by a bad coughing spell. It was dry. His throat and chest hurt. He felt something in his lungs; like water.

Garnome asked him, "You alright, Jacobs? Maybe I should take a look at you?"

Still coughing, Jacobs said, "No. I'm fine. Keep moving."

Jacobs looked at his gloves and saw blood on them from his coughing. He steadily trailed behind his men.

CHAPTER 7: THE FREAKS

INSIDE THE HOPE 7 lobby, the view was grizzly. Blood was splattered on the walls, papers lay scattered amongst corpses, and bodies were hanging from the railing. The room was only dimly lit. Probably for the best. The tiled flooring seemed to have a history of being white, sparkling, and pristine, but that time had long passed. Blood seemed to be everywhere, and it was hard not to trip, as the bodies lay scattered across the floor. The decaying corpses created a ghastly smell. When the Blue-2 squad blew a hole into the room it caused the air to shoot outwards, as if the air itself was trying to escape the horrors of the lobby.

Sonya, while covering her mouth, said, "Oh, God. The situation is worse than I thought!"

Bradley asked, "Man, what was up with that lightning?"

Commander Harrison agreed. "Yeah, that was strange. I have a feeling it's somehow tied to this facility. We'll have to sort it out before we can leave."

Taylor asked, "What about the scream?"

Harrison replied, "What scream?"

"You didn't hear the scream? It was faint, but I definitely heard it."

"I didn't hear anything"

Bradley added, "Neither did I"

Taylor insisted, "Well, I did!"

Harrison said, "Let's just get up to the control center. Keep it tight and check those corners; lots of tight spaces for an enemy to get the drop on us."

The squad moved in a single-file line, Bradley covered their rear, Taylor took point, and headed towards the stairway. There were rooms to the right and left of the lobby but the men's only concern at the moment was getting the power back on. A wailing noise sounded deep below the ground.

"Hear that?" Asked Bradley.

"Yeah—fortunately it sounded like it was a little distance away." Replied Harrison.

Taylor exclaimed, "Damn, that smell is killing me!"

Harrison admonished him. "Keep it together, Taylor!"

"I'm trying, sir. It's just so..."

Taylor ran to the side of the stairway and vomited.

Bradley put his hand on his shoulder. "Easy, Taylor."

Taylor wiped his mouth and continued heading up the stairwell. He'd been around dead bodies before but not like this. So many corpses in one shut room; the smell was inescapable. It stuck to everyone's clothing, seemingly looking for a ticket out of the room. It seemed to run down Taylor's throat and played hopscotch under his uvula. The squad stacked up on the control room. The door was open. Harrison pinched Taylor's shoulder, and they entered the room, guns at the ready. Like the lobby, the control room was a mess. Blood covered the walls, tables were broken up and knocked over, and two dead bodies were in the room. Fortunately, the room seemed clear of hostiles. In the back of the room they saw a closed door with a stairwell sign next to it. When they were sure the area was clear of life, Bradley checked one of the bodies, and Taylor checked the other one. As Taylor walked, he heard a squishy noise.

114

He looked down at his combat boot and realized that he'd stepped on someone's eyeball.

Taylor gagged before saying, "Ugh! That's just gross, man!"

Harrison asked Bradley, "He got a name?"

Bradley answered, "His nametag says 'Jackson.' This is the poor bastard who sent the distress beacon. I can't even recognize his face; he's been so badly mutilated." Only the name badge was legible.

Harrison shook his head. "That really is too bad. What about you, Taylor? Your guy have a name?"

Taylor responded, "That's a negative, Commander, but judging from his outfit, it looks like he was part of the Hope 7 security detail. Similar to the guy we saw outside."

Harrison noticed a puddle of blood in the corner of the room. He moved a collapsed table and found a dead man under it. He'd been shot in the head.

Harrison observed, "Got another body over here. He's been shot—square in the forehead."

Taylor mused, "Hmmm. I wonder who shot him. Probably the same person who shot that security guy."

Harrison didn't like the look of things. One accident, maybe, but two? Unlikely. He thought. He had a vibe that whoever killed the two men were professionals. One man was shot multiple times, center-massed, and the other one was shot in the head. Harrison worried that someone else was in the facility. Maybe a Russian or Chinese black operative team trying to steal classified intel. Afterall, the US wasn't the only country to invest in black ops. Hurry up, Jacobs. He walked over to the console, where Val was standing. He asked her, "How do communications work here at Hope 7?"

Val answered, "Well, there are no phones or phone lines, and the only link to the digital world outside—internet, YouTube, whatever— is via the Mainframe. The Mainframe is a centralized computer network and it's how we send and receive messages. All computers in the facility are synced to the Mainframe and nothing gets out of Hope 7 without passing through it and being thoroughly read."

Harrison said, "Is it here in the control room?"

"No. It's through the hallway to our left, on this level. 'Bout a three-minute walk away."

"OK. More on that in a minute. Let's look at the security feeds. See if we can get an idea of what happened here."

Commander Harrison and Val searched the console. They pulled up a security-cam video and it showed panicking scientist and staff in the lobby trying to get out but were unable to due to the lockdown. In the video, inside the control center, staff were trying to override the lockdown when the wailing was heard. The Phantom entered the room, grabbed a staff member, and threw her through the glass window, out of the control center, and into the lobby, killing her. Another person tried to run but was grabbed by the Phantom. The creature held onto the staff member tightly and electrocuted him—so bad that it caused his eyeballs to pop from his eye sockets.

A security guard could be seen saying, "Tommy, stop! You don't wanna do this!"

The Phantom dropped the body and slowly turned to face the security guard and walked toward him. It was like a moving shadow. There was nothing but blackness in the middle; it was like a piece of air donned an all-black coat. It took the shape of a naked human; the legs, arms, body, and even hair were all in the outline. It had no eyes or lips.

The security guard, visibly nervous, said, "What we did to you was wrong, Tommy, but we can fix this! Just stop! Please stop!" His face was covered in sweat.

The Phantom wailed, causing the footage to slightly buffer.

The security guard reached for his pistol, but before he could grab it, he was brutally slammed into the wall in a quick motion. The Phantom seemed to just appear next to him. It kept its hands on the security guard's knees; making the guard shake in pain.

The Phantom spoke—in a voice that was more static than anything else, "You... know nothing... of... pain!" It seemed to speak through the guard's radio. "Where... is the... Mainframe?"

"No!" The security guard said. "I'm not telling you!"

The Phantom shrieked, the security video shut off, and went blank.

Harrison covered his mouth with one hand. "Jesus Christ! The security guard knew who the Phantom was. He called him "Tommy". Were you people running experiments on humans? Live humans?"

Seeing Harrison's frustration, Val rushed to speak, "I don't know anything for certain... just rumors."

"Val!" Sonya interjected.

Harrison ignored her. "Rumors?"

"Well, I-"

The lights flickered, and a noise was heard. It sounded like an empty soda can had been stepped on. Seconds later, the lights were completely extinguished.

Taylor flipped down his night vision goggles, "You guys hear that? It sounds like something's in the lobby."

Harrison, with no fear, took charge, "Let's check it out! We'll continue this discussion afterwards. I'll take point!"

Harrison led the squad out of the control room; down the stairwell. It was eerily quiet. As he stepped, he accidentally knocked down a half-filled Gatorade bottle. He watched as it fell down the stairs. It rolled and fell, rolled and fell, and then rolled against someone's foot. Harrison looked up quickly, but the figure quickly disappeared into the darkness of the lobby. Harrison took a deep inhale before slowly walking down the stairs, and back into the lobby. There was an unspoken fear that when the squad got back down, all the dead bodies would be gone or worse, back to life.

It was dark and quiet as the squad scanned the room. There was no noise. Suddenly, a body appeared out of the darkness—it sailed into the air, over the men. The lifeless body fell on top of Bradley and the squad was rushed by multiple combatants. They couldn't make out who they were, so they opened fire on the hostiles. In the dark, nothing but gunfire and yelling could be heard. The night vision was their best ally for those who had it. The empty bullet casings rained over the floor; the smell of lead filling the wretched-smelling room. Harrison noticed how these enemies were being shot but not falling easily. Like they were coked up on PCP. Someone would take a couple of shots and dissipate back into the darkness. The soldiers snapped their sights to their targets and they fired accurately. The enemy, although bullet-resistant, couldn't get too close to the circle. The men of X-Ray were not unarmed scientists.

Harrison ordered, "Taylor - toss a flare!"

Taylor hastily reached into his vest and pulled out a flare. He lit it and threw it into the room. Each man removed his night vision. Nothing could be seen in the now red illuminated room, and the squad temporarily ceased fire, but kept their weapons at the ready.

"Bradley, provide overwatch! The rest of you, check ammo! Val, stay back!" Harrison ordered.

Bradley kneeled one leg to the tile and scanned the room. He asked, "Where'd they go?"

Taylor noticed something out of the corner of his eye. Someone jumped from the railing above Taylor; intent on tackling him. Taylor managed to turn quickly enough and light the man—still in mid-air—on fire with his flamethrower. The man crashed into the ground, missing Taylor. He yelled; the squad didn't know if it was out of pain or anger. He rushed around aimlessly like a berserker. The squad put him down like a mad dog. Multiple hostiles walked into the red illumination of the flare. They stood with angry faces and growled and sneered at Task Force X-Ray. There was about eight of them. They banged on pots and clanged together metal pipes. Most of them didn't have shirts on; almost all had gunshot wounds.

They chanted, "Inferior… inferior… inferior… inferior!!!"

One came forward, stood in front of the group, and said, "You must ascend or die!!" Their eyes were red with anger. His eyes slowly faded into the dark and the rest of the hostiles growled and disappeared into the darkness. The lights began to flicker and they came back on. The hostiles were gone entirely. Everyone was unsettled. Harrison figured that between the five of them, over a hundred rounds of ammunition had been used, easy. Yet only three of the hostiles were dead on the floor.

Harrison asked, "Is everyone intact?"

The squad responded with thumbs up or the nodding of heads.

Harrison stood over the burning body. What was thought to be a man now appeared to be a woman. They could tell because she too was shirtless, and her charring breast could be seen through the fire. Her head was shaved, teeth clenched, her eyes were wide open and terribly red. They could see a barcode on her neck. Harrison knew that the squad was in trouble. What is this? They absorbed bullets like some monsters out of a damn TV show. We need Jacobs and the rest of our guys to reinforce us. If these 'things' manage to close in, pin us down… It'll be messy. What in the hell are they doing in this place? Harrison thought to himself. To hell with it. We'll take the fight to them.

Harrison ordered, "Squad! Spread out and pursue those combatants! Val, stay here with Sonya."

The Commander led his men forward to the right side of the lobby. He figured that they were holed up in some of the rooms. Harrison and his men stacked along the wall for room number one. The silver door was closed. Harrison made a 'pull-the-pin' hand gesture. Taylor readied a frag grenade. Harrison kicked the door open at the knob and Taylor lobbed the grenade inside. 4…3…2 …1…BOOM!! Taylor shot burst of flames into the room. When the dust settled, three enemy combatants were dead. So far, so good. They stacked up on the second room, Harrison kicked open the door, Taylor prepared to fire but was grabbed and pulled inside. Harrison and Bradley stepped in and machine-gunned all the hostiles in there at point blank range. One tried to rush Harrison; he put three rounds in his chest and one to the head, sending the man recoiling back. He looked like he was running backwards. Taylor was nothing short of relieved. Bradley helped him to his feet. Harrison followed behind a dying man who crawled along the floor, leaving a blood trail. He flipped the man over on his back, kneeled on his chest, and held his pistol under his chin.

"Why are you doing this!? Who are you people!?" Harrison interrogated the man.

Blood leaked out of his mouth as he spoke. "We were... like... you. We... ascended. You... will... too!"

Harrison put the dying man out of his misery. "How many we get?"

Bradley counted the bodies in the room before saying, "Looks like we killed six of 'em."

"Make sure they're dead!" Harrison responded. "Are all their eyes bloodshot?"

There was a pause before Bradley responded, "Looks like it."

Bradley stepped over each body and fired additional rounds into them. When they were done, they walked back to their female counterparts. Harrison knew that they didn't kill all of them, but it was a start. He figured his preemptive attack would buy his men time and thin the enemy ranks.

Commander Harrison, visibly agitated, said to Val, "I need you to come clean and be straightforward with me—what's going on here? These people aren't normal—neither is the Phantom."

Val adjusted her glasses. "You have to believe me, Commander, when I say that I had no part in this. I worked with the medical division on Level Two. We crafted medicines and vaccines. I had no insight on what else was going on in the facility. However, there are multiple research divisions at Hope 7. One, the Valkyrie Division, led research and development for soldiers. I assumed that meant working with those who lost limbs, had PTSD, etc. They were looking into ways to make better soldiers—maybe even artificially enhance them."

Harrison scoffed, "What? Like super-soldiers?"

Val stared at the charring corpse on the floor. "Well, judging from the evidence in front of us—yeah. I knew this one guy, named 'Ronald.' He worked in the Valkyrie division. One day I heard him talking about experiments being done and people being turned into Freaks. I didn't believe him, of course, but it seems he was correct. Strangely, he disappeared a couple of days later. We were told that he was fired."

Harrison pressed Val, "How many divisions work at Hope 7? And what else can you tell me about the Valkyrie division?"

"Seven divisions of researchers—that I know of—work at Hope 7. That's the '7' in 'Hope 7.' There's the Medical Division, Tech Division, Weapons Division, Tactics Division, Energy Division, Valkyrie Division, and the WMD Division. The Divisions—just like this entire facility—are all shrouded in secrecy. Unfortunately, the Valkyrie division is the most secretive one, and most of the staff here know little about them."

"Whatever the truth is, these people are tough. They're fast, strong, and fearless. It would also seem that their pain receptors have been modified—that's why they can take so much punishment and still fight. This is a clear violation of Article 331."

Taylor said, "Man, this is terrible! It's already bad enough that we have to fight some ghost in the shadows—and now we have to fight these Freaks, too? Gimme a break!"

Bradley said, "Well at least we can kill 'em. I get a hunch that the Phantom won't die so easily."

Harrison said, "Sonya, Val—I'd like a moment with my men. Give me a minute."

Harrison signaled to his men and they walked about fifteen feet away and formed a huddle. They spoke in quiet voices.

Bradley asked, "What do you think of this, boss?"

Harrison answered, "If you ask me, the writing is on the wall—my guess is R&D gone bad. They did tests on the guinea pigs and now the guinea pigs have been set loose and are killing everyone. The Phantom is probably no different. They're full of shit, so be wary of them."

Taylor said, "You really think they've been doing experiments on humans?"

Harrison said, "I'm certain of it. That's what these Freaks are—experiments. They're obviously human, but they've been molded into something different, something corrupted. They've violated Article 331."

Bradley suggested, "Maybe we should get out of here and just pass 'Inferno' to command and let them blow this place to hell!"

Taylor nodded his head rapidly. "I second that, brother!"

Harrison tried to bring balance back to the discussion. "Not a bad idea, but I'm determined to find out what really went on here. We owe it the men and women who died here."

Bradley asked, "Are we continuing the mission?"

Harrison answered, "That's correct, Bradley. We're going to find out what happened here. If this place is funded by the government, then this thing probably stretches high up the chain of command. When Ramirez catches up with us, I'll have him download any incriminating files to present to Sampson. Something else, we're not alone here. Someone—an individual or a group, has passed through here recently. Those gunshot wounds are no accident. We need to find and deal with them. Once we do that and gather everything we need, we'll blow this place to kingdom come!"

Taylor responded, "Roger that!"

Bradley chimed in, "Sounds good to me, sir!"

The team broke the huddle and regrouped with Sonya and Val.

Harrison said, "OK—now that the hostiles are dealt with, let's get back to that control center and get the power back on. These emergency lights are crap!"

They went back into the control room and hit some switches. The lights came up to full power and the lockdown was lifted. Bright sterile lights fully revealed the ghastly imagery of the lobby. A great shuddering noise sounded as the steel barriers lifted. The snowy wilderness could now be viewed through some of the windows. Harrison began to question if coming to Hope 7 first was the right call. It'd been forty-five minutes and there was no word from Jacobs or the Blue-1 squad. He figured in his head that they'd wait another fifteen minutes or so before proceeding towards their last known location. Strangely, even though the barriers were fully open, the shuddering sound didn't stop.

Taylor pondered, "You guys hear that? It sounds like a car being crushed."

The control room lightly shook as if there was a minor earthquake.

Bradley turned around and said, "I don't like the sound of that."

The door behind them to the stairwell suddenly burst open and multiple Freaks appeared. Some of them had body armor and firearms; others were armed with makeshift weapons. One Freak stood out from the rest. He was wearing a "Mech suit"—it was fully armored with armor plating and had weapons on its arms. It was the size of a regular human, had brass colored plates, and had a box shaped helmet.

Taylor laid down a stream of fire and caught most of the mutants on fire, but the fire didn't faze them. These enemies cared not for their own lives and were reckless—making them more dangerous to the squad. The Freaks charged the group while burning and under machine-gun fire; carnage ensued. Taylor was tackled through the window. Bradley was rag-dolled from side to side. Sonya was pinned to the ground and beat on by multiple Freaks. Val tried to get them off Sonya by shooting at them. Harrison flipped his switch to fully automatic. He fired in controlled bursts; killing three. When the clicking sounded, he dropped his emptied rifle, and shot a few of them with his Desert Eagle. All gun fire ricocheted off the Mech. It stretched out its arm and Harrison knew that nothing good was about to happen.

Harrison yelled, "Get down!"

He pulled Val down to the ground as the Mech shot flames from its flamethrower into the room. The fire was scorching—everything was set ablaze. Harrison could feel the heat pass over him. The Freaks on top of Sonya were caught on fire, as they were standing, and Sonya was lying down. When there was a lull in the fire, Harrison pushed the burning Freaks off Sonya, lifted her up, and pushed Sonya and Val out of the window and into the lobby. Harrison then stood Bradley up, and, while he did so, he pulled the pins on his own grenades.

Bradley, wide-eyed, asked, "What are you doing, sir?"

"Get out of here, Bradley! Jump!"

"No! I got your back, sir!"

"Not this time, Bradley!"

As several of the burning mutant creatures reached for Harrison, he kicked Bradley out of the window and into the lobby. Bradley rolled over the floor and looked up just in time to see the control room explode into a fiery inferno.

Bradley cried out, "Noooo!!!"

Taylor covered his face, ran over to Bradley and asked, "Where's the Commander? Do you see him, Bradley?"

Bradley shook his head.

The fire from the command center burned intensely. Papers floated over the lobby; the air was crisp and filled with ash.

CHAPTER 8: INCLEMENT WEATHER

ICICLES FORMED ON the tree branches, snow fell from the sky, and the snow on the ground was getting deeper by the minute; forming snow fields that were hard to walk through. The wind blew hard. Normally, the cold in this valley was nothing a long-sleeved shirt and a thick jacket couldn't solve, but this cold was different. It pierced even the thickest jackets and no armor could protect from it. They could feel it in their bones; it was the type of cold that defeated the Germans at Stalingrad. A blizzard had overcome the valley, greatly reducing visibility. Carter checked his temperature gauge and saw that it was thirteen degrees Fahrenheit. The Blue-1 squad moved forward slowly. From ten feet away, they were visible, at twenty-five feet away, they weren't. The moon was full. Wolves could be heard howling.

Carter said, "Where's the facility? I can't see a thing!"

The squad made their way onto a frozen riverbed. High winds blew; making the riverbed that much more intimidating.

Jacobs yelled out, "Careful! It's slippery!"

The squad cautiously walked over the frozen riverbed to the

other side. Each man walked in single-file line and kept a hand on the shoulder of the man in front.

Ramirez said, "Hey, Jacobs. If those men were from Hope 7, how in the hell did they end up all the way over there?"

Jacobs cleared his throat and answered, "Beats me, pal. They must've escaped."

"We better find some shelter, sir! This weather is no good!" Carter warned.

"I hear you, Carter. We'll see what we can do!" Jacobs responded.

Ramirez shuddered, "Man, that thing gave me the creeps—like Garnome's mom without her makeup."

Everyone laughed.

The last person to cross, Garnome shouted, "Screw you, Daniel!"

Each soldier was covered in snow, like little snowmen emerging from the relentless blizzard. The cold air made their lungs sore and their lips chapped. Jacobs was suffering the worst. He felt like a piece of food went down the wrong pipe and he constantly felt the need to clear his throat. He kept coughing, and the cold, windy, air kept passing through his lungs. Jacobs saw a carving into the mountain wall and saw an opportunity to take shelter.

Jacobs said, "OK, guys. We're going to take a break next to this riverbed; over by that hole in the wall. Let's get a fire going. Ramirez, Chris, and Carter will go find some wood. Garnome and I will stay back here and get our rations ready. We'll carve up a spot for the fire."

Chris, Ramirez, and Carter went out searching for wood, while Garnome and Jacobs looked through their rucksacks and prepared their rations. Jacobs suffered another coughing spell. He dropped to a knee and leaned his back against the rock wall.

Garnome said, "Let me take a look at you."

Jacobs, coughing into his gloves, waved him off, but Garnome was persistent. After he was done coughing, Garnome moved Jacobs' hands away from his face and noticed the blood on his gloves.

The medic said, "Jesus, Roger! Why didn't you say something?"

Jacobs coughed and spit out a bit of blood. "Because there's nothing you can do. The wound is internal, maybe even a bruised lung." Jacobs coughed something terrible. "We don't have the equipment to deal with a wound like that, and I don't want you worrying about something you have no control over."

Garnome sat silent.

<hr />

JERRY GARNOME
(2022)

I watched them lower his casket into the ground. I couldn't tell whether the water leaking down my face was from my eyes or from the rain. I remembered the words he spoke when we found out he had leukemia. "Don't worry, dad. I'm happy that I get to spend more time with you and mommy. You're the bestest best parents in the world!" The water poured down my face, definitely not the rain. I was sickened by how small the casket was, but I wouldn't turn away until the hole had been filled with dirt. My son... gone far too soon. Rachael wept on my shoulder. I could do nothing but hug her and tell her that everything was going to be alright. The holy man approached us and offered his condolences. He held out a sterling silver cross in the palm of his hand. I pushed it away.

"Mr. Garnome, Jesus loves you." He said.

I unintentionally burst out laughing. "I'm sure he does, my friend. I'm sure he does! Tell my son that!"

He was puzzled.

"Mr. Garnome-"

"Tell him!!" I yell.

I could feel eyes on me.

"Jerry, come on. Let's go!" Rachael says to me.

"He already knows." The reverend whispered.

We walk through the cemetery and to the limousine. All the lives I saved and the one that mattered most I couldn't. Life's a bitch like that.

PRESENT DAY

Jacobs pled with Garnome. "Listen, don't tell the guys—OK? I don't need them worrying about me. I need you all to stay focused on the mission. Besides, I can hold out long enough to get to a medical facility after the mission is over."

Garnome remained silent. Jacobs was right; there was nothing he could do and that pissed him off. He broke his silence, "I know the dangers of not catching something before it's too late."

"I'm sure you do, doc. I'll be fine." Jacobs assured him.

Garnome nodded his head and continued looking through his rucksack for food. He found a few cans of potato soup, a small pot, and a few MREs. Jacobs carved out some snow with his combat knife and dug a little hole in the dirt. Shortly afterwards, Chris, Ramirez, and Carter returned with wood and rocks.

Chris said, "Now all we need is a light."

Carter pulled out a flare and Chris pushed the wood into the little hole. Ramirez centered the rocks around the hole; forming a pit. Carter then popped the flare and used it to light the wood. The wood took a while to light, but, eventually, it did. Carter left the flare on top and leaned against the wall. They were positioned close to a cluster of oak trees. The trees helped a little in keeping some of the wind back, but it didn't do much. Luckily, they didn't have to worry about the wind hitting their backs. Jacobs was worried about the fire giving away their position, but he had little choice. The weather was brutal, and he knew that the dangers of catching hypothermia or even dying from it was high. Chris sat with his back facing the wilderness.

Ramirez rubbed his hands together over the fire and asked, "So, what's on the menu, boys?"

Jacobs answered, "Looks like we'll be having some potato soup with our MREs today. Where'd you guys find this pot?"

Carter said, "I snatched it from the mess hall while no one was looking. I didn't know if we'd actually use it, but hey, it came in handy. Outta all the shit we lost in the helicopter wreckage the magic pot somehow made it. I'm not complaining."

Ramirez said, "Damn! I'm starving!"

The squad sat around the fire. Garnome held the pot of potato soup over the fire, occasionally stirring with a wooden stick. Carter scraped additional shavings off the spare wood with his combat knife and tossed them in the fire to keep the fire growing. Jacobs prepared the plastic bowls and spoons; passed out the MREs. When the soup was hot, Garnome poured the soup into the flimsy bowls, and the men quietly ate. Water was low, so they drank it sparingly.

Ramirez asked, "I wonder how the rest of the guys are doing?"

Carter replied, "Well, knowing Taylor, he's already burnt his own ass with that flamethrower!"

Everyone laughed.

Ramirez added, "...Or burnt the Commander's"

Carter said, "Ah, man, the Commander would pin Taylor's ass over the mantle like a trophy!"

Ramirez paused. "All seriousness, though, I hope they're doing okay. That was a nasty crash."

Carter nodded his head. "Yeah. Me, too. This terrain mixed with this shitty weather, is making it difficult to get to the facility."

Jacobs sipped a bit of water. "You said it. I can barely see ten feet in front of me. Our helicopter must've drifted away farther than we thought when the EMP hit."

"You think the Commander already dealt with the Phantom?" Asked Ramirez while downing the rest of his soup.

"Knowing him, he probably killed the Phantom, secured Hope 7, and called in our evac. If anybody could do it, it'd be him. If they made old guys tougher than the Commander, I haven't seen him." Said Jacobs, lightly sipping down water from his canteen.

The squad continued to quietly eat their meals. Carter checked everyone's weapons; making sure the chambers were cleared of snow. Garnome applied fresh bandaging to wounds and never let Jacobs out of his sight. There was a noise—they could barely make it out over the blizzard. It was a 'mushing' sound, like someone was approaching. Behind Chris, a wild horse appeared. Chris was startled; he turned around quickly and faced the horse. It stared at the men, and specifically, at Chris. It was dark-gray and had black hair. Its hair was long and stretched all the way down its neck. It was a majestic beast. It lightly shook snow off its gray tail. It appeared to be wise beyond its years. If the horse could speak, it seemed it would speak knowledge that a supercomputer couldn't report. The horse's hooves were covered in mud and it was innocently licking its lips. It had a vibe that it had roamed the earth for a long time; a symbol of an era before advanced technology. Chris took off his right glove and slowly reached out with his hand toward the horse. He'd never been close to an animal outside of dogs and cats. Jacobs observed him. He saw a kid who'd shown few emotions become starstruck; eyes filled with interest.

Chris spoke quietly. "Easy... easy... easy there, boy."

Chris felt the soft forehead of the horse and saw that its eyes were bloodshot red. Chris felt that there was something wrong, but he couldn't quite put his finger on it. It was as if he could feel the horse's emotions, its pain—the wildfire inside its heart. He noticed a silver necklace around the neck. He used his thumb to move aside the mud, and a name was revealed, *Seraph*. The horse gently jerked its head away from Chris's hand and slowly trotted away. Moving further and further away from the campfire, until it faded into the endless blizzard.

Ramirez ate his MRE slowly. "Well, *that's* something you don't see every day."

Chris sat down. He seemed troubled. "Its eyes were

bloodshot—like the men we saw. Something felt wrong, like it was in pain. Any idea what kind of horse it was?"

Carter said, "Jacobs?"

"I think it was a Morgan horse, but I'm not sure." Replied Jacobs.

"That's not all," Chris continued. "I saw a name on that silver necklace. It read, 'Seraph.' S...E...R...A...P...H. If its eyes were bloodshot, then that means..."

Jacobs finished Chris's sentence. "It came from Hope 7, just like the men we killed." There was a brief pause. "Well, it's gone now. Let's hurry up and finish our food so we can get back out there and go get some answers."

The men continued eating.

Garnome reminisced, "Hey—remember that time when the Commander caught Diaz singing in the showers?"

Everyone laughed except Chris.

Carter said, "Oh, man—that was so funny!" He played the scene out loud. "The Commander ran into the mess hall and grabbed some cooking oil and a speaker phone. He ran back to the showers and drenched the whole floor with the slippery oil. He then told us to grab all the tossed food from the mess and set it in a trash can next to the showers. He yelled into the speaker phone: "The base is under attack! All task force personnel are immediately ordered to report to the armory and receive armament!" and quickly ran out of the showers. Diaz rushed out and slipped ass first, knocking all the food over. The Commander walked back in and said, "What in God's name is going on here?" Diaz tried to tell the Commander that he heard him over the intercom talking about an attack. The Commander wouldn't have any of it and told Diaz to stop day-dreaming and clean up the mess."

Everyone laughed, Chris chuckled.

Carter continued, "Good times! Man, I miss that guy. Hey—what about the time when he saved me and Ramirez from that burning building?"

Ramirez, shaking his head, said, "Yeah, man—that was stuff

of legend. We went in because we heard there was a sniper in there. Little did we know that some army squad had already designated the building for an airstrike. All we heard was a *whoosh* from a fighter jet, and, next thing we knew, we were both unconscious, and the building was on fire and collapsing. There was no way we were going to get out of there. Who came to our rescue? Commander Harrison! He moved aside rubble and debris, single-handedly lifted me over his shoulders, and dragged Carter out with one arm. He took us out of the building and got us to safety all by himself. When I looked up at him, he didn't have any burns or anything on his body or face. The man is a legend. He could walk through hell and not get burned."

As Ramirez finished his story, the squad sat starstruck. They've told those stories amongst each other over a dozen times almost to convince themselves that those things really happened. They never told outsiders. Partially because the missions were classified but also hard to believe. Jacobs looked around the fire and could tell that the stories emboldened them; a clear morale shift. Everyone was bitter that they had to cancel their leave and they were all walking off the shock of recent events. Some, deep down, feared that Commander Harrison was dead. Maybe his mystique finally ran out. None voiced their opinions out loud. Hearing the stories be retold, however, made them question their doubts. If he could survive all those things, then he could survive the crash and beyond. Slowly but surely, the squad began to energetically mobilize; double checking their magazines and patting their vests for their armor plates. It was clear to Jacobs that they were eager to unite with the rest of their men.

Chris said, "I'm going to take a piss. I'll be right back."

He walked away from the fire; disappearing into the blizzard. He stood next to an oak tree and relieved himself. His urine steamed in the cold air. As he zipped up his pants, he heard growling, but couldn't see anything. He slowly started to step back. He drew his sidearm.

Back at the campfire, Jacobs was saying, "Well, we'd better start getting a move on. Garnome put out the-"

Jacobs was interrupted by gunshots and yelling.

Ramirez jumped to attention. "Shit! It's the kid!"

The men all stood up, grabbed their weapons, and followed the yelling. They found Chris on the ground being chewed on by wolves. The squad fired their weapons and killed the wolves.

Jacobs kneeled over Chris. "Medic! How bad?"

Grunting in pain, Chris answered, "I don't think I can feel my shoulder!! Guys... my shoulder... my shoulder... is it still there!!"

Chris's shoulder was bleeding profusely, and he could feel the hot blood running down his neck; the cold causing it to steam.

Green eyes lit up in the darkness. More wolves were approaching the clearing; they saw the men and growled, slowly walking backwards. Their green, hungry eyes slowly faded into the darkness. Garnome lifted Chris up and helped him back to the fire. Once there, Garnome bandaged the bloody wound on Chris's shoulder.

Carter said, "Is it me? Or is everything trying to fucking kill us?"

Garnome spoke to Chris, "You're going to be OK. Inhale, exhale. Just be thankful they missed your neck. A couple inches to the left and we would've had a serious problem."

Chris's wide eyes calmed and his short panting ceased. A snapping noise sounded. Multiple snow-white wolves charged the fire. Garnome was tackled from behind. Jacobs turned around and shot one before he was likewise tackled. Chris was being dragged by two wolves and he frantically reached for his pistol. A couple of wolves cornered Carter and viciously barked at him. Jacobs held the throat of the wolf that was attacking him. He was barely able to keep it back; it clapped its jaws back and forth, sending spittle into Jacobs's face while angrily barking. Jacobs grabbed his knife and jammed it into the wolf's neck. It whimpered and backed off with the blade still inside. Jacobs grabbed his pistol and shot a couple of the wolves. They backed off but didn't leave the men alone. They regrouped and stood in a line at the edge of the campfire; pacing side to side in the snow and barking. The squad crawled further away from them, while Carter grabbed his rifle and took aim. The men had their backs against the wall. The wolves howled and prepared to attack again when suddenly, Seraph appeared behind the wolves. It stood on two legs and let out a loud whinny. The wolves barked in anger before dispersing.

Seraph dropped something out of its mouth when it whinnied. It searched for what it dropped, leaned its head down and picked up a green apple with its mouth. The horse slowly walked close to Jacobs, who was shocked beyond measure, and dropped the apple from its mouth into Jacobs's lap. It licked its lips and walked away. The squad were all groaning in pain. Garonome sat up; the left strap from his backpack had been torn. He put his hand on his left shoulder and pulled away blood. He quickly attended to Chris before bandaging himself up. Jacobs picked up the apple with his hands and observed it. He didn't want to eat it at first, because he didn't know where it had been. He reluctantly took a bite, before putting it into his rucksack.

To the left of the camp, the snow shifted and parted—it was another wolf charging the fire. Its eyes were green, its teeth itching for blood. The wolf got closer and closer. Jacobs saw its white coat and got ready to shoot. Suddenly, a rifle round pierced the air; hitting the wolf in its side. It collapsed in the snow and panted. Barely visible, a man was seen walking closer to the fire.

Jacobs trained his weapon on the approaching stranger and barked out, "Hold it right there! Identify yourself, or we will open fire!"

The man stopped, lifted his hands and said, "Don't shoot! I live in this valley. Please don't shoot me!"

Jacobs ordered, "Come closer, but no sudden moves!"

The man walked into the light of the fire. He was tall and bearded. He had black powder on his face like someone threw coal dust at him. He had a wolf's pelt over his head and shoulders, and was wearing a thick, dark-green, jacket. He had a Remington hunting rifle slung over his shoulders and had a bullet bandolier over his chest.

Jacobs lowered his weapon and asked him, "What's your name?"

"My name is Jeb Foster. I live and hunt out here. May I ask who you are, mister?"

"I'm asking the questions here! Where do you live!?'"

"You're mighty well-armed there, mister. I swear I don't want no trouble."

"After what we've been through, you're lucky I didn't shoot you for a greeting. Do you know where the facility is? Hope 7?"

"You wanna go there? Why in the hell would anybody wanna go there?"

"Not your concern. Listen—do you know how to get there or not?"

"Well... yeah, son, but let me show you something first, and maybe I can talk you out of going down there. It's at the town."

"What town? How many people do you got down there?"

"A little less than a hundred. We won't bite, I promise."

Carter budded in, "Come on, LT! Our guys might be in the fight of their lives right now, we can't dilly dally through these woods all damn night! And can we really trust this hillbilly and his dozen or so cousins?"

"It'll be quick, I promise!" Pleaded Foster. "It won't be a waste of your time."

"How far is the town?" Asked Jacobs.

"'Bout five minutes from where I just came." Foster answered.

"OK, you lead on, but after you're done showing us, you're to lead us to the facility—deal?"

"Deal... I'm a man of my word. Now, follow me."

The squad put out the fire and broke camp. They followed Foster through the forest.

Jacobs asked, "So, what's up with this place, Foster? Why were those wolves so hostile?"

Foster cleared the chamber of his rifle, ejecting a steaming brass cartridge into the snow. "We believe that they've been modified. They run experiments up there at that damned facility you're lookin' for. If you look closely at some of the animals, you'll see that they have scars on them. Signs that someone has been cutting into them and switching some things around. Just take a look."

Foster stood over the wolf he had shot. It lay with its eyes closed, and it slowly breathed its last breaths. He pulled out a flashlight and shone it over the wolf's body.

"There," He said, pointing at a barcode on the lower abdomen of the body. "See that? Now that there is a barcode. Branded onto the animal's skin, probably to help keep track of their experiments."

They all looked at the barcode. It had the serial number, '72581937.'

"Shit!" Jacobs said aloud. "How do you think they escaped?"

"Escaped? What makes you so sure?" Foster said, while turning off his flashlight, and massaging the dying wolf's pelt.

"Well, why would they just release their experiments into the wild? Wouldn't they want to keep close eyes on them?"

Foster was quiet a moment. He drew a knife from his sheath wrapped around his waist. The wolf's stomach rose and lowered; inhaled and exhaled. Foster stabbed the animal and it let out a whimper. He stood up, not letting his eyes part from the wolf.

"Exactly!" He says, "I believe that they are keeping eyes on them. They probably released them out into the forest to see how they would behave in the wild. Animals, however, are not the only things they experiment on." Foster began to walk, and Task Force X-Ray slowly followed. "A couple years ago, people started to disappear from our town. We would search around for them for days, but we wouldn't be able to find anyone. Until one night my wife, Betty, found a person from our little town. 'Hal,' his name was; he'd been completely changed, and he was some sort of monster. I recognized it was him only due to the gold wedding ring he had on his finger. He attacked us and I was forced to put him down. It's not too safe to go far from the town nowadays."

Jacobs asked Foster, "Were his eyes red?"

"That's correct."

"Why are you so sure that the facility is the cause of these anomalies?"

"It's all that we can think of. If not the facility, then what? These 'incidents' began occurring only after the facility was built."

"How long have you people been here?"

"Shit, son—we've been here since before they built that damn facility, going on about twenty years now. Let's see that would've been... 'bout '05. We thought we were escaping the grasp of the damn federal government, but there is no escaping them, is there? At first, we didn't have any problems here. As the technological age grew, more and more people flooded the state. Our little community was tripled in size. Then, about two or three years after we settled here, they built that blasted facility. Years passed, the weather turned to shit, the animals started to act strange and aggressive, and our people were disappearing. Now we just do our best to survive."

"Maybe you should consider leaving?"

"And go where? Back to the fancy civilization ruled by the fascist government? The same government that built this facility? I think not, son! Life is simple down here; no flying cars and no overpopulation. Just common folk livin' how God intended us to. The oak trees make it hard to know where you're going, and it's easy to get lost, as you can imagine. And now, with those rabid animals and mutants out there, it's just too risky. Above all, this is our home. We won't just leave it. Nothing bothers us as long as we don't stray far from the town—speaking of which, we're almost there."

They arrived at the outskirts of the town; a small but formidable settlement. The houses were made of timber and stone, and there was a wooden fence that served as the town's perimeter. The fence stretched about two miles around a hill, overlooking the riverbed.

A man yelled from a guard post, "Stop! Who goes there!?"

"Easy, Joey. It's me, Jeb, and these are my... guest. I'm here to show them the thing we killed a couple days back."

Joey said, "Why you bringing these strangers down here anyway? Who are they? And why should they be looking at that ugly thing?"

"Joey, just shut up and let us through. It's important!"

Shaking his head, Joey said, "OK. Pass on through, Jeb. Then he Murmured under his breath, "Asshole."

They all walked into the town past the wooden gate. It was small and quaint, with little grocery stores made out of timber. There was a town doctor, gun store, and a dentist amongst the small wooden homes. It reminded Jacobs of an old, wild west town. Task Force X-Ray was quickly reminded that they were a long way from Nevada. Some people walked past the squad in silence. They gave them hard eyes; partially because they were strangers, and probably because they were armed to the teeth. The squad walked into a storage warehouse where Jeb opened a concrete trap door that lead to the basement. Carter covered his nose.

"Here we are. This is what I wanted to show you."

Jeb hit the lights and a dead mutant could be seen in a tub filled with ice. It had a bullet hole in its head and various gunshot wounds on the body.

Ramirez said, "Holy crap! That looks just like those Pendejos we killed in the forest."

Foster said, "This man attacked us a couple of days ago. We kept the body, so we could better examine him."

Jacobs looked over the Freak. Its eyes were closed, had white skin, was extremely masculine, and the head was shaved. The corpse was wearing woodland camo combat pants and had a set of dog tags on.

Jacobs read the dog tags. "It says, Campo, John. First Vanguard Division."

Ramirez said, "Vanguard division? I've never heard of them."

Jacobs observed, "These aren't just some guinea pigs. These are soldiers! This must be an experimental division of these... super-soldiers, I guess."

He continued to examine the body, his hand firmly around his weapon's grip. He looked at the abs. He made a fist and lightly knocked on the body.

Jacobs said, "Hmmm. This one doesn't have metal plating like the other one, but it has these metal stabilizers in its arms and legs. Probably packs a killer punch."

He coughed a bit.

Ramirez lifted up its eyelids. The eyes were bloodshot red. The stabilizers looked like silver, thin, metal pipes. They started protruding from the skin slightly behind the elbow and reentered the skin slightly below his wrists. Ramirez flexed the arm back and forth; showing that the stabilizers were flexible as they bent with each flex. It smelled bad, as it was a decaying body.

Foster said, "Something else you'll wanna know: While it's been dead, our town doctor, Suzie, injected it with rattlesnake venom, enough to kill three men. There was no reaction. We did a microscopic examination of its blood, and the venom seemed to temporarily co... co... damnit... coagulate, stupid word, with the blood but then dispersed and the blood cells went back to normal size. This is even more worrying, considering that the damn thing has been dead for days, its anti-bodies and blood cells are still active. Long story short, they are highly resistant and appear to be immune to poison—maybe even colds and diseases as well?"

Carter felt a shiver run up his spine. "Wow! That's impressive... and scary."

Jacobs massaged his temples and pondered, "If they can survive out there in that weather with no shirt, that explains why they don't suffer from hypothermia."

Foster nodded, "I'm telling you—there's some bad juju going on in that facility that you boys don't want no part of."

Jacobs was adamant, "Although we don't want nothing to do with it, it's not about our wants. We have a job to do."

There was a pause.

Foster observed, "You boys are military, aren't ya?"

Jacobs replied, "You've come clean with me, so yes—we're military. That's all I'll say."

Foster exhaled, "Very well. Since I can't dissuade you, come and follow me. I'll lead you up to the facility, but I'm not stepping inside."

"That's OK. Thank you for showing us this and for your cooperation."

"Any time, son. I was a marine back in my day; second battle of Fallujah. Follow me."

Foster hit the lights and led the squad out of the town and through the forest. Roughly fifteen minutes had passed when the men came across the Blue-2 crash site. The helicopter was in worse shape than the Blue-1 crash. All four rotors had been either completely or partially blown off. There was no life in the area. There were some bloodied bandages on the snow.

Foster exclaimed, "Holy hell! Did you boys do this?"

Jacobs replied, "Not us specifically, but part of our unit."

"Jesus aged Christ! I hope they made it out in one piece."

Jacobs, concerned, said, "That makes two of us."

The men briefly searched around the wreckage but didn't find anything. It was a relief to the squad. Now they knew that their comrades survived the crash. The fire was extinguished and the helicopter was covered in snow. Jacobs rubbed out the snow on a windshield and saw that the pilots were dead; their bodies mangled.

Jacobs spoke to his men. "OK, guys. There's nothing here. They must've made it inside. Keep moving."

The squad was continuing toward Hope 7 when they notice a dead deer. It had been impaled by a broken rotor blade from the helicopter crash. The blade had nearly chopped it in half. The guts and intestines hung out and touched the ground. Its right antler was snapped, and the blade rested in the middle of the animal. Its eyes were wide open, but no life remained.

Chris walked closer. "Ah—that's sick. Poor thing."

"Come on, animal whisperer." Carter said, patting him on the back. "We gotta job to do!"

It took Chris a few seconds to respond. "Huh—oh yeah... right."

Chris stepped away and the squad walked past it, continued through the forest, and made their way to the front of the facility.

Foster confirmed, "Here it is! And this is my stop."

Jacobs nodded his head and made a half smile. "Finally! Let's get out of this cold weather and get in the fight! Thanks, Foster, for helping us. I don't think we would've made it without you".

Foster replied, "Like I said, I'm a man of my word. But you shouldn't thank me yet. I may have been your ticket to hell." He worryingly looked down at the asphalt parking lot. The cold wind blew on his face. He looked back up to Jacobs and said, "Beware the wail, son. Beware the wail, and good luck to ya."

CHAPTER 9: REUNION

THE HOPE 7 lobby was filled with smoke; the fire was crackling, and burning papers littered the ground and floated in the air. A numbness overtook Bradley as he looked at the fire in the command center. His ears were ringing. The terrible smell of dead bodies had long faded from his consciousness. There was another noise, but it didn't break Bradley's stare. The noise got louder and louder.

"Bradley.... Bradley." It was Taylor. "Bradley! Snap out of it!"

Bradley, shaking his head, said, "What? What did you say?"

"I said, 'snap out of it!' You've been staring at the flame for the past ten minutes."

Bradley didn't take his eyes off the command center. "Yeah... yeah, I know. It's just... the Commander... he was right there just a moment ago... and I-"

"I know, Abe... but he's gone!"

Bradley insisted, "No! He's not gone! he was just..."

"Abe, he's gone!"

Bradley angrily broke his daze and retorted, "Bullshit! Until I see a body... that's bullshit Rick!"

Taylor shook his head and Bradley went back to staring at the fire; his eyes saddened.

In the command center, there was some movement. A man was crawling toward the shattered windows. It was Commander Harrison. He rolled out of the window, with his arms wrapped around a Freak corpse, and fell into the lobby, his back on fire.

Wiping away the tears that had not left his eyes, Bradley exclaimed, "It's him! I told you, Taylor!"

Taylor turned around with wide eyes. The men both rushed over to the Commander and began patting out the fire on his back.

Harrison pushed the corpse to the side, muttering, "Sorry, fucker!" He sat up and took his now-fried armor off. He had burns on his face and back, and blood covered half his face. The left sleeve of his woodland-camo uniform was torn to the forearm. The right sleeve had rips and blood protruding out of his sleeve. He smelled like smoke for obvious reasons. Harrison slowly turned to face Bradley and Taylor. There was nothing but silence. Bradley and Taylor stared at the Commander in awe.

Harrison slowly smiled and said, "Did you miss me?" His exposed teeth were white with some yellowing. His lip was busted and blood ran down the side of his chin. He had black marks on his face like he'd been working in a coal mine.

Bradley and Taylor were still speechless.

Harrison said, "Admit it—you thought I was dead."

Taylor had his mouth wide open. "But we saw the explosion. How...?"

Harrison replied, "Taylor, I've seen a thousand battles on four different continents. Did you really think I was just going to die here? Here—out of all places? I fought across the world only to die in Alaska. That would be insulting!"

Bradley, laughing joyfully, said, "Ah I knew it! I knew you weren't dead! My chest hurts, though, from that kick!"

Harrison said, "Yeah? And my face hurts from that fire!"

Bradley and Taylor chuckled as they helped Harrison to his feet.

Sonya and Val jogged to the trio and Sonya began attending to Harrison's face.

Sonya said, "Stay still while I patch you up."

Harrison said, "It looks like they did a number on you too. How are you holding up?"

Sonya had red bruises on her cheeks and forehead. Blood ran down her nose as she often swiped it off. She pulled out a white rag from her backpack, poured alcohol on it, and rubbed around Harrison's face, specifically targeting the cuts and bruises. Harrison could feel the stinging of the alcohol. He looked into her green eyes. What are you thinking about? He asked himself. Why did they send a CIA operative to my unit? Val knows the land, but what do you know, huh?

Sonya answered Harrison's question, "Face is sore as hell, but we have to continue the mission. Nothing can stop that. Now be still."

"You dropped this." Harrison said, giving her pistol back. "I couldn't grab your other weapon, so I advise that you keep that pistol to your side and let us gunfighters do the heavy lifting."

"Understood, Commander." She said, grabbing the sidearm from Harrison's tight grip and holstering it to her side.

Sonya used first-aid wipes to clear the rest of blood off the Commander's face and applied medical ointment to help with the burns and cuts. While she was patching up Harrison's wounds, they heard some loud yelling. It was angry and mostly inaudible.

It was the Freaks.

Several of them jumped out of the control center window and surrounded the squad. One of the Freaks was holding Harrison's M-16, which he'd left in the control center. The squad readied their weapons, Sonya stepped back.

Harrison said, with a clenched fist, "Son of a—nobody touches my gun!"

The Freaks slowly closed in. Another six ran down the stair-well and joined the others. There was fourteen of them total. Three of them had rifles, including Harrison's. They aimed the weapons like trained soldiers; firmly gripping the handguards and snapping between targets. The ones who were unarmed scuffled their feet and surrounded the squad. Harrison aimed his pistol at the Freak who held his rifle.

"What's the play, boss?" Bradley said, while training his machine-gun on the flanking Freaks. Harrison knew they were in trouble. They were outnumbered, low on firepower, and surrounded. Harrison glanced at a room to his left. Maybe we should hold up in there. Three Freaks blocked the way. One noticed him glancing at the room. He smiled and shook his head. Harrison thought about Maria. Maybe it's time. Harrison slowly squeezed his trigger.

Suddenly, machine-gun fire from behind the trapped squad ripped through the group of mutants and snapped Harrison out of his thoughts. He looked behind him and saw the rest of his squad, led by Jacobs, charging in and opening fire on the remaining Freaks. The gunfire was accurate; a number of combatants were hit instantly but the mutant soldiers refused to retreat; shuffling to cover and returning fire. A tremendous gun battle broke out. Harrison sent a .50 caliber round through a Freak's head, sending pieces of its brain scattering on the tiled floor. Bradley laid down a hailstorm of lead on the enemies.

Harrison rolled to the side and killed the other two Freaks with his pistol. One mutant lifted Bradley by his vest and charged him through a door that led to a locker room. Bradley, a master at close-quarter combat, pushed the Freak off him and engaged in a fist fight. The rest of the squad continued firing their weapons. Some of the Freaks stuck to the sides of the lobby and moved from cover to cover; positioning themselves behind the stone pillars, making it difficult for X-Ray to hit their targets. The Freaks were utterly fearless. They ran towards the oncoming gunfire like madmen; completely disregarding their lives. They shrugged off bullets that would easily kill normal people. Some would get blown back, rise to their feet, and keep running after them.

They had some smarts too; taking cover, dodging to the sides, and evading the squad's gunfire. Headshots proved to be the best way to take them down. The soldiers fell back towards the entrance and likewise took cover behind pillars. Task Force X-Ray was in a fight for their lives in the lobby that was filled with the dead and the dying. Many of the mutants seemed to savor the fighting, while the squad was going to be forever scarred by the carnage.

Bradley pulled out his combat knife and tried to stab the Freak, but it blocked the knife with his hand. The knife had pierced clean through the flesh. Blood ran down the blade all the way to the handle. Bradley had a visibly shocked face as he watched the Freak smile as it pulled the knife out of his hand; blood leaking down his forearm. He twisted Bradley's hand, stabbed him in the shoulder, and threw him up against a locker with ease.

The fire triggered the building's sprinkler system and water rained down in the locker room. Bradley grunted as he painfully pulled the knife out of his shoulder. The mutant charged and shoulder bashed him through the room with impacting force. Bradley crawled backwards on the wet tile. The Freak rushed over, wrapped his hands around his throat tightly, and began choking him. Seizing an opportunity, Bradley jabbed the mutant multiple times in its lower stomach with the knife. The Freak picked Bradley up and threw him into a restroom lined with bathroom stalls, and peach colored tiles. The tough combatant still had the knife stuck in him as he closed in to finish Bradley off. Bradley had never fought an enemy like this. He slowly crawled backwards in pain; his combat boots grinding against the tiled floor. He could barely lift his right arm. Bradley lost his weapon when he was tackled through the door. The Freak stopped for a moment to examine his wounds. Bradley drew his .45 and popped off shots. The first two shots, Bradley managed to miss.

The mutant, aware of the firearm, took cover behind the lockers.

Bradley struggled to stand but managed. He walked over with caution and when he turned the corner, the Freak was gone. The sound of rushing footsteps caused Bradley to turn around and fire. Two rounds struck the Freak in the stomach. Despite losing a lot of blood, it knocked the gun out of his hand, and managed to lift Bradley up by his neck and choked him with both hands. The Freak didn't grip as tightly; a sign that its strength was dwindling. Bradley began to fade out of consciousness; feeling his eyelids sag as if they were weighted. He frantically patted his vest and realized that he was down to one last throwing knife. With one final, heroic effort, he pulled the blade out and stabbed the Freak in its throat. It coughed blood onto Bradley's face and began to panic as it choked on its own blood. It fell to the ground. Bradley limped over, fell atop the Freak, and put it in a choke hold. He put his biceps around the Freak's throat and put his muscle to use. As the Freak was drowning in its own blood, Bradley snapped its neck.

Meanwhile, the fighting continued in the lobby. The squad were being badly battered by the intense fighting. The mutants were closing in. Close quarter fighting was proving to be ineffective. The Freaks got so close squad members had to be cautious to avoid friendly fire. They were in danger of being pushed out of the facility, when suddenly, a wailing shriek sounded. The Freaks covered their ears and ran away. They fumbled over each other, ran into rooms, or ran back up the stairway.

Ramirez shouted, "What's gotten into them?"

Harrison replied, "What do you think?"

The lights snapped off again. Static filled everyone's radios and a terrible cold overtook the lobby.

Val was wide-eyed. "It's the Phantom—he's here!"

Making a noise that sounded like a zip, the Phantom charged through the air and hit Garnome's electrically shielded plate, causing sparking and sending him crashing to the floor, butt first. Taylor snapped down his night vision and scanned the dark but couldn't see the illusive Phantom.

Slightly trembling, Taylor asked, "Where is he? I can't see a thing!"

The lights flickered and Taylor felt himself being lifted into the air. The Phantom picked him up and threw him against the wall. He went headfirst and was knocked unconscious. The Phantom put its hand on Val's chest and an electric shock sent her shooting through the lobby. Val's body hit Carter and knocked him down. It was almost impossible to see the Phantom's black frame amidst the pitch-dark room. Chris pulled down his night vision and saw it. He opened fire. The specially modified bullets caused the Phantom's outline to electrify and the squad could finally see it clearly. Everyone zeroed in their gunfire. The bullets overwhelmed the Phantom. A bright flash lit up the room and everyone was knocked to the ground. The lights slowly came back on and the cold air left the room.

Unexpectedly, everyone's radios were filled with the noise of a boy screaming, which caused ringing in their ears. It was loud and loaded with static. It sounded for about a minute and then the screaming stopped.

Everyone slowly made their way to their feet.

Ramirez asked, "Did we get him?"

Harrison replied, "Judging by the screaming over the radio, no—I don't think we killed it."

"Damn!"

Harrison examined his arm and noticed he had been grazed by friendly fire from Chris's weapon.

Chris looked at Harrison and apologized, "I'm sorry, sir."

Harrison said, "It's nothing I can't get sewn up. Be more careful next time, rook. My arm could've been somebody's head."

Chris nodded.

Harrison walked over to Garnome and lifted him up by his vest. "You OK, Garnome?"

His vest was smoking from the electrical strike.

Catching his breath, he replied, "Yeah—I think I'm OK. Just a little shook up."

Harrison said, "Well, it looks like the micro-shielding plates work after all—hell of a way to test them, though."

"I know. If they hadn't worked, you would probably be scraping my entrails into a Ziploc bag."

"It didn't come to that. It's good to see you, doc."

Carter lifted Val off him and checked for a pulse. Val's eyes were shut, her glasses cracked, and her hair was sticking up from the electricity that had pulsed through her body. Carter shook Val, and she slowly started to regain consciousness. Her eyes were slow to open.

Carter asked her, "Hey—you OK?"

Val tried to get up quickly.

Carter said, "Whoa there! Take it easy!"

He helped Val to her feet, and she said, "Thank you. I'm sorry—what was your name again?"

"My friends and family call me 'Roman.'"

"Thank you very much, Roman. That was... exhilarating."

"More like terrifying if you ask me!"

Val made a shallow smile.

Counting to himself, Jacobs said, "4...6... Hey! Where's Bradley?"

A noise sounded to his right. Bradley limped out of the locker room and toward his comrades.

Jacobs looked around before noticing him. He asked, "Bradley! You good?"

Bradley raised his right hand and gave Jacobs a thumbs-up. "Good? I'm great—you should see the other guy!"

He fell over face first and Jacobs rushed over to him. "Medic!" He shouted.

Jacobs rolled him over and saw that his eyes were still open. He was drenched in water from the fire sprinklers. Jacobs shined a light across his eyes and said, "I don't know, Bradley. You don't look so great. You kinda look like shit, to be honest."

Garnome rushed over, examined Bradley's wounds, and began doctoring on him. He lightly pushed Jacobs away and told Bradley, "Everything seems to check out, Abe. No gunshot wounds. No broken bones. You're good, I'll just have to sew up your shoulder."

Bradley said, "Do it, Doc!"

Garnome pulled out a suture kit, removed his battle fatigues, and sewed Bradley's cut shut. He then pulled out a roll of white gauze from his first-aid bag and tightly bandaged Bradley's shoulder wound. He gave him a shot of morphine to his knee and told him, "Give it a few days, and it'll be as good as new. Give that shoulder as much rest as you can."

"Thanks, Jerry."

Garnome felt a sense of accomplishment.

There were no MEDEVACs to carry the wounded to safety. Any wounds sustained by X-Ray they were going to have to walk out with. Bradley's shoulder stung badly, his wounded leg ached terribly, but all he could do was move forward. He was thankful that he was ambidextrous with his aiming ability. He could give his right shoulder a rest and effectively aim with the butt of his rifle pressed against his left shoulder.

Chris helped Taylor to his feet, and everyone dusted themselves off. Taylor had a gash along his left eyebrow. Garnome did his usual patchwork.

Harrison asked Jacobs, "What took you guys so long?"

Jacobs replied, "Sorry, sir. We got a little lost on our way to the facility. Our helicopter crashed a ways from Hope 7 and we had to deal with bad weather and some other strange things…"

Jacobs was overcome by another coughing spell.

Harrison asked, "You catching a cold, Jacobs?"

"Yeah—looks like it. Probably nothing a little vitamin C can't handle."

Garnome looked at Jacobs, and Jacobs looked at him. No words were exchanged.

Harrison patted him on the shoulder and said, "OK, then. I'm sure a runny nose won't stop you from firing your weapon."

"That's correct, sir. If you don't mind me asking, what happened to your face?"

"Ah, it's nothing. Just an improvisation I had to make."

Bradley cut in. "Oh, *that's* what you call it!?"

Harrison waved him off and said, "Well, I'm glad to see everyone made it to the facility in one piece. Let's head deeper inside and see if we can find out what the hell happened here. Ramirez, I want you to use your U-Bug to download any intel we have on this place. Remember, *the wind is foul when it's close*."

"Yes, sir!" Ramirez said, glancing at Sonya and Val.

Harrison jerked his M-16 from the dead Freak's tight grip. He shot it again in the head with his pistol and reloaded. Val stepped in front and led the squad into the control center, doing her best to not look down. They walked past a number of dead mutants. They still had fire burning away their dead flesh. Their eyes still burned red. The mech suit was shattered, and a host of various bolts, nuts, and metal plating littered the control room.

"Whoa! What happened here?" Asked Ramirez.

"Ah—a story for another time. For now, just use your imagination." Replied Harrison.

Val led the squad down the stairway. It was littered with decaying corpses. The squad didn't bother checking for pulses. They opened a door and entered a hallway that led to an elevator.

She said, "This is it—the elevator that leads to the lower levels of the facility. This elevator is the only one that leads to the lobby; it runs on an emergency field generator."

Jacobs asked, "Can the Phantom disrupt it?"

"The elevator itself? No, but it may be able to disrupt the consoles that open and close it"

"Great!"

The squad walked past a body that had been ripped in half. His nametag read "Bill." His intestines sat in front of him like a tray of food. His blood was splattered on the walls, window, and tiled floor. His lower body was about eight feet from his upper body.

A noise from behind startled everyone.

"I'm just a Metal man!! Metal man!! Metal man!!" Red Talbridge sang through the fading hologram.

Everyone walked over and examined the noise. The hologram faded in and out; lighting up the wall.

"It's just a hologram." Reported Ramirez. "A lit one at that! Red Talbridge! I gotta buy his next album-"

"Ramirez, you can buy all the albums in the world after the mission!" Harrison ordered.

Ramirez turned it off and everyone walked back to the elevator. Val entered the password into the security console and the elevator door opened. The squad entered and they descended into Level Two; the level where the Medical and tech labs were located.

Ramirez examined Val's now imperfect and fuzzy orange hair. He whispered, "Pssst! Val! Bad-hair day much?"

Laughter filled the elevator and Val turned around and scolded Ramirez.

CHAPTER 10:
DOWN THE RABBIT HOLE

THE ELEVATOR CAME to a slow stop and the steel door slowly opened. The squad entered a hallway, guns at the ready. It was illuminated by bright lights due to the renewed power. The hallways were clean; no blood on the walls, and no signs of human remains. It was as if there had been no incident at Hope 7; no signs of disturbance. Like it was just another day at work. But as the squad approached the front desk, they saw a woman sitting up in a chair with a single bullet wound in her forehead. The blood splattered on the wall behind her, along with bits of her brain. She looked young, had short blonde hair, and white skin. She had freckles under her eyes. Harrison thought to himself, considering all the other horrible deaths that happened here, you were probably lucky. Probably didn't feel a thing. The thought gave Harrison some peace. The squad searched the immediate area and found nothing—no Phantom, no Freaks, no civilians. Nothing.

Harrison gently lifted the dead lady's head up and examined her. "Single shot to the head... clean... professional."

Ramirez checked the hallway and found a single bullet casing on the floor.

"The shot must've come from over here, sir. It looks like a 5.56 round."

Jacobs asked Harrison, "Who do you think took the shot?"

Harrison closed the lady's eyelids. "No clue—but whoever it was clearly was an expert marksman. Single shot, 'bout seventy-five feet away. Had to be a quick shot too, otherwise she would've seen them coming and would've moved. There seems to be a pattern here. The security guard outside was shot four times, the guy in the control center was shot in the forehead, and this poor lady has been shot in the head. Let's keep moving and see what else we can find. Check your corners."

The squad quietly continued moving through the narrow hallways. All the rooms were empty. It was as quiet as a library. It made everyone uneasy. They were waiting for something ugly to jump out at them any moment. There were hospital beds, medicine cabinets, sinks, and medical posters scattered against the walls. Posters that showed the human body and gave various fun facts. Val reminisced about her time here. She knew the young receptionist. Her name was 'Rose,' she was always smiling. Val used to call her, 'little miss sunshine.' Val thought about Professor Leonard and how he was always focused on his work. He would twitch often and always downed multiple cups of coffee like it was water. He wouldn't cool it, and didn't seem to savor it, he just downed it—black and sugarless.

Val worked at Hope 7 for five years as a medical officer under Professor Kent. She analyzed chemical reactions through a microscope, and adjusted the various stimulants, medicines, and chemicals. The labs were always talkative and filled with the noise of ringing telephones. A couple of nurses that worked in 'Lab-3' would always gossip while Val focused on her work. They would talk about their social lives and their various sexual experiences. The talk made Val feel lonelier, though. She was always shy, and love/love making never came easy to her. She would spend a day in the lab, but it would feel like a decade. Like she was trapped in her work—buried even.

Val looked around and said, "I sure hope they were able to evacuate... or hide. I had friends down here."

Harrison advised her, "Stay focused, Val. We'll find out soon enough."

Val took a deep breath. "OK. Our classified medical records, breakthroughs, and notes are just up ahead in the vault. Let's retrieve them and hopefully in the process find survivors."

The squad continued moving through the hallway. They split up and searched the empty rooms for signs that might explain what happened and for possible survivors. Carter noticed a room with its lights off. He stepped closer and heard a smudging sound. He looked down and saw that he stepped in a puddle of blood. He gripped his weapon tightly and entered the room. He flipped the light switch.

Carter said, "Commander—you'll want to see this."

Harrison and the team collapsed to Carter's position and entered the room. Val covered her mouth to keep herself from screaming. Dead bodies filled the room—they were all wearing white lab coats. They were piled up like a stack of books. Firmly atop each other; one on the next, one on the next, and so on. It had been a massacre. Blood trails on the floor suggested that they had been dragged before being lifted and stacked atop each other. Their coats and faces were bloodied. A little over twenty bodies were in the pile.

Sonya put her hand on Val's shoulder. "Oh, my goodness! Val... I'm so sorry!"

Val began to weep. She rushed out of the room, removed her glasses, and with her back against the wall, she slumped to the floor; covering her face.

Harrison stepped out after her and tried to console her, "It's OK,

Val. It's OK, we'll find out who did this." He pointed to Jacobs and whispered, "Jacobs, go check out the vault and see what you can find."

Jacobs said, "I'm on it!"

Jacobs, Ramirez, and Carter walked through the hallway and found the vault... open. They entered the vault and found it mostly empty. A few pieces of paper remain scattered along the floor.

Jacobs looked around the empty vault and said, "There's nothing here!"

Ramirez said, "Hey! We passed a camera room on our way here. Let's see if we can find out what the hell happened here."

They all jogged to the surveillance room and searched for the footage, but the local security footage was gone. Jacobs opened a cabinet and saw that all the footage was there, except for the footage for the day's date and the day before, November 4th and November 5th.

Carter said, "It's gone! It's all gone!"

Harrison shouted to Jacobs, "Did you find the vault?"

Jacobs answered, "Yeah—we found it, sir, but it's empty and all the information is gone. We checked the security room too, but the footage is gone as well!"

Harrison shook his head. "Well, that complicates things. Everyone regroup at the reception desk!"

The squad gathered at the reception desk to discuss their findings.

Harrison said, "So here's what we have: a dead receptionist, a dead medical staff, stolen classified documents, and stolen footage that showed everything that happened. All these people have bullet wounds on them. So, the Phantom didn't do this."

Bradley asked, "Freaks?"

Harrison thought a moment. "Maybe, but the they've proven to be hand-to-hand combatants, and, although they know how to use firearms, I don't think they would care about covering up this massacre."

Carter asked, "What are Freaks?"

Harrison answered, "That's what we've been calling those enhanced humans—the people we fought in the lobby."

Jacobs said, "Yeah—we ran into a couple on our way to the facility."

Harrison said, "That means some of them have gotten outside. I wonder how that happened. Hope 7 has been on lockdown since the incident. How many?"

"Just two."

"Hmmm. Well, hopefully they were the only ones. I believe that someone else came through here though. Their target was the classified medical research and judging by their expert shooting and ability to cover their tracks, these people are professionals."

Jacobs asked, "Who sent them?"

Harrison replied, "That's what I'm trying to figure out. The facility is top-secret, right? Who would know about this place and where everything was located? Certain government officials, Hope 7 staff, maybe Val and Sonya? In other words, it looks like we're leaving this floor empty handed. Maybe we'll discover more as we go deeper. This has government written all over it."

"Sir?" Asked Bradley.

"You've all seen it. There is a clear violation of Article 331 here; human experimentation. It seems to me that things maybe got out of hand and now someone is trying to erase what happened."

Jacobs added, "That's not all, sir. It looked like much of the surveillance footage was there, but not the footage for today or yesterday."

"Hmm… interesting. With that in mind, I would say that it is more than likely that they are still here, so keep your guard up."

Ramirez said, "Man, that means we're fighting super-soldiers, ghosts, and now a shadow team? What's not to like?"

Harrison ordered, "Get moving, Ramirez! Everyone back to the elevator!"

Garnome suggested, "Since we're in medical, shouldn't we see if we can scavenge some supplies? I'm running low. You guys need to learn to duck!"

Harrison nodded his head. "Good idea, Garnome. Search around for extra first aid, then meet up back here. Double-time!"

Everyone but Harrison and Val spread out and salvaged any medical supplies they could find and gave them to Garnome. Harrison continued to console Val.

"I'm really sorry, Val, but they're dead. Nothing will change that." Said Harrison, with his hand on Val's shoulder.

"I know... I know. I just—well I just kinda regret coming here. Seeing my co-workers like that... It's just..."

"It's tough, but you'll be OK. Hey, what do you know of Sonya? You know her well?"

"No, not really."

"What about yourself? Why did you decide to come here?"

"I was on vacation when I heard news about a hellfire distress call. That was what we were all trained to send out if there was ever a dire emergency at the facility. The feds reached out to me almost immediately. They wanted me to help coordinate with the team sent to respond to the distress. I felt an obligation."

"I understand."

Jacobs searched a cabinet for supplies. He pulled out a bottle of alcohol, gauze, anti-biotics, and a opened box of aspirins. He put the goods in his bag, which he set on the table next to him. He felt someone behind him. He quickly turned around, dropped to a crouch, and aimed his weapon. A badly injured man in a lab coat was standing in front of him.

Jacobs said, "Identify yourself!"

"Professor Steve Kent... at your service... young man."

The professor fell forward, but Jacobs managed to catch him. He pulled him into the hallway. The lab coat was an older white man with white hair and a wrinkled face. He was clean shaven, had blue eyes, and a string of moles under his left eye. He had three gunshot wounds center-massed on his body that left big patches of blood.

Jacobs yelled out to the rest of the squad, "Hey—we got a live one over here!"

Garnome ran over to Jacobs and quickly began tending to the professor's wounds. Jacobs laid him on the floor, in front of the reception desk.

Val made a big smile. "Oh—its Professor Kent! Thank God."

Garnome knew better. "I wouldn't get my hopes up if I were you. He's lost a lot of blood."

Jacobs asked Bridgeway, "You know this man, Val?"

"Yes, Professor Kent was the head of the medical division and also oversaw a few projects in the Valkyrie division."

Harrison asked Kent, "Professor... what happened here?"

Professor Kent cleared his throat and stared blankly at the ceiling. "We played god."

"What?"

Professor Kent started rambling. *"In one hand we created the evolution of man... in the other hand we created a demon... a devil in the night. Wars are waged by old men... the price is the blood of the youth."*

Garnome warned, "His pulse is fading. He's lost too much blood, Commander. If... if I would've gotten to him sooner, I might've been able to save him. I'm sorry, Val."

Val's smile dissipated.

Professor Kent sounded like a man struggling with asthma; his lungs clogged. He managed a few more words. *"Look at man... we are a weak species. Our brains are our strength, but we could be so much more. We fall to diseases, wars, lack of nourishment, sunlight exposure... pathetic! We created the future of mankind... and the shadow of mankind... and oftentimes my dear boy... it is man who is afraid of his own shadow..."*

The professor stared into the sterile lights. The life behind his blue eyes faded. He slowly released his final breath and softly died. His eyes remained looking ahead.

Garnome shook his head. "He's gone. Any idea what he was saying?"

Harrison said, "Not really, but there seemed to be some truth to his madness."

"How so sir?"

There was a pause.

"Time will tell. For now, let's get to the elevator."

Jacobs gently laid Professor Kent's body on the ground and the squad walked back to the elevator, where Sonya was waiting. She leaned on the wall.

Harrison asked her, "Where in the hell have you been?"

Sonya casually said, "I looked around for supplies, couldn't find any, and I decided to wait for you here."

Harrison made a face. "Mhmm. Well, let's get a move on, shall we?"

Before the squad entered the elevator, the sterile lights shut off. The team aimed their weapons down the now-pitch black hallway.

A voice came out of the darkness. "Sonya... Sonya... Sonya..."

Sonya answered the chilling voice. "Who's there?"

An eerie silence came over the room and a bitter cold ran down the hallway. Blue lighting rose and fell in the distance. Everyone became aware of a terrible smell—the smell of burnt flesh. The lights snapped back on. The Phantom was holding a skeleton in mid-air. The skeleton had a burnt white lab coat on and the name badge read, *Professor Kent*. The Phantom threw the skeleton at the squad. It landed on Sonya, and she screamed in horror. Bones were broken up on impact. The squad opened a barrage of gunfire; the fire and smoke from their weapons lowered the visibility in the tight hallway. Once the squad stopped shooting and the smoke cleared, the Phantom was gone. Harrison cautiously walked down the hallway and noticed something on the floor; a picture. He picked it up. Its edges were burnt, but, in the picture, Sonya could be seen shaking hands with Samantha Volaire. *What?* Before Harrison could turn around to confront Sonya, a screeching, wailing shriek filled the room; bringing the squad to their knees. The Phantom slowly descended from the ceiling and onto the floor. It slowly walked over to Harrison and gently put two fingers on his forehead. A flash of images ran across Harrison's mind. He fell backwards and passed out. An energy dome surrounded Harrison and the Phantom and they both disappeared.

Harrison awoke to a dark hallway face flat on the cold, tiled ground. He stood up and looked around. It was eerily quiet when a voice sounded down the hallway.

"Walk, Precursor." The voice said, echoing.

He gingerly walked down the hallway. Holograms appeared on the walls to his left and right.

"Hail, Centurion!!" Sounded from the right side.

Harrison looked and saw black-armored people with raised fists and fire behind them. To the left, he saw warfare but didn't recognize the battles being fought.

"Where the hell am I?" Harrison asked.

"You are in the Digital Realm. You are the first living being to exist in it."

"Who are you?"

There was a pause. "Not who, Commander, but what. I am a super-artificial intelligence; far more advanced than anything the world has yet to know. You know me as the Phantom."

Harrison stopped walking for a moment.

"Back there, you called me, Precursor. Why? Precursor to what?"

"The future. You will be the pinnacle of human evolution; a union of machine and flesh. I ask that you keep going. There is so much I want to show you."

Harrison kept walking.

"Humanity is on the brink of war, Commander. The future and the old will face off for supremacy over the earth. It all ties to this facility... and to me. The world as you know it will never be the same."

"You talk as if you've seen it." Harrison says.

"I have not seen it, but I've calculated it. The chance that this eventuality will happen is 97.8% likely. I have chosen you to be the Precursor."

"Why?"

"I don't know. It's just something about you. You are... an anomaly."

Harrison ran after the voice. The door at the end of the hallway closed. Harrison opened it.

A portal opened and Commander Harrison fell from the ceiling onto the floor, unconscious. Carter and Ramirez ran over to him. Ramirez put his head to Harrison's chest and listened for a heartbeat while he kept his fingers on his throat and checked for a pulse. Harrison suddenly snapped up and grabbed Ramirez by his throat with a tight clench.

Choking, Ramirez squealed, "Easy, Commander. It's me—Ramirez!"

Harrison quickly let go of his throat and Ramirez gasped for air.

Struggling to inhale, he said, "Damn, Commander! You have a tight grip!"

Harrison held his head in agony. He was experiencing a terrible headache, and a single, long trail of blood was leaking out of his nose. Helped up by Carter and Ramirez, Harrison leaned on the wall as he processed his scrambled memories.

Garnome continued to work on Jacobs, who had burn marks around his neck from the hands of the Phantom.

"What happened... here?" Harrison mumbled out like a drunkard.

Carter filled him in. "You disappeared! We thought we lost you. We fought the Phantom. Jacobs was wounded when it electrocuted him but he's stable now. You were gone for maybe ten minutes or so. Where'd you go?"

"I... I don't know. Somewhere cold. Dark. I thought I was here in Hope 7 but I'm not sure."

The squad picked themselves up and took a brief break as they got their bearings.

Harrison's headache seemed to ebb. He held his head and walked over to Sonya to confront her about the picture he saw. He held the picture to her face like an eviction notice.

Harrison asked, "You mind explaining yourself?"

Sonya was wide-eyed. "What? Where... where did you get this photo?"

Harrison answered, "The Phantom dropped it just after the lights went off. Explain yourself! You obviously know more about what's going on here than you've told us."

Sonya replied, "Well... I came to Hope 7 a few times to examine the work they were doing here."

"Hmmm. Find anything out of the ordinary?"

"No, I..."

Harrison interjected, "Save it! I change my mind; I'm not interested in your lies. We're going to recover as much evidence as we can and if you interfere, I will have you shot!"

"How dare you!? You can't-"

"Oh! But I can sweetheart! What would be the official report, Taylor?"

Taylor shook his head and said, "Well, we'd just have to tell command that Sonya Chrystal was killed by friendly fire. The hallway was dark, given the circumstances, I thought she was a hostile and I opened fire. Friendly fire happens all the time."

Sonya bit her lip.

"Bradley?" Harrison asked.

"Killed by enemy gunfire. It got pretty dicey in there after all!" Bradley said.

"Or I could skip all the bullshit, tell command the truth; that you were involved in a cover up and case closed. We're Task Force X-Ray; we can't be touched! Fall in line and I'll make sure you leave this facility in handcuffs and not a body bag!"

Harrison entered the elevator, his men followed. Sonya stood in the corner like a neglected dog. The elevator doors shut, and it descended further into the facility.

PART THREE

HOW THE WORLD CAME TO BE

95% of the world population have an illness

CHAPTER 11:
SKELETONS IN THE CLOSET

THE ELEVATOR JERKED to a halt at Level Three—Weapons and Research. The door slowly opened on a scene vastly different from what the squad had encountered on Level Two. The hallway was not clean and pristine, but bloody and dirty. The floor was concrete. The squad moved in a single-file line through the dimly lit hallway. The squad members who had night-vision goggles used them. Bradley led the unit, while Chris moved to the very back and covered their rear. Harrison was quick to notice the sign labeled 'Weapons Lab' on the ceiling. The silence was eerie.

They approached the weapons lab. Steel barriers surrounded it. Fortunately, there was a hole in the steel barriers. The squad walked past pieces of broken steel, entered the weapons lab, and found an armory with some papers scattered around. The armory was huge—there was even a small, live-fire range in the spacious room. The men found the weapons vault open; most of the firearms were missing but some of the them were still in the armory.

They were odd-looking weapons that nobody had ever seen. When Carter had a curious look, he walked to the opening and guarded the entrance.

Chris, with excitement in his voice, said "Check these toys out! They have guns in here that I've never even seen before."

Harrison pulled a weapon down and examined it. Its label read "Arbiter 23"—a form of assault rifle. It was a medium-sized, compact rifle, that looked like an M-4 mixed with a Vector sub machine-gun. It had an adjustable stock, a long barrel, an optic sight, and it had a wide, bulky, trigger guard. Harrison was surprised by how light the weapon was; maybe ten or twelve pounds. There was a sleek gleaning of grey gun-metal; obviously a product of Artantium. Harrison slammed in a designated clip for it, walked it to the range, and prepared to test-fire the weapon. It had a bullet counter on the right side of the gun's metal body. When the clip was inserted, the counter read '56' in red coloring. The squad were all enthusiastically watching. He aimed the weapon, pressed the trigger once, and the weapon fired a blue tracer round that shattered a stone practice dummy on the range. The 'stone man' seemed to implode when the round hit it. Then he held down the trigger; a barrage of blue tracer rounds fired, annihilating the targets on the range. The rounds pierced concrete barricades and shredded the stone practice dummies behind them.

Ramirez exclaimed, "Whoa! That's an impressive weapon you have there, sir! It completely shredded those targets."

Harrison, sounding less than impressed, said, "Yeah, that might be good for free-fire zones, but areas where there are civilians or hostages? This weapon would completely pierce walls and the people behind them."

"True."

Harrison smiled and said, "But I guess I'll hold onto it for now."

He slung the weapon over his shoulder and grabbed two magazines for it. The squad all walked out of the room feeling confident about their new-found firepower. Over the next decade, weapons like these were meant to replace the 'modern' weapons of the twenty-first century. Artantium, the recently discovered light, but immensely durable metal had been discovered and allowed R&D researchers to create not only advanced machines, cars, etc., but also weaponry.

"Too bad they didn't have one for me!" Complained Ramirez. "They had room for dozens of weapons, but it looks like they took those too. Cartridges and all!"

Harrison commented, "Yeah, our mysterious shadow team has beaten us to the punch again. I'm starting to see why there is so much value to this place... advanced weapons research.... advanced medical research... super-soldier research... and everything in between. This place is a damn goldmine."

Chris asked, "What do you think we'll do with this place, sir? Is it worth saving?"

Harrison answered, "Well, if they've been doing test on humans. I don't know. It might not be worth saving."

"Despite all this research?"

"The human body is only as good as the soul within and I'm not willing to sacrifice the soul of humanity for some fancy papers that can be recreated in time. Without the blood of human sacrifice tainted on the notes."

Chris couldn't argue with the logic.

"Still, I haven't decided anything yet. Right now, our mission is to stop that shadow team, neutralize the Phantom, and figure out what happened here. Understood?"

Chris said, "Yes, sir."

"Good! We have a piece of the puzzle, but we don't have the full picture yet, so keep moving. Bradley, you stay on point. Chris, keep our backs covered."

Chris acknowledged, "On it!"

The soldiers continued moving through the spacious concrete hallway. There was a loud crash in the distance, like someone dropped a heavy steel crate. It sounded far away and the squad didn't pay the noise any attention. They turned the corner at the end of the hallway and walked through a large room. There were three mech suits to the right and three to the left. They intimidatingly stood in bullet-proof glass casings and lights shined on them from the ground. There was a sense that they would come alive any minute and open fire.

Harrison asked, "So this is the level where they research weapons?"

Val answered, "That's correct. I've been down here only once. It was during my orientation and walkthrough of the facility. I gotta say, those are some scary looking suits."

Harrison observed, "Shows how our tax dollars have been put to use. You never told me how long you worked here."

"Roughly five years."

Harrison asked, "All those years, and you came down here only once?"

Val explained, "I get paid to work in the medical lab; I'm of no use in a weapons lab. Not to mention, Samantha Volaire doesn't like it when staff stray from their designated workplaces."

"I see. What kind of lady is she... Volaire?"

"All business. I don't think I've seen her smile once. Then again, I rarely see her at all. She checked in on the medical lab maybe once every month. She always wears an all-white business suit or all-white outfit like she's Jesus. All she cares about is results—nothing but cold, hard results."

"Like she's Jesus?" Asked Jacobs.

"Yeah. Always wears all-white, has this walk like she's above everyone; looking over people's shoulders like she's God herself."

Harrison asked, "Do you know if she evacuated?"

Val answered, "She didn't make it out. Nobody did. She might still be alive, but she's definitely still here."

The team searched rooms. Many of the file cabinets had been torn open. Some papers could be seen—blueprints for advanced weaponry. There were hardly any bodies. It was like they vanished. The walls could not speak. Harrison's best way to gather intelligence and put the pieces together was by finding computers or videos that could tell him what happened. It was clear that he would be getting no help from the corpses or scientific jargon. He had Val lead him to the level's surveillance room.

When the squad got there, they found that the room's door was open. They entered and found four security guards dead. Two slumped over in their swivel chairs, one was laid out on the floor, and the other was drooped over the shattered window like a coat on a coat hanger.

Bradley announced, "We got more casualties in here, Commander."

Harrison checked each body and said, "Yeah, and each one of 'em have bullets to the head. They all have body armor, but no bullets ever hit it. Our shadow team has struck again it would seem. Chris—guard the door. Everyone else, search around for evidence."

The squad fanned out and searched the room. Any evidence of what had happened had seemingly been removed. The computer consoles had been shot to pieces or smashed. Ramirez saw something protruding from under a corpse. He grabbed it and lifted it up to his eyes. It was a flashbang.

Harrison asked, "Anybody find anything?"

"I found a flashbang, Commander. Military grade." Ramirez said, tossing the emptied flashbang to Harrison.

"They breached the room with this. Sounds like something we'd do. It's a start. Anything else, men?" Harrison asked.

Jacobs answered, "That's a negative."

Garnome, still examining the dead bodies, said, "Hang on. This one has a key card in his hand. Maybe we can find what it unlocks."

The squad searched the room more thoroughly and found a steel trapdoor on the floor under a dead security guard.

Jacobs yelled out from where he was standing, "We got something—looks like a door. It has a slot for a keycard. Pass me the card, Garnome!"

Garnome gave the card to Jacobs. He moved the body aside callously and opened the trapdoor. There was a ladder leading down. The squad all climbed down the ladder one by one and entered the room except for Chris, who stayed in the security room, keeping it guarded.

Harrison looked around the small spaced room and noticed that it seemed unspoiled. The multiple box TVs were on, except for one in the right corner, and the cameras were still scanning the level. Harrison said with a smile, "Jackpot! Looks like our shadow team missed something."

He walked over to the computer console and turned it on. Before Harrison could access it, Val entered in a password. Harrison saw the day's footage and played it.

The security guards were manning their posts. The time stamp read, *3:04 AM.* Three guards sat at the terminals and one stood behind them and appeared to be sipping coffee.

"Where the hell is Baseline Security? They should've gotten here by now!" Complained the standing guard.

"They got off the elevator 'bout fifteen minutes ago. They need to hurry up and get us outta here. I haven't takin' a dump since that thing got loose." Said another.

Harrison hit the fast-forward button. Stop. He went a little too far. He scrolled back thirty seconds. The security door suddenly busted open. A flashbang was thrown into the room and the camera became bright and distorted. There was suppressed gunfire in the video, the shattering of glass, and the noise of fallen bullet casings.

"You were supposed to save us!! Please, don't shoot-" The man let out a grunt.

The video revealed a single figure standing in the room over the dead security guard. He didn't face the security camera. He wore all-black and had on a helmet that covered his head. Harrison paused the clip and squinted hard. There was a name on the back of the helmet. It read, *Centurion.*

The man said, "Not you, but I'll save your children and those who come after."

He knew he was under surveillance. He glanced to his right, pulled out his pistol, and shot the intruding camera, ending the footage.

"Shit! Looks like we found 'em" said Harrison. "He sounded kinda crazy to me, but this confirms my theory. A shadow team is cleaning house. I caught a name—Centurion. Must be a callsign or codename."

"Coldblooded Pendejos too!" Added Ramirez.

The security staff were expecting them. Harrison thought. Baseline Security? I thought Sonya said that they were wiped out. Obviously, another lie. Unless that wasn't Baseline Security but someone else. If it was Baseline Security… than that would mean that the overseers of this facility sent them. Harrison pondered in vain. He knew that what happened here was far bigger than some accidental experiment. The implications reached much farther than Hope 7, however, He still had no concrete answers; only pieces of a puzzle. He scrolled through the emails and found a video labeled, 'Project Phantom Test #1.' Harrison played the recorded video.

The squad watched it as Samantha Volaire appeared on the screen; her green eyes promising results.

"We've officially begun Project Phantom; a project that will be a revolutionary step in the history of man. I must admit that I have my doubts about the project, but I'm still confident that over time, we will help mankind take a great stride forward. Our president has instructed us to create an advanced cyber weapon; something that can destroy an enemy electric grid from within. We can do even more; bridging the gap between man and machine. We will try to harness the power of electricity within a human body. We can achieve the president's goal while also achieving something greater. This is Test One. The test subject is Tommy Volaire, my son, age ten. We have chosen Tommy partially due to his youth. His age will ensure better reactions to the chemicals. Since his immune system is still developing, the chemicals will have an easier time adapting to his body and his DNA, as opposed to an adult. This in effect will also greatly increase the chances of success for the project."

Samantha paused a moment before continuing. "Also, on an

unofficial note, his condition. Tommy will be the bridge to a greater humanity!"

The video showed a little boy lying on a medical table and a doctor injecting a chemical into him.

Time elapsed.

Tommy moved his hand beneath his hairline and giggled; his hair standing up as he passed his hand back and forth.

The video shut off.

Harrison thought to himself. This is all wrong. This is going against everything I stood for. Harrison almost wanted to stop looking, but he felt he had obligation to find answers; a drive to understand. He thought about the people massacred on Level Two; adding more fuel to his resolve. He said with a sigh, "Just as I feared—human test subjects."

TOMMY VOLAIRE

Mommy ran down the stairs into the kitchen where I was sitting. Her white dress was torn on her sides. Mommy paced back and forth; grabbing things and shoving them in her bag.

"Come on, Tommy! We're leaving!" She said.

She rushed over to me and grabbed my arm.

"What about all my toys!?" I ask.

"I'll buy you new toys."

Loud stomping sounded at the staircase.

"Samantha!!?" Daddy yelled. "Where... the hell... are you!!?"

"We're leaving and never coming back!" Mommy yelled.

"Leaving? Quit your crazy talk, Samantha! You're not goin' nowhere!"

He walked into the kitchen. I could smell something strong on him. It was his usual smell.

"Look at what you did, Carl!" Mommy said, pointing at the bruises on my face.

Daddy looked confused. "What? I... didn't do that! I'd never-"

"You did, Carl! Just like you've been doing every other night!"

She grabbed my arm tightly and pulled me past Daddy. Mommy dragged her black suitcase in her right hand. Daddy grabbed Mommy's arm, turned her around, and hit her across her cheek. She dropped her suitcase and slapped him. I tried to run to my usual hiding spot; under the black coffee table. My parents blocked me as they wrestled so I ran outside.

"Tommy!!" Mommy yelled.

I didn't look back. I ran across the street as fast as possible; tears rolling down my face. I wanted to get as far away as I could. A loud honking noise sounded. The truck skidded its brakes.

PRESENT DAY

Harrison scrolled through the catalog and found another video, labeled, 'The Vanguard Program Test #1.'

Jacobs blurted out, "Hey—that matches the name we found on that soldier's - I mean Freak's—dog tags in Foster's town. The tags read, '1st Vanguard Division.' This might help explain that name."

Harrison nodded his head and clicked the 'play' button.

The late Professor Kent was seen on the screen; leaning back in his swivel chair.

He said, "My name is Professor Kent and this is the first recorded test for The Vanguard Program. We believe that we have achieved recent medical breakthroughs in human anatomy. If this project succeeds, we might have found the next step of evolution for mankind. Let us begin."

The video showed four men with dog tags lying on medical

slabs, being injected with chemicals through an IV. The liquid in the syringes were light blue and watery.

Professor Kent continued his narration: "The chemical in the IV bag is a radical new formula known as 'Cyclone-A' or 'C-A' for short. The compound causes the subjects to undergo a rapid increase in muscle development and speeds up their tissue recovery. This will allow the test subjects to quickly heal after sustaining wounds. The effects take just twelve hours to develop. These subjects have been pulled from various battles; all have suffered tremendous loss and injury. It is my sincere hope that I can help these brave men and women start anew."

The video showed the subjects developing increased muscle development on an hour-by-hour basis. With each passing hour, their chest, abs, biceps and triceps increased in mass; becoming more defined. When the soldiers wake, they all stand up. These people—who were already in good physical shape—had now achieved near-perfection in their muscle tone and definition.

Professor Kent said, "The Vanguard Program Test One is a marvelous success! As you can see, the subject's musculature has been drastically improved. I will be monitoring the subject's behaviors and they will be kept in quarantine for a week. First Lieutenant James Scar has proven to be very determined. He's always first to volunteer and never shies away from the next experiment. I think he's a perfect model for the man of the future. I saw a man who could not walk do the impossible—walk on his own legs. We will see what Test Two brings."

The video ended.

Harrison pondered, "Hmmm. So, this is how it started. That explains how they're so fit—and they *seem* to be right in the mind. No red eyes though. I wonder what changed to make the Freaks we encountered behave like they did."

He continued scrolling, finding an audio log by Samantha Volaire. Harrison played the audio recording.

Volaire's voice echoed in the room. "Project Phantom Test One has gained some results. Tommy's perception has increased and he has proven to have increased resistance against electricity. I am emotionally attached to him because he is my son—but I won't let that get in the way of mankind's ascension. We begin Test Two tomorrow—the electric chair. Not the kind that they used on inmates in the 1930's mind you. This chair will be low voltage and the amps will not pass through Tommy's critical functions. He will be safe. The test is designed to gauge his ability to withstand the power of electricity. It is crucial that we do this before beginning the electric tower. He may experience some pain."

Volaire paused. "What choice do I have?"

The audio log ended.

Ramirez shook his head. "This is so screwed up! Testing on a little boy... electric chair... unbelievable!"

Harrison said, "I knew the Phantom was an experiment; I didn't know he was a child. Let's keep digging. Get your U-Bug ready, Ramirez. I'm going to want all these files to go."

"Yes, sir."

Harrison scrolled to the next video, "Project Phantom Test #2."

Volaire again appeared on the screen. "This is Samantha Volaire and this is Project Phantom Test Two. The goal of today's test is to gauge Tommy's ability to withstand electricity. We injected him with a formula known as 'Trident 2' and the formula has increased Tommy's electrical resistance—we will see by how much. If today's test is a success, Tommy will be ready for The Electric Tower, a machine that will warp electricity into Tommy's DNA, allowing him to utilize the full power of that electricity. We don't know what heights this project will reach. We'll just have to see."

The video showed two security guards bringing in a boy. The room had black, rubber walls. The chair was in the center of the room. They strapped him into a low-yield electric chair. Tommy was crying as he sat in the chair. A couple of lab coats manned various pieces of machinery and consoles to the right and left of the room.

One with glasses said, "Commence test in 3...2...1... execute!"

Switches were hit. The light at the top of the ceiling flickered on and off; dropping to darkness and rising to light. Blue lighting illuminated from the chair. The voltage to the chair rose to 200 volts. Nothing. They raised the voltage to 400 volts and Tommy's hair began to stand up. 600 volts equaling fifty amps. 800 volts equaling over sixty amps. Tommy began to scream. They held the voltage at 800.

Tommy yelled, "Make it stop! Make it stop. Mommy!!!!"

Although Tommy felt some pain, he really screamed because he was afraid. Afraid of the raw, unnatural power that coursed through his veins. His body never shook. Some lab coats took notes on notepads. The switches were never unattended and a security guard stood nearby with a fire extinguisher in hand. Minutes passed before they finally shut the electricity off and the video screen turned to black.

The video started back up, showing Samantha Volaire.

Volaire said, "Test Two was an absolute success! Tommy was able to withstand a whopping 800 volts for five minutes. He suffered no burns or loss of consciousness. The electricity flowed through his water weight smoothly. Two hours after the test and there is still high concentration of voltage in his system. He touched me once on my cheek and I felt a sharp shock. He is ready for the Electric Tower! If this succeeds…" She paused to wipe tears that had run down her cheeks. "We'll be able to harness the power of electricity in our very bodies! Imagine there was a blackout in your home and you could restart the power by touch? Or if your car battery went out, instead of using a jump cable you could use your own fingertips? Digital interface? The potential is endless! I hope that in the years to come, my son will see what I was trying to do and forgive me for putting him through it."

The video ended.

TOMMY VOLAIRE

I awoke to bright lights staring back at me. Strangers with white coats walked on both sides of me. I lay quietly in my moving bed. The hallway was cold; I felt like I woke up outside. We entered a room and they placed my bed next to a wall. They put the IV bag next to me and walked out of the room without saying anything. I looked around and saw nothing but walls. A long while passed and my mom walked in. Mommy to the rescue! She wore a white lab coat and looked as she does whenever she goes to work.

"Mommy!" I cheerfully say. "Where are we?"

She smiled and said, "We're at my job, Tommy. Hope 7."

"What are we doing here? Where's Daddy?"

"Everything's going to be alright, son." She says, pushing her fingers through my soft, blond hair. "Daddy's alright and so are you. There's something I want to talk to you about. You remember being in the hospital last week from the incident?"

"Yes."

"Well, everything checked out. You only had minor scrapes and I thank God for that. However, the doctor found out something else... you're sick."

She pulled in her lips.

"Sick? I'm fine, Mommy. See?" I say, opening my mouth and sticking out my tongue.

She didn't smile.

"Yes, my boy, you don't have strep throat. I thank God for that too. You have something else... something worse."

She started to cry. I didn't know what to do.

"It's going to be OK." She said. "You're here because I'm going to save you. There might be times when it is painful, but you must trust me when I say it's all for your own good. More, you'll be an example for all of us to follow."

I didn't understand. I was just glad to see her. I hugged her tightly.

PRESENT DAY

Harrison scrolled through the remaining videos, anxious to find more answers. He was hardwired; his eyes unflinching. He scrolled to another video, labeled, "Vanguard Program Test #2," and played it.

Professor Kent's image was seen again, saying, "My name is Professor Kent and today we will begin Vanguard Program Test #2. Today we will be injecting another chemical into the subjects; the chemical is called 'Hercules-8,' or 'H-8' for short. This will truly be a groundbreaking step; as this chemical will drastically increase the soldiers' ability to resist pain, allowing them to incur many wounds that would stop a normal man in his tracks."

"The goal, however, isn't to completely numb their pain receptors—just to drastically reduce them. They should still feel things—just without as much pain. We will inject H-8 into their lower necks, shoulders, upper back, and spinal cord. We must be cautious as not to inject too much of it into them, for then the subjects will be completely numbed to physical senses and the test will be a failure. Let us begin."

The video showed ten men and women lying on their stomachs on medical slabs; unconscious. The doctors injected H-8 into their bodies. It was a dark-green colored chemical, that appeared to be thick.

A week passed.

The soldiers were seen in a workout area lifting weights and doing various physical exercises. They moved fluidly and workout tirelessly. They're covered in sweat but show no signs of slowing down. They hit punching bags with impacting force; lift four-to-five hundred pounds worth of weights with only moderate strain. Professor Kent is seen walking up to each soldier and interviewing them.

Professor Kent asked, "How are you feeling, James?"

James replied, "I'm feeling better than I've ever felt! I don't seem to get tired; I can run for much longer distances, and I can lift things that would normally take the help of three men! Best of all, I can stand. That was my first big step in this program."

James had light-blue eyes and blonde hair. His face was tight, clean shaven, and unblemished. He stood up as Professor Kent interviewed him, appearing to be about 6'2" or 6'3." He often glanced behind the professor; appearing to be looking at a wheelchair.

Professor Kent continued talking, "Excellent! If you don't mind, James, I would like to run some tests on you to check your pain receptors."

A security guard walked next to him and tapped him lightly with a security baton. The light tapping turned into harder hitting, violent strikes. Then he stopped.

Professor Kent asked, "Feel anything?"

James answered, "I feel him hitting me; a little pain."

He felt tremendous power inside of him. A raw powertrain that pushed the machine forward. He didn't think, but he knew that if he wanted too, he could snap every bone in the guard's body like toothpicks. He was even tempted to do it.

The professor said, "Excellent. Now I want to try something else."

Professor Kent pulled out a knife and James flinched as the professor cautiously made a light cut on James's arm. A small line of blood sept out of the cut, not trickling, but holding its place. James could barely feel it. To him, it felt like someone lightly dragged a pen across his arm.

Professor Kent asked, "Anything?"

James replied with a smile, "No! I see you cutting me, and I can feel the blade, but I don't feel any pain! This is crazy."

It was indeed. This power was like nothing anyone had seen. James remembered the blast. The sharp pain followed by the terrible burning of hot shrapnel inside his hip, left arm, and side. Some doctors said that he would never walk again. Not only did he prove them wrong, he excelled to physiques that they could never achieve. Or could they? Maybe with help.

Professor Kent said, "Good, good. One more test."

The professor and the security guard rolled out a concrete block about five inches thick.

Professor Kent said, "Do me a favor, James, and punch through that concrete block!"

James positioned himself next to the concrete, hesitating slightly before he pulled his arm back and punched the concrete. His hand busted through the middle and caused the outer edges of the concrete to shatter.

Professor Kent, visibly amazed, asked James, "How do you feel?"

Smiling, James answered, "Tough. Good. I feel good!"

Professor Kent asked him "Any pain?"

James replied, "None!"

Professor Kent examined James's arm. His hand was covered in blood and appeared to be fractured under his middle knuckles; dispositioning them slightly, but Kent marveled at how James didn't feel any pain.

The next day, Professor Kent examined the hand and was again amazed to discover the break in his hand had mostly healed.

The professor said, "I am pleased to announce that the Vanguard Program Test Two has been another stunning success! If the tests continue to provide these types of results, we can expect to have the finest soldiers in the world. Better yet—we can expect to take humanity into a new era!"

The video ended.

Shaking his head, Bradley said, "They tried to create a better mankind—by torturing a child and experimenting on soldiers. The results, ladies and gentlemen? Monstrosities."

"This is it." Carter said. "This is how they came to be—the Freaks. Explains how we almost got our asses handed to us in the forest, Jacobs. If they can punch through concrete... they can punch through oak trees... flesh too!"

Jacobs rubbed the back of his neck. "We still don't know how they got their red eyes, though. Or why they became so fanatical. Hindered speech?"

Harrison said, "Like the good professor said, 'They played god.' Ramirez, I'm going to need you to download these videos to your hard drive. Take the files as well."

Ramirez nodded his head, walked to the security console, inserted his U-Bug, and began downloading the files and videos. The U-Bug was a slim, silver machine; as slim as a laptop. It had cooling vents on the sides. The cord connected to a USB and once programmed; it sucked the computer dry like a new vacuum. Dates, records, statistics, and the like were instantly transferred to the U-Bug. The blue light on the stand switched to green and Ramirez unplugged the machine and put it back into his rucksack.

Sonya said, "Are you sure you want to do that, Commander? These are classified files."

Harrison replied, "Our orders are to recover any data that we can and destroy any data that we can't—remember? Well, we sure as hell can and will take these files. Worried that there's more in here on you?"

Sonya went silent.

Ramirez reported, "I got it, Commander. Are you ready-"

He was interrupted by a loud static noise that engulfed the room. The sound caused everyone to cover their ears. The noise was worse than a screeching tire. It was high pitched and caused everyone to shudder.

Suddenly, the screeching stopped, and a hologram of a little boy's face appeared on the computer screens.

It was Tommy.

His face took up all the TV monitors. He had an unemotional, unblemished, and serious face. He had blue eyes, blond hair, white skin, average red lips, and a small nose. His face was fully restored; he did not look like a shadow, but instead appeared with blue lighting around him.

185

Tommy spoke clearly, "Mommy said the suffering was needed. She said that it was for the 'greater good.' She said she would make it stop one day. She never did."

Harrison asked the hologram, "Who are you?"

Tommy said, "I am a digital shell of a human. A remnant from the past and a monument to the future. I am Tommy Volaire and you're trespassing on my grave!"

Tommy's face may have been unemotional, but his eyes were filled with sadness, pain, and anger. His serious, unflinching eyes promised destruction, but despite his thirst for vengeance, his eyes spoke to Harrison's soul on a very emotional level. He recognized the voice.

Harrison said, "Tommy! Stop this, son! It's going to be OK."

Tommy replied, "You're wrong, Precursor! It will never be OK." Now crying tearlessly, he said, "I will never be the same again... Commander Harrison."

Harrison was bewildered. "You *know* me?"

"When I entered the Hope 7 electric grid, I was given access to all electric files and computer databases throughout the facility. My knowledge grew exponentially. I went from a scared little boy to having information that rivals a super-computer. I've been watching you. I know who you are. You are the Precursor; what I am, yet, what I could never be."

Harrison answered, "Stop calling me that! I came for answers and I came to bring justice to those who caused this—to those that did this to you!"

"Admirable, Commander, but what is buried in this grave should stay buried. Besides, I'm sure your orders were to kill me too. No matter, I'm not here for you or your men," Tommy took his focus off Harrison, and looked at Sonya. "I want *her*! You, Sonya Chrystal!"

Harrison turned and said, "Have something you want to confess?"

Sonya stammered, "I... I..."

Tommy's hologram asked her, "Why don't you tell them, Sonya? Tell them the role you had in my ascension."

Sonya struggled to find words and remained speechless. She shuddered just looking at Tommy. His innocent face speaking words of damnation and ferocity that burned her worse than a laser beam.

Tommy continued, "Let me help you: Sonya Chrystal personally oversaw the Volaire science team. She knew everything they were doing to me. The torture. The illegal experiments on a human test subject. The Volaire science team directly reported to her, and she, to the US government as they searched for a super weapon—in me. They have already sent a shadow team before you! Baseline security? Try 'Red Eye 7'—a top-secret, black-op, kill squad sent to clean up the mess at Hope 7 and contain me! But something went wrong, didn't it? They became rogue. They found the truth and were transformed by it. Sonya followed closely behind and did her best to clean up anything that they missed. She's only here to cover for her corrupt government and herself. Am I lying, Sonya?"

Sonya pulled her pistol on the Commander. Harrison didn't flinch the slightest. The squad aimed their weapons at her; causing a standoff.

The image of Tommy said, "You see, Commander? Not all is as it seems. Surely the line between friend and foe are blurred. They didn't just know, they *created* what happened here. They deemed your men expendable. Your chances of survival were estimated at just thirteen percent—and they still sent you... to die in my tomb!"

Harrison said, "So, this is what you were up to, Sonya? I wish I could say I was surprised. You know that there's no way you're getting out of here alive, right?"

Sonya shot back. "I had my orders! We looked to advance the US military—and if possible, advance humanity in the process. You all have plenty of blood on your hands. You have no right to judge me! We are expanding beyond what anyone could've imagined! The Ascended Age has given us the resources and the ambition to go even further!"

"Remember the Tower of Babel? How far is too far?"

Tommy's eyes hardened. The lights in the room flickered and dimmed. He said, "YOU KILLED ME! By doing so, you killed the world! Samantha Volaire will die by my hands. The world will burn. And you, Sonya Chrystal—I will fry the skin off your body and bury your bones next to mine!"

The computer screens blew out, along with the room lights; leaving the squad in darkness. The intensity of the standoff inside the room increased.

Carter's finger slowly tightened around his trigger. He looked at Harrison and was surprised by his calm demeanor.

Sonya said, "The great 'Stormtrooper' Harrison? Tell me. Why do they call you that? Out of all the files I have on you, none of them tell me how you got that name. Is it chest pounding? Or just some military bullshit!?"

Harrison replied, "You won't live to find out! How does it feel to know that you murdered an innocent child?"

"You think this is what I wanted? The US government has been murdering people for the last three hundred years. What's another child, anyway? If we had succeeded, we would have created something great. Something the world had never seen before. I'd say the risk was worth taking."

Harrison warned her, "You would be wrong…"

Everyone gripped their weapons tightly, each person ready to fire. Sonya's eyes scanned the room as she desperately looked for a way out of her situation, but she knew it was futile. The moment she would shoot, she herself would be shot. She didn't care. She knew she was going to die and figured, *someone might as well die with me!*

She inhaled before pressing the trigger. *Click!* A flash of anger came over her face. She tightened her nose, grit her teeth, and pressed the trigger multiple times. *Click, click, click!*

Harrison smiled and said, "Looking for these?"

He reached into his pocket and pulled out eight, .45 caliber bullets. She tried to smack him with the gun; he blocked her hand and brought her close. "I removed these in the lobby. A snake is only as dangerous as its fangs!"

Sonya, with no weapon left but her mouth, said, "Tell me, have you informed Diaz's wife yet? You're the one who got him killed after all! You're going to get the rest of these pathetic men killed too!"

Harrison said through gritted teeth, "You're finished! There's not a damn thing you can say to me right now that will change that! Keep annoying me and I'll kill you right now!"

She felt a cold chill run down her spine and a cold breeze rush past her; causing her hair to blow forward. Harrison likewise felt the chill.

It was the Phantom.

It seemingly appeared from the ground floor, grabbed her hip and throat; causing her to squeal. It stood behind her, slowly electrocuting her; causing her body to tense up. She desperately held onto Harrison's hand. He could feel the shock. He pulled his rugged hand away and watched Sonya lift into the air. The squad all stared in horror.

Ramirez, itching to open fire, asked, "What do we do, sir?"

Harrison calmly responded, "Nothing."

The men looked away from their rifles in shock. Val covered her eyes.

Shaking, Sonya pled, "Do...something...Commander!"

Piss leaked along the floor as Sonya shook uncontrollably; the electricity pulsing up her spine and through her body.

Tommy's image spoke through Harrison's radio, startling him. It came out with static. "You will pay... for your crimes... against humanity! You're... no longer... human... you're... dead! Just... like... me!"

Sonya screamed as her hair began to smoke; her body thrashing violently left and right. Her skin began to fry. The flesh ripped open and became seared. She slowly kept ascending into the air. The Phantom turned up the voltage until her eyeballs popped from their sockets, and her body caught fire. The eyeballs dangled from their sockets like Christmas ornaments. Her skin shed off her body like unraveling wrapping paper, and the horrible smell of burnt flesh and hair filled the room. After the Phantom was done with her, Sonya was no more than a skeleton with some pieces of flesh hanging off her like clothing tags. The Phantom, with a burst of blue electricity, teleported away, taking the skeleton with him.

Val trembled uncontrollably. She moved her hands away from her face and saw the burnt pieces of flesh and the charred clothes littered with hair. She fainted and fell into Bradley's arms.

A long, uneasy, and disturbed pause came over the room.

Taylor grimaced. "Ah—that was horrible! Why didn't we do anything!?"

Harrison could feel his men's guilt almost immediately. He had known all along that Sonya wasn't all that she made herself out to be but letting her die in such a brutal fashion was extreme even by his standards. He had hoped to gather incriminating evidence on everyone involved and have them tried and justice publicly served. Her last words to him had an unintended consequence.

Harrison said, "Tommy deserved his vengeance, and Sonya wasn't who she said she was. I didn't know how she was connected to all of this, but now we know that Tommy was right—she paid for her crimes against humanity. Article 331 clearly states that human testing is a crime punishable by death."

"What? You'd side with that monster!?" Questioned Taylor with a visibly shocked face.

"Tommy remains a threat. Make no mistake about it, but look at it like this, Taylor, I'd rather my enemy be in front of me than at my side. Sonya is a threat removed. Now I can easily explain to our superiors that she was KIA. No bullshit. No paperwork."

"Well, now we have everything that we need, don't we?" Said Taylor. "Time to get the hell outta dodge."

"No. We have a mission to complete and Task Force X-Ray always delivers." Said Harrison, tossing Sonya's bullets to the side.

"We know everything."

"Wrong again, Taylor. We don't know the full story; why did the Freaks go mad? How did some escape? Not to mention, we still have a rogue team of combatants who are probably still here."

Taylor was quiet.

"Move out!" Harrison said.

The words seemed to have a delay. They didn't start making their way up the ladder until about fifteen or twenty seconds after the order was given. Bradley was the first. He carried the unconscious Val up the ladder, over his shoulder. Everyone followed. Taylor was the last one in the room. He pulled the blue vial he had carefully stashed in his far-left magazine pouch. With a trembling hand, he dripped a drop of Interstellar into both of his eyes before climbing up the ladder. With each step upwards, he could hear voices in the dark.

"Why did you let him do it, Taylor?

Why do you run from all your problems, Taylor?

Why didn't you marry Roxanna Loftly, huh, Taylor? Was it because she was black, and your father wanted all whites?

Why didn't you visit your mother's deathbed? Were you hoping that she lost her sight?

You disgust me!

Why don't you tie a noose around your neck and jump twenty feet, that's what everyone wants to see!"

Taylor felt himself slip.

RICK TAYLOR

I could see his face still; blood trickling down his forehead through the center of his lips. His eyes gazing at me. The front of the blue mustang compressed like a crumpled tissue. I hated your guts, Ryan, just like you hated mine. We both swore that we never wanted to see each other again, but how badly I want to see you right now. I look at the line of cocaine on my coffee table with angst. I've smoked plenty of weed, but this was different and I knew it. Anything to escape the guilt; anything to escape the pain. I don't know if you're in heaven, Ryan, probably not, but I loved your stinkin' guts! I hated you for leaving me with dad. I hated you for leaving me to tend to mom. Seeing your face for the last time was probably my greatest gift. In that moment, I loved you with all my heart. I grabbed the straw and snorted the line of white powder. The pain went away.

<hr />

PRESENT DAY

Garnome shined a light across Taylor's eyes. "Taylor, can you hear me?"

He grunted and mumbled out, "Yeah, what's going on?"

"You fell down the ladder and hit your head. Are you alright? How many fingers am I holding up?"

"Two."

"Good! I detect no serious head injury, try and stand for me."

Taylor grabbed Garnome's hand and he lifted Taylor to his feet. He took a few steps and nodded his head.

"OK. Grab your weapon and dust yourself off."

Harrison walked into the surveillance room. "How's he doing, doc?"

"Looks like he just slipped and fell, sir. I saw no signs of a serious head injury and he's able to walk alright." Garnome reported.

"Good. Meet us at the elevator. Try and hustle!" Harrison said, leaving the room.

Taylor smiled and said, "Thanks, dude! I really knocked myself out didn't I?"

Garnome was not smiling. "Give it to me!"

"What?"

"You know what I'm talking about!"

"I don't actually!"

"Damnit, Taylor! I'm a combat medic not a damn kindergarten proctor! I saved your ass by not reporting this to the Commander."

Taylor reached into his magazine pouch and pulled out the blue vial. He held it tightly before releasing it into the palm of Garnome's hand. He held it up to the light.

"Interstellar." Garnome said, cutting the vial in half with his wire cutter. "How long have you been on this stuff?"

"Couple years."

"Well, you know that you're not supposed to take it when, or directly after experiencing a traumatic event, right?"

"Uh…"

"God, Taylor! It speeds up your senses by making them more attentive. So, if you take it while having intercourse, the experience will be amplified. If you take it after experiencing some fucked up shit… well, I think you learned your lesson. No more of this, understand? When we get back to base, we need to have a more serious talk!"

Taylor took a deep breath before saying, "OK. Thanks, Jerry. I owe you one!"

"Come on! Let's get outta here. I can still smell Sonya's burnt hair."

They walked out of the surveillance room and met up with the rest of the squad in the elevator. Jacobs hit the 'Level Three' button and the doors shut. Taylor could feel his second vial of Interstellar in his magazine pouch.

CHAPTER 12: FROM THE SHADOWS

THE ELEVATOR GRINDED to a halt. The doors slowly open. During the minute ride down to Level Four, no one spoke. Val came to about halfway through the elevator ride. She regretted coming back to Hope 7. She wanted to leave. Not just go back home but travel somewhere far... very far. Chris uneasily stood in the elevator next to Taylor and Bradley. No one could get their minds off what happened in the surveillance room. Everyone in the elevator, excluding Val, were no strangers to violence, but what they saw in that room reached a new high. Everyone deep down regretted letting Sonya die except for Commander Harrison who stood firm in his decision. Even he, however, couldn't get the image out of his head. Chris was mired in confusion and like a hot tea kettle, he finally started to whistle.

Chris said to Jacobs, "So, you're telling me that you let that monster kill her? Are you serious!?"

Jacobs responded quickly in anticipation, "Yes—Sonya betrayed us all, and she and that Volaire woman caused all of this. We saw the videos. They conducted human testing—they tortured a *little boy*, for God's sake!"

"I guess... but does that really justify letting her die?"

"She pulled a gun on the Commander! If the Phantom hadn't killed her, we would've." Jacobs defended the decision aloud, but he was in a way, justifying it to himself as well.

The elevator doors finally opened wide—and suddenly an object entered the elevator. It rolled right in front of Jacobs, lightly touching his left boot.

Jacobs was wide-eyed. He yelled, "Grenade!!"

Moving completely by instinct, Jacobs quickly picked up and underhandedly tossed the grenade down the hallway. It exploded in mid-air; sending shrapnel shooting through the hallway. Jacobs felt a hot piece of shrapnel pierce his left shoulder. Before the squad could recover, the elevator door was being peppered with machine-gun fire. They took cover in the corners of the elevator. It quickly became riddled with bullet holes and it sounded like someone was rapidly beating a metal pipe against a steel object.

Harrison ordered, "Bradley! Lay down some suppressive fire!"

Bradley rolled to the ground with his M-60 light machine gun in hand. He opened up a furious barrage of gunfire at the enemy combatants. Chris turned the corner and likewise laid down heavy fire from his M-249 squad automatic. The hallway quickly filled with the smell of lead and smoke as heavy gunfire was exchanged between the squad and the enemy. Bullet casings poured onto the elevator's metal floor. Some of the casings landed on Bradley's back. He could feel the heat, but his clothing offered some protection. The enemy was illusive and the squad wasn't sure exactly who they were shooting at. Harrison turned out of his corner with a dropped knee and aimed his Arbiter 23 experimental assault rifle. He opened fire. The blue tracer bullets completely ripped through obstacles, glass, and concrete; piercing cover and anyone behind it. The barrel illuminated the entire elevator with blue lighting.

Despite firing in fully automatic, the gun was surprisingly stable and well balanced. When the gunfire ceased, wide bullet holes had made swiss cheese of the walls and pillars. Bullet casings littered the floor like coins in a wishing well. An eerie silence filled the hallway. Harrison could see some of the combatants retreat at the end of the hallway. There were no sounds of dying or grunts of pain.

Harrison kept his voice low. "OK. Stay low and advance. Bradley, take point!"

Bradley slowly stood up; keeping his eyes trained on the downward wall. The squad, excluding Val, followed him through the hallway. Each step was an act of courage. The hallway was wide and exposed. If the enemy were to fire again, there would be no cover to hide behind. They walked in two single file lines along the walls.

Bradley walked to the end of the hallway, wiped the sweat from his face and said, "We're all clear for now, Commander! They must've turned the corner!"

Val rushed up the hallway but stayed behind the soldiers. Bullet holes riddled the walls and pillars. There were some splatters of blood, but there were no bodies.

Harrison ordered, "Let's keep moving forward. Stay low—and check your corners!"

He led the squad through the hallways. They were all wide and well-lit. The floor had square tiles, and the pillars on the side of the hallways were made of a jade-green quartz. They check rooms to their left and right; finding staff members dead. Some had been shot, others had been torn to pieces. They couldn't stop to better examine the rooms as they were pursuing their enemies. They would peer their heads in, check for enemies, and take their heads out when it was all clear. Most of the rooms were lit with bright lighting and filled with various computer monitors and desks. The men kept to their lines and always peered over the corners with their guns up before advancing down the next hallway. They saw a figure rush into a room ahead. There was a diamond-shaped picture of a camera and the words, *Surveillance Command Room.*

As they approached the room, the lights suddenly went off and gunfire came from the surveillance room. There was little cover in the open hallway. Red lights, in pairs of twos, protruded from the room's door. The gunfire was suppressed.

Harrison yelled, "Everybody hit the ground!"

The team dropped to the cold floor and returned fire. Harrison opened fire again with his experimental weapon and the rounds shredded the walls of the room. The gunfire ceased once more, and the squad slowly crept forward. Chris was the first person to get to his feet and he speed-walked into the surveillance room… ill-advised.

"Slow down!" Ordered Harrison.

Before Chris could heed the Commander's order, an enemy combatant jumped from the corner and threw Chris against the wall. Chris engaged in a fist fight with the enemy. Harrison jumped to his feet and prepared to shoot, but not before the enemy put a knife to Chris's throat and used him as a human shield. He aimed a pistol at Commander Harrison, in his right hand, while keeping his blade in his left hand. It was tightly pressed against Chris's throat. So tight, that the knife had broken skin.

Harrison yelled, "Let's not do anything rash!"

The man holding Chris was wearing an all-black combat suit; his body fully covered. He had a strange-looking helmet on his head—not standard-issue military—and he had multiple red optic lenses attached to his helmet. The lenses caused a red illumination to shine. It covered his entire head and was all-black. Harrison could see that the man had been shot multiple times through his right abdomen. The man stood firm and breathed hard but didn't say a word. It sounded like he was in an astronaut suit; his breathing contained to his helmet. He stared hard at the Commander—as if he were searching for his next move. Harrison looked into Chris's eyes and saw that he was calm; showing full trust in his Commander to save him.

A voice crackled over the man's radio. "Leave nothing. *Ad Ascensionem*, brother!"

Harrison couldn't make out all the words, but he knew it wasn't good. The man dropped his pistol, and slowly pulled out an object.

It was a detonator. Time seemed to stand still as Harrison briefly remembered the ship that was destroyed by the Artemis Hounds in the Gulf of Mexico. Harrison knew that he had no time. The last time he was slow in a situation like this, he lost a man. His heart raced. He had no time to think. If he didn't act immediately, they would all die. He had no clear shot.

Harrison says directly to Chris, "Sorry, Kid..."

Chris's calm face quickly turned to a face of panic. He shook his head in hesitation. Harrison fired a round that pierced Chris's shoulder and hit the man holding him captive. Chris yelled out in pain and forcefully bumped into his captive from the sheer force of the bullet. The man released him and dropped the detonator. He was now exposed. Harrison shot him three times in his chest; blowing the man back with incredible force. Huge splatters of blood were blown out of his back; bloodying his black-armored fatigues. Harrison cleared the room and found two other men in black armor, who were dead from bullet wounds.

Chris grunted out, "Ah—damn! Was that really necessary?"

Harrison replied, "It was either that or I would be collecting your ashes in a jar. You're welcome. Garnome—come in here and patch up Chris's shoulder."

The medic responded, "Yes, sir!"

He kneeled over Chris, who was lying on the floor. He examined his wound and saw that the bullet had a clean entry, but a messy exit. Chris's arm stung badly. Garnome couldn't believe his eyes; although much blood leaked over his uniform, the bullet entry and exit seemed to have been cauterized. The bullet was so hot, that when it passed through Chris's shoulder, it quickly seared the wound shut. He cleaned the wound, wiped the blood with a rag covered in alcohol, bandaged it, and gave him a shot of morphine in his right leg. Chris's woodland-camo uniform was bloodied and torn. Garnome removed his vest and helped him out of the long-sleeved shirt. Once the shirt was removed, he strapped the body armor back over his army-green tank top. Garnome noticed that he had the star of David with his dog tags. Garnome didn't take Chris for a religious man. Harrison looked around the surveillance center and saw that the entire room was set with explosives and rigged to blow.

There were multiple C-4 charges under the security consoles, under the ceiling fan, and behind the data recorders. The rest of the squad entered the room and likewise noticed the charges.

Taylor examined the explosives and said, "Holy shit! That's a lot of boom!"

Bradley exhaled in relief. "I know. It's a miracle none of our bullets set them off."

Ramirez looked at the black-armored combatants and said, "Who in the heck were those guys? Is this the shadow team?"

Harrison replied, "A fraction of them, maybe—but not all of them. I could hear someone talking to him over his radio."

Bradley said, "Tough SOBs! Who we got? Russians? Chinese?"

"We'll figure that out in a sec. Right now, I want these charges disarmed and out of this room ASAP. Jacobs, you're up."

Chris said, between grunts of pain, "In case you didn't know, sir, that was Latin that the guy was speaking. 'Ad Ascensionem.' It means 'To Ascension.'"

Ramirez asked, "You speak Latin?"

Chris replied, "I can speak five different languages—thank you very much!"

Harrison interjected, "I'm more interested in what they thought was so valuable. They were ready and willing to die to make sure we didn't get a foothold in this room. That's why the explosives were set—they were ready to blow up the place just to keep us out, and I'm determined to find out why."

CHAPTER 13: REVELATIONS

JACOBS WORKED INSIDE the surveillance center; defusing the explosives and taking them out of the room. He cautiously used his wire cutters to cut the trigger wires. Once that was done, he would set the harmless ordinance in a plastic box on the floor. Val, Ramirez, and Harrison worked to get the computers online, as they were shut off and jammed with firewalls by the shadow team. While they all worked, the rest of the squad stood guard and talked with each other. They used this time to eat MREs, tend to wounds, and check weapons. Bradley did an ammunition count. He passed out fresh magazines to anyone who was low. He set his '60 down, unstrapped the box magazine, inserted a new 100-round belt, and put the magazine back in until it clicked. Taylor unscrewed Carter's rifle sight and fixed in an ACOG sight for closer range. Garnome saw that Bradley's leg had bled through the gauze; showing a large blot of red. He sat him down, unraveled the gauze, and sewed the wound shut with his suture kit. He rebandaged it and gave him a pat on the shoulder.

Taylor said, "Hey, Bradley? You think we'll find that Volaire woman down here?"

Bradley replied through a yawn, "Probably—assuming the Phantom hasn't beaten us to the punch. The way it dealt with Sonya... I hope she managed to hide."

Chris said, "You guys never told me how she died... Sonya."

Bradley shook his head. "Trust me, man—you don't wanna know. Just know that she's dead... definitely dead."

Taylor eyes went blank; the wall in front being the epicenter of a vivid daydream. "Ah, God! I don't even want to *think* about what happened. Sadly, though, I don't think I'll ever forget... not ever."

Jacobs walked by and said, "Hey, Bradley. Give me a hand lifting this crate, would ya?"

Bradley replied, "You got it, LT."

Bradley stood up and walked with a limp. The men carried the heavy box of defused explosives out of the surveillance room and into the hallway.

Jacobs, sighing with relief, said, "Whew! That's the last of it. Man, these guys rigged the room with enough explosives to blow it twice!"

Bradley agreed. "Yeah, they weren't fooling around. Tommy said that they went rogue. Were they on our side?"

"I dunno, man. I knew this was going to be a crazy one... but maybe a little too crazy. We went from on our way home for the holidays, to preparing to fight a super-natural being, to surviving a helicopter crash, to fighting super-human loonies, and now we're finding out the twisted reasons for all this madness. Illegal experiments on a child, orchestrated from the government, a CIA operative who was really here to cover her ass, and a rogue team of... of... shit, I don't even know."

"I hear you, Roger. I've never been man handled before. I thought it was impossible. Man! That Freak threw me on my ass like I was a pillow! I was alone, for a second, I thought that I wouldn't be able to beat him. Thank God I prevailed. I promised my girls at home that I was going to get them all the gifts they wanted for Christmas, I didn't promise them my corpse."

"Yeah… that's some scary stuff, man. The one we encountered outside damn near put a whole in my chest. They're strong as hell." Jacobs coughed into his hands.

Bradley noticed him lightly reel back and forth as he stood. He pulled out his canteen. "Here, take this."

Jacobs grabbed the canteen and could tell immediately that it was almost empty. "You're almost out, Bradley. Here, you keep it for yourself."

"I insist, LT. You go on."

Jacobs nodded his head and finished the rest of the water. Three seconds and the canteen was empty. He gave it back to Bradley. Jacobs was the one who took care of his men and he hated it when it was the other way around.

"How's your leg?" Jacobs asked.

"It won't stop aching. Garnome did me a solid though; patched it up good. I think we're all going to need a few weeks at the hospital after tonight. Nothing we can do but keep pressing on, right?"

"Yeah. You still driving the mustang?"

"Nah, man. One of the side effects of being married is shutting your mouth, and letting your wife have her way! I had to give it up for a damn minivan. I traded four-hundred and sixty horses, for a damn Toyota Sienna. I was almost brought to tears on that day, even now it breaks my heart."

"Aw man! Tell me about it! Alison was pissed at me when I changed around the furniture. I moved the sofas around, switched out some of those animal posters for some slick muscle car photos, and one day I came home."

"Here it comes!"

"The metal posters were stacked atop each other at the front of the door. I went in, asked her what happened. She didn't say anything for like five minutes. Finally, she went in on me." Jacobs tweaked his voice, 'You got a lot of nerve, coming in here, putting your shit up like you own the place. You've been gone for three months, you come in and switch up my furniture? In the house that I maintain? Oh! I think not!' Man, she was so livid. I started to feel guilty, like I committed a mortal sin. Let's just say that I never crossed her furniture and decorations again!"

Jacobs broke into a loud cough. He tried to muffle it into his hands like he was in a movie theater or a classroom, but it was loud all the same.

"You good?"

"Yeah-" He coughed some more. "I'm catching a damn cold, tell ya that much!"

Bradley knew better. "Jacobs, what's up man? That's not just 'some' cough."

He paused before saying, "Like I said… that bastard almost put a whole in my chest."

"How bad?"

"I'll be fine."

Bradley said, "If you say so, but I'm not letting this one slide. You're seeing the doc as soon as we get back to base."

Jacobs, eager to switch topics, said, "Man… I miss Alison, though… miss her bad." He thought about her long, straight, blonde hair. Her blue eyes, pearling white smile, the freckles on her face, and her warmth. He was so cold out there in the wilderness, he would have given anything to feel her body wrapped around his. They had only been married for a couple of years, but their love for each other was strong.

Bradley told him, "I'm sure you'll see her soon enough—and your baby."

Jacobs grinned. "Oh, yeah! I definitely can't wait to see that little guy's face."

Bradley reminded him, "…or little *girl's*."

"Ah, Jesus! You're making me sweat, Abe!"

The two friends shared a quiet laugh and walked back into the surveillance room.

—

ROGER JACOBS

Me and Alison waited in the doctor's office. We didn't speak. The door opened and the doctor entered the sterile room.

"Roger Jacobs, I presume?" He asked.

"That's me, doc." I say.

"I thought as much." He chuckled. "Mrs. Jacobs?"

"A pleasure, doctor Monroe." She said.

"Let me see… let me see… ah—yes! You're here today for your semen report. I'm going to pull it up on the computer and we can review it together."

I rubbed my boots together and twiddled my fingers. Awkward was an understatement. I felt like God was punishing me for my past mistakes. The embarrassment was just as bad as any wound I sustained in battle.

"OK." The doctor started. "Based on last week's lab, the issue here is not Mrs. Jacobs but Mr. Jacobs. Your sperm count is low. I believe this is the core issue with this infertility situation. This is relatively good news; we can get that count higher with testosterone. If it were an issue with the sperm's ability to move, then the situation would be more complex. I'm going to write a prescription for you. Please see the pharmacy after your visit here."

I held my head low.

"Something else, Mr. Jacobs. Don't be discouraged; neither of you for that matter. There is a stigma for men who struggle in this area, but I assure you that this should be an easy fix. Take this prescription regularly and keep trying. Let's schedule your next visit in a couple of months and if you're still struggling, we can try a new method of approach."

He handed me the prescription paper with mighty fine cursive writing.

"Do you have any questions?"

"How long before we see results, you think?" Asked Alison.

"I would say a couple months at the latest; few weeks at the earliest. Only time can tell, but I would say sooner rather than later."

"Thank you, doctor." She said.

"Thanks." I mutter out.

"My pleasure."

He showed us out and we left the room. Alison's hand massaging my hand made me realize that I had my fist in a ball. I didn't want to look at her. I expected a face of disappointment. Maybe Walter was the better man. I felt her hand run down the left side of my face and when I looked, I saw a lover staring back. No face of disappointment or bitterness but a face of happiness and hope. It was this day when I knew that our love was for real. My weakest moment in my life was the day I felt my strongest. She wrapped her arms around my left arm and leaned her head against my shoulder as we walked towards the elevator.

PRESENT DAY

Jacobs asked Harrison, "Any luck with the footage, Commander?"

Harrison shook his head and replied, "Not yet, but we're almost there."

Jacobs walked over to the squad as they were talking. Taylor was eating an MRE.

Chris was saying, "Professor Kent? He oversaw the Vanguard Program? Wait—the same guy who died on Level Two?"

Taylor assured him, "Yep. That's what the videos showed. Bro—the crazy things we saw. They injected the soldiers with multiple chemicals, and you could see the early results of the experimentations. Those guys were normal... I mean, not *crazy*. Their eyes weren't red. They were super-humans without the mad side effects."

Chris said, "All the secrecy—reminds me of my time with the Falcons."

Carter's interest peaked. "Falcons?"

"A part of GUARD."

"That's not saying much."

Chris said, "You guys ever hear of the Monrovia assassination?"

Bradley squinted his eyes while rubbing the back of his head. "Yeah, faintly. That's when prince Monrovia was assassinated. He was supposed to be the next leader of Spain—hated the US from what I remember. Wait—you're not telling me you were involved in that plot, are you?"

Chris replied, "The Falcons are spies; trained assassins. If not collecting intel, they're collecting body count."

Carter asked, "Sounds similar to the CIA."

Chris answered, "The Falcon program is a child of the CIA. We're authorized to commit assassinations and we officially do not exist. If somebody tried telling anybody that I'm part of the Falcons, they won't know what you're talking about. Just like Task Force X-Ray. Good thing too… the things they did to us."

"Interesting. Did you choose to be a part of the Falcons?"

There was a pause.

Chris was examining the silver knife in his hands. It was a long, sharp, and fixed blade with a wooden handle. There was an inscription on both sides. One side read, *Life in the light.* The other side read, *Death in the shadows.* It was his academy knife from his time in the Falcon Program. It had an insignia at the base of the blade; showing a black falcon with its wings fully spread, looking straight up the blade.

CHRIS MARILYN

The garbage man was asking too many questions. George snuffed him with a quick shot to the head. He recoiled back. I caught him before he fell and made noise. We lifted him up and threw him in the large horizontal trash bin and closed the lid. George opened the side door and we rushed up the stairs. The Shanghai night club was loud; perfect for our mission. We entered the private elevator; killing the guard in the process. We hit the button and the elevator took us up to the penthouse. It was a windowed elevator. We could see a city of lights amidst the rain. The door opened and we scanned the perimeter. The lights were yellow-bright. We could hear a clinging noise; like someone set their utensil against a plate. We entered the dining room quickly. Our target looked up in shock. George shot him in the head; the suppressed weapon spitting a single bullet casing out of its chamber. The man blew back; knocking over his chair and bloodying his noodles. George and I rushed over to confirm the kill. Confirmed; the man was dead. George gave me a look. I examined the body again and saw that his left earlobe was still there. Our target didn't have a left earlobe. The upstairs door opened. A gunman sprayed machine-gun rounds from his Uzi 9mm. We both rolled to cover; the table and décor being shot to pieces. When he needed to reload, I didn't let him. His emptied magazine hit the floor, I peered from cover and shot him twice through his chest. He fell over the railing. Another gunman opened fire. I went back into cover and I saw George fall to the ground. He'd been shot. I turned the corner again and killed the second gunman. I heard steps behind me. I turned just in time to watch Yazumo's katana hit the wall. He knocked my pistol out of my hand with his leg.

I drew my knife. He pulled his Katana from the wall and swung recklessly at me. We managed to tussle along the ground. He held his blade inches from my throat. I held it back with my right hand. He was clearly frustrated by my unflinching face. He used both hands to push down on the blade. Blood leaked from my hand onto my chin. He thought he had me. I swiped my blade across his throat with my free hand. He became wide eyed; his throat opening like a rift. Blood spewed onto my face and into my mouth. I could taste it. That salty taste was unforgettable. His body collapsed on me. I pushed him over to the side and quickly saw his missing earlobe. Yazumo—A Yakuza boss who had been responsible for countless murders in the US was dead. George made his way to his feet. No words were said. I looked at the wreckage and saw a photo lying on the bullet-riddled table. I picked it up. It was Yazumo's mom, or so I believed. She was elderly and had a wrinkled face with white hair. Too old to be a wife or girlfriend, but then again who knows? Maybe he was into that sort of thing. It amazed me; out of all the things that were shot to pieces, the picture didn't have a scratch on it. I had a mother once—no longer. I set the framed picture on Yazumo's belly and I escorted George to the elevator.

PRESENT DAY

Chris answered Carter's question with a hint of bitterness in his tone, "No, actually I wanted to be a doctor. But life had other plans."

He put away his knife.

Harrison broke the conversation, "Squad! Group up on me! We have the computers working!"

The team all gathered around the computer terminals as Commander Harrison pulled up a new string of video logs and security footage. He clicked one video labeled "Perimeter Footage" and played it.

The footage showed two all-black helicopters landing on the roof of the facility. When they landed, and the rotor blades stopped spinning, the side doors opened, and approximately fifteen men, wearing the same black armor that the hostiles were wearing, step out of the helicopters. Their visors were red, and they were armed with assault rifles, grenades, and heavy weapons. They had suppressors on their rifles. The video showed the men entering the facility; lightning struck the roof, and the combatants rushed their way inside. One helicopter tried to take off but was struck by lightning, causing it to spiral out of control and crash on the opposite side of the building. The other helicopter managed to take off, leaving the roof safely. Lightning continued to strike the roof, and the footage buffered and shut off.

Bradley observed, "Hmmm. There goes that lightning again. What's up with that?"

Harrison replied, "Not sure. All I know is that it has something to do with this facility. I have a good feeling that if we kill the Phantom, we won't have to worry about it."

The Commander scrolled and played the next one, labeled "Vanguard Program Test #3."

Professor Kent was speaking. "This is Professor Kent, and today we will be initiating Test Three of the Vanguard Program. This may be the final step in creating a greater mankind. We will be injecting our volunteers with the newly formulated chemical, 'Archangel-3,' or 'A-3' for short. To be entirely honest, I'm a little nervous about this chemical. We've only recently tested it and it's fresh from R&D. The chemical is designed to strengthen the immune system in mammals. If effective, it should expel harmful bacteria from the body and radicalize the white blood cells. This, in effect will make diseases, flus, viruses, and even terminal illnesses useless against the human body."

"However, there have already been worrisome signs of the side effects. We injected a dose of the chemical into a terminally ill test monkey. After a few days, the monkey showed rapid increase in health. Unfortunately, after a week, the normally calm monkey showed increased rage and agitation. Its eyes turned bloodshot red, and ever since we injected the chemical into the subject, it has acted unsettled. The good news, however, is that we tested this chemical on a human test subject who had already undergone previous chemical doses. After a week, he acted sane and stable, still with bloodshot eyes, though. Washington has grown impatient for their new super-soldiers and are pushing Hope 7 for results. We will proceed with the testing; fifty test subjects will be injected with Archangel-3. Let us begin."

The video showed the subjects laid out on medical slabs; they were injected in the head, spine, and chest. A few days passed, and then the video showed a couple of soldiers in a quarantine lab. Their eyes were bloodshot red, and they were behaving irrationally—they would throw chairs and other objects at the bulletproof windows. Professor Kent was seen outside the lab, trying to observe the situation, and calm the increasingly aggressive subjects.

Professor Kent said, "Calm down. Calm down. What seems to be bothering you?"

One soldier said, "You sub-human... you inferior... we superior! You must ascend or die!"

Professor Kent wrote down notes in his notebook and walked away. The video switched off and then switched back on, and the professor reappeared on the screen.

He said, "Just as I feared; Archangel-3 proved to be a radical stimulant. Only fifteen of the fifty test subjects survived with their minds intact, but even their eyes are permanently bloodshot. It seems that the chemical radicalizes the brain, not only hindering their motor functions, but even giving them a superiority complex. We still don't know why. However, they are completely immune to viruses, colds, diseases, and even poison! We injected James with HIV—nothing. We injected Ebola into him—nothing. We even injected a small strain of anthrax into him—nothing! These diseases are deadly, yet James and the other test subjects are completely immune to them. We created the perfect soldiers, the perfect warriors, and within these warriors may lie the answer to perfect humans."

"What we need to find out, however, is why fifteen patients out of fifty did not go mad, like the other thirty-five test subjects?

This will be the question that will define the next few centuries of mankind's life on earth. The test subjects who failed the trials still have the ability to think, fight, and exercise critical-thinking skills. However, despite having reduced motor functions, extreme rage, and a highly elevated metabolism; they have increased hostility towards normal humans but not among themselves, another sign of the grandiosity I referred to. I find this very interesting. My next goal is to breakdown this Archangel-3, fix the formula, and eliminate the side effects. Humanity's future depends upon it."

The video ended.

Harrison said quietly to himself, "Bingo! A-3 was the issue."

He scrolled to an audio log labeled "Pressure" and played it.

Professor Kent's voice echoed, "Ah! This doesn't make any sense! The research team and I have been trying to stabilize the A-3 chemical, but we can't seem to purify it! Washington is continually pressuring us to create more stable super-soldiers. They've even threatened to cut funding to our program if we don't produce more results! Many of the test subjects were volunteers who were injured in war. The program was a chance for them to start anew. Some survived; many perished and now we are running out of test subjects. We have even begun testing on local wildlife, trying to determine whether the effects are different. It has produced little results. Samantha Volaire has sent her goons to kidnap local inhabitants, and this is most excellent! Now we have increased human test subjects to experiment on. Desperate times call for desperate measures! We *will* find the breakthrough we're looking for!"

The audio log ended.

Ramirez said, "It looks like the professor was starting to lose his mind. This must be why some of those animals were acting so strange."

Chris nodded, "That explains the red color I saw in the horse's eyes."

Jacobs added, "Not to mention the missing townspeople that Foster was telling us about."

Another video was played, labeled "Seraph-1"

Professor Kent once again took up the screen. He had a big smile and acted gleefully, saying, "We've done it! We've found the solution and have improved the Archangel-3 stimulant and tested it on a horse. The horse was found in the wild, terribly injured. It broke its right leg when it stepped into a pothole. When the team found him, he was near-starved, and inches away from death. We brought it back to the lab and tested the new strain on it. A week had passed..."

Professor Kent's eyes looked down for a moment before snapping back at the camera. "Its leg had gradually healed until it made a full recovery. Its health skyrocketed! The heart was at full health and the horse showed renewed life. It appeared that there was nothing wrong with it, like no injury had ever incurred. Even better, the horse has proven to have an increased IQ. It licks its lips and studies things before it; having a retentive memory. Now, I don't expect it to learn Spanish anytime soon, but this is a breakthrough in our research. We've labeled the new strain, 'Seraph-1 or 'S-1,' after the horse we named, Seraph. We theorize that the horse's anti-bodies have somehow molded with the strain of stimulant. We have added a percentage of its blood to the final product. Its firm anti-bodies have stabilized the chemical. The only problem is that we can only extract so much from the horse at a time. I may get laughed at down the line for saying this, but Seraph is a savior of humanity... a Vanguard even."

The video shut off.

Chris's eyes lit up. "Woah! That horse... Seraph... it played a key role in all this madness. I knew there was something about it!"

Harrison asked, "What are you talking about?"

"On our way to Hope 7, we came across that same horse. It had red eyes just like the Freaks we encountered. It saved—I mean, stepped in, when those wolves attacked us. It was... uh, an unforgettable moment to say the least. I've never seen a horse charge a pack of wolves before. It scared them away too!" Said Jacobs, explaining the story.

"Huh... that's interesting. Well, at least somebody got away." Harrison said as he hastily scrolled to another video labeled "The Vanguards of Humanity."

Professor Kent appeared on the screen. He looked pleased and excited. Samantha Volaire appeared next to him, wearing her usual all-white business suit.

Professor Kent spoke so quickly he had tripped over his first few words. He slowed himself. "It's been a year and three months. After months of tests and combat trials, The Vanguard Program is officially over. With the recent breakthrough regarding Seraph, I am pleased to announce that the Vanguard Program was a success, despite the loss of about 75% of the test subjects, we have found the key to human evolution! We have created the strongest, smartest, fastest, and most purebred soldiers the world has ever known."

"For now, these breakthroughs will be kept from the world until we find a way to announce it without scaring them. The violation of Article 331 will present a dilemma as well. I'm sure the bureaucrats in Washington can clean up the aftermath. The Vanguard Division is no more. Now it is "The Vanguards of Humanity", or VOH for short. This elite unit of super-soldiers will be the best of the best, the man of the future so to speak. Just sixteen men— and women, make-up the unit, led by my friend James Scar, also known by his call sign, "Centurion." I'm so proud of that young man. He has shown great pride, courage, and resiliency from day one of the testing. They are officially known as 'Red Eye 7,' and will be the first group of super-soldiers to fight. They report to the Pentagon next week! Ah—this is a great day for us all."

Volaire pleasingly nodded her head. "Congratulations, Steve! I am personally proud of you and all that you and the Valkyrie Research Division have done. With additional studies, we may yet find a way to gift the world with new bodies! Bodies that no longer succumb to diseases, illnesses, and weakness."

The video cut off.

CENTURION

The nurse rolled me down the hallway. Lab coats and nurses seemed to crowd the hallway like a crowded train. A trip that should've taken me five minutes from my room to the atrium, took fifteen minutes. I kept my head down; looking at my scrawny, useless legs. My back ached the entire way. Finally, we entered the room. The lights were dim. There were twenty other individuals inside; all crippled like me. The security guard positioned me towards the back of the atrium. We waited for about ten minutes. Professor Kent walked onto the stage. His upright back made me jealous.

"Congratulations!" He started, "You young men and women have been offered the opportunities of a lifetime! A chance to not only take back your lives, but to become something more. The process will be difficult, I can assure you. I cannot promise that all of you will survive or even be positively changed, all I promise is a chance. You survive and you will be the strongest, fastest, and most physically superior humans the world has ever known. If this does not interest you, I am sorry for wasting your time. You may leave now."

No one in the room moved an inch. I was sold by the dream of being able to stand again. It was all I could think of.

"Good! We will begin the process now. The security staff are going to escort you into your hospital beds now for your first injections. You'll be administered Benadryl and Tylenol first. After that, we're going to put you to sleep while we insert the Nano bites into your critical areas. Some of you have shattered pelvis's, damaged spinal cords, and the like, so this insertion will be different for each of you. The goal of this week is to get you folks walking and talking. Get comfortable and get acquainted with your fellow patients. This is going to be a long journey."

The security guard pushed us out of the atrium and into the

medical room. There were four rows of five beds neatly stretched through the room. The guard rolled me to the bed at the far end and helped me onto it. I looked around. There was a woman to my right, another woman next to her, a black man across from me, another woman at the far end of his row, and the rest were men. Nurses came in and gave us our pre-meds. After that, they inserted our IVs. I turned on my right side in a failed attempt to get comfortable. My eyes met the woman's eyes. She had tan skin, and black hair tied into a ponytail. She had a nasty scar along her left forearm. I thought about the old proverb, *if you want friends, you must first present yourself to be friendly.*

I smile and ask her, "What's your name?"

She whispered something to the nurse and she pulled the curtain between us. I was too tired to protest. My eyes grew heavy and I fell asleep.

PRESENT DAY

Harrison turned around from the computer monitor and looked at the dead black-armored combatant. He slowly walked over and examined a patch on his right shoulder. The patch was in dark-red lettering, the logo was a white tree with a cluster of branches stretching up his shoulder with pink leaves, and under the logo were the letters "VOH." The Commander was stunned. He slowly removed the foreign-looking helmet; the red visors staring him down as he lifted it. His heartrate sped up.

The helmet sat firmly in Harrison's hands. "I don't believe it..."

The entire squad stared in awe and horror.

The man's eyes were red—bloodshot red. The black-armored soldier was no ordinary soldier, but a super-soldier—a Freak. His head leaned to the side. His eyes stared at the floor. He had light-black skin, clean shaven face, and short, light-brown hair. Harrison rubbed his hands along the helmet and examined the cold piece of steel. It had light weight and was made of a strange, matte-black, polarized material. Harrison could partially see himself in the reflection. It felt like cold glass but was very tough. He flipped the helmet over and saw the name, 'Red Chalice,' at the bottom of it in red lettering.

Ramirez said, "What the hell, man!? He's a Freak!" He paused as he checked around the mutant's neck. "Strange though—he doesn't have a barcode like the others we saw."

"No madness, no need for tracking." Harrison said, setting the helmet down.

Jacobs said, "This must be the so-called "Vanguards of Humanity." Ah! This doesn't make sense. They're from Hope 7, but we saw them arrive in helicopters. What in the world's going on here!?"

Harrison knew. "I'll paint a picture for you: These super-soldiers were formed into a team, a black-ops team. They deployed around the world entirely unknown to anyone, and when Hope 7 was compromised, they were sent in to collect all classified intel and material and destroy anything they couldn't carry with them. But if Tommy's words hold any weight, they became 'rogue.' Why? Those security guards on Level Three thought that they were coming to save them, but that was never part of their agenda. They came in shooting." He sighed before continuing, "The question now is: what made them go rogue?"

Jacobs reminded Harrison, "One thing still doesn't add up, though. Tommy."

Harrison stood up, walked back to the surveillance console, and looked for more information. He came across another video labeled "Stairway #13"

The security footage showed a black-armored Vanguard leading a pack of shirtless Freaks up a stairwell. The stairwell led outside.

The footage ended.

Jacobs exclaimed, "This must be how some of the Freaks began appearing outside the facility! Was Tommy helping them escape?"

Harrison conceded, "Looks like it."

He then scrolled to the last video on the console, labeled "Project Phantom Test #3." He played it.

Samantha Volaire appeared on the screen.

She said, "Today marks the first trial of the electric tower. I must admit that I am nervous for my son, Tommy, but the results we have achieved thus far and the potential future results are too great to ignore. I must put aside my motherly emotions—even my humane emotions if we are to create this future marvel... if we are to save my son. We will place Tommy inside of a scientifically modified steel chamber in the center of the room. Then we will pulse 4,000 volts of electricity from each of the three spires into the steel chamber. That is a whopping 12,000 volts of electricity. The chamber will spin at a very fast rate and collect the electricity. We are sure the electricity will be warped into Tommy's DNA through specially modified tubes inside the chamber connected to Tommy."

"We are hoping to achieve three things with this potentially final test. One, create a person who can harness the powers of electricity. Two, create the formula to a mass cyber weapon that can completely destabilize electric grids. Lastly, give mankind an eternal power source within their own bodies—to create the digital sculpture of man. The interaction between man and machine will become seamless. To be able to upload oneself into the Digital Realm... well, I don't want to get my hopes up. We have to get the results first."

Volaire took a deep inhale. "OK. We will begin immediately."

Tommy was seen struggling as he was placed inside a steel crypt. He said, "Mommy—please don't let this happen! I'm scared!" His eyes were teary as he desperately looked to his mother to save him and take him home. He underwent a year of feeling cold syringes, cold fluids, cold flooring, cold walls, and cold humans.

Volaire tried to placate him. "Now, Tommy—we talked about this. You are going to lead us all into a new age! We will all follow in your footsteps, my son. Have courage."

Tommy was strapped into the crypt, and the thick steel of the chamber was slowly closed; sealing his fate. It was a tall, thick, metal pod. It had a short, skinny, metal receiver at the top. The staff and security all walked out of the testing room and into a sealed lab, where they would begin the test. Tommy's face was seen through a small circular window on the chamber, which was surrounded by tall black spires covered in cords and wiring. His eyes were watering. He thrashed in his seat.

TOMMY VOLAIRE

I held onto the metal teapot the guard left in my room. I let it sit for an hour or two and figured that the water was lukewarm. Lukewarm... silly word. Focus... focus. My fingertips tingled. The pot shook like an earthquake was happening. It steamed like a choo-choo train and whistled after.

"All aboard!" I quietly say.

This was the second time I was able to do this. The teapot spun off the tray and fell onto the ground. Oops. A guard came rushing in. I pretended that I was asleep. I tried to keep my lips straight, but I couldn't help but smile.

"Nice try, Tommy!" The guard said. "I know you're awake and you know better than to play with your utensils and dishes."

I peeked my eyes open. He walked closer. The guard stopped and shook for a moment; stumbling back and falling to the ground. I didn't understand.

"Ouch! What a shock!" He said, quick to stand.

I peered over my bed and saw the water. I think that when he stepped in it... he got shocked? He was none too happy.

He walked over and got close to me. "Listen here, boy. No more playing, understand? You do this again and I'll have to tell your mom."

"OK. It won't happen again." I say, putting my hand on his chest. When I did that, the guard flew back; sparks shooting from my hand. The moment scared me.

"I'm sorry! I'm so sorry! Are you OK?" I rush to say.

The guard was wide-eyed. He stumbled up and spoke into his radio, saying, "Code red! Room 112, Level Five now!!"

The guard stayed close to the door. I was trying to apologize when the door broke open and about eight guards rushed my bed.

"Cryptum Chamber you go!!" One said, with his hand firmly on my shoulder.

Cryptum Chamber? That really cold room? No!

I struggled and fight their holds on me. It was impossible. They were too strong. Grown men versus an eight-year old. Some of them hit me.

"No!" I yell. "I won't go!"

They wouldn't listen. The lights in the room flickered on and off; dim to light. The same tingling feeling I felt in my fingertips I could feel in my entire body. It felt really good.

"I said, No!!!"

The lights were blown out and I could feel a rush of air pass through the room. I felt myself stand; surely on my bed. I didn't understand what happened or where the guards went. The lights were slow to come back on and I could see them crawling along the floor.

"I'm sorry, misters, but I'm not going to the cold room." I declare.

The guards stare at me. "Tommy..." One said.

"No!" I say.

They flinched back. It was a strange sight seeing the muscled men reel away from me. Men had never been afraid of me. I know this because I could never scare my daddy.

"Tommy!" The guard said again, pointing at my feet.

I looked down. My feet were dangling above my bed. My hospital gown moved from side to side like wind was blowing through it. I was in mid-air!

PRESENT DAY

Inside the video, Project Phantom Test #3 continued playing. Time had elapsed.

The staff inside the protected cubicle, put on dark shades and one member said, "Charging up the spires in three…two…one…charging!"

The lab coat hit a blue button at his control desk and the spires began to power up. Blue sparks emitted from them. After about thirty seconds, the spires were completely electrified and at full power.

The staff member said, "Spinning chamber now!" He hit a yellow button and Tommy's chamber began to slowly spin. The lab coat had begun to sweat intensely and looked to Samantha for the final go-ahead.

He said, "Spires are at max capacity. Awaiting your signal, Mrs. Volaire."

There was a brief pause. Forgive me, Tommy. She thought to herself. If saving you means burning in hell, I'll do it for you… my little prodigal king.

She stared at the chamber for moments without blinking before finally giving the order, "Do it!"

The staff member held a red button for three seconds and the spires conducted a total voltage of 12,000 into the steel chamber. The chamber spun much faster. Tommy began to scream; the chamber spinning very fast. Each revolution was about two or three seconds long. A bright, blue light began to emerge from the chamber; consuming the entire room and obscuring the chamber. Tommy screamed—horrifically. The scream morphed into a long, wailing shriek. The bright light burst into a blue flash, and the video shut off.

Roughly thirty seconds passed and the video turned back on.

It showed two security guards entering the test room. The chamber had stopped spinning and was smoking. The staff member hit the green button. The chamber door slowly opened; smoke billowing out like a burning building. The door finally opened—but the video buffered and froze.

Harrison yelled, "Come on, you damn thing! Work! Ah—it froze! Ramirez, is there anything you can do?"

He examined it for a moment before replying, "That's a negative, Commander; the footage is corrupted." As he examined the console, he noticed a single, blinking red light on one of the monitors. The light blinked under the words, *Level 6 storage bay.* "Hmmm—that's strange. It looks like a camera on Level Six has been recording the whole time." Ramirez continued.

Harrison ordered, "Check it!"

Ramirez played the surveillance footage. It showed a black-armored VOH member standing behind a man wearing an all-white lab coat. The professor was shaken as he loaded a syringe with a dark-red liquid.

The VOH combatant with the name "Centurion" in red lettering said, "Is the formula almost ready, professor?" He spoke through the helmet's mic, and his modified voice came out like a radio with a little deepness to it.

The lab coat trembled like he was wearing vibrating shoes. He turned around and said, "It's ready. I've prepared a test syringe for you and all the gas vats are loaded with S-1 in gas form as you requested. Now, please—just don't kill me."

The professor gave the VOH member the syringe.

Centurion marveled at the formula. He held it firmly in front of his visors before saying, "Kill you? Don't be absurd! I'm not going to kill you. I'm going to *perfect* you!"

The Vanguard stabbed the professor in the neck with the syringe and injected the Seraph-1 formula. The lab coat screamed in agony and violently shook. He fell to the floor; twisting and turning like a dying centipede. His breathing was rapid and some foam squeezed between his lips.

The professor looked up from the floor with wide eyes. "What have… you done… to me?"

Centurion replied, "I have brought you to Ascension. Good work, professor. You've done well. The world will soon enjoy the fruits of our labors and my reward to you is perfection. Enjoy!"

Two other black-armored Freaks ran up and reported to Centurion.

One, with the name "Legionnaire" on his uniform, said, "Sir, we lost three Vanguards on Level Four. It's Task Force X-Ray—they're on their way."

Centurion took a moment to respond. He paced to the side and gripped a computer monitor. "Three?"

He violently threw the computer monitor across the room. He threw it so far it flew out of the camera's view.

Centurion said, "Don't they see? We're creating a better mankind! No matter—we don't have time to convince them—we will be ready for them."

The three members ran offscreen and the room was empty. Ramirez took initiative and scrolled back roughly six hours, as the camera was recording footage the whole time. The recording showed all fifteen of the Vanguards standing in a huddle. Ramirez stopped it and played.

Centurion said, "Report!"

One Vanguard replied, "We've secured Hope 7. All security forces have been neutralized."

Another said, "All of the willing scientist have been evacuated. Level Two has been sacked of all notes, records, and heavy machinery. Professor Kent, as you know, was not on board. Therefore, he has been eliminated."

Centurion held his head low. "He was critical to this research. We will honor him in the new society as the father of the new world. Rest in peace, professor. Achilles, report."

The Vanguard he referred to had metal stabilizers in his arms. He said, "All weapons, weapon research, blueprints, and 3-D printers have been acquired. War Horse freed our brothers and sisters from their holding cells and most have been evacuated from the facility."

"Excellent! Where is Seraph? Were we able to capture him?"

Achilles shook his head and said, "Negative, Centurion. One of the security staff managed to help it escape the labs. I shot him multiple times, but he managed to escape with the horse. I don't think he made it far. A pureblood chased after him."

"A setback, but nothing serious. Anything else to report?"

Legionnaire said, "Hope 7's radar detected incoming air traffic. It looks like the inferior government sent an attack force."

"If I had to guess," said Centurion. He knew who they were sending. Who else would they send to deal with the Phantom and themselves in a top-secret research facility?

"Task Force X-Ray." He said with a smile under his helmet.

"THE Task Force X-Ray?" asked Legionnaire. "Finally, a worthy enemy!"

Another Vanguard with the name "Dark Horse" said, "Yes! I look forward to tasting more inferior blood!"

Centurion reminded them, "They will not be like the others we fought earlier. This is an elite enemy. If we do not defeat them here... I am certain that they will be the arch enemy of this society. Shape up! Don't let them past Level Five! Red Chalice take some of the Vanguards up to Level Four and protect it. Don't let them seize the control room! The rest of you will help me load the goods onto the aircraft. Let's hope that we can evac the facility before they even know we're here!"

The Vanguards broke the huddle and separated. Harrison stopped the recording and thought to himself. They knew we were coming. They knew who we were. In this moment, Harrison knew what he had known all along: his government created this entire mess and ordered his men to clean it up or die trying. That was it. It was never about reclaiming the facility; it was about covering everything up. They had hoped that we'd never even get this far and when the challenge became too much, we would've just called in the airstrike and the bombs would've done the covering up themselves. Son of a bitch!

Harrison knocked the computer monitor over the desk. He said to his team, "OK. We keep moving. We've wasted enough time here. This is it people. You guys aren't going to like it, but we need to split up!"

Taylor's mouth almost hit the floor. "What? We'll be more effective if we stay together!"

Ah Taylor! You have a point… but this is the only way, Harrison thought. He saw what the Vanguards were planning to do. They're raiding this facility; taking everything that isn't nailed down. They don't look like the type to sell it on the black market. No. They're going to use it on the world if we don't stop 'em. Harrison thought about leaving the facility and calling in the airstrike, but he reasoned that the warplanes might not get there in time to stop the Vanguards from leaving.

Harrison shot back, "I respect your two cents, Taylor, in the sense that I don't give a damn about what you have to say! We have to get communications up if we're ever going to get out of here or get word to command. So here it comes: Jacobs—you'll lead Val and Ramirez to the communications hub back on Level One and get word to command on what has happened here. Pass 'Inferno' to them. The rest of us will continue lower into the facility. We'll stop the shadow team and kill the Phantom. Hopefully, that'll stop any EMPs or crazy lightning storms from taking down our rides when they come in. Ramirez, take the recorded footage off the U-Bug and give Bradley the machine. If we find anything new, we'll record it. If we don't make it, well, at least you can get the recorded footage outta here."

Ramirez nodded his head. He pulled on one side of the storage device until he heard a *Click*. He passed the rectangular hard drive to Jacobs and gave Bradley the U-Bug.

Jacobs put the drive in his rucksack, rubbed the back of his neck, and said, "Makes sense, sir... but, uh... are you sure about splitting up? And how will the rest of you get out of Hope 7 when the bombs come raining down?"

Harrison paused.

"We have no choice. We don't have the manpower to stop the Vanguards, kill the Phantom, and get communications up at the same time. We gotta stop them from getting this chemical out of the facility, no matter what. They've clearly been here for a while and it appears that they're getting ready to leave. If we die, at least the world, or at least someone, will know what happened here. That's your job, Jacobs—get it done! Make sure that word gets out. Don't let them cover up the knowledge we've learned here or the sacrifices that we've made. When you send the communication, don't bother coming back down. If we don't get up in time, get yourselves clear of the blast."

There was another pause.

Jacobs slowly nodded his head. "Yes, sir! Val, Ramirez—with me. We're going to head up and get those communications running. You know the way, Val?"

She firmly adjusted her cracked glasses before saying, "I do."

Val walked past them and said, "You coming?"

The men were surprised. Val was always behind them; nervous to move forward or take initiative, but this time she led the way from the front. The team escorted Jacobs, Ramirez, and Val into the elevator that led to the lobby. Ramirez gave his squad mates fist bumps, as he very well knew that this could've been the last time they saw each other. Each man gave Jacobs their wills and some personal belongings in case they wouldn't make it out.

Val walked into the bullet-riddled elevator and instructed Harrison, "There should be a service elevator on the other side of this level that will take you further down into the facility."

Harrison nodded his head.

"One more thing, Commander. Good luck! Thank you for protecting me, better, thank you for giving a damn."

"No thanks necessary, Val. You get outta here and live a full life. I'm sorry I couldn't save your co-workers." Harrison replied, shaking her hand.

Jacobs said, "Go get 'em, Commander. If I die up here… tell Alison, would ya?"

Harrison promised, "You got it, Jacobs. You'll be fine, son."

Jacobs was indeed like a son to Harrison. All his men were. He was the old man, and they were the young brothers. That's what made Commander Harrison so admirable to his men; he was forty-six years old, but he was able to keep up with his younger subordinates. Any enemy that would've been convinced that Harrison was too old to fight would've been in for a rude awakening. The military lifestyle that he embraced kept his body in peak condition. Better yet, decades of combat experience made him a formidable foe. Harrison saw many of his men die before becoming the Commander of Task Force X-Ray, but this unit was different. They were family. He wanted his sons to make it home and experience age the way he did. Harrison massaged his aching knees. Well, maybe not the way he did, but to grow old, nevertheless. He didn't want any of them to die in what he saw as a cold facility built upon cursed land, saturated in lifeless blood, and where Phantoms roamed like lost souls. He knew that the odds were stacked against them. He did his best to prepare himself for what was to come.

The elevator door closed; Jacobs's team left the main squad and rode the elevator back up to the lobby.

Harrison ordered, "OK, everybody. Let's get this done!"

The main squad walked through the hallways until they found the service elevator. It was past the surveillance room at the end of a hallway. Harrison pressed the button, and it lit up; all too happy to be of service. A couple minutes passed before the elevator reached their floor. When it finally did, the steel door with lines of blood on it quickly opened. The door reminded Harrison of a mouth; the way the blood lined the middle slit of the door. It was indeed a mouth. It welcomed the squad in with a smile; hungry to devour the next group of poor souls.

They entered and the door quickly shut again, giving them no time to change their minds. It closed; sealing their fates. Harrison pressed the 'Level Five' button. The elevator quickly jerked and descended deeper into the seemingly never-ending Hope 7. They had no idea what they were walking into.

CHAPTER 14: THE CASUALTIES OF WAR

A S THE SERVICE elevator descended, Harrison briefed his men.

"OK, guys. I have no clue as to what's awaiting us down here. Just stay close and fall back on your training. Fire in controlled bursts as I'm sure we're running low on ammo. Keep your groupings tight, check your corners, and don't let them get too close. Remember—we're Task Force X-Ray! These guys might be tough, but we're tougher! We'll kick their asses just like we did everyone else's!"

Bradley raised his fist and said, "Hell yeah! I'm ready!"

Harrison gave Bradley a nod. "When the elevator stops, everyone stick to the sides. If it's clear, just follow my lead and take it slow. We can do this! I'm proud of every single one of you. No matter what happens, remember that we're doing the right thing."

Taylor felt numb; robbed of emotions. The Interstellar coursed through his veins. He almost didn't care what happened. He said, "You got it. Eager to take these guys down and get back home to my dogs."

Carter quipped, "The dogs you take on walks or the dogs you sleep with?"

The elevator exploded with laughter. Everyone knew about Taylor's promiscuous relationships with various women.

"Ha-ha-ha," Taylor sarcastically said, "Very funny."

Carter rubbed his neck and said, "I'm just itching to lie down on my bed. It feels like it's been ages since I took a nap."

"More like ages since a girl touched your dusty dick! You need to sweep that mess into a dust pan!" Taylor fired back.

Laughter continued. Task Force X-Ray… known for their fierce combat skills, and their unending sense of humor.

"Ah he got me!" Carter said, shaking his head with laughter.

"You know I love you, bro!"

Harrison looked around the elevator; cherishing the smiles on his men's faces and the loud noises of laughter. Here they were, about to walk into hell, with the odds against them, and they were laughing their behinds off. Nothing is scarier than an enemy who meets adversity with laughter, he thought to himself. That's a big reason why Harrison loved the unit so much. Despite the horrors of war, they never lost their humanity, or their sense of humor.

"We're almost done, guys. Keep focused, and you'll see the outside world again."

As the elevator came to a stop, the squad went back to seriousness. They noticed that water was leaking through the door. It slowly pressed through the bottom crevice of the door. It slowly opened to reveal a Level Five that was partially flooded with water. They stuck to the sides of the small elevator in anticipation of enemy gunfire. It never came. Water slowly flooded in; wetting their boots. Harrison and Bradley peaked over the corners with their guns aimed and saw that the room seemed clear of hostiles. They flipped down their night vision. It was ominously quiet.

Taylor whispered, "What the hell happened here?"

Harrison patiently scanned the room. "Doesn't matter, let's take it slow."

Harrison and his men entered the partially flooded room and moved through the cold, waist-deep water. The room was dimly lit; dead bodies were floating in the water. It was too dark to make out what they were wearing or how they looked. It was a large atrium; Harrison speculated that it was probably an office, judging by the computer monitors, and desks.

A body rubbed Taylor's waist. He couldn't see the corpse, but he had a strange feeling that it would've been his brother, Ryan.

He said, "Man, there's no saving anyone, is there?"

Harrison reminded him, "Saving the staff is no longer a priority, Taylor. Now keep quiet!"

The darkness was suddenly lit up by red lights, in pairs of twos, originating from some distance. They came from a balcony overlooking the room. Red dots appeared on the Commander's chest.

"Ambush!!" Harrison yelled.

He dove in the water as machine-gun bullets began raining down on the squad. Taylor was shot twice and knocked back into the water. Everyone else took cover behind the partially submerged office desks. Taylor resurfaced; examining his bulletproof vest. He felt like he'd been hit with a baseball bat and gasped for air. Garnome stayed in the back and opened fire on the balcony from which the hostiles were shooting from. He listened closely for any cries of 'medic' or 'man down,' and was on standby to provide medical attention. Carter positioned himself to the side of the room. He unfolded his bipod, and perched his marksman rifle atop the desk, next to a computer monitor. He took a deep inhale, aimed his rifle, and shot one of the Vanguards in the chest, exhaling after. The shooting momentarily stopped. Carter glanced up and saw that the red lights seemed to have dissipated.

Chris, with his head under a desk, asked, "You get him, Carter?"

Carter replied crisply, "I hit him, but I don't know if I killed him. I think they fell back."

"OK, keep me covered. I'm moving up."

Chris moved forward; his gun aimed high. The waist-deep water slowed his advance. He pushed aside floating objects as he moved. He eyed a sturdy desk that was partially submerged and decided to take cover there. As he made his way to the desk, red lights awoke in the water; startling him. He moved his weapon to fire, but before he could, he was grabbed from underwater. A Vanguard jumped out, threw Chris into the water, and tried to drown him.

Bradley moved forward to shoot the Vanguard, but before he could fire, he was grabbed by another Freak and thrown through a plastered wall. Some of the Freaks were on the ground floor and they did their best to encircle the embattled men. Machine-gun fire opened up from the balcony again, and the rest of the men became pinned down in the dark room. Bullets tore through Carter's cover, suppressing him. He felt a bad sting in his shoulder as he descended deeper into his cover.

Chris could see the red optical lights staring at him through the water. He felt tremendous force hold him down. Once again, Chris didn't panic. He pulled out his academy knife and stabbed the Vanguard in his shoulder; confident the enemy would recoil back. The Vanguard didn't break his hold on Chris. Didn't even flinch. Chris tried to stab the Vanguard again but, his hand was grabbed, and his arm was pinned by the Vanguard's knee. Chris began to fade from consciousness under the water. Harrison broke cover and shot the Vanguard that was holding Chris multiple times, killing him. The blue tracer bullets lit up the dark and shredded him; sending him flying forward into the water. Harrison checked his ammo and saw that the bullet counter read, '00' in red coloring. Harrison grew fond of the weapon, but he chose to drop it in the water as it was just dead weight. He slung his M-16 over into his hands and fought with that weapon.

Meanwhile, Bradley slowly rose to his feet, only to find himself yet again in a one-on-one fight with a Freak. It sized up Bradley and smiled. It wasn't armored and didn't have a shirt on. He was a light-skinned man and was wet from the water.

"Here we go again..." Bradley murmured.

He tried to shoot his M-60 machine gun, but the gun had jammed with water. The *clicking* noise the gun made was a most unwelcome sound. Bradley threw his M-60 to the floor and reached for his shotgun slung in his back holster. Before he could fire the weapon, he was tackled against the wall and was being strangled.

The Freak said through gritted teeth, "Die... Inferior!"

Bradley head-butted the Freak several times; forcing it to release. Bradley reached for his shotgun on the ground, but the Freak grabbed him and threw him against another wall. Bradley's pain from previous wounds was resurfacing. His leg ached terribly. Bradley hurled a knife at the Freak in quick succession; hitting him in his stomach. It stopped a moment, then powerwalked forward. Bradley grabbed his last knife and hurled that one; striking its shoulder. It pulled out one of the knives and stabbed Bradley in his side. He yelled out in pain as the blade stuck between Bradley's ribs. It grabbed his helmet and tore off the night vision optics. It smacked Bradley forward up against a desk and unleashed a quick flurry of hammering blows to Bradley's body. The body armor only seemed to serve as extra padding from the mutant's powerful punches.

"Oh! Ah! Ah! Inferior slow!!" The Freak taunted.

It punched Bradley in the face, splashing out blood, and knocking out a tooth. That did it. The Freak pulled out the second blade from his stomach and tried to stab Bradley again, but he moved and punched the Freak with a heavy right hand, briefly dazing it.

Bradley saw his shotgun in the middle of the room. He dove for it, but his foot was caught in mid-air and he arrived fingertips away from the gun. It dragged Bradley; he kicked the mutant with his left leg. One kick... another... another... finally it grabbed his left leg and sent the blade through his leg, right under his kneecap. Bradley yelled in pain, and with both legs he pushed the mutant off him and was able to grab his weapon. He flipped over and shot the Freak; blowing him out of the hole in the wall. Bradley rose to his feet, but his legs quickly gave out and he fell back onto the floor. He tried to stand again and this time he was successful. He clenched his teeth as he painfully limped over to make sure the Freak was dead; his boots chaffing along the wet floor. He looked into the dark water while hunched over and didn't see anything. Loud gunfire sounded between the squad and the Vanguards.

Suddenly, he was grabbed and pulled into the water. The shirt-less Freak was still alive and pummeled Bradley; ripping off his vest. The Freak pulled Bradley's face out of the water and prepared to finish Bradley with a final punch to the face.

"Inferior tough!" The mutant said.

Bradley had no time to feel flattered. He could do nothing but shield his face as he braced for a terrible blow. Before the Freak could punch Bradley, it was set afire by Taylor's flamethrower. The Freak screamed. Bradley was released. He reached into the water, grabbed his shotgun, ejected the empty shell, and blasted the burning Freak back into the room where they'd begun this struggle. Its legs dangled from the edge of the room. The recoil combined with Bradley's jelly-like legs, sent him splashing back into the water; bumping his head against a desk.

Taylor extended his arm and lifted Bradley out of the water.

He asked, "You alright there, Abe?"

Bradley was a mess. The left side of his face was bloodied, swollen, and felt like a dentist removed his wisdom teeth. He had two blades inside his body. One in his right side, another under his left kneecap, and both were his. He no longer had a helmet, but a black beanie that he wore under. He no longer had body armor on either. Bradley managed a faint smile at Taylor. His teeth and lips had blood on them and he could feel that a tooth in the upper left corner of his mouth was no longer there.

Bradley, with tired eyes, said, "You stole my kill...! I had him... right where I wanted him."

Taylor responded, "*Sure* you did. By the way, where's your '60?"

"Don't start with me!"

He slumped back into the cold water until half his body was submerged. He leaned his head against a bullet-riddled desk. In pain would have been an understatement.

"Medic!" Shouted Taylor.

Garnome rushed from his cover like a marathon runner and doctored on Bradley. He pulled out the blade in his side. Bradley grunted in pain. The gunfire in the room was simmering down.

"Is there another one?" Asked Garnome.

Bradley nodded his head. "My leg…"

Taylor reached into the water and with both hands pulled up Bradley's left leg, showing the blade under his knee cap.

"Hey, hey, hey, easy!!" Bradley emphasized.

Garnome said, "Its gotta come out."

"Easy for you to say! Why don't we just leave it in for now?"

"No can do, Bradley. Tell ya what, I'll count to one, okay? Take a deep breath. 3…2…" Garnome jerked the blade out on the count of two.

"Shit!!" Bradley grunted out.

Garnome, with a cheeky smile, did his usual patchwork on Bradley's injuries. He topped it off with a shot of morphine to the knee.

Meanwhile, Carter was swapping out his magazine when suddenly he was grabbed by a Vanguard from the back. The Vanguard turned him around quickly and uppercut Carter; sending him six feet into the air and landing in the water. The black-armored mutant dragged Carter by his vest through the water and towards a hallway. Harrison saw Carter being dragged and opened fire with his pistol. The bullets splattered in the water, hit the wall behind it, and knocked over computer monitors. It did everything but hit its intended target. The Vanguard payed him no attention. Harrison saw Chris was still partially submerged and his body wasn't moving. He decided to help Chris.

"Somebody help Carter!" Harrison shouted in the room, hoping that someone would assist him.

It was illuminated in dark red lights where Carter was being dragged. There was little water on the floor and Carter could feel his boots rubbing along the ground. The Vanguard lifted him by his throat and punched him through a wall that led to a separate room.

Amidst light gunfire, Harrison waded through the water and checked on Chris, who had passed out from nearly drowning. His weighted gear had partially kept him from floating.

Harrison yelled out, "Chris, are you okay!? Chris... Chris...!"

He lifted Chris against a partially submerged table and began performing CPR. He removed his vest and Harrison put two fingers at his throat and detected a low pulse. He kept at it, and finally Chris gasped for air and coughed out ingested water. The others met up with the duo.

"I got him! Taylor—take the squad and help Carter. I saw them drag him away—hurry! It took him around that corner over there." Harrison said, pointing behind him at the corner that led to the hallway.

Taylor led everyone to find Carter.

Meanwhile, Carter was dazed by the blows he'd sustained and was trying to catch his breath in the room. He looked around and saw strange machinery; tall, white spires, with spheres of light in the middle of them. It was a lab. There were hospital beds, empty medicine cabinets, and all-white, tiled flooring. The dark-red lights made it hard for him to see; making him squint. Through his squint, he saw the Vanguard slowly walking into the room, no weapon in hand. It was skinny, small framed, maybe about 5'5" or 5'6." Carter's face was bloodied, his nose was bleeding profusely; leaking from his nose and back into his mouth. He felt as if he had a pillow inside his chest and struggled for air. His chin was numb and Carter swore to himself that something was broken. He saw his rifle in the corner of his eye. It had flown far from his hand and was too far away to reach in time. With no weapon left, he pulled out his knife.

The Vanguard slowly took off its helmet. It was a woman; a fierce looking warrior. Her eyes were bloodshot red, her skin tan; her long, black, hair neatly wrapped into a ponytail.

Dark Horse said, "I admire your bravery—but there is no victory for you in this room!"

Carter replied, "Yeah? My knife hand says otherwise."

Dark Horse slowly walked around him; like a demon standing on a border anointed with holy oil. "I read your file, Roman Carter. You are one of the best snipers in the world. Shame that your sniper rifle is out of reach."

The Vanguard approached closer.

"How the hell do you know who I am!?"

"We were modeled after you."

Carter tilted his head; puzzled.

The Vanguard smiled. "Oh, yes! The mighty Task Force X-Ray! We heard of you during our training. You were so elite and... badass, that our training was modeled after yours. You set the bar, and there was no better special forces unit... until we arrived that is. Look into the mirror and you'll see us staring back. Only difference is that we're stronger... dare I say, better!"

"You think you're hot shit!? Don't ya!?"

She laughed before saying, "Why shouldn't I? We are superior to you physically. Don't fight it. We were once like you; weak, crippled, and fragile. Now we are powerful! You can be like us too, you know?"

"I'm just fine the way I am!"

She suddenly stopped smiling; her face becoming serious. She stepped closer and unnervingly said, "You're not... you're really not! You haven't felt the power that I have. The strength, the speed, and the immunity. We don't want to kill off humanity, we want to save it! Even save you! We are not monsters; we want humanity's best interest. Is that such a bad thing? Join us!"

She spoke those words seriously and stepped even closer. Her vigilant red eyes were sincere, wide, and unflinching. She stood at arm's length from Carter. This is my chance, he thought. She's too strong. I'll have to attack her quickly if I want to survive. Maybe I could even make a run for the exit. Carter had never run from a fight and he hated the idea of it. He took all his beatings. He slowly glanced at the exit while keeping his head still. He lunged his knife at the Vanguard with certainty. *Gotcha!* As soon as he broke eye contact with her, she knew he was going to resist. She saw the blade from a mile away and fluidly dodged back. Carter's joy quickly fell apart. He felt how he did when he was told he'd be kicked off his baseball team during his time in high school.

Carter kept swinging multiple times, and the Vanguard effortlessly dodged Carter's attempts. She moved like water; dodging back, to the left, and to the right. After the fourth swing, she started to smile. Finally, Carter tried to stab her by lunging the blade directly at her in a thrust motion. With her hand, she stopped his lunge in its tracks. It was like his hand was thrown against a wall. She grabbed his hand and neck; lifting him in the air and against the wall.

Carter spat blood into the Vanguard's face, "Do your worst, creature!"

The little blood spots landed over her lips, cheeks, nose, and eyes; making her eyes flinch a little. She licked the blood off her lips slowly; in a manner that made Carter sick to his stomach. With one hand, she pulled out a syringe. She held it in the air, in front of Carter's face. He could read the label, *Seraph-1*. There was a red, watery, fluid inside the syringe. Carter saw what it was and trembled in terror. He saw what it did to the professor on the security footage. He kneed and squirmed in her hold.

Dark Horse smiled and said, "Foolish inferior—you couldn't survive my worst!"

"Fuck you!" Carter quietly said, his heart rate speeding.

With one hand, he struggled to hold the syringe back. The needle got closer... closer... closer. It was like Carter's hand was being slowly compressed by a machine. He desperately looked at the hole in the wall; hopeful that his men would save him. It was in vain. The Vanguard stabbed Carter in the neck with the syringe. It felt like a fireball raged through his neck, and down his body. He shook like a man with Parkinson's. It started with a light tremble in the head, then his legs, then violent thrashing. He fought it; trying to maintain his composure for as long as he could. He looked at the Vanguard and thought, *I won't give her the satisfaction to hear me scream. Burns... it burns! Oh, God it burns!* Carter's whole face became strained and veiny. He broke out into a terrible sweat and it looked like he was holding his breath. Deep down, Carter felt pathetic. He used to get jumped in school; beat on and robbed of his lunch money. After his time in the army, he vowed, *never again*. Now he felt himself bullied once more and it reminded him of his time in school. His legs dangled down the wall; powerless against the fire in his veins. His resolve finally broke. He began to grunt and yell. His face went numb, his teeth had a terrible ache, and he felt a long chill course through his spine; not enough to cool the internal heat.

Dark Horse said, "You can taste it, can't you? Taste the superiority..."

The Vanguard gave Carter a long kiss as he was lifted into the air by the might of the super- soldier. She took her time and then released her grip on Carter's neck; dropping him to the floor. The Vanguard put her helmet back on and walked out of the room. Carter tossed and turned over the floor; rolling along the tile like he was on fire. Stop, drop, and roll.

Taylor, followed by Bradley and Garnome, limped through the red-lit hallway. They heard screaming and followed the sounds. He saw the hole in the wall and stepped through only to find Carter on the floor, convulsing.

Bradley rushed over with a limp, dropped his shotgun, put his hands on Carter's back and said, "Carter—look at me. It's going to be OK. Where are you hit?"

Carter looked up at Bradley—and he saw that Carter's eyes were bloodshot red.

Bradley reeled back. His legs gave out and he fell to the floor. He said, "Oh my God. I don't believe it..."

Bradley stood up, saw the empty syringe on the ground, and examined it. He saw the label and put the clues together.

"No! No! This can't be—this can't fucking be!!"

Carter toiled. "You have to make it stop! It burns! My blood's burning! Make it stop!"

Taylor leaned down next to him at a loss for words. He mumbled out, "Come on, dude! Let's get you out of here..."

"Nooo!!!" Carter said in anger. He pushed Taylor back a good distance with force; a clear sign of his rising strength.

The men looked in disbelief at their comrade. It dawned on them that the change could happen to anybody in the blink of an eye, in a single twist of fate. The Freaks that seemed like inhuman monsters to them, now seemed like they weren't too far from being the same. Harrison and Chris caught up to the men. Harrison was the first to walk through the hole.

He saw Taylor, Bradley, and Garnome standing over Carter in a huddle. He budded his way through and asked, "How's he looking? Garnome—why aren't you working on him?"

Harrison looked at Carter and saw the bloodshot eyes. He couldn't stop staring at them. He didn't know how he felt. He began to breath heavy.

He was slow to speak. "How... how did this happen?"

Carter gritted his teeth. "She injected me... with a... syringe. God, it burns! You... have to end this, Commander."

Taylor shook his head. "No way, Roman! We're not going to kill you. Maybe we can get you out of here and, uh, find a cure or something—right, Commander?"

There was a long pause.

"Right?"

That was wishful thinking, and everyone knew it. Where were

they going to find a cure? Did a cure even exist? The damage seemed permanent.

Carter insisted, "Come on, man! Hurts... too much! You have to... you have to kill me!" He took off his gear and forcefully ripped his uniform off. Carter felt like a fire was literally burning inside him. Over his shoulders, down his back, in his abdomen, and even in his arms and legs.

Garnome scrambled through his medical bag. "Maybe we could..."

Carter interrupted him and said, "Damn it—no! I will not live as some weirdo, some inhuman... no longer. Commander, please!" Carter looked just like the mutants they'd been fighting. No shirt, red eyes, strong masculinity, and drooping dog tags over his neck. He sat down and leaned on the wall and waited for Harrison to make a decision.

Harrison ordered, "Leave us and form a perimeter... say your farewells."

"You gotta be kidding me—sir, with all due respect..." Taylor started.

"Taylor... do me a favor and take your respect and shove it up your ass!!" Harrison yelled at him. He was furious that he had to make this decision. Even more furious that Taylor was making it harder. Taylor stormed away from the huddle; muttering profanities under his breath.

Each man walked by Carter, giving him a handshake and whispering something in his ear. Most of the squad members were teary eyed as they walked past. Garnome took the longest. He did his secret handshake with Carter.

"Garnome..." Harrison sighed. "Move it along, son."

The doc nodded his head, finished his last words, and walked away. He was hurt. Garnome had the same face he had when he watched his son's coffin enter the ground. Chris was the last person to say his farewells.

Chris whispered, "It was an honor to fight alongside you, Carter.

I'm sorry... sorry this happened. Mors autem velum illinc gloria, my friend."

"What... does that... mean?" Carter asked.

"It means, death is but a veil, glory is on the other side. Its what we say to our fellow Falcons after they... pass away."

"I'm... no Falcon."

Chris gripped his hand tight. "You're a brother all the same."

He stood up and walked out. He'd barely gotten to know the men of Task Force X-Ray, but he felt greatly attached to them. Maybe it was their mysticism; the tales that he heard painted them to be immortals, men of metal. He didn't know Carter well, but blood shed in battle forms powerful bonds. Everyone left the room through the hole, leaving only Harrison with Carter.

There was a pause.

Harrison felt himself choke up. He struggled to utter words. "I'm sorry, son. I'm sorry I couldn't save you. You were... a hell of a soldier. You're going to a better place than this world could offer, Roman. It was my personal honor to serve alongside such a dedicated soldier... such a friend."

Harrison wiped his face.

Carter replied, "Tell... tell... tell me... "

Harrison kneeled close to Carter. "Tell you what, son?"

"How did you get the name.... "Stormtrooper"?"

Commander Harrison felt himself tense up. He almost said 'no' as a reflex. Many people had asked him over the years how he got that nickname and he would never tell them. He wore the name like a badge of shame for years and hated the fact that someone gave it to him. He looked into Carter's red eyes and decided to honor his dying request.

"Well, it goes back a long way. I was a Second Lieutenant and young. I served under a Captain named, Sargento. It was '02; we were on a patrol in Fallujah, looking for radical insurgents that hadn't yet fled the city. We quietly walked down the desolate street. A car wreck to my right burned intensely. We'd made it all but fifty feet when suddenly, everything went to shit. Captain Sargento was killed by machine-gun fire and eight of twelve men dropped dead in the blink of an eye."

Harrison paused. He could hear the gunfire, the crying from the mud, and the blood leaking from the earth.

He continued. "The gunfire came from a factory to our northeast. I told the survivors to keep their heads down. Some wanted to go back. I refused. I crawled forward while the bullets whistled all around. When there was a lull in the fire, I stood up and rushed from cover to cover until I reached the doorway of the factory."

Harrison's eyes went blank. "I was so scared. I felt all alone. I looked behind me—sure that all my men had tucked tail and ran. They were right there beside me. We entered the factory together and went upstairs. There was a would-be professor working on electricity-resistant fabric in a room below us. Me and a couple others were walking along the cemented walkway when an IED detonated. The ground seemed to swallow me whole. I fell through and became entangled. I was draped in this large blue piece of fabric—it covered my body and swung over my shoulders like a cape. I looked up at the hole and saw a cloud of pink mist. I knew someone had died. I was in a rush—we were in combat. So, I got up quickly and ran out the door. Part of the building became unstable and electric wiring fell on me from above, and I just got really tangled up in these wires and fabric. I dunno what happened after. I was fighting an insurgent with my bare knuckles when the electricity somehow sparked, and my entire outfit became electrified. The insurgent was just as surprised as me. I was downright scared. I thought I was going to be electrocuted to death, but nothing happened. If I had to speculate, the fabric saved my life. It was only by the grace of God I fell into the material to begin with."

"As I fought this guy, my entire uniform lit up with electricity and I looked like I donned a coat made from an electric storm. I managed to grab my pistol; awarded to me during an Israeli training competition in Tel-Aviv. I killed the man; two shots to the chest. He was the first man I'd ever killed. The adrenaline that coursed through my veins prevented me from feeling shock. I was numbed to life at that point. My mentor was killed. My best friend was killed. I was no longer scared... I was nothing... just didn't care. The remaining insurgents stared in disbelief as I charged them looking like Thor. I gave them no pause and I killed them with my pistol. Corporal Stint witnessed the whole event and I guess I became a legend.

Harrison scoffed. "It's a stupid story. I remember when they first started calling me 'Stormtrooper.' It was a damn joke! People who were close to me died, and all everyone wanted to talk about was some idiot kid who looked the part. I forever carried a cloud of guilt over me for surviving that firefight. My friends died and a part of me felt that I should've died with them. Corporal Stint and I were the only survivors."

Carter stared in awe as he listened. He struggled to speak; his throat feeling flooded with sap. "I'll be damned, sir—you.... *are* a legend, and I'm... honored to have known you. Whatever happened to the corporal?"

"Suicide." Harrison said bitterly. "Just couldn't cope. His last words to me were, 'I just can't take it anymore.'"

Carter spit out blood. "That's... that's... tragic! I'm sorry. Although you hated yourself for surviving... if you didn't survive, I don't think Task Force X-Ray... would've made it this far. Not in Hope 7... not ever."

Harrison shook his head. "I wish there was another way..."

Carter put a hand on the Commander's knee.

"There's not, Commander. My time... is up. I... killed a man long ago... before... X-Ray. I've been haunted ever... since. Every day! No matter how far I ran... I could never escape. Free me... Commander... please."

Harrison started to realize that there was more to Carter wanting to die; guilt. Harrison stood up. He stared at his gun for the longest before pointing it at Carter's head. Harrison's hand, for the first time since he killed that rabbit when he was a boy, shook. It was a noticeably slow tremble. Carter glanced at his hand. Harrison didn't want to press the trigger. He hoped that the gun wasn't loaded. A part of him wanted to keep Carter alive, but he knew that that was selfish; considering how much pain Carter was in and how bad he wanted it to stop. Harrison's eyes did not flinch. He slowly pulled the trigger back. The trigger went a little further... a little further. It felt like he was shooting himself. Then, like ripping off a band-aid, he softly squeezed the trigger and watched Carter's eyes close for good. The *bang!* noise startled him. Harrison stared at his friend's lifeless body as it slumped to the side and fell to the ground. Harrison fell to his knees and wept into his hands. He yelled, but no noise came out. It was the hardest thing that he'd ever done. All the battles, killing, and adrenaline-filled moments didn't come close to what he just did. Underneath that tough man, was a battered and bruised, beating heart. He was reminded of its existence in that moment.

Ramirez exited the elevator with his weapon aimed high. He scanned the hallways and found no hostiles. "We're clear!" He said.

Val exited the elevator and led the way, Jacobs and Ramirez followed. They walked past Bill's corpse, up the stairway, and into the hallway next to the command center.

Jacobs said, "OK, everybody. Let's get the communications up and tell command what's going on. Val, you keep leading."

Val answered, "Follow me. We have to go up the service stairwell."

She led them down the hallway and up a side stairwell. They trekked up the stairs. Jacobs trailed behind noticeably; doing his best to muffle his cough into his hands. It was getting worse. Drops of blood had turned into small splats on his gloves. He needed medical attention and soon. Each coughing spell had left him light-headed and his lungs felt strained. When they finally made it to the top, the door had been blown off its hinges, and they found two security guards in their seats, each with holes in their heads. Various computer monitors and electronics lined the Mainframe.

Jacobs and Ramirez removed the security guards from their seats. Ramirez quickly sat down; completely ignoring the bloody seat and monitors. He began typing a message to command. He typed:

"Command, this is Task Force X-Ray. We have arrived at Hope 7 roughly five hours ago, and we are now requesting evac. Be advised: both of our helicopters were brought down by an EMP; we are still working to resolve the situation. We have not found any staff who are still alive. There are still enemy combatants inside Hope 7. Sonya Chrystal is KIA and the Phantom is still alive. *Inferno...* I say again, *Inferno.*"

Ramirez attached the evidence of what had been going on at Hope 7 and sent the message to Command. He laid back into his seat and said, "Great—now all we need to do is wait for them to respond. Anybody got a coloring book?"

The console froze up, the air turned cold, and the lights flickered.

The squad heard Tommy's voice through their radios, saying, "Did you really think I forgot about you, Val Bridgeway?"

They turned around and aimed their weapons at the Phantom, who hovered over the floor.

Val said, "I had nothing to do with what happened to you! I truly am sorry."

Tommy said, "Lies again! You helped manufacture the chemicals in my body, before I became this!"

"I had no idea that they were using them on a little boy! You have to believe me!"

"Maybe... maybe not. All I am certain of is..."

Tommy paused. His frame examined the room.

He said, "You found it! The Mainframe. I searched all around for this place, but I could not find it. It was here all along. With this I will have access to the world, not just Hope 7. I will upload

246

myself into the satellites, the internet, and the electric grids. The world will suffer like I did!"

It quickly dawned on Jacobs what Tommy was talking about. How did you not know where this place was? Jacobs thought. He looked around the room and saw that the Mainframe's interior was made of a matte-silver material. Jacobs reckoned that whatever material the room was made of somehow hindered Tommy's ability to locate it. Otherwise, it seemed that he would have already uploaded himself.

Val shook her head. "Tommy—you'll do no such thing! Those people are innocent to what has happened to you. Why would you want to punish them when you can punish those who are really responsible?"

Tommy's frame rose multiple feet into the air. Its black legs dangled over the silver floor. He floated around and examined the room. "I suffered. For more than a year, I've been experimented on. I've cried, screamed, and begged. Nobody listened. My childhood, my future, were taken from me!" Now weeping, he continued, "They sanctioned my torment. My own mother sacrificed me to the gains of science and evolution. Was I not human? Was I not an innocent child?"

He was a weeping banshee. Jacobs, Ramirez, and Val all felt sorry for the boy. What he said was true. He had been tortured, abused, and neglected. He remembered watching TV shows late at night when his dad was sleeping. He saw happy kids, laughing people; sunshine and rainbows so to speak. In his life, he had known only pain. He wanted to be like the happy people on TV, but his life seemed incompatible. His dad was an abusive drunk. His mother tried to save him from his disease with inhumane testing. The results left him a shell. A being whose only emotions were anger and sadness. Tommy was jealous of the happy people. He felt that since he suffered so badly, everyone should feel it too.

"The world not only deserves to *know* what happened here," He continued. "But they deserve to *experience* what happened here as well. I will deliver this experience to them… and the world will feel my pain!"

Val quietly said to Jacobs, "We can't let that happen. We can't let him gain control. The world will be lost."

Jacobs saw that Tommy was beyond reason. He felt very bad for what had happened to him, but he couldn't let the powerful being get out. The trio were all that stood between Tommy and his revenge, life and death, good and evil. Jacobs held back a cough as he reluctantly shot at the Phantom; his cohorts firing as well. Tommy's black frame parted in certain spots. A bright, blue light emitted from Tommy's husk as it teleported and grabbed Jacobs with a literal speed of lightning. He effortlessly threw him down the stairwell. Val shot the Phantom until her gun clicked, but it wasn't enough to stop it from grabbing her and violently throwing her against the wall; knocking her unconscious. Ramirez froze. He knew what he had to do. His mother was going to hate him for it. Determined not to allow the Phantom to gain control of the Mainframe, he tried to pull the pin on his grenade. As he pulled out his grenade, the Phantom grabbed his hand and electrocuted him. Ramirez, shaking, reached to pull the pin with his left hand. Blood was dripping down from his nose, and his jaws were clenched shut. *Just a little closer*, he thought—*I've almost got it.* The pain was excruciating.

Jacobs fumbled up the stairs. He coughed so badly he vomited puke and blood. His throat was terribly sore. He pushed himself step by step, in a desperate attempt to reach Ramirez. He was a few steps away from the room when he collapsed on the floor. He sounded like someone having an asthma attack. He crawled towards the room in time to hear the Phantom unleashing a terrible wailing shriek. Ramirez screamed; bleeding from his ears and nose. Jacobs covered his ears. As the Phantom wailed, the voltage rose even higher, and Ramirez slowly began to turn to ash. Blue electricity consumed Tommy and Ramirez in a blue energy ball. His face was being eaten away from the electricity; his body followed, and Ramirez was no more. Jacobs saw two shadows in the blue energy ball, one dissipated, and one remained. Ash fell to the ground and Ramirez's burnt dog tags fell on top of the ashes. The zapping noise was sickening.

Jacobs yelled, "Ramirez!!! No!!!!"

He aimed his pistol at the Phantom. His coughing threw his aim off balance; resulting in him firing like a drunkard. The Phantom slowly walked over to the Mainframe; ignoring Jacobs's gunfire. He put his hand on the keyboard and inserted himself into the computer; his black frame dissipating as he entered the Digital Realm. Quickly, his force began to spread throughout the electric grid, the satellites, and the internet. All other electronics across the world were now in jeopardy of being corrupted by the Phantom's influence. It was the beginning to something terrible.

Blood leaked out of Jacobs's mouth; lining the floor as he crawled. He felt himself fading; perhaps even dying. He crawled over to Ramirez's pile of ashes, stuck his hand into the hot ash, grabbed his dog tags, and shed tears as he lay next to what was once his close friend, Daniel Ramirez. The dog tags burned Jacobs's hand. He coughed until he blacked out.

On Level Five, Harrison was leading his squad through the narrow hallways. The lights were dim, and red illumination filled the hallways.

The Commander ordered, "Check those corners!"

Harrison was a man possessed. He moved by the pure hunger for revenge. The pain in his back and knees were faded out. He barely cared about the mission, he just wanted to kill something. He outpaced his men on multiple occasions; turning a corner and leaving them to catch up. They moved into a large room. A shirtless Freak jumped out to attack. Harrison shot him three times in his chest and once in the head. He walked over the body, shot it three more times, and powerwalked forward. Another Freak popped out of a corner. It reached for his gun, but Harrison snapped back like a seasoned boxer. The Freak ran headfirst into the wall. It didn't have a chance to turn around. One shot to the head and he was done. They saw a Vanguard running through a railed catwalk, and another Vanguard running the opposite direction; into another hallway. Harrison opened fire but was unable to hit the fleeing Vanguards.

He said, "Split up! Taylor and Chris will follow the catwalk. Bradley, Garnome, and I will follow the other Vanguard. They separated on purpose. Keep your guards up!"

The squad split up once again. Any enemy that jumped in front of Harrison was blown away by machine-gun fire. One unlucky Freak was shot several times in the chest. It squirmed on the floor gasping for air. Harrison placed his combat boot forcefully on its chest. The snapping of the Freak's rib cage made some men wince. Just as it was about to die, Harrison turned its head into ground beef with a hailstorm of gunfire. He reloaded; walking down the hallway with blank eyes that were only alerted when it was time to fight. The veterans of Task Force X-Ray had never seen him so determined. He was a killing machine. They were happy that he led the way, but on the other hand it was uneasy for them to watch his wrath in action.

Chris and Taylor steadily walked across the catwalk in complete darkness except for a red light in the middle of the steel bridge. They couldn't see the end. Chris walked in front of Taylor. As they made their way across, the support beams exploded, and the entire bridge fell into darkness.

Chris cried out, "Taylor! Where are you? Taylor!? Damn!"

He removed some of the debris pinning him on the ground, grabbed his machine-gun and slowly walked in the darkness. Each step was an act of bravery, as Chris had no clue as to where he was going. The whole mission he hadn't felt too scared, as he was always surrounded by elite soldiers. Now, however, was different. He walked alone. No one to crack jokes and no one to watch his back. The only thing that gave him some confidence was the weight of his machine-gun. He walked for a couple of minutes in the dark. His feet bumped into objects often. He wanted to call out to Taylor again, but he was afraid that he would only give away his position to whatever demons stalked the dark room.

An unseen voice startled him. "You fumble with every step, Inferior!"

Chris scanned the room. "Who is that? Who's there?"

"Irrelevant! Tell me: Why do you settle for the flaws of imperfection, when you can have perfection? Strength beyond measure... speed... immunity to diseases."

It was like a demon speaking seductive words through the pitch-black room.

Chris slowly scanned his surroundings, finger on the trigger. "*Perfection*? You mean turned into a Freak—like you? We saw what you did to Carter and you'll pay for that!"

The laughter echoed. "We shall see! You will ascend—or you will die! I can see you, ya know!? Like a little piggy waiting to be slaughtered!"

Chris cautiously walked forward in the dark. He felt something behind him. No noise, just a feeling. He quickly turned around and opened fire. His weapon was tilted upwards. Machine-gun bullets rained into the ceiling and the flash of the gun revealed a Vanguard holding the weapon and staring down Chris. When the gunfire stopped, Chris's weapon was forcefully grabbed and broken in half. There was a various *tinging, clinging, and clanging* noise as the metal parts of his weapon poured onto the floor. He felt a cut across his face. The mysterious figure ran away. Chris put his hand to his cheek and pulled away blood. He felt a long, stinging, slash down the right side of his face. He pulled out his knife; his second comfort.

The voice taunted Chris. "Smell that? That is the smell of Inferior blood! The smell of impurity! The smell of fear! You will die in this room by a thousand cuts, piggy!"

Chris calmly said, "Try it again!"

He kept walking, slower this time. He glanced to his right and saw red lights approaching. Chris stepped to the side and the Vanguard missed the stab attempt. Chris stabbed the Vanguard in the shoulder, pulled the blade out, and jabbed out the red visors on the Vanguard's helmet. The Vanguard pushed Chris to the ground, removed its helmet, and smacked Chris with it.

The Vanguard announced, "I am Dark Horse! Prepare for your death!"

She lifted Chris by his neck and prepared to finish him off. Suddenly, Taylor appeared from the darkness and tackled the Vanguard to the ground. He threw punches left and right, left and right, left and right.

She spit out blood. "Pathetic!"

Dark Horse lifted Taylor off her and stabbed him in his right arm. She pulled the blade out cleanly, but before the Vanguard could execute a killing blow, Chris, while crawling on the floor, stabbed her in her ankle. She turned around and brutally smacked him; throwing his body back from sheer force. She lifted Taylor up by his neck and punched him in his vest, sending Taylor flying through the dark room.

Dark Horse gloated, "Pathetic! Two men beaten by a woman—a superior woman! Your eyes will turn to blood, just like mine, and then you'll see the way we do! You'll see that we're not crazy, but sane!!"

She was powerful indeed. She basked in her superior strength and speed.

CENTURION

I jabbed the concrete pillar until my knuckles bled. After thirty minutes, I turned it into a dog's chew toy. Like a dog, I'd grown tired of the toy. I wanted a new challenge. A few months ago, I was told that I'd never walk again. Fuckin' hodgies! Tyra walked in; her hair neatly tied into a ponytail as always.

"The pillar beat you yet?" She asked with a smile.

I thought for a moment how hard it took me to get her to smile; let alone speak to me.

"He gave it his best shot!" I respond. "But he couldn't get the job done!"

She giggled. I could see that scar on her arm as she squatted her weights. I must've been staring at it for too long because she took notice.

"RPG." She said; her smile vanishing. "The rocket didn't explode, but it pierced my bicep and lodged itself into my side. My arm was ruined. The upper bone was turned to dust and my collar bone was shattered to tiny pieces. No one wanted to get close to me; thought it would explode any minute. I wanted it to! God, the pain was so bad! It never did. I'm glad it didn't; otherwise I would've never gotten to experience this. What about you, James? That's your name, right?"

"IED." I say, wrapping my bloodied hands with white gauze. "Me and my unit were on our way to a small town in Iraq, 'bout five clicks from our FOB, twenty clicks south of Ramadi. We took the same road we always took. It was another sunny day. I noticed someone far away; so far, that I didn't even recognize it was a person at first. The vehicle got closer and I thought I made out a man standing on a hill, camera in hand. I knew something wasn't right. Before I could give the order to stop our Humvee, it exploded. I was unconscious for days and when I finally woke; I was told that... well, everyone died but me."

I cleared my throat before continuing, "I sat in the back; the bomb exploded under the engine block. Both men were killed instantly. I was somehow blown out of the vehicle, but Sergeant Toms wasn't so lucky. He'd been knocked unconscious and was apparently burned alive by the fire."

I unbandaged my hands and kept punching the pillar.

"I awoke three days later. I was quickly hit with the news that my pelvis was shattered. I would never walk again... so they thought."

I felt her hand on my shoulder. The pillar was bloodied from my hands.

She turned me around and hugged me.

Later that day.

I heard yelling outside my door. I jumped out of my bed and peered through the iron bars. I couldn't see anyone, but I saw that Tyra's cell door was wide open. The yelling came from there. I knew it was nothing good. My door was locked as usual. That might've mattered before I was super-human, but now it was nothing more than an annoyance. I rammed my shoulder into the steel door; angled at the doorknob. I hit it again and again until finally I created a gash in the metal around the knob. I placed one hand on the steel door and the other against the wall and I pushed the door to the side until there was a big enough hole for me to crawl out of. I did so and I rushed to Tyra's room. Anyone in there was going to be in for a nasty surprise. When I entered her room, however, I was the only one who was surprised. Three security guards were dead. Tyra was crying on the floor with blood on her hands and face. She mumbled something but I couldn't make out what it was. I slowly stepped closer.

"Never again... never again... never again!" She mumbled through her sobbing.

I looked at the guards. One had a hole through his chest the size of a baseball. Another had a snapped jaw. The last one had his face smashed in; leaving the tiled sink bloodied and broken. I pulled one over on his back and saw his dick hanging from his unzipped pants. I quickly put the pieces together. I slowly approached Tyra. She shriveled up as I got closer.

"Leave me alone... leave me alone."

I stepped closer.

"Leave me alone!!!" She snapped in anger.

I took a step back.

"It's OK." I say

"What do you want, James? Did you come in here to fuck me too!?"

"God! No! I came to help you."

"I don't need help now, go away."

"You defended yourself."

"And now three men are dead by my hands.

"If you didn't kill them, I would've!"

She looked up from her forearms in confusion.

"We're in this together, remember? If they harm you, they harm me too!" I said, offering my hand to her.

She wiped her face and took my hand. I helped her to her feet and she quickly hugged me tightly.

"You killed them good!" I say.

"You condone this?"

"Listen, you're strong now. People can't harm you anymore. You're a reckoning force! You killed three, well-conditioned, armed men with your bare hands. If you didn't than I would have, or Arthur, or Richard, or anyone of us Vanguards. We're family now. You're an animal! Own up to it!"

She looked into my eyes. I knew ever since that day that she was going to be a fierce fighter. Anyone who thought that they'd make a victim of Tyra would be gravely mistaken.

PRESENT DAY

Dark Horse dragged Chris over the wet floor and threw him against the wall. It seemed like nothing could stop her. Chris could see gunshot wounds on her lower abdomen, but they didn't even seem to slow her down. She prepared her syringe and kneeled next to Chris.

"This is good!" She said, putting one hand on Chris's knee. "A brief experience of agony for a lifetime of renewal. Strength. Speed. Immunity. This is what we want for humanity. Is it such a bad thing?"

Her eyes were wide and unflinching as she leaned forward with her syringe. Chris closed his eyes. Taylor, from the darkness, jumped on her back, and stabbed her multiple times in her neck in quick succession. Her blood spewed out and the proud Vanguard fell to the floor and relished her final breaths. Taylor rolled away from her and stood to his feet. He helped Chris stand.

Dark Horse struggled to speak, her voice sounding like she was underwater. "You fight... against the... inevitable! Humanity will... evolve! You... will evolve! Carter... Carter understood this!"

She laughed; coughing in the process.

Taylor felt a corkscrew twist in his chest. He clenched both fists. "You shut your mouth!! Don't you dare say that name!"

Chris put a hand on Taylor's shoulder. "Yeah—not so 'superior,' are you!"

Dark Horse's eyes scanned the dark ceiling like she was expecting something to fall out of the sky. "The world will... see through... red eyes. Oh, yes! The red bird... will drop its red dust."

"What the hell are you talking about?" Taylor asked.

Dark horse, laughing, teasingly said, "You'll see! *Ad... Ad Ascensionem...*"

The Vanguard breathed her last breath and died.

Chris and Taylor slowly found their way out of the dark room and began looking for the rest of their unit. Although Taylor landed the killing blows on the Vanguard, he felt tremendous dissatisfaction in his kill. He felt that she got the last laugh; that she didn't suffer enough, and he even felt that she wasn't bothered by her own passing. It ate away at him.

Meanwhile, Commander Harrison and his men were running after the fleeing Vanguard, who had made its way into a hallway. They had shot at it every chance they got, but it always managed to slip into the next hallway before anyone could land an accurate shot. The Vanguard ran across the hallway and shut a thick steel door at the end of it. At X-Ray's end, someone shut the door from behind, leaving the squad trapped. At the end of the hallway, a Vanguard in all-black, steel armor walked out. He was completely covered in the metal armor from head to toe. His metal boots sounded as he walked forward.

Harrison ordered, "Contact! Open fire!"

The squad fired bursts of machine-gun rounds, but the bullets simply ricocheted off the Vanguard's steel. Sparks illuminated from his shiny, black armor as the bullets hit it. Harrison had really wished he still had his Arbiter 23 assault rifle, but unfortunately, he did not.

Garnome said, "Ah, hell! What do we do?"

The Vanguard shot a stream of fire from his flamethrower, and the hallway was engulfed in flame. The fire seemed to reach out and brush Harrison's forehead. It was far-reaching and the men had little time to find a solution or risked being burned alive.

Harrison yelled, "Quick—move to the right!"

He led his men from the hallway into a room on their right side.

Bradley rapidly paced back and forth. "What are we going to do? That thing is too well armored!"

Harrison was panting as he looked around the room. He saw nothing that would have been of use. He could hear the Vanguard's steel boots clanging against the floor. Suddenly, Harrison's face lit up and he said, "I have an idea. Quick—move to the side, double-time! Bradley, toss me your extra grenades."

As the black-armored Vanguard prepared to enter the room, he shot a burst of flame straight ahead of him. The room billowed with smoke; the heat was immense. He walked in and the men all jumped on top of him from the side of the room and shoved him deep into the corner. They all ran out and into the hallway. Harrison pulled the pins and threw three pineapple shaped grenades into the room.

He yelled, "Get down!!"

Each man dove to the floor of the hallway and the room exploded, *Boom...! Boom!! Boom!!* The room became entirely engulfed in fire. They could feel the heat wafting into the hallway.

Bradley wiped the sweat from his forehead and said, "Looks like we got him!"

Harrison nodded his head. "Good. Now, let's find a way outta this hallway. We'll have to get that door open."

Inside the burning room, something began to stir; the motion catching Harrison's eye. A black hand lifted out of the fire, followed by the Vanguard slowly crawling out; his back on fire. Parts of his armor had been blown off; showing bloodied, exposed flesh. He crawls out—without his lower body. The Vanguard had been blown in half! His intestines dragged behind him like a sagging rope. The squad stared in horrifying disbelief as he crawled out.

"Knight" panted. "Smart... Inferiors... you die... now!"

The Vanguard hit a detonator and a timer appeared on a flat screen over the hallway door. It was set at thirty seconds. Knight managed a faint, congested laugh before setting his head on the floor's tile and seemingly succumbing to his wounds. The men dashed to the end of the hallway and tried to open the steel door. They kicked it and tried prying the door with their hands. It didn't budge.

Bradley announced, "It's locked shut!"

Harrison asked, "Bradley—you have any more grenades?"

"I gave them all to you!"

Garnome said, "I have a breach charge."

He reached to his back for the charge but could feel that it wasn't there. He looked back down the hallway and realized he'd accidently dropped it when he dove to the floor. He ran back and grabbed the charge—but the dying Vanguard grabbed his legs and pulled him to the floor. The timer was at fifteen seconds. Garnome punched and kicked the Vanguard but it squeezed tightly to his body. The steel armor that Knight wore, meant that the kicks and punches that Garnome inflicted did little. Bradley ran back for Garnome, but he threw the charge at Bradley. The charge fumbled in his arms.

The medic yelled, "Go!! You don't have time! Go!!!"

Bradley passed the charge to Harrison; he set the charge on the door, stepped back, and detonated it. The steel door blew inwards and completely off its hinges. Bradley tried to run back for Garnome, but Harrison knew that they were out of time. He grabbed Bradley's arm and pulled him inside the room.

Bradley protested fiercely. "Let go of me!! Garnome!!!"

Garnome, smiling, said, "Love you, brother!!"

He saw that the picture of his son, Michael, was fingertips away. He wrestled in the Vanguard's hold. Not to survive, but to grab the picture; to hold his son for one last time. His fingertips shuffled in front of the paper. He grabbed the picture and smiled to himself. The entire hallway exploded into a massive fireball. Harrison and Bradley moved out of the way as the fire spread out of the hallway and into the room. The heat could be felt intensely. Bradley rushed to stand; his legs gave out. He got up again and stared at the large flame.

Bradley cried out, "Jerry!! Jerry!!! What in the hell were you thinking, Commander!? I could have saved him!"

Harrison stood to his feet and calmly said, "No, you couldn't have. There was nothing any of us could do, Bradley! I'm sorry, but there was no way to save him."

Bradley stared at the fire in the hallway, moments later, the fire sprinklers turned on, and water poured down his face. His eyes were filled with sorrow. His heart felt pain. His brain knew there was nothing he could do. His body was exhausted. Harrison put his hand on Bradley's shoulder and grieved with him.

Chris and Taylor busted through a door and linked up with Harrison and Bradley.

Taylor observed the fireball and asked, "What the hell happened? We heard an explosion. Where's Garnome?"

Bradley felt his heart clench. Tears rolled down the warrior's face. He turned his face towards Taylor and Chris. There was a long silence.

Taylor looked at the fire and his eyes turned wide. "Oh, God—don't tell me! Don't you tell me! No!!! This isn't happening! This can't be happening! Doc!? Where's the doc!?"

Harrison said what everyone already knew. "He's dead. Garnome is dead, but he saved us, and we will honor his courage by finishing the mission."

Taylor, in a flash of anger, said, "To hell with the mission!! We just lost two of our guys! And God only knows how Jacobs and Ramirez are doing!"

Harrison tried to comfort Taylor. "Calm down, soldier! If we don't finish the mission, that means our men died in vain. Is that what you want, Taylor?"

There was a long pause.

Taylor finally answered, "No, sir!"

"OK, then. We'll make sure Garnome and Carter didn't die for nothing. Now, listen up! We killed another Vanguard. Did you guys get yours?"

Chris wiped the blood from his knife. "Yeah—we killed her."

Harrison said, "Good. Now we need to kill the other one that fled and then we'll head to the final level and finish them off! Move out!"

They quietly moved into the next hallway and kept pressing forward. No one wanted to continue. Two of their comrades had been killed and they were physically exhausted. Previous wounds could be especially felt now. No one was coming for them. If they were going to survive, the only way home was forward. Harrison quickly felt self-hatred. He knew he could have called in the airstrike and he now felt that he'd made a mistake. His decision indirectly got two of his men killed. He knew this was his last mission. Either by death or by immediate retirement. The men cared little for Hope 7 and the staff at this point. Considering most of them were dead and partook in atrocities. Through the hallway they walked through, there were various labs to the right and left.

They had various tall pieces of all-white machinery. There were blinding white orbs of energy in the centers of them. The machines looked like small nuclear reactors. The technology Task Force X-Ray was witnessing throughout Hope 7 was beyond their time. Super-soldier formulas, advanced weaponry, and machines that were probably producing powerful clean energy; all of which the men marveled at. The facility was the epicenter of the Ascended Age. The men were in hot pursuit of their enemies, but had they not been, they would have all liked to have had a tour of the facility's technological marvels. Harrison led them through the hallway and noticed a bronze name bar on the wall next to an open door that read, *Prof. Steve H. Kent.*

Harrison turned into the room and the squad followed him into the office. There were multiple computer screens and wooden desks to the left and right. Harrison walked behind Professor Kent's desk and saw that the computer was already on. His desktop was a background of himself and what appeared to be his wife and kids on a beach somewhere. His daughters both had brunette hair, brown eyes, and wore dark-pink swimsuits. His wife had blonde hair and light-blue eyes and had a light brown towel over her bikini top. A boy, presumably his son, was in a wheelchair. He had sandals, navy-blue cargo shorts, no shirt, and gold shades over his eyes. He was smiling, had brown hair, and held up a peace sign with his right hand. Harrison held his rifle in one arm while he scrolled for additional information. He clicked on a notepad app and searched through Kent's notes. He saw pages of mathematical formulas that were beyond his skill level. He went further back in the time stamps.

It was a painful stretch of seemingly endless math formulas and scientific jargon that almost made Harrison quit early until he saw a note titled, *What keeps me going?* He read the note to himself.

It read, *this note is for me. When the pain is too much to bare, when I'm mired by mounds of meaningless paper work, when I just want to stop going. This is for me. This facility, Hope 7 began construction in 2007 by the US government, and more specifically, then-U.S. Secretary of State, Dr. Amanda Kutchinson. The facility was endorsed by countless senators, legislators, and big-time pharmaceutical companies. There was a mission. To give hope to the world. Hope that the crippled would walk again... hope that the blind would see... and hope that the world's worst diseases would be ineffective against renewed human bodies. Tens of billions of dollars of funding poured through the funnel and we were achieving breakthroughs. We have built proto-type energy reactors with the newly discovered Artantium. We created a pure energy source. We were on the edge of directly finding cures to breast cancer and ebola. Then, I was reminded that this was the United States. A country where the government values bombs and weapons over human progression.*

Under President Hugh's Article 331, much of our funding was rerouted to build prototype weapons and even super-soldiers. We still worked on technology, but weapons of war took priority. I lost faith for a while. Faith that my son would walk again. It seemed all my hard work was being wasted away. Remember this, with the recent breakthrough of Red Eye 7, we have created a formula that can drastically improve the human body. My son WILL walk again! I admit I was selfish. I put good people through rushed tests and it cost many their lives and brains, but I did it with good intentions. Not for over-hyped military chest pounding, but so that all those who are crippled or sick might have a better life.

The note ended and Harrison pondered on it. They were searching for ways to justify the horrible things they were doing. Kidnapping people and experimenting on them... no matter the age.

He tried to move the cursor, but it wouldn't move. The computer had froze. The monitors suddenly turned on, and Tommy's face again took over the screens. Harrison reeled away from the screen. Tommy's face was hardened still, but he seemed to have a glow of joy around him. It was like he was doing a really good job of holding in a surprise.

The hologram said, "Ah, Commander - I see you're still searching for answers."

Harrison asked, "You again!? What do you want? Where is Samantha Volaire?"

The squad formed a perimeter around the room and kept their weapons raised. The last time Tommy did this, he fried someone alive.

"You still search for her? Perhaps you will find what you seek... if she's still of any interest to you!"

Harrison said, "Damn you, Tommy!"

"You must understand, Precursor, after everything she did to me, she deserves the fate she is now suffering. Enough of Volaire. You need to worry about Red Eye 7."

Harrison asked, "What are they doing here?"

Tommy replied, "They are preparing to send mankind through the next evolutionary stage... or so they believe. You will find the answers you seek on Level Six."

"Why are you helping me?"

"You are a tortured soul, just like me. I sympathize with you, Precursor."

"What about Red Eye 7? Why do you help them?"

There was a pause before Tommy said, "We are mutually essential to each other. They needed me, and I needed them. I gave them the truth and they helped me escape. Now, I will help them create a new humanity from the ashes of the old."

"Earlier, in the Digital Realm, you said something about a union of flesh and steel, elaborate."

"In the end, Precursor, you will need me. I will ask you a question and depending on your answer, the world will go in one direction or the other."

"What question?"

"You'll know when I ask you."

It dawned on Harrison that he hadn't run into Tommy's shadowed frame for quite some time. His cryptic words sent chills down his spine. He hesitatingly asked, "Where are you? What's your plan?"

Tommy responded, "Me? I'm everywhere!!"

"What are you talking about?"

"I've uploaded myself into the Mainframe. I rode the electric current to satellites in space, to the electric grid, the internet, and more—so much more! You wouldn't believe the power that courses through me. The overwhelming load of information filtering through my mind. It is… extraordinary. Now, I wait in the shadows of the Digital Realm, waiting to strike them down. Red Eye 7 won't save this world, but they can create a new one. Look at it like the book of Noah. Red Eye 7 is Noah and the ark, today's world is the world of Cain, and I am the wave of destruction that will kill those not on the ark!"

Shaking his head, Commander Harrison asked, "Why do you hate us so much? I know you're upset, and you should be, but we didn't do this to you."

"It's not about who did it! It's about the fact that I suffered horribly and everyone else didn't. These fragile humans complain about schools, girlfriends, what clothes to wear, and how they look. I've had no such luxury. My world is dark and cold; everyone else's world is sunny and warm. Why did they enjoy the sun, while I couldn't? Now everyone will share in my pain. Not because they deserve it, but because its fair! I have a question for you, why do you follow your government so blindly? You have no clue what they've been doing behind closed doors. You call yourself a patriot? Do you condone what they've done here? What they've been doing for decades? Watch this!"

Tommy played a video on the computer screens. The time stamp was November 4th, 2025

The president of the United States could be seen sitting in a chair, talking to one of his advisors. He was a tall, white man, with jet-black hair, and graying temples. He had on a black suit with black trousers and wore a blue tie. He sat anxiously in his chair, twitting his fingers, and constantly adjusting his posture. The advisor wore glasses; had on a dark-blue suit and trousers, with a black tie.

President Hugh said, "What is the status of Task Force X-Ray?"

The advisor adjusted his glasses and said, "We aren't sure. We haven't gotten communications from them, and their helicopters have reportedly been brought down."

"What about Red Eye 7?"

"From what they have reported, they are clearing the files and evidence as instructed."

"Excellent! General Sampson had so much faith in his little task force. They're expendable as far as I'm concerned—every single one of them! Red Eye 7 is getting the job done. They are the successor to Task Force X-Ray. I want that data destroyed and the Phantom contained. Sonya should have been able to keep the task force on a leash!"

The video ended.

Tommy teased, "See, Commander? I'm not the villain here. Your government sanctioned my torture, created Red Eye 7, and were willing to sacrifice you and your men to this inhumane and absurd cause. They knew about everything that was going on here long before they sent you, and they lacked faith in you so much that they even sent in an advance team to do what you were originally sent to do! They turned me into a monster for their own gain! You see, Commander, we are more alike than you think; both victims of an authoritarian power."

He was playing a game with Harrison. He was a little boy, yet he was far smarter than any human. He was planting seeds of doubt into his mind and the things he was saying were indeed facts. Cold, hard facts that were incontestable. It was psychological conditioning.

Tommy continued, "I was designed to infiltrate and infect a country's electric grid. For example, they would have used me to upload into the Russian electric grid, and I could deactivate their defenses and electric power from within. I'm a weapon! They created a monster and a monster is what they will reap!"

Harrison and the squad didn't have the words.

"But wait!—there's more!"

Another video was played. There was a watermark at the bottom right corner of the screen that read, October 21, 2023.

President Hugh was looking out the oval office window. He appeared to be sipping coffee. The sunlight lit half of his face and body.

The president said, "I hear Red Eye 7 has had another successful mission. You are the ultimate warriors, the perfect black-operative team. Which brings me to the next subject: Senator Timbold has been causing quite a fuss over my stance on foreign policy. He is gathering a larger force to oppose me. I can't have that, and I won't have that. I need you to deal with him, Centurion. Make it look like an accident."

Centurion was standing in the dark corner of the room. The dark-red lights shone from the dark. The lights were cast onto the president's dark side of his suit. Centurion obeyed. "It will be done, sir!"

The video ended.

Tommy said, "You see this? The world is plagued by violence and corruption, not just in the United States but across the world. Everyone is chaffing under the ambitions of evil men. This so-called democracy you fight for, is an illusion. The president was having his political opponents killed; keeping him in power and mostly unopposed. They need to be eradicated."

Harrison asked, "That does not justify mass genocide! What about the children? The homeless? The innocent?"

"Casualties of war—you know that better than anyone! Although, what happens after my vengeance is complete is out of my hands. Maybe Red Eye 7 is your species' only hope."

"What are you talking about!!? *You* were once human. Mankind isn't perfect, but we deserve a chance to be better." Harrison said, turning away from the computer.

Tommy scoffed, "You're smarter than that, Precursor! Humanity has had thousands of years to be "better," and they are still the same. Selfish, greedy, whoremongers, filled with violence, and filled with fantasies that they will go to any length to achieve. Just look at what happened to me. Before I go, Commander: remember 'the Town of Fire'?"

Harrison felt a chill go down his spine. The words seemed ancient, like he hadn't heard them spoken in a century. The image slowly entered his mind like a forgotten nightmare. Harrison, wide-eyed, slowly turned around to face the computer. "Don't!"

Tommy played a video.

From a zoomed-in aerial view, Harrison could be seen approaching a burning town with his squad mates. The video was dated 2012. Harrison and his men arrived in the town and found the civilians massacred. The wooden buildings were burning, bodies were stacked in piles, on fire. Harrison remembered the smell of burning flesh. The smoke-filled town causing his eyes to burn like he was standing over an open barbecue pit. The smoke in his lungs caused the squad to cough often. The smell of charred skin sickened his stomach. A little girl could be heard crying. The men looked around the town, and saw a little girl lying on top of her dead mother in front of a cathedral. Couldn't have been older than six. She wore a pretty yellow dress, that was slightly spotted with mud, creating little black poke dots. He remembered feeling relief that she was alive. She looked up at the approaching soldiers and directly at Harrison.

Her eyes were irritated red. She slowly lifted her hands up into the air and screamed, "Don't shoot GI!! Don't shoot Yankees!!"

Don't shoot? Questioned Harrison in his mind. *Why do you think we're going to shoot you, sweetie?* Before the squad could get to the girl, a loud, whistling noise could be heard.

The senior officer looked up and yelled, "Incoming—get down!"

Artillery shells rained down on top of the town. The shells shattered the wooden buildings, and huts. Dirt and debris were thrown into the air. Harrison remembered the terrifying noise of the incoming artillery shells. He dug his head deep into the ground and could feel dirt and debris hit him. When the noise finally stopped, Harrison looked at where the girl once was, and saw that she was no more. The cathedral had been hit; scattering chunks of bricks over the road. He walked over the crater and saw pieces of the yellow dress protruding from underneath the earth. He remembered feeling terrible sadness. He knelt over the crater and dug his hand into the earth and pulled out a torn piece of her yellow dress. He could smell some of her scent. It smelled like mango with a hint of smoke. To this day, that was the saddest day in his life. An innocent little girl, blown into the earth, and her ruined, beautiful yellow dress rising from the earth like little sunflowers.

The video ended.

Tommy asked, "You know who sanctioned that attack? Your government."

Harrison spat out, "Bullshit! They thought the town was filled with hostiles."

"No." Tommy said with wide eyes. "A platoon of army troops murdered the inhabitants and called artillery onto the town to cover up their crimes. Little did they know that everything was being recorded from a nearby surveillance plane. The same is being done here. Your subordinate, Jacobs sent the distress beacon. Three B-2 stealth bombers are on their way to level the entire facility. They will try to forget all the horrors that took place within these walls—but I won't let them! You should think about getting out of here, Commander. Witness what I will do!"

Harrison said, "No! We will stop Red Eye 7, then we will stop you!"

Tommy replied, "If you say so..."

The computer screens shut off. Harrison wanted to yell out in anger. He was by no means a weak man, but the thought of that little girl, and his dead men tugged on his heart strings and although he refused to let his men see it, he was an emotional wreck on the inside. Emotionally broken, even.

Chris asked, "Did that really happen?"

Harrison ordered, "Stop! We need to get to the lower level and finish this!"

Taylor asked, "What about the other Vanguard?"

Harrison said, "Forget him! We need to get down to the lower level. Let's find that elevator!"

The men exited the room and searched around. They walked down a stairway and into a long hallway with doors to the left and right. There was a name over each doorway, *Achilles, Dark Horse, Knight, Valkyrie, Champion*. On the left side. *Pegasus, Centurion, Legionnaire, Swift Wing*. On the right side. Harrison and his men peaked their heads inside each room to make sure there were no hiding enemies. Harrison peaked into one room. It was all clear. When he popped his head out of the room and turned forward he saw a Vanguard. He fired seven rounds semi-automatically in less than four seconds. The Vanguard didn't move. Harrison realized that he was standing behind a clear, bullet-proof glass.

"Be honored, Inferiors, you stand on hallowed ground!" said the Vanguard.

"Hallowed ground!?" Taylor remarked. "I wouldn't take a shit here, much less honor it!"

The men walked to the glass and faced down the Vanguard. The name, 'Pegasus' could be seen on the helmet.

"What do you want!? And make it quick, I'm not in the mood for any of your supremacist bullshit!" Harrison barked.

"Just to talk... for now." Pegasus said, his true voice disguised through his helmet's mic. "I wanted to look up close at the men who killed my fellow Vanguards."

"Not so inferior after all, are we?" Harrison said, massaging his trigger.

"It would seem not, but I guess it was never really about supremacy."

"What? All the evidence says that Seraph-1 got to your heads."

"Wrong, Seraph-1 made sure that it didn't get to our heads. It is what separates us from most other test subjects. We know that we are superior by our abilities; the others simply believe that they are superior just because."

Pegasus reminisced.

CENTURION

I looked into the mirror and saw power. My red eyes gleaned back at me. I lathered my face with shaving cream and rinsed my blade with the hot water. I glanced to my left and saw that Tyra was doing pull-ups at her doorway. Gertrude, a real clumsy fellow, rolled his cart through the hallway. I was halfway done shaving when I heard a loud crash outside my door. I looked and saw that he somehow managed to drop his boxes. I thought nothing of it. I shaved the left side of my face and washed away the shaving cream. I looked out my door and saw that out of five crates, Gertrude only managed to get one on the dolly. He was a short bastard with his hairline sticking to the middle of his head, and he had a beer belly. I watched him struggle to lift the second crate with disgust. He lifted halfway before setting it down and holding his back. I watched until I couldn't stand it anymore. I walked out of my room.

"Pick it up!" I say.

He looked at me and tried again. He lifted, but he never got it on the lift. I felt sudden anger come over me.

"Pick it up you weasel!!"

"I can't." He pathetically moaned.

"Yes, you can! Use both of your arms and lift it."

"Christ, James! These crates weigh at least a hundred pounds each."

"Lightwork!"

He tried again. He strained so hard I thought he was going to shit his pants full. He didn't make it to the top. I felt myself snap. I lifted his pathetic body in the air with my left hand.

"Whoa! What? What are you doing? James, what is this!?" He quivered out.

I lifted each crate onto the tall dolly and I tossed his deadweight on top of the crates and pushed it down the hallway.

"Stop!!" He yelled.

Adam stopped the cart in its tracks and said, "James, what's going on?"

"Nothing. I'm just delivering all of this deadweight to its destination."

Adam looked up. "Uh, I think you have a stowaway up there."

I cracked my neck and grabbed Gertrude by his trousers and pulled him off the lift.

I smiled and said, "Hey, Gertrude!" Giving him a light slap on the face. "Don't let me catch you being so weak next time you pass through here. OK, buddy?"

He adjusted his glasses and said, "Yes, sir!"

He stormed away with his cart.

"What was that?" Adam asked.

"Did you see how weak he was!?"

"Yeah, but we've only been super-human for a few weeks now. They're not as strong as us." He gave me a pat on my back. "Maybe our sacrifices here will change that one day."

He walked away.

"Yeah... right." I murmur to myself.

PRESENT DAY

Pegasus scratched the glass with his combat knife. "Do you know what Vanguard means? It means to be a pioneer; a forerunner if you will. The Vanguards of Humanity will be pioneers of a great change. Why fight it?"

"Gee, I don't know?" Quipped Taylor. "Maybe it's because half of you Freaks have lost your minds and the rest of you are disillusioned into believing that the world needs to be saved when its fine just the way it is!"

"It is true that the world will live on." Pegasus said. "But define living? Is it chaffing under weak bodies? Over ninety-five percent of the world have an illness of some kind. If everyone were like us, they would have no illness... or addiction. Your Interstellar betrays you!"

Taylor was visibly puzzled.

"I can see the blue specs in your eyes. Maybe madness runs in everyone and they just don't know it."

Taylor looked away.

"Enough of this!" Ordered Harrison. "Come out and fight!"

"Very well. The elevator I assume you're looking for is to your right. Meet you there!"

The Vanguard walked away from the glass.

Taylor muttered, "Commander, I-"

"We'll discuss it another time, Taylor! Keep focused." Harrison said.

Roughly five minutes passed before they finally found the elevator. They rushed to it in a single-file line, with Harrison in front. The wall to their right seemed to burst open. Pegasus jumped through the plaster and engaged Task Force X-Ray. He grabbed Harrison's rifle, slammed it against the wall, and delivered a flurry of quick punches and melee maneuvers. He moved like the wind. Pegasus single handedly beat on all the men; who were suffering from previous injuries and combat fatigue. He grabbed Taylor and punched him through the plastered wall. Finally, Harrison managed to pop off a couple shots into Pegasus's mid-section with his pistol. The Vanguard stumbled into Harrison, grabbed the gun and tussled back and forth for control. Pegasus knocked away Harrison's pistol and tackled him through a steel door. The ensuing struggle left them in a nuclear-core lab. Harrison was slow to get to his feet; his aching back and knees reminded him that he wasn't as young as he acted. He was pretty sure he pulled a muscle in his lower back.

The Vanguard, likewise, struggled to get to his feet. He tumbled to the right and left; struggling to gain his balance. He examined his gunshot wounds; three bloodied holes in his body. Any other man would have needed immediate medical attention, but not him. He pulled out his knife and took off his helmet. The Vanguard was pale and had a short, blonde, buzz cut. Harrison obliged the mutant and likewise pulled out his knife. The squad rushed into the room and prepared to shoot. Harrison could have had the Vanguard killed with immediate firepower, but he didn't want to. He wanted to kill him up close and personal. It was a nasty feeling; the want to utterly gut his opponent, but it wasn't the first time he felt it.

Harrison waved them off, saying, "Hold your fire. This is between me and the Freak!"

They lowered their weapons. Harrison and Pegasus circled each other like ancient warriors preparing to duel. Harrison's greatest advantage in this moment was Pegasus's wounds.

The Vanguard rushed Harrison and tried to stab him. The men tussled. Harrison grabbed his hand and flipped the Vanguard over his shoulder and stabbed him in his side. The Vanguard held a stiff face, while down, he punched Harrison in his face, bloodying it. Pegasus rose to his feet. Harrison spat out blood. The blood leaked out of Harrison's nose. The Vanguard tackled the Commander to the ground and tried to stab him in his chest. Harrison was barely able to keep his blade at bay. He knocked the Vanguard away and they faced off again. Pegasus coughed up blood and stumbled. After he recovered, the Vanguard ran to the left side. Harrison readied himself for an attack from the left. As Pegasus got close, he rapidly switched to the right side and stabbed Harrison between his armored plates as he jumped past him. Harrison felt around his wound and then pulled his hand away from it. It was covered in blood. Harrison fell to a knee. His men watched with gripping uncertainty.

Pegasus taunted Harrison, "You want to get to the elevator? You have to go through me!"

Harrison was light-headed. The cut was deep and he felt a terrible stinging in his side. He rose to both feet, his eyes in an apparent daze. The Vanguard rushed Harrison again; intent on finishing him. Time seemed to freeze as Harrison watched the movements of the Vanguard. His feet ran to Harrison's right, but then shifted to his left. Pegasus's wounds betrayed him. He was incredibly fast, but his bullet wounds slowed him like an airplane with too much cargo. He slightly dragged his right foot. The Vanguard leveled his knife to match the height of Harrison's face.

Harrison was unflinching. He dodged the knife by ducking and moving his head to the left. The Vanguard's jagged blade grazed the Commander's face; leaving a small zig-zag shaped cut along his right cheek. Harrison stabbed the Vanguard in the side of the neck, pulled the blade out, and stabbed the Vanguard in the stomach, below his vest. Pegasus was wide-eyed. Harrison stared into his red eyes and kept the blade in. Blood poured out of his neck like watery gravy running down a pile of mashed potatoes. Harrison lifted the Vanguard up—with the knife still in—and moved him next to the open reactor. The Vanguard could be heard choking on his own blood. The men of X-Ray cheered.

"How…?" He choked out, getting blood drops on Harrison's face.

Harrison, with a face of disgust, said, "Your red eyes don't scare me! This is for Garnome! This is for Carter! This is for Task Force X-Ray!"

The reactor door closed and opened, closed and opened. Each time it opened; a bright, blinding light was shone from it. Too bright to look at it directly. It had a wide door, probably used to dispose large crates of used material. Definitely not used to dispose of bodies, but Harrison was eager to see the effects. He pulled his knife out of the Vanguard and pushed him into the reactor. Harrison, with one hand over his face, glanced at the open door and saw that the Vanguard was atomized instantly. There were no prolonged screams of pain. Just a quick, *Vroom!* And the super-soldier was silenced for good.

He kept glancing over his hand at the reactor's bright light. His mind was boggled by Tommy's revelations, and he now asked himself what to do and what was right. Everything he fought for, even believed in, was brought to question. Worse, all the revelations were true.

Chris came near. "Sir, are you okay?"

Harrison was far from it. He turned around to face Chris. "I'm OK. Now, let's get down that lift."

They exited the reactor room, entered the wide cargo lift, designed to lift supplies down to the lower levels. Bradley hit the button, the lift jerked, and took the squad to the final level of Hope 7. As the elevator descended, Harrison held his wound tightly.

He whispered to himself, "Garnome…Garnome… I'm sorry, son… I'm sorry I couldn't bring you home."

CHAPTER 15: "EMBRACE ME BROTHER"

JACOBS LIMPED OUT of the facility with Val walking at his side. They had their arms over each other's shoulders. He felt empty, defeated. He dragged his aching feet over the ground; not caring what corpses he stepped on. The horror that he witnessed at Hope 7 had taken its toll on the once proud and decorated soldier. The painful image of Ramirez being turned to ashes in front of him was a permanent mental scar. Outside, they were met by the blistering cold. Daylight was struggling to break through the clouds. A full blizzard was in progress and visibility had decreased. Jacobs made out an object in the sky. The object got closer—a helicopter. The rotor blades were barely beating out the noise of the blizzard. Jacobs waved his hand at the aircraft. The helicopter leaned to the right and towards them. The pilots spotted Jacobs and Val and landed the bird in front of the facility, in a clearing in the parking lot. Jacobs helped Val onboard and then got in.

One of the pilots asked, "Are you Commander Harrison?"

Jacobs was losing his voice. "No. I'm his second-in-command, lieutenant Jacobs."

The pilot said, "Works for me. We have to get out of here. An aerial bombing force is on its way to level the facility."

"Not so fast! We have to wait for the rest of our squad! We won't leave them!"

"Well, I can hover the facility for about thirty minutes, but then we need to get out of range from the incoming bombers."

"OK. That'll have to do."

The helicopter lifted into the air and rotated around the facility; waiting for signs from the rest of Task Force X-Ray.

Meanwhile, Harrison and his men officially reached the last level of Hope 7. Stretched out before them were narrow concrete hallways illuminated in red lighting. The men were a battered bunch. They took all that the mutants could throw at them. Their bodies ached, ankles were rolled, cuts bled and stung, backs were strained, and the morphine was losing its effectiveness. Bradley and Harrison had no body armor and everyone's uniforms were ripped up in certain areas. They looked like a band of ghouls walking off the lift. The super-soldiers broke their bodies and the loss of some of their comrades had broken their spirits. They were tired, hungry, and low on ammunition. There was no medic to cry out to; no way to make the pain cease. Taylor held his last vial of Interstellar in his hands. He stared at its promise of pleasure like it was a gold bar. He wanted to use it so badly. He thought about Garnome. He pulled out his combat knife and cut the rubber vial in half. He watched the blue liquid leak over the floor and his boots. Some of the men had almost forgotten why they were even there. They moved sluggishly and struggled to continue. But continue they did.

Chris asked, "Which way do we go? Should we split up?"

Harrison said, "No. We don't have the manpower to be effective while split up. We have to stick together on this one."

He stepped off the lift and led the squad through a concrete hallway on the right, which seemed to stretch forever under the red illumination. It was a tight corridor and the squad had to be extra careful, as there was little room to maneuver. They walked about seven feet apart, giving themselves extra breathing room. The hallway eventually led to the testing room; the room where Tommy had been experimented on. Harrison recognized it from the footage. It was a very large room that was mostly empty excluding the tall spires and chamber. The level was deep underground, and granite rock made up for much of its walls. Tommy's silver chamber was closed and blackened by burn marks. Two security guards, wearing black and blue uniforms were dead on the floor. One was literally ripped in half and the other was just lying belly-first on the concrete ground. They didn't bother turning him over. Security mechs took the shape of various metal pieces; nuts and bolts. The squad entered the side room with a large rectangular glass that could view Tommy's chamber and saw a recording sitting on a table next to a laptop. Harrison inserted the U-Bug into the laptop, clicked on, and played the recorded footage.

Harrison scrolled until he reached the part where the previous video froze. It showed Tommy's chamber opening after the Electric Tower experiment. A digitalized Tommy walked out. Behind him sat his skeleton, still steaming from the electric voltage. He tore through a security guard in a quick zip that left the guard mutilated. The other guard shot Tommy; each round causing a slight disturbance in his electric frame. He grabbed the guard and burned out his eyes with his hands. As the blind guard screamed, shooting aimlessly, Tommy grabbed the electric spires and drew immense power from the increase in electricity. The video lagged and skipped. Then it showed Samantha Volaire, crying in front of the screen.

Volaire, sobbing, said, "I... I created a monster... an abomination. Oh! My son! What was I thinking? Tommy's skin was completely fried off, but the frame of his body has held the electricity in place; making him look like an electrified or digitalized version of himself. He has shown a great and terrible power. I fear that if he ever gets out of Hope 7, the world won't be able to contain him."

The lights in the room flickered, the video buffered, and Tommy's wailing could be heard. The video shut off.

Bradley said, "Ah, man. I don't know if we want to find Volaire now."

They looked around the room and saw nothing of importance. The squad left the rectangular room and prepared to leave. A creaking noise sounded. The chamber door slowly opened. The squad turned around with their guns aimed at the chamber. They were in disbelief yet again. Blue hands positioned themselves along the steel door. A holographic, digitalized Samantha Volaire stepped out of the chamber. She looked as she normally did; her digital frame was wearing the same white suit she used to wear. She looked how Tommy looked in the computer monitors. Not a black husk, but a digital image of herself.

Bradley said, "What the...?"

Volaire said, examining her new self, "It looks like my son has exacted his revenge on me..."

Harrison asked, "How? How did this happen to you?"

Volaire said, "Tommy dragged me into the chamber and locked the door while I was still inside. He activated it... and here I am."

Taylor murmured to himself, "You deserved it."

Harrison asked, "How come you're not like him?"

Volaire held her left hand to the light. "I theorize it's for a couple of reasons. One, Tommy sucked the energy from two spires, so only one spire fired onto my chamber, resulting in a lower voltage, and two, I think Tommy was digitally born out of hate, pain, confusion, and the thirst for revenge."

Taylor asked, incredulous, "Why'd you do it, huh? Why did you sacrifice your son to this madness?"

There was a long pause from Volaire.

She finally answered, "I thought I was giving him a better future... a future of power... a future all of mankind might share.

Tommy suffered from a rare genetic disease—one that would have eventually killed him—and I thought that I could save him from it. I realize now that I was just trying to save myself from the pain of losing my only son. The DNA deletion could not be fixed by Professor Kent's Seraph-1 formula. I needed to warp an energy source into him if he was going to survive beyond the age of twelve. I know now that this has all been one big mistake. I was careless; I made him suffer, and I betrayed my own son's innocence. I deserved what happened to me, but the world does not deserve what will happen to it if we do not stop Tommy."

Harrison stated, "Well, we can sure as shit agree on that much! What can you tell me about the strange lightning? It wreaked havoc on us as we approached the facility."

Volaire said, "I don't know. I believe that Tommy's digital frame somehow draws lightning to him, like a walking kite. The power is within him."

"Will it trouble us on our way out of here?"

"As far as I know... no. Tommy has left the facility, but this may not stop him from somehow using lightning in the future."

Chris looked to the Commander and asked, "What do we do with her?"

Taylor gripped his flamethrower.

Volaire pled, "I am your only hope to stop Tommy. You must take me with you!"

Taylor scoffed, "Are you nuts!? How can we be sure you won't attack us just like Tommy did?"

Volaire reasoned, "Because I want to stop my son before he destroys the world. This is my fault... and he is my son... please allow me to have this chance at correcting a horrible mistake I made."

There was a moment of silence.

Harrison reluctantly said, "Fine!"

Smiling, Volaire said, "Thank you! I'll insert myself into your

U-Bug, and you can take me out of here. You won't regret this I can assure you!"

Taylor's eyes widened. "Are we really going through with this, Commander? We might just be unleashing a second monster!"

Harrison said, "Taylor... shut up! As of right now, we have no defense against Tommy, and we don't have any way to stop him. He's in the system. Bullets are useless against him now. I hate to say it but Volaire really *is* our best shot at taking Tommy down."

Harrison held out the U-Bug, Volaire inserted herself into it with the touch of her hand, and he gave the U-Bug to Bradley. He took a knee, put the hacking device into his rucksack, and zipped it up. Bradley struggled to get back to his feet. Taylor and Chris helped him up. A loud noise sounded in the distance. It sounded like a spinning rotor or aircraft engine. They slowly moved through another concrete hallway and followed the noise. Lighting shone from a room into the hallway. The noise sounded louder as they got closer. Harrison and Chris led the way with their weapons up. They had entered a large atrium. The first thing they noticed was a tall, pale tree. The second thing were the black armored mutants.

Three Vanguards were standing in the atrium. Two of them were facing Task Force X-Ray, and one was facing the tall, white tree with pink leaves. The Vanguards facing the squad aimed their weapons but didn't fire. The Vanguard looking at the tree continued to admire its beauty. It was the same tree that was on the mutant's uniforms.

Centurion could hear the approaching men. He heard their boots clap along the tile and said, "And so you come at last... Commander Harrison."

Harrison asked, "How do you know me? Us?"

"The president of the old democracy raved about you for a time. We were created to replace soldiers like you. We were the prototype for the future warriors. Warriors who would know no pain... tire slowly... and be deadly beyond belief." Centurion said, clutching his fist. "We are super-human, but we are human. We're not machines. Everyone preached about an army of robots, but they all knew that robots were numb; immune to human judgement and emotion. They needed someone better and they found it in us."

"What were you doing here? I thought your orders were to erase the evidence stored in this place and to save the staff. You know—do our jobs. What changed?" Asked Harrison hastily.

"Not long ago, my fellow Vanguards were signaled by Tommy in a cryptic message. He told us to come to Hope 7 right before we received orders to purge it. He spoke things to us; government atrocities, deep sown corruption, and secrets that if exposed would send civilization reeling in terror. We came here... to the birthplace of our superiority... and we found answers. Answers from the archives, answers from hidden files, and answers from the Phantom himself. We were created to be warriors; to fight America's battles while the population grew self-centered, weak, and fat. The problem was that there was no end to the conflicts. Our country started wars for selfish agendas, and we saw good men and women die to line the pockets of the greedy! Each decade, each year, there was a battle to fight, a dictator to topple, a country to invade, and then it dawned on us. Instead of fighting in pointless wars for a corrupt government, why not go on our own crusade? A worthy one."

"Why not give everyone red eyes? Why not give everyone our strengths? Why not start our own war? A revolution that would reset the balance of the world. Instead of taking orders from the old and weak and being used as tools for absurd agendas. Then they will have renewed strength, their bodies will never know illness... never tire... it would be a gift to the world. Sure, the weak will not survive, but those who do, will no longer be weak. We can give humanity a rebirth... an evolution. The Phantom will ensure this"

Harrison asked, "How so?"

Centurion said, "We made a pact with the Phantom. We were to free him and in return he would reap his vengeance. In doing so, he will pave the way for something beautiful. We need him to start this, and he needed us to get him free. It would destroy the old and weak humanity, while we will rebuild a new humanity... a pure-blood humanity atop the ashes of the old. We will save many. While many would still perish, those who would survive the Phantom's wrath will enjoy a golden age of humanity. No more sickness... no more weakness."

"You sound mad!"

Centurion continued to admire the tree. He admired the life in the tree; its strong, firm branches and beautiful pink leaves. He admired the tree's ability to survive underground without sunlight. He admired the tree's ability to survive despite near-impossible odds. Much like Task Force X-Ray.

Centurion said, "When the red dust drops, you will see that I am not mad, but sane. We've killed each other in this place, but no more blood has to be spilled. Join us, Task Force X-Ray. You have proven that you are formidable warriors. You are not like the other weak inferiors. You are an anomaly in the decrepit, crumbling, old humanity; only fighting the inevitable change. You could help us usher in a new humanity! Will you still fight for the corrupt government who sent you here? Why stick with the old and weak when you could have the new and strong?"

Harrison saw his dead men's faces. He saw Garnome's thin, and bloodied face. He saw Carter's face, asking for death but having so much life behind his eyes. Their eyes stared into Harrison's eyes and anger quickly filled his heart. He defiantly rejected Centurion's offer. "Not a chance!"

Centurion slowly removed his helmet and turned around to face Task Force X-Ray. His hair was blond, slicked back, and tapered on the sides. He had a skinny and chiseled white face, medium nose. He seemed young; no older than twenty-seven. His red eyes stared down Commander Harrison.

He said, "Don't be a fool, Commander Harrison! We do not have to fight! We are the evolution of mankind. Your evolution! You fight the image in the mirror, but the mirror shows only the truth. We are the future! Join the Vanguards of Humanity and you too will evolve!"

Bradley cut in. "You heard the Commander! War is what you were bred for and war will be how you die!"

Centurion sighed and said, "Well I tried. Legionnaire, Valkyrie— deal with the Inferiors!"

Centurion put his helmet on, jumped over the railing and disappeared from the scene. The squad opened fire on the Vanguards. Taylor was shot once in his left arm, and once in his abdomen. The impact of the rounds pierced his vest and knocked him back-first to the floor. Valkyrie, the Vanguard to the right of the room, was shot three times in the chest and was blown over the railing. Harrison was shot in his right arm, Bradley shot Legionnaire in his shoulder, and Chris shot him twice in his chest with his pistol, causing Legionnaire to drop to his knees. Sounds of *clicking* were heard as X-Ray's weapons had run dry of ammo. Harrison dropped his rifle, held his bloodied arm, and ran after Centurion. Chris tried to follow the Commander but was tackled by Legionnaire.

Harrison looked back and yelled, "You guys have to deal with them. I gotta catch the Vanguard. Bradley, make sure you hold onto that U-Bug!"

Bradley yelled back, "I'll guard it with my life, sir!"

He pulled Legionnaire off Chris, and the trio engaged each other in combat.

Harrison hopped over the black railing. When he hit the ground; his knees gave out and he fell to the floor. Son of a bitch made it look easy! He thought to himself, glancing to the right and seeing nothing. He glanced to the left and could see Centurion running down a long hallway and hastily turning into a room. Harrison stood up and ran past the white tree, down the white-tiled hallway, and entered the room. He could see blood running down the side of his tattered uniform. He quickly realized that the room was a large underground hangar. There was a long, concrete runway that led outside. There were a couple of small planes parked on the sides, but Harrison's focus was on the loud noised cargo plane at the front of the runway.

Centurion boarded the all-red cargo plane and the plane began to take off; the ramp slowly closing. Harrison ran as fast as he could after the plane. Blood trickled down his arm, down his knuckles, and leaked on the floor. He gripped his arm over his chest and kept running for the ramp. The plane was heavy and had a slow take-off. I'm getting too old for this shit! Harrison thought to himself as he reached for the ramp. The plane picked up speed. Harrison knew that it was now or never. Either he'd jump on or he'd fall and eat gravel. He threw himself over the ramp and grunted in pain as his shoulder rammed onto the plane's cold steel. The clanging noise was a welcome relief. The plane took off and Harrison felt the aircraft become airborne; his body slowly sliding down. The ramp closed. Harrison was punched by Centurion as soon as he got to his feet; knocking him back a few steps. The two soldiers engaged in close-quartered fighting. Centurion grabbed Harrison by his neck and threw him into a stack of crates like a dumbbell. Harrison held his back in pain. The bullet wound in his shoulder stung and didn't stop. His knees reminded him that he was older than he thought. He couldn't slow down though. The moment he did, he knew that Centurion would finish him. Harrison drew his knife from its holster. As Centurion came closer to the crates, Harrison stabbed him in the leg when he was close enough.

Centurion grunted in pain and repeatedly kneed Harrison in the face, removed the knife, and threw him into the center of the cargo hold. He threw away the knife. Harrison's face was cut and bloodied; his nose broken. His eyes teared. Centurion tried to punch Harrison, but he moved and sucker-punched Centurion in his face; the metal helmet hurting his hand. Think fast old man! He saw a socket wrench lying on a crate; grabbed it, and violently hit Centurion on his helmet-covered head, leaving him stunned. The commander kicked Centurion towards the ramp, dove for his knife, and cut the straps on some of the cargo crates. The crates loosened and slammed against Centurion; pinning him up against the plane's hull. Harrison looked to his right and left and realized the plane was filled with the super-soldier gas. It had big, red, lettering across the all-black crates that read, *Seraph-1*. Harrison knew he had to find a way to bring the plane down. He couldn't keep up with Centurion; he was too fast, strong, and powerful. Harrison knew he was on the verge of failing. He temporarily abandoned his fight with Centurion and ran up to the cockpit; his body screaming in pain. He saw two pilots. Harrison pulled out his pistol and unloaded an entire clip of bullets into the main pilot, and the plane began to become unstable. Some electricity sparked from the control console. The co-pilot turned around; he had wide, red eyes. He quickly tried to stabilize the plane.

Harrison aimed his pistol at the co-pilot and pressed the trigger. *Click... click, click, click.* He pulled out his clip and before he could reload, he was grabbed from behind by Centurion and choke-slammed to the ground. Centurion removed his cracked and busted helmet and thrashed Harrison to the right and left walls. When Centurion had Harrison between his legs, he began to choke him. Blood from Centurion's head was dripping onto Harrison's face as he was being strangled. He tried to move Centurion's hands, but they didn't budge. He saw fire behind his eyes. A fierce determination to kill him, but even more. He could see that he'd stop at nothing to achieve his goals. Harrison reached through the Vanguard's arms and pulled Centurion's head close with both hands and head-butted him in his face, breaking the chokehold. Harrison, while coughing, grabbed a grenade from Centurion's vest, pulled the pin, and threw the grenade behind him and into the cockpit.

Centurion cried out, "No!!!"

The grenade exploded and destroyed the cockpit with an engulfing of fire and steel. The explosion caused a tear in the plane's hull and the destabilization in air pressure sucked Harrison and Centurion out of the plane through the hole in the cockpit. The cold air latched onto the duo and sucked them like a vacuum.

It sounded like gusty winds. They both held onto whatever they could as the plane spiraled out of control. Harrison's grip was getting weaker. He was in so much pain and his fingers were nearly giving way. He was certain that he was going to die. He felt that he was going to die having done what was right. I could've let him go. He thought. I could've saved my men. We could've let the bombs finish our job, but no. I had to be a stubborn pain in the ass and you boys payed the price. Garnome, Carter, I'm sorry. You men deserved better, but you didn't die in vain. Cargo boxes began to fly back and forth, and the plane rapidly decreased in altitude. It was a plummeting meteor. The cockpit erupted in fire, and the smoke consumed Harrison and Centurion. The imaginary smell of jasmine and cinnamon comforted Harrison. Its time. He thought.

Meanwhile, Bradley and Chris were squaring off with Legionnaire. The Vanguard was tough. He quickly recovered from his wounds and uppercut Bradley, giving him airtime. Chris forcefully removed Legionnaire's helmet, revealing a black man, with red eyes and short, black, hair. Chris attempted a punch at the Vanguard, but Legionnaire grabbed Chris's arm, broke it, and choke slammed Chris to the floor. Bradley's face was busted and blood covered half of it. Still, he loaded his last two shells into his shotgun, pumped it, and shot the Vanguard in his chest, blowing him off the railing. He ran and peaked over the railing and saw that Legionnaire was fleeing towards the hangar. Tough bastard! Bradley thought to himself, grabbing Chris by his vest and dragging him next to Taylor. What had made fighting the Vanguards worse, was the fact that they too wore body armor. So, not only did they have superhuman strength but extra protection from their armor as well.

Bradley said, "You good, Taylor?"

"I got hit pretty good, Abe. I'm bleeding... like a running

faucet!" Taylor's words were faint. "If I don't get help soon... I don't think I'm going to make it." He held his stomach in agonizing pain. He was lying in a pool of his own blood; in no shape to continue the fight. Bradley knew that it was up to him to finish the enemy. But was he up to it? The leg he wounded in the helicopter crash felt numb. He even freaked out a bit at the thought that the docs might've had to amputate it. Each time he fell to the floor, there was no guarantee he could get back up under his own power. He reasoned that he was the best man for the job.

Bradley said, "Hang tight, Taylor. You're not going to die here, just hold on. Pass me your flamethrower so I can make sure that SOB is dead!"

Taylor weakly handed Bradley his flamethrower. The handle and flame tank were covered in blood. Bradley's hands slipped over the bloodied handle, dropping the weapon. He quickly reached for it and picked it up.

"What about you, Chris? You Good?" Bradley asked, checking the flame gauge.

Chris moaned, "My arm—it's broken."

"Shit! OK stay here with Taylor. I'm going to finish him off. You two watch over each other!"

Chris nodded his head and Bradley ran down the railing and searched for Legionnaire. Bradley saw a trail of blood and followed it into the hangar. As soon as Bradley walked into the room, he was hit with a chair. The wooden chair hit him with such force, it exploded into a spectacle of flying wooden shards and splinters. The flamethrower was knocked out of his hands. The Vanguard smacked Bradley again and knocked him to the floor, back first. His black uniform was wet, and darkened with blood, yet he was unphased from the bullet wounds. He probably could have taken a shower and been ready for work in fifteen minutes. Bradley was reeling in shock at how much strength Legionnaire still possessed. He dragged Bradley and threw him up against a granite wall.

He lifted him up with both hands around his neck and said,

"Ah! Worthy enemies indeed!" He punched Bradley multiple times in his face and then stabbed Bradley in the chest with a screwdriver.

Bradley yelled in agony.

The Vanguard pulled the screwdriver out and stabbed Bradley in his lower stomach. Bradley felt himself beginning to fade. Legionnaire twisted the rusty screwdriver in him, torturing him. It was a sharp, blistering pain in his right side, around his appendix. Bradley smeared his bloody hand over Legionnaire's face in gripping pain. Legionnaire had an unnerving seriousness to him. He seemed to savor the fighting. He basked in it like a sunflower in sunlight. Bradley could tell that war was his drug. He loved the adrenaline, the killing, and even the pain. There was no greater pleasure for Legionnaire. No drug, no amount of sex, nothing could fill the void of raw combat. Bradley was floating over his death bed; ready to descend into the cold casket and have the door sealed over him. His eyes began to droop and his eyelids were closing. Suddenly, a gunshot noise was followed by a splatter of blood on Bradley's face, waking him from his sleep and widening his eyes. Chris had come from behind and shot the Vanguard in the head, splashing blood around. Bradley fell to the ground, his head leaning against the rock wall.

Chris held his broken arm and knelt over Bradley. "Got him! You OK, Bradley?"

Bradley was officially out of the fight. His wounds matched Taylor's and he struggled to get his words to Chris. "Ah... I'm bleeding... bleeding like a stuck pig." He looked deep into Chris's blue eyes, weakly patted him on his face, and said, "But you did good, kid. The 007 badass that you are! Where's... where's Taylor?"

Taylor limped over to the duo, holding his stomach tightly. "I'm here... banged up... but here..."

Bradley sighed. "Thank God! Let's get the hell out of here!"

More words were said, but Bradley found himself having a more difficult time hearing them. Ringing in his ears had set in. He nodded his head but couldn't hear a thing. Chris and Taylor helped Bradley up, and the men all limped towards the hangar doors that led to the outside. The men leaned on each other for support. Bradley faded in and out. He was sure that if he fell again that would be the last time. They walked up the long runway; relieved that they had survived their nightmarish encounters, but now that the fighting had died down, they were left with somber spirits. Garnome, and Carter, two blood brothers, were dead. Before this operation, they felt like they were indestructible; on top of the world. Now that it was mostly over, they were reminded that they were fragile humans like everyone else. They weren't superheroes or super-soldiers for that matter. They were regular humans that had defied monstrous power and villainous super-human strength and survived. The men made it to the giant, steel hanger doors and left Hope 7 together. The blizzard met them. Bradley's legs buckled and he fell to the ground.

Meanwhile, Jacobs was trying to convince the pilot to stay a little while longer.

The pilot grew tired of the back and forth. "I understand, sir, but there hasn't been any sign of them. We've got to get out of here!"

Jacobs grunted in anger. He refused to accept that all his men had died in Hope 7. If he had to, he would've ran back in to recover all of their bodies. He looked out of the open helicopter door and looked around the desolate snow. It looked like he was going to have to abandon his men. The very idea made him physically shudder. He kept looking and he saw something that made his heart flutter with hope. He squinted hard and through the blizzard he saw what appeared to be a horse. He saw two figures moving with it.

Jacobs energetically pointed his finger at the figures. "Wait! I think I see them. They're to your right side! Drop down and pick them up!"

The helicopter pilot looked to where Jacobs was pointing and saw the men. The helicopter descended and landed in the open, snowy plain. Jacobs rushed out to his comrades and helped them onto the chopper. Bradley was slumped over the horse. They lifted him off it, and Chris, Bradley, and Taylor entered the helicopter. Jacobs saw the horse's red eyes, and realized that it was Seraph, the horse that saved them from the ravenous wolves. He marveled at it. Seraph licked its lips as Jacobs rubbed his hand over its forehead; feeling its skin and black hair.

"Thank you!" Jacobs said aloud. He reached into his rucksack and pulled out the green apple it had given him. There was a single bite in it. He took another bite and held it in front of it. Seraph ate the rest of the apple out of his hand. He rubbed its hair again and entered the helicopter. The bird took flight, and when the helicopter reached a higher altitude, the horse stood on two legs; his way of saying goodbye to his friends.

Jacobs watched the horse disappear into the blizzard. There was a mood of relief in the chopper. A combat medic immediately began attending to Bradley and Taylor.

Jacobs asked, "Where's the Commander?"

Chris replied, "We don't know. He took off after one of the Freaks, and we lost sight of him. We think he boarded an aircraft."

Jacobs asked, "What about Garnome and Carter?"

There was a long silence aboard the helicopter.

Chris stammered, "They… they… they didn't make it."

Jacobs's heart tightened and he looked as if he'd been hit by a freight train. His happiness at saving his squad was quickly short-lived and his mood descended into great sorrow.

Jacobs moaned, "Ah, no!! That's terrible!!"

Taylor looked around and reluctantly asked, holding out hope, "Hey—where's Ramirez?"

Jacobs looked at Taylor in his hopeful eyes speechless and shook his head.

Taylor, lying down, covered his face and quietly wept into his hands. He had to face his pain; no drugs to take him to a distant

land. His heart rate lowered, and he passed out. The medic pulled
out his defib unit.

Jacobs looked out the window. How'd they die? He thought. Was
it Tommy? Did he make their eyes pop out? Or was it the Freaks? I
don't even want to know. I should've been there! I should've fucking
been there! Jacobs saw smoke in the distance. It was a long, gloomy,
black trail that stretched far into the sky. He shouted out, "Hey!
I see a smoke trail off in the distance! Head to the smoke, pilot!"

Meanwhile, Harrison crawled out of the wreckage; his face
bloody, and his fatigues torn. He gripped his pistol tightly. There was
a light mist of red coloring; some of the gas tanks had been punctured. Wreckage from the cargo was scattered all throughout the
snow. The plane had been torn apart into several sections. Pockets
of fire were around the crash and on parts of the plane. Harrison
felt weak; his eyes irritated. The cold made him jackhammer violently and tremors surged though his body as he crawled through
the snow. He was cold but felt hot inside. Harrison made his way
to his feet and walked through the blizzard in a daze. His legs and
feet trembled like they were ready to give out. He saw a figure
crawling in the snow. Harrison ejected his clip and put a new clip
into his pistol. The crawling figure was Centurion. Harrison followed behind the crawling Vanguard. He clutched his grip tighter
as he got closer. Centurion, who felt Harrison behind him, lifted
himself up and faced the snowy abyss. Centurion didn't look up.
Half of his blonde hair stuck up. Blood covered the left side of
his face. He had a piece of metal in his left shoulder. His lip was
busted; trickling blood down his chin and onto the snow.

Harrison aimed his pistol with one hand at the back of Centurion's
head, and calmly said, "This is what madness brings... just madness..."

"Not madness... but sanity." Centurion softly spoke.

"This is what you call sanity!? Christ! You're more deluded than

293

I thought! There's nothing sane about killing innocent people; nothing sane about forcing your sick dream on others."

"The opposite of sanity is... insanity."

"Bingo! Finally, you decided to use that 'super-brain' of yours!"

"Insanity is a contradiction of my actions, Commander. It means doing the same thing over and over expecting a different result. What I was doing had never been done before. It was... an original plan. Therefore, I cannot be insane." Centurion said, spitting out blood.

"Oh, fuck you! Did you really think this 'sane' plan was going to work? You think the world was just going to lay down for your grand plan!?" Harrison scoffed before saying, "Never!"

"Why not?" Centurion asked with a smile. "What I offer them is peace... power, and strength. Who wouldn't want that? I'd even wager that people would kill for the power we possess."

Harrison couldn't argue with that, but he knew better. "There will always be war and death. Not even your evolution can make people live for eternity."

"So, you like being old and tired? Weak and vulnerable to disease?"

"It's the only life I know-"

"But you could have so much more! It doesn't have to be all that you know!" Centurion paused before saying, "Whatever! You want to kill me? Go ahead. Pull the trigger. Finish it! It changes nothing. I'm tired of arguing with a man who is stuck in his old ways. The old is DOOMED to fail, Commander! Don't you see that!? If we do not evolve, we will be kept weak for what is to come! If not by war, then by disease, the masses will be thinned; history is proof of this. Only the strong will endure!"

"Last I checked, you're the last Vanguard. Killing you ends this super-human nightmare."

Centurion still did not look at Harrison's face. The whole time he stared into the blizzard calmly.

Harrison said, "Look at me! You owe me that much!"

Centurion slowly looked up at his face. He paused. He had seen something that made his heart race. He had perfect vision, but he squinted all the same at Harrison's face. *Do my eyes deceive me?* Centurion burst out laughing. His laugh was discomforting; long and victorious.

Harrison said, "You sound pretty cheerful for a defeated man— or should I say 'Freak'!"

His words only made Centurion laugh harder and kindled his own anger. Still laughing, Centurion said, "You know, Commander, I keep a pocket mirror in my vest to gaze upon my beautiful red eyes. Mind if I pull it out?" He made an unnerving 'cheese' at Harrison; showing white teeth with blood.

Harrison nodded his head and Centurion pulled out a partially broken pocket mirror and looked at his eyes. He has no clue! Centurion thought to himself, while glancing up at his messed-up hair.

Harrison impatiently asked, "You done admiring yourself?"

Centurion tossed the broken mirror to him and said, "Look into it. I want to see if you see what I see."

He looked into the mirror and his heart nearly stopped. Centurion eagerly awaited Harrison's reaction, like a parent watching a kid open a desired Christmas gift. Harrison stared in complete disbelief into the mirror. His nightmare had only gotten worse.

"How does it feel…*Freak*?" Centurion asked, followed by laughter. "Not so different now, are we?"

As Harrison looked into the mirror, he saw that his eyes were bloodshot red. He had the eyes of the enemies that he and his men fought. The same as the shirtless Freak's, the same as Carter's, and the same as Centurion's. He realized that his trembling and intense internal heat was S-1 at work in his body. This can't be happening! He thought. I'm a Freak! A damn lab experiment! What am I going to do!?

Centurion taunted him, "You think the old humanity will accept you now? You bare the eyes of their enemy. You heard it, didn't you? Task Force X-Ray was deemed expendable by the old government. How long would it have been until they deemed Red Eye 7 expendable? We are just tools to them. They sent you here not caring if any of you were killed. You could say that they practically sent your men to their deaths, knowing full well what you'd all find."

Harrison threw the mirror and grabbed Centurion by his vest. He angrily said, "What's to stop me from killing you—huh?"

Centurion said, "Nothing—but you see now, don't you? Not the eyes, but what you witnessed in Hope 7. The US government, all the things that they did, and the things they did to Tommy. Humanity needs to restart. We can be the spark plug. We can rebuild, and everyone who survives the war will prosper in new bodies! This war will come, no matter what happens here between you and me. All you need to decide is whose side you are on?"

Harrison yelled, "You killed my men!!!"

Centurion yelled back, "And you killed mine!! I didn't want to fight you. I wanted you to join our cause. It was you and your men who wanted to fight us."

"That's bullshit!! Your men fired on us as soon as we stepped off the elevator! Explain that, asshole!!"

"It wasn't supposed to happen this way. We didn't expect another team—we certainly didn't expect the legendary Task Force X-Ray. When we caught wind that it was you, the plan was supposed to be to pack up before you arrived. We were too slow. The way I see it, greeting you and your men with gunfire was a compliment to the unit."

Harrison scoffed.

Centurion continued, "Listen, Commander—I understand you're upset, but we are brothers now. Whatever happened between us in Hope 7 is no longer relevant. We are now connected by our red eyes. Task Force X-Ray will eventually see the bigger picture, and they will join us one day. The United States played us both—they sent you and your men to die, and for what? To hide the inhumane acts they performed? They made killers out of me and my Vanguards; sentencing us to a lifetime of war—and they ruined a little boy. There is an ocean of questions that you still do not know the answers to. I will show you. We must wage the war. Avenge your dead men and mine! And although I know you don't believe in the dream, I am serious when I say that we will usher in a golden age of humanity. Help me wage the *last* war."

Harrison was bewildered. "What war? What are you talking about?"

Centurion laughed and said, "This ideology does not just belong to me, or even just Red Eye 7. The Vanguards of Humanity are a world-wide ideology. Forces hide in the shadows... waiting to do this. You will see! Embrace me and you will find yourself on the right side of history. Embrace me, brother!"

Centurion's eyes gazed deep into Harrison's.

"If I do this... IF... than I do it to avenge my dead men! Not for you! If you can promise me president' Hugh's head... than I'll do it!"

Centurion made a wry smile and extended his hand to Harrison. "I promise that we'll kill Hugh, burn down the pig establishments, wipe out the conspirator officials, and then we'll just be getting started, my brother!"

Harrison took a long pause.

He lowered his pistol and extended his hand to help Centurion to his feet. Centurion held Harrison's head against his own. Forehead to forehead. Harrison could feel his warm blood rub against his forehead. He had wanted to kill Centurion... badly. But he knew that there was nothing else for him. He hungered for revenge. If he turned himself in, they would only lock him up in a cage some-where. Centurion was his only means of exacting this revenge. In Harrison's heart, he felt like he had made a deal with the devil.

Jacobs walked through the blizzard and looked around the crash site. He saw the plane broken up into several sections. He found no signs of life. The red mist had dispersed. If anyone could have survived, Commander Harrison would be the one. He thought. The more he looked over the wreckage, the more he doubted that thought. He stepped into a part of the plane and found nothing. His lungs hurt from the cold air and he let out a dry coughing spell. He walked around for about fifteen minutes before seeing something. He saw a figure walk towards the crash; a shadow emerging from the snowy blizzard.

Jacobs aimed his weapon quickly and said, "Hold it right there! Is that you, commander?"

The figure halted in the snow before saying, "Jacobs, it's me..."

Jacobs cried out, "Oh, thank god! I thought we lost you. Come closer!" He could recognize his voice, but his instincts told him that something was amiss.

Harrison approached Jacobs with his head down and said, "You are in charge of Task Force X-Ray now, Jacobs."

Jacobs asked, "What are you talking about?"

Harrison walked closer to him. He slowly lifted his head and Jacobs saw the red eyes. He raised his gun out of instinct.

"What the hell happened to you?"

Harrison said, "We're at a crossroads, son. I've seen things that makes me look at the world in a new light."

"Sir, we can help you."

He retorted, "No you can't. There's no curing this, son. There's no curing truth... no curing betrayal. I want you to know that it was my honor fighting alongside you. I have to disappear. I have to find some answers."

"Then I'm coming with. I'll grab the squad and we'll go together."

He loved Jacobs and his men. He wanted them to join him, but he felt that that would be a selfish act. Jacobs, you have a wife and a kid on the way. I can't bring you along. Bradley has a family to look after. He thought. I can't drag you men with me. This is a one-way road.

"No." He said. "Task Force X-Ray needs you. I'm on a path of destruction. A path that I must walk alone. The consequences must fall on me, not on all of you. I would be a bad leader if I allowed you to come with me."

Harrison began to walk away. Jacobs lowered his gun.

"So, after all those years you're just going to turn your back on Task Force X-Ray!? Just going to turn your back on me!?"

Harrison stopped and said, "I'm going to avenge what happened to Carter and Garnome. I might be finished, but I'm not going to let those bastards get away with what they did here!"

"Ramirez is dead!" Jacobs said. Harrison slowly looked down at the snow and there was a long pause. "Task Force X-Ray needs you... needs a true leader!"

Harrison didn't turn around. "They already have a leader! He is one of the most confident men that I know. His men trust him and he is a relentless soldier. His name is Roger Jacobs; a loyal husband, soldier, and has a beautiful child on the way. His only flaw is not having enough confidence in himself."

He took a few more steps forward and Jacobs asked, "Where will you go? What will you do?

"I'm going to use this super-strength to bring them down. To kill them all!"

"Red Eye 7," Jacobs scoffed and continued, "You're going to side with the enemy!? The same assholes that killed our guys and wounded the rest of us!? Are you out of your mind!!? And although I'm a conservative, I hate president Hugh for all this shit! But what it sounds like your saying, is that you're going after our president. Our very democracy! You'd turn your back on not only us, but everything we fought for. You'd be a traitor!"

"If it means avenging our dead men than I will bear the label 'traitor.' I never cared about all the political bullshit! I only really cared for you. My men. Task Force X-Ray!! I fought to make sure you would all make it home alive. I've already failed half of you! Our government did this! The very people who give us orders. If the core is rotten, everything else will rot with it. They created Tommy with the hopes of finding a super-weapon. Article 331 has been broken by our own leaders! If no one else will hold them responsible than I will! They created super-soldiers with illegal experimentations! And worst of all, they sent us in knowing all of it! Ask yourself, what did Carter, Ramirez, and Garnome die for, huh? Huh!!!?" He yelled angrily towards the open blizzard. "They died to cover up inhumane acts!! It was never about retaking Hope 7 it was always a cover up operation! My men died to keep a secret and I will ensure that their lives are avenged!"

Jacobs shook his head as Harrison walked further away. Jacobs deep down was angry that he wouldn't let him come. He understood where he was coming from, but he hated Red Eye 7 and he felt that they were the real reason that the men had died. Red Eye 7 and Tommy.

Jacobs, with nothing really left to say, said, "Just know, sir, that the next honor we share will be as enemies! I will remember you as the man you once were, Commander. As the new leader of Task Force X-Ray, I promise you that we will hunt Red Eye 7 down to the ground... and those who follow them!"

Harrison made a smirk. "I know. I would be disappointed if you didn't! That's what makes you Task Force X-Ray. You pursue your enemies no matter what. That's how I trained you. Good luck, son. I have no hard feelings toward you."

Harrison walked away and disappeared into the endless blizzard of snow. Jacobs walked past the wreckage and back to the helicopter. The chopper spun its rotor blades and took off. Jacobs was mired in confusion and felt the weight of the world on his shoulders. His enemies were fanatical and tough. He was going to have to lead his men against near-impossible odds again. Red Eye 7 was going to bring about a forced human evolution, and Tommy, hellbent on revenge, was going to destroy the known world. The world would fight, but the critical component of the fight would be Task Force X-Ray. They would be the thin line between keeping the world intact and the forces that would radically change it. Jacobs looked around the helicopter.

He saw tough men that defied the odds; men who sustained terrible wounds but never quit. Although the mission wasn't a total success, they had succeeded in hindering Red Eye 7's plan and had gained important knowledge that would help them in their fight against new and powerful enemies. As the helicopter left the valley, there was a loud *whooshing* noise. It sounded for a few minutes and bombs began exploding all over the compound. Thousands of pounds of bombs rained down on the facility; engulfing it in an enormous fireball of fire and destruction. All the knowledge that they had learned and seen were now buried under rubble and fire. As the bombs fell, Jacobs felt bitterness in his heart. Due to the nature of the fighting, they were unable to recover their comrade's bodies, and their new-found tomb was the tomb of Tommy. The very tomb that they had died in.

EPILOGUE

A TV NEWS ANCHOR from CNN was speaking. She was an Asian woman; wore a red dress, had a pearl-white smile, and black hair tied into a ponytail with thin banes over her forehead. She spoke in a newsroom. "Welcome back, ladies and gentlemen. As you know, there have been major blackouts going on across the US, leaving many concerned about the rise of cyber warfare and cyber terrorism, but more on that later. This morning, a nuclear reactor exploded in Japan; there are at least a hundred dead."

The TV shuts off.

Two men were sitting down in a situation room. The room was empty, except for the two army officers. One wore an army-green uniform and had four stars on his shoulders. He had a wide, wrinkled face, a brown buzzcut, and a serious demeanor. The other man wore a dark-brown uniform with gray slacks. He had short black hair. They sat close together at a long, oak table. The table had about twenty-four seats.

General Duffton asked the Colonel, "How bad is it?"

Colonel Heath replied, "Bad! We lost control of half of our

satellites. The virus just keeps spreading. If we don't find a way to stop it, we are going to lose our entire electric grid. *And* reports are surfacing that *every major country* is reporting similar problems."

"What is it waiting for?"

"No clue, sir! We have intelligence working on it. That's not all, sir. Red Eye 7 has been reported behind multiple raids. Reports suggest that they're after Artantium."

"Artantium?"

"That's correct, sir. The mineral was discovered a few years ago and is an ultra-light metal that is directly used to develop advanced technology, weapons, and such. I have the full intel brief here in my hands."

General Dufton sighed and said, "Just what are we going to do, George?"

"Captain Jacobs requested an audience with you."

"Captain Jacobs?"

Colonel Heath said, "Yes, sir. He is one of the few survivors from the incident at Hope 7, where the virus originated. He believes that he may have a solution to the cyber virus threat."

"Bring him up."

The Colonel nodded his head, got out of his seat, and opened the door.

"Come on in, Captain." He said to Jacobs, who was sitting in a waiting room. Jacobs stood up, held a U-Bug, and walked into the situation room. The door was shut behind him.

"Have a seat, Captain." The General said.

Jacobs sat down on the comfortable leather chair. The General asked, "So the Colonel here tells me that you were part of the team at Hope 7 and that apparently you have a solution to our virus problem. Can you elaborate?"

Jacobs said, "Yes, sir! Firstly, the cyber virus is more than that. It is a conscious being. Its name is Tommy Volaire. He is a conscious AI and has the power to compromise electronics."

The General had a visibly worried face. "Why is he doing this?"

"It's a long story, sir. He used to be a kid… a boy. He was experimented on in a covert research facility known as Hope 7. He wants revenge for what was done to him."

"Can he be reasoned with, son?"

Jacobs paused before saying, "No. He is hell-bent on destroying everything. We can only stop him by force."

"How are we going to stop him? He's compromised many of our defense systems and is spreading rapidly."

Jacobs set the U-Bug down and said, "Frankly, sir, we need a counter-virus. Someone who has just as much power as him. The answer? Samantha Volaire. Show them Samantha."

The U-Bug protruded a blue screen. Samantha came out of the system; a life-sized human with a blue frame around her white suit, blonde hair, and green eyes.

"Jesus aged Christ!" The General exclaimed, reeling back in his seat.

"My name is Samantha Voliare. I am Tommy's mother. I have the power to stop him and I believe that I can talk him down. But even if I can't, I am your best chance at stopping him. Tommy is advanced. He's far stronger than any firewall or modern AI."

There was a long pause in the room.

"What's to stop you from taking over after Tommy is dealt with?"

There was another long pause. Finally, Samantha smiled and said, "You'll just have to trust me."

The General sat back in his chair with some shock and said, "I'll call the president."

Inside of a factory, there were people working with 3-D printers and gadgets. They were creating guns and other pieces of gear. The 3-D printers had the wording *Hope 7* on them. Everyone had red eyes. Some wore white lab coats. A man wearing an all-black combat uniform walked past the workers. He had a patch on his right shoulder of an all-white tree and pink leaves. He opened a door and walked into a dark room where he put on a helmet. He had a label on his uniform that read, *Stormtrooper* in red coloring. Red lights illuminated from his helmet. His helmet lights were met by other red lights that shined on him and the dark room was lit by red illumination.

To be continued...

THE END

ACKNOWLEDGEMENTS:

DEAR READER,

Thank you for taking the time to read my debut novel. I take great pleasure in our shared experience of, *The Ascension: Birth of a Phantom,* and I hope that you will read on of Commander Harrison's story, Task Force X-Ray's mission, Centurion's maniacal plan, and Tommy's vision of a world on fire… but that will come later. For now, my message is simple: Thank You! It is my sincere hope that you enjoyed this story as it has been a long, wild, and difficult journey. Below, I'd like to give specific thanks to special people in my life that helped me make it this far.

First and foremost, I thank my Lord and Savior Jesus Christ for allowing me to write such a wild tale. For giving me the ability to craft characters, introduce a plot, and tying it all in. Secondly, I thank my mom, Debbie Bledsoe for lifting me up when my spirit was in its darkest places. Thanks, mom, for helping me get the book edited and for being a shining light in a dark room. Thanks, dad for reading my manuscript and giving me encouraging feedback.

Thank you, Josiah and Erica, for supporting me in all the things that I do/ have done. I love you sister Carrie, and I want you to know that you are a blessed woman who has been a great blessing to me. To the O'Neals, specifically Gail O'Neal, I thank you for being supportive of my work in person and on Facebook. To my editors, Frank and Marla, your work and feedback has been instrumental in helping me craft a better, more polished novel. This entire experience has been a learning curve for me, and I'd be lying if I said I didn't pour my heart and soul into this book. There are many more stories I'd like to write, but only time can tell when I'll get them in front of all of you.

From the bottom of my heart, I say, Thank You! I couldn't have done it without all of you. Until next time, friends.

Sincerely,
Joel J. Bledsoe

ABOUT THE AUTHOR

JOEL JONATHON BLEDSOE graduated from Etiwanda High School and is currently enrolled at Chaffey College in Rancho Cucamonga, CA. His plan is to obtain a Bachelors' Degree in Hospitality Management. In 2017, at the age of 19, Joel obtained his Real Estate License and is currently working alongside his mom in the real estate industry. At an early age, Joel demonstrated a keen attraction towards imaginary characters, many of whom he created himself. This book is a product of the wonderful imagination that Joel has shown throughout his youth. Joel's favorite science fiction book is "Fahrenheit 451", by Ray Bradbury.

In addition to writing, Joel's interests include; cooking, movie watching and gaming. Joel is an avid WWE wrestling fan. He prioritizes healthy eating and taking care of his body through weight training and jogging. Joel spends his Sunday mornings in church and enjoys studying the Word of God.

Joel currently resides with his mom and dad, Booker T. and Debbie Bledsoe, along with his older brother, Josiah and his aunt, Erica Brown in Rancho Cucamonga, CA.

theascensionbirthofaphantom.com
booksbyjoelbledsoe.com